Praise for *Anna Dressed in Blood*

"*Anna Dressed in Blood* is a dark and intricate tale, with a hero who kills the dead but is half in love with death himself. By the end of the book, you will be, too. Spellbinding and romantic."
　　　　　—Cassandra Clare, #1 *New York Times* bestselling author of the Mortal Instruments series

"It's the old boy-meets-girl story, if the boy is a wry, self-destructive ghost hunter bent on avenging his father and the girl is a homicidal ghost trapped in a house full of everyone she's ever murdered. Needless to say, Cas and Anna are my new favorite twosome. When I got to the last page, I flipped back to the first."
　　　　　—Holly Black, *New York Times* bestselling author of *Book of Night*

"I loved Cas! And the world he inhabits is terrifyingly vivid and utterly compelling. Get ready to sleep with the lights on because this book has teeth. Sharp ones."
　　　　　—Stacey Kade, author of the Ghost and the Goth series

"*Anna Dressed in Blood* is easily one of my favorite books of all time and is exactly what I'd hoped it would be: gorgeous, brutal, heartbreaking, merciless, and cool as hell. This is the kind of book I've been dying to read!"
　　　　　—Courtney Allison Moulton, author of *Angelfire*

ANNA DRESSED IN BLOOD

KENDARE BLAKE

TOR PUBLISHING GROUP

NEW YORK

This is a work of fiction. All of the characters, organizations, and events
portrayed in this novel are either products of the author's imagination
or are used fictitiously.

ANNA DRESSED IN BLOOD

Copyright © 2011 by Kendare Blake

A Tor Teen Book
Published by Tom Doherty Associates / Tor Publishing Group
120 Broadway
New York, NY 10271

www.tor-forge.com

Tor® is a registered trademark of Macmillan Publishing Group, LLC.

The Library of Congress has cataloged the hardcover edition as follows:

Names: Blake, Kendare.
Title: Anna dressed in blood / Kendare Blake.
Description: First edition. | New York : Tor, 2011. | "A Tom Doherty
Associates Book."
Identifiers: LCCN 2011018985 (print) | ISBN 9780765328656 (hardcover) |
ISBN 9781429982818 (ebook)
Subjects: CSH: Ghosts—Fiction. | Wiccans—Fiction. | Cats—Fiction. |
Blessing and cursing—Fiction. | Horror stories.
Classification: LCC PZ7.B5566 Ann 2011 (print) | DDC [Fic]—dc23
LC record available at https://lccn.loc.gov/2011018985

ISBN 978-1-250-90787-5 (second trade paperback)

Our books may be purchased in bulk for promotional, educational, or
business use. Please contact your local bookseller or the Macmillan Corporate
and Premium Sales Department at 1-800-221-7945, extension 5442,
or by email at MacmillanSpecialMarkets@macmillan.com.

Second Tor Teen Paperback Edition: 2023

Printed in the United States of America

0 9 8 7 6 5 4 3 2 1

ANNA DRESSED IN BLOOD

CHAPTER ONE

The grease-slicked hair is a dead giveaway—no pun intended.

So is the loose and faded leather coat, though not as much that as the sideburns. And the way he keeps nodding and flicking his Zippo open and closed in rhythm with his head. He belongs in a chorus line of dancing Jets and Sharks.

Then again, I have an eye for these things. I know what to look for, because I've seen just about every variety of spook and specter you can imagine.

The hitchhiker haunts a stretch of winding North Carolina road, bordered by unpainted split-rail fences and a whole lot of nothing. Unsuspecting drivers probably pick him up out of boredom, thinking he's just some college kid who reads too much Kerouac.

"My gal, she's waiting for me," he says now in an excited voice, like he's going to see her the minute we crest the next hill. He taps the lighter hard on the dash, twice, and I glance over to make sure he hasn't left a ding in the panel.

This isn't my car. And I've suffered through eight weeks of lawn work for Mr. Dean, the retired army colonel who lives down the block, just so I could borrow it. For a seventy-year-old man he's got the straightest back I've ever seen. If I had more time, I could've spent a summer listening to interesting stories about Vietnam. Instead I cleared shrubs and tilled an eight-by-ten plot for new rosebushes while he watched me with a surly eye, making sure his baby would be safe with this seventeen-year-old kid in an old Rolling Stones t-shirt and his mother's gardening gloves.

To tell the truth, knowing what I was going to use the car for, I felt a little guilty. It's a dusk blue 1969 Camaro Rally Sport, mint condition. Drives smooth as silk and growls around curves. I can't believe he let me take it, yard work or no. But thank god he did, because without it I would have been sunk. It was something the hitchhiker would go for—something worth the trouble of crawling out of the ground.

"She must be pretty nice," I say without much interest.

"Yeah, man, yeah," he says and, for the hundredth time since I picked him up five miles ago, I wonder how anyone could possibly not know that he's dead. He sounds like a James Dean movie. And then there's the smell. Not quite rotten but definitely mossy, hanging around him like a fog. How has anyone mistaken him for the living? How has anyone kept him in the car for the ten miles it takes to get to the Lowren's Bridge, where he inevitably grabs the wheel and takes both car and driver into the river? Most likely they were creeped out by his clothes and his voice, and by

(8)

the smell of bones—that smell they seem to know even though they've probably never smelled it. But by then it's always too late. They'd made the decision to pick up a hitchhiker, and they weren't about to let themselves be scared into going back on it. They rationalized their fears away. People shouldn't do that.

In the passenger seat, the hitchhiker is still talking in this faraway voice about his girl back home, somebody named Lisa, and how she's got the shiniest blond hair and the prettiest red smile, and how they're going to run off and get married as soon as he gets back hitching from Florida. He was working part of a summer down there for his uncle at a car dealership: the best opportunity to save up for their wedding, even if it did mean they wouldn't see each other for months.

"It must've been hard, being away from home so long," I say, and there's actually a little bit of pity in my voice. "But I'm sure she'll be glad to see you."

"Yeah, man. That's what I'm talking about. I've got everything we need, right in my jacket pocket. We'll get married and move out to the coast. I've got a pal out there, Robby. We can stay with him until I get a job working on cars."

"Sure," I say. The hitchhiker has this sadly optimistic look on his face, lit up by the moon and the glowing dashlights. He never saw Robby, of course. He never saw his girl Lisa, either. Because two miles up the road in the summer of 1970, he got into a car, probably a lot like this one. And he told whoever was driving that he had a way to start an entire life in his coat pocket.

The locals say that they beat him up pretty good by the bridge and then dragged him back into the trees, where they stabbed him a couple of times and then cut his throat. They pushed his body down an embankment and into one of the tributary streams. That's where a farmer found it, nearly six months later, wound around with vines, the jaw hanging open in surprise, like he still couldn't believe that he was stuck there.

And now he doesn't know that he's stuck here. None of them ever seem to know. Right now the hitchhiker is whistling and bobbing along to nonexistent music. He probably still hears whatever they were playing the night they killed him.

He's perfectly pleasant. A nice guy to ride with. But when we get to that bridge, he'll be as angry and ugly as anyone you've ever seen. It's reported that his ghost, dubbed unoriginally as the County 12 Hiker, has killed at least a dozen people and injured another eight. But I can't really blame him. He never made it home to see his girl, and now he doesn't want anyone else to get home either.

We pass mile marker twenty-three—the bridge is less than two minutes away. I've driven this road almost every night since we moved here in the hopes that I would catch his thumb in my headlights, but I had no luck. Not until I got behind the wheel of this Rally Sport. Before this it was just half a summer of the same damn road, the same damn blade tucked under my leg. I hate it when it's like that, like some kind of horribly extended fishing trip. But I don't give up on them. They always come around in the end.

I let my foot ease up on the gas.

"Something wrong, friend?" he asks me.

I shake my head. "Only that this isn't my car, and I don't have the cash to fix it if you decide to try to take me off the bridge."

The hitchhiker laughs, just a little too loudly to be normal. "I think you've been drinking or something tonight, pal. Maybe you ought to just let me off here."

I realize too late that I shouldn't have said that. I can't let him out. It'd be my luck that he'd step out and disappear. I'm going to have to kill him while the car is moving or I'll have to do this all over again, and I doubt that Mr. Dean is willing to let the car go for too many more nights. Besides, I'm moving to Thunder Bay in three days.

There's also the thought that I'm doing this to this poor bastard all over again. But that thought is fleeting. He's already dead.

I try to keep the speedometer over fifty—too fast for him to really consider jumping out, but with ghosts you can never be sure. I'll have to work fast.

It's when I reach down to take my blade out from under the leg of my jeans that I see the silhouette of the bridge in the moonlight. Right on cue, the hitchhiker grabs the wheel and yanks it to the left. I try to jerk it back right and slam my foot on the brake. I hear the sound of angry rubber on asphalt and out of the corner of my eye I can see that the hitchhiker's face is gone. No more easy Joe, no slicked hair and eager smile. He's just a mask of rotten skin and bare, black holes, with teeth like dull stones. It looks like he's grinning, but it might just be the effect of his lips peeling off.

Even as the car is fishtailing and trying to stop, I don't have any flashes of my life before my eyes. What would that even be like? A highlight reel of murdered ghosts. Instead I see a series of quick, ordered images of my dead body: one with the steering wheel through my chest, another with my head gone as the rest of me hangs out the missing window.

A tree comes up out of nowhere, aimed right for my driver's side door. I don't have time to swear, just to jerk the wheel and hit the gas, and the tree is behind me. What I don't want to do is make it to the bridge. The car is all over the shoulder and the bridge doesn't have one. It's narrow, and wooden, and outdated.

"It's not so bad, being dead," the hitchhiker says to me, clawing at my arm, trying to get me off the wheel.

"What about the smell?" I hiss. Through all of this I haven't lost my grip on my knife handle. Don't ask me how; my wrist feels like the bones are going to separate in about ten seconds, and I've been pulled off my seat so that I'm hovering over the stick shift. I throw the car into neutral with my hip (should have done that earlier) and pull my blade out fast.

What happens next is kind of a surprise: the skin comes back onto the hitchhiker's face, and the green comes back into his eyes. He's just a kid, staring at my knife. I get the car back under control and hit the brakes.

The jolt from the stop makes him blink. He looks at me.

"I worked all summer for this money," he says softly. "My girl will kill me if I lose it."

My heart is pounding from the effort of controlling the lurching car. I don't want to say anything. I just want to get it over with. But instead I hear my voice.

"Your girl will forgive you. I promise." The knife, my father's athame, is light in my hand.

"I don't want to do this again," the hitchhiker whispers.

"This is the last time," I say, and then I strike, drawing the blade across his throat, opening a yawning black line. The hitchhiker's fingers come up to his neck. They try to press the skin back together, but something as dark and thick as oil floods out of the wound and covers him, bleeding not only down over his vintage-era jacket but also up over his face and eyes, into his hair. The hitchhiker doesn't scream as he shrivels, but maybe he can't: his throat was cut and the black fluid has worked its way into his mouth. In less than a minute he's gone, leaving not a trace behind.

I pass my hand over the seat. It's dry. Then I get out of the car and do a walk-around as best I can in the dark, looking for scratches. The tire tread is still smoking and melted. I can hear Mr. Dean's teeth grinding. I'm leaving town in three days, and now I'll be spending at least one of them putting on a new set of Goodyears. Come to think of it, maybe I shouldn't take the car back until the new tires are on.

CHAPTER TWO

It's after midnight when I park the Rally Sport in our driveway. Mr. Dean's probably still up, wiry and full of black coffee as he is, watching me cruise carefully down the street. But he doesn't expect the car back until morning. If I get up early enough, I can take it down to the shop and replace the tires before he knows any different.

As the headlights cut through the yard and splash onto the face of the house, I see two green dots: the eyes of my mom's cat. When I get to the front door, it's gone from the window. It'll tell her that I'm home. Tybalt is the cat's name. It's an unruly thing, and it doesn't much care for me. I don't care much for it either. It has a weird habit of pulling all the hair off its tail, leaving little tufts of black all over the house. But my mom likes to have a cat around. Like most children, they can see and hear things that are already dead. A handy trick, when you live with us.

I go inside, take my shoes off, and climb the stairs by two. I'm dying for a shower—want to get that mossy, rotten feeling off my wrist and shoulder. And I want to check my dad's athame and rinse off whatever black stuff might be on the edge.

At the top of the stairs, I stumble against a box and say, "Shit!" a little too loudly. I should know better. My life is lived in a maze of packed boxes. My mom and I are professional packers; we don't mess around with castoff cardboard from the grocery or liquor stores. We have high-grade, industrial-strength, reinforced boxes with permanent labels. Even in the dark I can see that I just tripped over the Kitchen Utensils (2).

I tiptoe into the bathroom and pull my knife out of my leather backpack. After I finished off the hitchhiker I wrapped it up in a black velvet cloth, but not neatly. I was in a hurry. I didn't want to be on the road anymore, or anywhere near the bridge. Seeing the hitchhiker disintegrate didn't scare me. I've seen worse. But it isn't the kind of thing you get used to.

"Cas?"

I look up into the mirror and see the sleepy reflection of my mom, holding the black cat in her arms. I put the athame down on the counter.

"Hey, Mom. Sorry to wake you."

"You know I like to be up when you come in anyway. You should always wake me, so I can sleep."

I don't tell her how dumb that sounds; I just turn on the faucet and start to run the blade under the cold water.

"I'll do it," she says, and touches my arm. Then of course she grabs my wrist, because she can see the bruises that are starting to purple up all along my forearm.

I expect her to say something motherly; I expect her to

quack around like a worried duck for a few minutes and go to the kitchen to get ice and a wet towel, even though the bruises are by no means the worst mark I've ever gotten. But this time she doesn't. Maybe because it's late, and she's tired. Or maybe because after three years she's finally starting to figure out that I'm not going to quit.

"Give it to me," she says, and I do, because I've gotten the worst of the black stuff off already. She takes it and leaves. I know that she's off to do what she does every time, which is to boil the blade and then stab it into a big jar of salt, where it will sit under the light of the moon for three days. When she takes it out she'll wipe it down with cinnamon oil and call it good as new.

She used to do the same thing for my dad. He'd come home from killing something that was already dead and she'd kiss him on the cheek and take away the athame, as casually as any wife might carry in a briefcase. He and I used to stare at the thing while it sat in its jar of salt, our arms crossed over our chests, conveying to each other that we both thought it was ridiculous. It always seemed to me like an exercise in make-believe. Like it was Excalibur in the rock.

But my dad let her do it. He knew what he was getting into when he met and married her, a pretty, auburn-haired Wiccan girl with a strand of white flowers braided around her neck. He'd lied back then and called himself Wiccan too, for lack of a better word. But really, Dad wasn't much of anything.

He just loved the legends. He loved a good story, tales

about the world that made it seem cooler than it really was. He went crazy over Greek mythology, which is where I got my name.

They compromised on it, because my mom loved Shakespeare, and I ended up called Theseus Cassio. Theseus for the slayer of the Minotaur, and Cassio for Othello's doomed lieutenant. I think it sounds straight-up stupid. Theseus Cassio Lowood. Everyone just calls me Cas. I suppose I should be glad—my dad also loved Norse mythology, so I might have wound up being called Thor, which would have been basically unbearable.

I exhale and look in the mirror. There are no marks on my face, or on my gray dress button-up, just like there were no marks on the Rally Sport's upholstery (thank god). I look ridiculous. I'm in slacks and sleeves like I'm out on a big date, because that's what I told Mr. Dean I needed the car for. When I left the house tonight my hair was combed back, and there was a little bit of gel in it, but after that fucking kerfuffle it's hanging across my forehead in dark streaks.

"You should hurry up and get to bed, sweetheart. It's late and we've got more packing to do."

My mom is done with the knife. She's floated back up against the doorjamb and her black cat is twisting around her ankles like a bored fish around a plastic castle.

"I just want to jump in the shower," I say. She sighs and turns away.

"You did get him, didn't you?" she says over her shoulder, almost like an afterthought.

"Yeah. I got him."

She smiles at me. Her mouth looks sad and wistful. "It was close this time. You thought you'd have him finished before the end of July. Now it's August."

"He was a tougher hunt," I say, pulling a towel down off the shelf. I don't think she's going to say anything else, but she stops and turns back.

"Would you have stayed here, if you hadn't gotten him? Would you have pushed her back?"

I only think for a few seconds, just a natural pause in the conversation, because I knew the answer before she finished asking the question.

"No."

As my mom leaves, I drop the bomb. "Hey, can I borrow some cash for a new set of tires?"

"Theseus Cassio," she moans, and I grimace, but her exhausted sigh tells me that I'm good to go in the morning.

Thunder Bay, Ontario, is our destination. I'm going there to kill her. Anna. Anna Korlov. Anna Dressed in Blood.

"This one has you worried, doesn't it, Cas," my mom says from behind the wheel of the U-Haul van. I keep telling her we should just buy our own moving truck, instead of renting. God knows we move often enough, following the ghosts.

"Why would you say that?" I ask, and she nods at my hand. I hadn't realized it was tapping against my leather bag, which is where Dad's athame is. With a focused effort, I don't take it away. I just keep tapping like it doesn't matter, like she's overanalyzing and reading into things.

"I killed Peter Carver when I was fourteen, Mom," I say. "I've been doing it ever since. Nothing much surprises me anymore."

There's a tightening in her face. "You shouldn't say it like that. You didn't 'kill' Peter Carver. You were attacked by Peter Carver and he was already dead."

It amazes me sometimes how she can change a thing just by using the right words. If her occult supply shop ever goes under, she's got a good future in branding.

I was attacked by Peter Carver, she says. Yeah. I was attacked. But only after I broke into the Carver family's abandoned house. It had been my first job. I did it without my mom's permission, which is actually an understatement. I did it against my mom's screaming protests and had to pick the lock on my bedroom window to get out of the house. But I did it. I took my father's knife and broke in. I waited until two a.m. in the room where Peter Carver shot his wife with a .44 caliber pistol and then hung himself with his own belt in the closet. I waited in the same room where his ghost had murdered a real estate agent trying to sell the house two years later, and then a property surveyor a year after that.

Thinking about it now, I remember my shaking hands and a stomach close to heaving. I remember the desperation to do it, to do what I was supposed to do, like my father had. When the ghosts finally showed up (yes, ghosts plural—turns out that Peter and his wife had reconciled, found a common interest in killing) I think I almost passed out. One came out of the closet with his neck so purple and bent it looked like it was on sideways, and the other bled up through the floor like a paper towel commercial in reverse. She hardly made it out of the boards, I'm proud to say. Instinct took over and I tacked her back down before she could make a move. Carver tackled me though, while I was trying to pull my knife out of the wood that was coated with the stain that used to be his wife. He almost threw me out the window before I scrambled back to the athame, mewling like a kitten. Stabbing him was almost an accident. The knife just sort of ran into him when he wrapped the end of his rope around my throat and spun me around. I never told my mom that part.

"You know better than that, Mom," I say. "It's only other people who think you can't kill what's already dead." I want to say that Dad knew too, but I don't. She doesn't like to talk about him, and I know that she hasn't been the same since he died. She's not quite here anymore; there's something missing in all of her smiles, like a blurry spot or a camera lens out of focus. Part of her followed him, wherever it was that he went. I know it's not that she doesn't love me. But I don't think she ever figured on raising a son by herself. Her family was supposed to form a circle. Now we walk around like a photograph that my dad's been cut out of.

"I'll be in and out like that," I say, snapping my fingers and redirecting the subject. "I might not even spend the whole school year in Thunder Bay."

She leans forward over the steering wheel and shakes her head. "You should think about staying longer. I've heard it's a nice place."

I roll my eyes. She knows better. Our life isn't quiet. It isn't like other lives, where there are roots and routines. We're a traveling circus. And she can't even blame it on my dad being killed, because we traveled with him too, though admittedly not as much. It's the reason that she works the way she does, doing tarot card readings and aura cleansing over the phone, and selling occult supplies online. My mother the mobile witch. She makes a surprisingly good living at it. Even without my dad's trust accounts, we'd probably be just fine.

Right now we're driving north on some winding road that follows the shore of Lake Superior. I was glad to get out of North Carolina, away from iced tea and accents and hospitality that didn't suit me. Being on the road I feel free, when I'm on my way from here to there, and it won't be until I put my feet down on Thunder Bay pavement that I'll feel like I'm back to work. For now I can enjoy the stacks of pines and the layers of sedimentary rock along the roadside, weeping groundwater like a constant regret. Lake Superior is bluer than blue and greener than green, and the clear light coming through the windows makes me squint behind my sunglasses.

"What are you going to do about college?"

"Mom," I moan. Frustration bubbles out of me all of a sudden. She's doing her half-and-half routine. Half accepting what I am, half insisting that I be a normal kid. I wonder if she did it to my dad too. I don't think so.

"Cas," she moans back. "Superheroes go to college too."

"I'm not a superhero," I say. It's an awful tag. It's egotistical, and it doesn't fit. I don't parade around in spandex. I don't do what I do and receive accolades and keys to cities. I work in the dark, killing what should have stayed dead. If people knew what I was up to, they'd probably try to stop me. The idiots would take Casper's side, and then I'd have to kill Casper *and* them after Casper bit their throats out. I'm no superhero. If anything I'm Rorschach from *Watchmen*. I'm Grendel. I'm the survivor in *Silent Hill*.

"If you're so set on doing this during college, there are plenty of cities that could keep you busy for four years." She turns the U-Haul into a gas station, the last one on the U.S. side. "What about Birmingham? That place is so haunted you could take two a month and still probably have enough to make it through grad school."

"Yeah, but then I'd have to go to college in fucking Birmingham," I say, and she shoots me a look. I mutter an apology. She might be the most liberal-minded of mothers, letting her teenage son roam the night hunting down the remains of murderers, but she still doesn't like hearing the f-bomb fall out of my mouth.

She pulls up to the pumps and takes a deep breath. "You've avenged him five times over, you know." Before I can say that I haven't, she gets out and shuts the door.

CHAPTER THREE

The scenery changed fast once we crossed over into Canada, and I'm looking out the window at miles of rolling hills covered in forest. My mother says it's something called boreal forest. Recently, since we really started moving around, she's developed this hobby of intensely researching each new place we live. She says it makes it feel more like a vacation, to know places where she wants to eat and things that she wants to do when we get there. I think it makes her feel like it's more of a home.

She's let Tybalt out of his pet carrier and he's perched on her shoulder with his tail wrapped around her neck. He doesn't spare a glance for me. He's half Siamese and has that breed's trait of choosing one person to adore and saying screw off to all the rest. Not that I care. I like it when he hisses and bats at me, and the only thing he's good for is occasionally seeing ghosts before I do.

My mom is staring up at the clouds, humming something that isn't a real song. She's wearing the same smile as her cat.

"Why the good mood?" I ask. "Isn't your butt asleep yet?"

"Been asleep for hours," she replies. "But I think I'm going to like Thunder Bay. And from the looks of these clouds, I'm going to get to enjoy it for quite some time."

I glance up. The clouds are enormous and perfectly white. They sit deadly still in the sky as we drive into them. I watch without blinking until my eyes dry out. They don't move or change in any way.

"Driving into unmoving clouds," she whispers. "Things are going to take longer than you expect."

I want to tell her that she's being superstitious, that clouds not moving don't mean anything, and besides, if you watch them long enough they have to move—but that would make a hypocrite of me, this guy who lets her cleanse his knife in salt under moonlight.

The stagnant clouds make me motion-sick for some reason, so I go back to looking at the forest, a blanket of pines in colors of green, brown, and rust, struck through with birch trunks sticking up like bones. I'm usually in a better mood on these trips. The excitement of somewhere new, a new ghost to hunt, new things to see . . . the prospects usually keep my brain sunny for at least the duration of the drive. Maybe it's just that I'm tired. I don't sleep much, and when I do, there's usually some kind of nightmare involved. But I'm not complaining. I've had them off and on since I started using the athame. Occupational hazard, I guess, my subconscious letting out all the fear I should be feeling when I walk into places where there are murderous ghosts. Still, I should try to get some rest. The dreams are particularly bad the night after a successful hunt, and they haven't really calmed down since I took out the hitchhiker.

An hour or so later, after many attempts at sleep, Thunder Bay comes up in our windshield, a sprawling, urbanesque city of over a hundred thousand living. We drive through the commercial and business districts and I am unimpressed. Walmart is a convenient place for the breathing, but I have never seen a ghost comparing prices on motor oil or trying to jimmy his way into the Xbox 360 game case. It's only as we get into the heart of the city—the older part of the city that rests above the harbor—that I see what I'm looking for.

Nestled in between refurbished family homes are houses cut out at bad angles, their coats of paint peeling in scabs and their shutters hanging crooked on their windows so they look like wounded eyes. I barely notice the nicer houses. I blink as we pass and they're gone, boring and inconsequential.

Over the course of my life I've been to lots of places. Shadowed places where things have gone wrong. Sinister places where things still are. I always hate the sunlit towns, full of newly built developments with double-car garages in shades of pale eggshell, surrounded by green lawns and dotted with laughing children. Those towns aren't any less haunted than the others. They're just better liars. I like it more to come to a place like this, where the scent of death is carried to you on every seventh breath.

I watch the water of Superior lie beside the city like a

sleeping dog. My dad always said that water makes the dead feel safe. Nothing draws them more. Or hides them better.

My mom has turned on the GPS, which she has affectionately named Fran after an uncle with a particularly good sense of direction. Fran's droning voice is guiding us through the city, directing us like we're idiots: Prepare to turn left in 100 feet. Prepare to turn left. Turn left. Tybalt, sensing the end of the journey, has returned to his pet carrier, and I reach down and shut the door. He hisses at me like he could have done it himself.

The house that we rented is smallish, two stories of fresh maroon paint and dark gray trim and shutters. It sits at the base of a hill, the start of a nice flat patch of land. When we pull up there are no neighbors peeking at us from windows or coming out onto their porches to say hello. The house looks contained, and solitary.

"What do you think?" my mom asks.

"I like it," I reply honestly. "You can see things coming."

She sighs at me. She'd be happier if I would grin and bound up the stairs of the front porch, throw open the door and race up to the second floor to try and call dibs on the master bedroom. I used to do that sort of thing when we'd move into a new place with Dad. But I was seven. I'm not going to let her road-weary eyes guilt me into anything. Before I know it, we'll be making daisy chains in the backyard and crowning the cat the king of summer solstice.

Instead, I grab the pet carrier and get out of the U-Haul.

It isn't ten seconds before I hear my mom's footsteps behind my own. I wait for her to unlock the front door, and then we go in, smelling cooped-up summer air and the old dirt of strangers. The door has opened on a large living room, already furnished with a cream-colored couch and wingback chair. There's a brass lamp that needs a new lampshade, and a coffee and end table set in dark mahogany. Farther back, a wooden archway leads to the kitchen and an open dining room.

I look up into the shadows of the staircase on my right. Quietly, I close the front door behind us and set the pet carrier on the wood floor, then open it up. After a second, a pair of green eyes pokes out, followed by a black, slinky body. This is a trick I learned from my dad. Or rather, that my dad learned from himself.

He'd been following a tip into Portland. The job in question was the multiple victims of a fire in a canning factory. His mind was wound up with thoughts of machinery and things whose lips cracked open when they spoke. He hadn't paid much attention when he rented the house we moved into, and of course the landlord didn't mention that a woman and her unborn baby died there when her husband pushed her down the stairs. These are things one tends to gloss over.

It's a funny thing about ghosts. They might have been normal, or relatively normal, when they were still breathing, but once they die they're your typical obsessives. They become fixated on what happened to them and trap themselves in the worst moment. Nothing else exists in their world except the edge of that knife, the feel of those hands around their throat. They have a habit of showing you these things, usually by demonstration. If you know their story, it isn't hard to predict what they'll do.

On that particular day in Portland, my mom was helping me move my boxes up into my new room. It was back when we still used cheap cardboard, and it was raining; most of the box tops were softening like cereal in milk. I remember laughing over how wet we were getting, and how we left shoe-shaped puddles all over the linoleum entryway. By the sound of our scrambling feet you would have thought a family of hypoglycemic golden retrievers was moving in.

It happened on our third trip up the stairs. I was slapping my shoes down, making a mess, and had taken my baseball glove out of the box because I didn't want it to get water-spotted. Then I felt it—something glide by me on the staircase, just brushing past my shoulder. There was nothing angry or hurried about the touch. I never told anyone, because of what happened next, but it felt motherly, like I was being carefully moved out of the way. At the time I think I thought it was my mom, making a play-grab for my arm, because I turned around with this big grin on my face, just in time to see the ghost of the woman change from wind to mist. She seemed to be wearing a sheet, and her hair was so pale that I could see her face through the back of her head. I'd seen ghosts before. Growing up with my dad, it was as routine as Thursday night meatloaf. But I'd never seen one shove my mother into thin air.

I tried to reach her, but all I ended up with was a torn scrap of the cardboard box. She fell back, the ghost wavering triumphantly. I could see Mom's expression through the floating sheet. Strangely enough, I can remember that I could see her back molars as she fell, the upper back molars, and that she had two cavities in them. That's what I think of when I think of that incident: the gross, queasy feeling I got from seeing my mother's cavities. She landed on the stairs butt first and made a little "oh" sound, then rolled backward until she hit the wall. I don't remember anything after that. I don't even remember if we stayed in the house. Of course my father must have dispatched the ghost—probably that same day—but I don't remember anything else of Portland. All I know is, after that my dad started using Tybalt, who was just a kitten then, and Mom still walks with a limp on the day before a thunderstorm.

Tybalt is eyeing the ceiling, sniffing the walls. His tail twitches occasionally. We follow him as he checks the entirety of the lower level. I get impatient with him in the bathroom, because he looks like he's forgotten that he has a job to do and instead wants to roll on the cool tile. I snap my fingers. He squints at me resentfully, but he gets up and continues his inspection.

On the stairs he hesitates. I'm not worried. What I'm looking for is for him to hiss at thin air, or to sit quietly and stare at nothing. Hesitation doesn't mean a thing.

Cats can see ghosts, but they don't have precognition. We follow him up the stairs and out of habit I take my mom's hand. I've got my leather bag over my shoulder. The athame is a comforting presence inside, my own little St. Christopher's medallion.

There are three bedrooms and a full bathroom on the fourth floor, plus a small attic with a pull-down ladder. It smells like fresh paint, which is good. Things that are new are good. No chance that some sentimental dead thing has attached itself. Tybalt winds his way through the bathroom and then walks into a bedroom. He stares at the dresser, its drawers open and askew, and regards the stripped bed with distaste. Then he sits and cleans both forepaws.

"There's nothing here. Let's move our stuff in and seal it." At the suggestion of activity, the lazy cat turns his head and growls at me, his green reflector eyes as round as wall clocks. I ignore him and reach up for the trap door to the attic. "Ow!" I look down. Tybalt has climbed me like a tree. I've got both hands on his back, and he has all four sets of claws snugly embedded in my skin. And the damned thing is purring.

"He's just playing, honey," my mom says, and carefully plucks each paw off of my clothing. "I'll put him back in his carrier and stow him in a bedroom until we get the boxes in. Maybe you should dig in the trailer and find his litter box."

"Great," I say sarcastically. But I do get the cat set up in my mom's new bedroom with food, water, and his cat box before we move the rest of our stuff into the house. It takes only two hours. We're experts at this. Still, the sun is beginning to set when my mom finishes up the kitchen-witch business: boiling oils and herbs to anoint the doors and windows with, effectively keeping out anything that wasn't in when we got here. I don't know that it works, but I can't really say that it doesn't. We've always been safe in our homes. I do, however, know that it reeks like sandalwood and rosemary.

After the house is sealed, I start a small fire in the backyard, and my mom and I burn every small knickknack we find that could have meant something to a previous tenant: a purple beaded necklace left in a drawer, a few homemade potholders, and even a tiny book of matches that looked too well-preserved. We don't need ghosts trying to come back for something left behind. My mom presses a wet thumb to my forehead. I can smell rosemary and sweet oil.

"Mom."

"You know the rules. Every night for the first three nights." She smiles, and in the firelight her auburn hair looks like embers. "It'll keep you safe."

"It'll give me acne," I protest, but make no move to wipe it off. "I have to start school in two weeks."

She doesn't say anything. She just stares down at her herbal thumb like she might press it between her own eyes. But then she blinks and wipes it on the leg of her jeans.

This city smells like smoke and things that rot in the summer. It's more haunted than I thought it would be, an entire layer of activity just under the dirt: whispers behind peoples' laughter, or movement that you shouldn't see in the corner of your eye. Most of them are harmless—sad little cold spots or groans in the dark. Blurry patches of white that only show up in a Polaroid. I have no business with them.

But somewhere out there is one that matters. Somewhere out there is the one that I came for, one who is strong enough to squeeze the breath out of living throats.

I think of her again. Anna. Anna Dressed in Blood. I wonder what tricks she'll try. I wonder if she'll be clever. Will she float? Will she laugh or scream?

How will she try to kill me?

CHAPTER FOUR

"Would you rather be a Trojan or a tiger?"

My mother asks this while she's standing over the griddle making us cornmeal pancakes. It's the last day to register me for high school before it starts tomorrow. I know that she meant to do it sooner, but she's been busy forming relationships with a number of downtown merchants, trying to get them to advertise her fortune-telling business and seeing if they'll carry her occult supplies. There's apparently a candle maker just outside of town that has agreed to infuse her product with a specific blend of oils, sort of a candle-spell in a box. They'd sell these custom creations at shops around town, and Mom would also ship them to her phone clientele.

"What kind of a question is that? Do we have any jam?"

"Strawberry or something called Saskatoon, which looks like blueberry."

I make a sour face. "I'll take the strawberry."

"You should live dangerously. Try the Saskatoon."

"I live dangerously enough. Now what's this about condoms or tigers?"

She sets a plate of pancakes and toast down in front of me, each topped with a pile of what I desperately hope is strawberry jam.

"Behave yourself, kiddo. They're the school mascots. Do you want to go to Sir Winston Churchill or Westgate Collegiate? Apparently we're close enough for both."

I sigh. It doesn't matter. I'll take my classes and pass my tests, and then I'll transfer out, just like always. I'm here to kill Anna. But I should make a show of caring, to please my mom.

"Dad would want me to be a Trojan," I say quietly, and she pauses for just a second over the griddle before sliding the last pancake onto her plate.

"I'll go over to Winston Churchill then," she says. What luck. I chose the douche-y sounding one. But like I said, it doesn't matter. I'm here for one thing, something that fell into my lap while I was still fruitlessly casting about for the County 12 Hiker.

It came, charmingly, in the mail. My name and address on a coffee-stained envelope, and inside just one scrap of paper with Anna's name on it. It was written in blood. I get these tips from all over the country, all over the world. There are not many people who can do what I do, but there are a multitude of people who want me to do it, and they seek me out, asking those who are in the know and following my trail. We move a lot but I'm easy enough to find if they look. Mom makes a website announcement

whenever we relocate, and we always tell a few of my father's oldest friends where we're headed. Every month, like
clockwork, a stack of ghosts flies across my metaphorical
desk: an e-mail about people going missing in a Satanic
church in northern Italy, a newspaper clipping of mysterious animal sacrifices near an Ojibwe burial mound. I trust
only a few sources. Most are my father's contacts, elders in
the coven he was a member of in college, or scholars he
met on his travels and through his reputation. They're
the ones I can trust not to send me on wild-goose chases.
They do their homework.

But, over the years, I've developed a few contacts of my
own. When I looked down at the scrawling red letters, cut
across the paper like scabbed-over claw marks, I knew that
it had to be a tip from Rudy Bristol. The theatrics of it.
The gothic romance of the yellowed parchment. Like I was
supposed to believe the ghost actually did it herself, etching
her name in someone's blood and sending it to me like a
calling card inviting me to dinner.

Rudy "the Daisy" Bristol is a hard-core goth kid from
New Orleans. He lounges around tending bar deep in the
French Quarter, lost somewhere in his mid-twenties and
wishing he were still sixteen. He's skinny, pale as a vampire, and wears way too much mesh. So far he's led me to
three good ghosts: nice, quick kills. One of them was actually hanging by his neck in a root cellar, whispering
through the floorboards and enticing new residents of the
house to join him in the dirt. I walked in, gutted him, and
walked back out. It was that job that made me like Daisy.

It wasn't until later on that I learned to enjoy his extremely enthusiastic personality.

I called him the minute I got his letter.

"Hey man, how'd you know it was me?" There was no disappointment in his voice, just an excited, flattered tone that reminded me of some kid at a Jonas Brothers concert. He's such a fanboy. If I allowed it, he'd strap on a proton pack and follow me around the country.

"Of course it was you. How many tries did it take you to get the letters to look right? Is the blood even real?"

"Yeah, it's real."

"What kind of blood is it?"

"Human."

I smiled. "You used your own blood, didn't you?" There was a sound of huffing, of shifting around.

"Look, do you want the tip or not?"

"Yeah, go ahead." My eyes were on the scrap of paper. *Anna*. Even though I knew it was just one of Daisy's cheap tricks, her name in blood looked beautiful.

"Anna Korlov. Murdered in 1958."

"By who?"

"Nobody knows."

"How?"

"Nobody really knows that either."

It was starting to sound like a crock. There are always records, always investigations. Each drop of blood spilled leaves a paper trail from here to Oregon. And the way he kept trying to make the phrase "nobody knows" sound creepy was starting to wear on my nerves.

"So how do you know?" I asked him.

"Lots of people know," he replied. "She's Thunder Bay's favorite spook story."

"Spook stories usually turn out to be just that: stories. Why are you wasting my time?" I reached out for the paper, ready to crumple it in my fist. But I didn't. I don't know why I was being skeptical. People always know. Sometimes a lot of people. But they don't really do anything about it. They don't really say anything. Instead they heed the warnings and cluck their tongues at any ignorant fool who stumbles into the spider's den. It's easier for them that way. It lets them live in the daylight.

"She's not that kind of spook story," Daisy insisted. "You won't ask around town and get anything about her—unless you ask in the right places. She's not a tourist attraction. But you walk into any teenage girls' slumber party, and I guarantee you they'll be telling Anna's story at midnight."

"Because I walk into a ton of teenage girls' slumber parties," I sighed. Of course, I suppose that Daisy really did, back in his day. "What's the deal?"

"She was sixteen when she died, the daughter of Finnish immigrants. Her father was dead, he died of some disease or something, and her mom ran a boarding house downtown. Anna was on her way to a school dance when she was killed. Someone cut her throat, but that's an understatement. Someone nearly cut her head clean off. They say she was wearing a white party dress, and when they found her, the whole thing was stained red. That's why they call her Anna Dressed in Blood."

"Anna Dressed in Blood," I repeated softly.

"Some people think that it was one of the boarders that did it. That some pervert took a look at her and liked what he saw, followed her and left her bleeding in a ditch. Others say it was her date, or a jealous boyfriend."

I took a deep breath to pull me out of my trance. It was bad, but they were all bad, and it was by no means the worst thing I'd ever heard. Howard Sowberg, a farmer in central Iowa, killed his entire family with a pair of hedge shears, alternately stabbing and snipping as the case allowed. His entire family consisted of his wife, his two young sons, a newborn, and his elderly mother. Now that was one of the worst things I'd ever heard. I was disappointed to get to central Iowa and discover that the ghost of Howard Sowberg wasn't remorseful enough to hang around. Strangely enough, it's usually the victims that turn bad in the afterlife. The truly evil move on, to burn or turn to dust or be reincarnated as dung beetles. They use up all their rage while they're still breathing.

Daisy was still going on about Anna's legend. His voice was growing lower and breathier with excitement. I couldn't decide whether to laugh or be annoyed.

"Okay, so what does she do, now?"

He paused. "She's killed twenty-seven teenagers . . . that I know of."

Twenty-seven teenagers in the last half century. It was starting to sound like a fairy tale again, either that or the strangest cover-up in history. Nobody kills twenty-seven teenagers and escapes without being chased into a castle by a crowd holding torches and pitchforks. Not even a ghost.

"Twenty-seven local kids? You've got to be kidding me. Not drifters, or runaways?"

"Well—"

"Well, what? Someone's pulling your chain, Bristol." Bitterness grew in the back of my throat. I don't know why. So what if the tip was fake? There were fifteen other ghosts waiting in the stack. One of them was from Colorado, some Grizzly Adams type who was murdering hunters on an entire mountain. Now that sounded like fun.

"They never find any bodies," Daisy said in an effort to explain. "They must just figure that the kids ran away, or were abducted. It's only the other kids who would say anything about Anna, and of course nobody does. You know better than that."

Yeah. I knew better than that. And I knew something else too. There was more to Anna's story than Daisy was telling me. I don't know what it was, call it intuition. Maybe it was her name, scrawled out in crimson. Maybe Daisy's cheap and masochistic trick really did work after all. But I knew. I know. I feel it in my gut, and my father always told me when your gut says something, you listen.

"I'll look into it."

"Are you going?" There was that excited tone again, like an overeager beagle waiting to have his rope thrown.

"I said I'll look into it. I've got something to wrap up here first."

"What is it?"

I briefly told him about the County 12 Hiker. He made some asinine suggestions on how to draw him out that were so asinine I don't even remember them now. Then, as usual, he tried to get me to come down to New Orleans.

I wouldn't touch New Orleans with a ten-foot pole. That town is haunted as shit, and all the better for it. Nowhere in the world loves its ghosts more than that city. Sometimes I worry for Daisy; I worry that someone will get wind of his talking to me, sending me out on hunts, and then someday I'll have to be hunting him, some ripped-up victim version of him dragging his severed limbs around a warehouse.

I lied to him that day. I didn't look into it any further. By the time I had gotten off the phone, I knew that I was going after Anna. My gut told me that she wasn't just a story. And besides, I wanted to see her, dressed in blood.

CHAPTER FIVE

From what I can gather, Sir Winston Churchill Collegiate & Vocational is just about like any high school I was ever at in the United States. I spent all of first period working out my schedule with the school counselor, Ms. Ben, a kindly, birdlike young woman who is destined to wear baggy turtlenecks and own too many cats.

Now, in the hallway, every set of eyes is on me. I'm new and different, but that's not the only thing. Everyone's eyes are on everybody, because it's the first day of classes and people are dying to know what their classmates have turned into over the summer. There must be at least fifty makeovers and brand-new looks being tried out somewhere in the building. The pasty bookworm has bleached her hair white and is wearing a dog collar. The skinny kid from the track team has spent all of July and August lifting weights and buying tight-fitting t-shirts.

Still, people's eyes tend to linger on me longer, because even though I'm new, I don't move like it. I'm barely looking at the numbers of the rooms passing by. I'll find my classes eventually, right? No reason to panic. Besides, I'm an old hand at this. I've been to twelve high schools in the past three years. And I'm looking for something.

I need to be plugged into the social pipeline. I need to get people talking to me, so I can ask them questions that I need answers to. So when I transfer in, I always look for the queen bee.

Every school has one. The girl who knows everything and everybody. I could go and try to insta-bond with the lead jock, I suppose, but I've never been good at that. My dad and I never watched sports or played catch. I can wrestle the dead all day long, but touch football might knock me unconscious. Girls, on the other hand, have always come easy. I don't know why that is, exactly. Maybe it's the outsider vibe and a well-placed brooding look. Maybe it's something I think I see sometimes in the mirror, something that reminds me of my father. Or maybe I'm just damn easy on the eyes. So I scour the halls until I finally see her, smiling and surrounded by people.

There's no mistaking her: the queen of the school is always pretty, but this one is downright beautiful. She's got something like three feet of layered blond hair and lips the color of ripe peaches. As soon as she sees me, she dips her chin. A smile comes easily to her face. This is the girl who gets everything she wants at Winston Churchill. She's the teacher's pet, the homecoming queen, and party central. Everything I want to know, she could tell me. Which is what I hope she'll do.

When I walk by, I pointedly ignore her. A few seconds later she leaves her group of friends and jumps in beside me.

"Hey. Haven't seen you around here before."

"I just moved to town."

She smiles again. She's got perfect teeth and warm chocolate eyes. She is immediately disarming. "Then you'll need some help getting acquainted. I'm Carmel Jones."

"Theseus Cassio Lowood. What kind of a parent names their kid Carmel?"

She laughs. "What kind of a parent names their kid Theseus Cassio?"

"Hippies," I reply.

"Exactly."

We laugh together, and mine isn't completely false. Carmel Jones owns this school. I can tell by the way she carries herself, like she's never had to kneel down in her life. I can tell because of the way the crowd is flitting away like birds from a prowling cat. Just the same, she doesn't seem haughty or entitled like many of these girls do. I show her my schedule and she notes that we have the same fourth period biology class and—even better—the same lunch hour. When she leaves me at the door of my second period, she turns back and winks at me over her shoulder.

Queen bees are just a part of the job. Sometimes that's hard to remember.

At lunch, Carmel flags me down, but I don't go over right away. I'm not here to date anyone, and I don't want to give her the wrong idea. Still, she's pretty hot, and I have to remind myself that all that popularity and ease has probably made her unbelievably boring. She's too much of the daylight for me. Truth be told, so is everyone. What do you expect? I move around a lot, and spend too many late nights killing stuff. Who's going to put up with that?

I scan the rest of the lunchroom, making a note of all the different groups and wondering which one would be most likely to lead me to Anna. The goth kids would know the story best, but they're also the hardest to ditch. If they got the idea that I was serious about killing their ghost, I'd probably wind up doing it with a gang of black-eyeliner-wearing, crucifix-carrying, Buffy the Vampire Slayer wannabes twittering around behind me.

"Theseus!"

Shit, I forgot to tell Carmel to call me Cas. The last thing I need is for the "Theseus" thing to get around and stick. I make my way to her table, seeing eyes growing wider as I do. Ten or so other girls probably just developed instantaneous crushes on me, because they see that Carmel likes me. Or so the sociologist in my brain says.

"Hey, Carmel."

"Hey. How are you finding SWC?"

I make a mental note never to refer to it as "SWC."

"Not bad, thanks to your tour this morning. And by the way, most people just call me Cas."

"Caz?"

"Yeah. But softer on the *s*. What do you get for lunch around here?"

"Usually we do the Pizza Hut pizza bar over there." She gestures vaguely with her head, and I turn and glance vaguely in that direction. "So, Cas, why did you move to Thunder Bay?"

"Scenery," I say, and smile. "Honestly, you wouldn't believe me if I told you."

"Try me," she says. The thought occurs to me again that Carmel Jones knows exactly how to get what she wants. But she's also given me the opportunity to be completely frank. My mouth actually moves to form the words, *Anna, I'm here for Anna,* when the damn Trojan Army rolls up behind us in an assembly line of Winston Churchill Wrestling team t-shirts.

"Carmel," one of them says. Without looking I know that he either is, or was until very recently, Carmel's boyfriend. The way that he says her name sticks to his cheeks. From the way that Carmel reacts, with a lifting of her chin and an arch of her eyebrow, I figure that he's more of the ex type.

"You coming out tonight?" he asks, completely ignoring me. I watch him with amusement. There's a blue light special on territorial jocks in aisle four.

"What's tonight?" I ask.

"The annual Edge of the World party." Carmel rolls her eyes skyward. "Something we've been doing forever, on the night of the first day of school."

Well, forever, or at least since *The Rules of Attraction* was released.

"Sounds cool," I say. The Neanderthal behind me can

no longer be ignored, so I put my hand out and introduce myself.

Only the dickiest of dicks would refuse to shake my hand. And I have just met the dickiest of dicks. He nods his head at me and says, "What's up." He doesn't introduce himself back, but Carmel does.

"This is Mike Andover." She gestures to the others. "And Chase Putnam, and Simon Parry, and Will Rosenberg."

They all nod at me like total assholes except for Will Rosenberg, who shakes my hand. He's the only one who doesn't seem like a complete douche. He wears his letter jacket loose and with his shoulders hunched like he's sort of ashamed of it. Or at least ashamed of its present company.

"So, are you coming, or what?"

"I don't know," Carmel replies. She sounds annoyed. "I'll have to see."

"We'll be at the falls around ten," he says. "Let me know if you need a ride." When he leaves, Carmel sighs.

"What are they talking about? The falls?" I ask, feigning interest.

"The party is at Kakabeka Falls. Every year it moves around, to keep the cops off. Last year it was at Trowbridge Falls, but everybody freaked out when—" She pauses.

"When what?"

"Nothing. Just a bunch of ghost stories."

Could I be this lucky? Usually I'm a week in before there's a convenient segue into haunting talk. It's not exactly the easiest thing to bring up.

"I love ghost stories. In fact, I'm dying for a good ghost story." I move to sit down across from her and lean forward on my elbows. "And I do need someone to show me around the Thunder Bay nightlife."

She looks directly into my eyes. "We can take my car. Where do you live?"

Someone is following me. The sensation is so acute that I can actually feel my eyes try to slip through my skull and part the hair on the back of my head. I'm too proud to turn around—I've been through too much scary shit to be put off by any human attacker. There's also the slight chance that I'm just being paranoid. But I don't think so. There's something back there, and it's something that's still breathing, which makes me uneasy. The dead have simple motives: hate, pain, and confusion. They kill you because it's the only thing they have left to do. The living have needs, and whoever is following me wants something of me or mine. That makes me nervous.

Stubbornly, I stare ahead, taking extra long pauses and being sure to wait for the walk signals at every intersection. In my head I'm thinking that I'm an idiot for putting off buying a new car, and wondering where I could hang out for a few hours to regroup and avoid being followed home. I stop and strip my leather backpack from my shoulder and dig around inside until my hand is clutching the sheath that holds my athame. This is pissing me off.

I'm passing by a cemetery, some sad, Presbyterian thing that isn't well-kept, the grave markers adorned with lifeless flowers and ribbons torn by the wind and stained dark with mud. Near me, one of the headstones lies on the ground, fallen down dead just like the person buried underneath it. For all its sadness, it's also quiet, and unchanging, and it calms me a little. There's a woman standing in the center, an old widow, staring down at her husband's grave marker. Her wool coat hangs stiff on her shoulders and there's a thin handkerchief tied beneath her chin. I'm so caught up in whoever was following me that it takes me a minute to realize that she's wearing a wool coat in August.

There's a hitch in my throat. She turns her head at the noise and I can see, even from here, that she doesn't have any eyes. Just a set of gray stones where her eyes used to be, and yet we stare at each other, unblinking. The wrinkles in her cheeks are so deep they could have been drawn in black marker. She must have a story. Some disturbing tale of woe that gave her stones for eyes and brings her back to stare at what I now suspect is her own body. But right now I'm being followed. I don't have time for this.

I flip open my backpack and pull my knife out by the handle, showing just a flash of the blade. The old woman draws her lips back and opens her teeth in a silent hiss. Then she backs away, sinking slowly into the ground as she does, and the effect is something like watching someone wave from an escalator. I feel no fear, just a bleak embarrassment that it took me so long to notice she was dead. She might have tried to give me a scare had she gotten close enough, but she's not the kind of ghost that kills. If

I had been anyone else, I might not have even noticed her. But I'm tuned in to these things.

"Me too."

I jump at the voice, right at my shoulder. There's a kid standing beside me, been standing there for god knows how long. He's got ragged black hair and black-rimmed glasses, a skinny, lanky body hidden under clothes that don't fit right. I feel like I recognize him from school. He nods toward the cemetery.

"Some scary old lady, huh?" he says. "Don't worry. She's harmless, here three days a week at least. And I can only read minds when people are thinking about something really hard." He smiles out of one half of his mouth. "But I get the feeling that you're always thinking really hard."

I hear a thump from somewhere nearby and realize that I've let go of my athame. The thump that I heard was the sound of it hitting the bottom of my backpack. I know he's the one who was following me, and it's a relief to have been right. At the same time, I find the prospect of his being telepathic disorienting.

I've known telepaths before. Some of my dad's friends were telepathic to varying degrees. Dad said it was useful. I think it's mostly creepy. The first time I met his friend Jackson, who I'm now quite fond of, I lined the inside of my baseball cap with tinfoil. What? I was five. I thought it would work. But I don't happen to have a baseball cap or any foil handy right now, so I try to think softly . . . whatever the hell that means.

"Who are you?" I ask. "Why are you following me?"

And then I know. He's the one who tipped off Daisy. Some telepathic kid who wanted in on some action. How else would he know to follow me? How else would he know who I am? He was waiting. Waiting for me to hit school, like some freaky snake in the grass.

"Wanna get something to eat? I'm starving. I haven't been following you very long. My car's right up the street." He turns around and walks off, the frayed ends of his jeans scraping along the sidewalk in a little shuffle. He walks like a dog that's been kicked, head low and hands stuffed into his pockets. I don't know where he picked up his dusty green jacket, but I suspect it was from the Army surplus store I passed a few blocks back.

"I'll explain everything when we get there," he says over his shoulder. "Come on."

I don't know why I follow, but I do.

He drives a Ford Tempo. It's about six different shades of gray and sounds like a very angry kid pretending to drive a motorboat in the bathtub. The place that he takes me to is a little joint called The Sushi Bowl, which looks like absolute crap from the outside, but inside it's not too bad. The waitress asks if we'd rather be seated traditional or regular. I glance around and see some low tables with mats and pillows around them.

"Regular," I say quickly, before Army Surplus Psycho can pipe up. I've never eaten anything perched on my knees before, and just now I'd rather not look as awkward as I feel.

After I tell the kid that I've never eaten sushi, he orders for us, which does nothing to help me shake the feeling of disorientation. It's like I'm trapped in one of those omniscient dreams where you just watch yourself do stupid shit, yelling at yourself about how stupid it is, and your dream-self just keeps doing what it's doing anyway.

The kid across the table is smiling like an idiot. "Saw you with Carmel Jones today," he says. "You don't waste any time."

"What do you want?" I ask.

"Just to help."

"I don't need any help."

"You already had it." He hunkers lower as the food arrives, two plates of circular mystery, one deep fried and the other covered in small orange dots. "Try some," he says.

"What is it?"

"Philadelphia roll."

I eye the plate skeptically. "What's that orange stuff?"

"Cod roe."

"What the hell is cod roe?"

"Cod eggs."

"No thanks." I'm so glad there's a McDonald's across the street. Fish eggs. Who the hell is this kid?

"I'm Thomas Sabin."

"Stop doing that."

"Sorry." He grins. "It's just that you're so easy sometimes. I know it's rude. And seriously, I can't do it all the time." He stuffs an entire circle of fish egg–encrusted raw fish into his mouth. I try not to inhale while he chews. "But I *have* helped you already. The Trojan Army, remember? When those guys came up behind you today. Who do you think sent that to you? I gave you the heads-up. You're welcome."

The Trojan Army. That's what I thought when Mike and Co. walked up behind me at lunch. But now that I think about it, I'm not sure why I'd thought that. The only view I'd had of them had been out of the corner of my eye. The Trojan Army. The kid had put the thought in my head so smoothly, like a note dropped onto the floor in a conspicuous place.

Now he's going on about how it isn't easy to send things like that, how it had given him a bit of a nosebleed to do it. He sounds like he thinks he's my own little guardian angel or something.

"What should I be thanking you for? Being witty? You put your personal judgment into my head. Now I have to go around wondering if I thought those guys were douche bags because I really thought so, or just because you thought so first."

"Trust me, you'd agree. And you really shouldn't be talking to Carmel Jones. At least, not yet. She just broke up with Mike the Meathead Andover last week. And he's been known to hit people with his car just for ogling her while she's in the passenger seat."

I don't like this kid. He's presumptuous. And yet, he's earnest and well-meaning, which softens me a little. If he's listening to what I'm thinking, I'm going to slash his tires.

"I don't need your help," I say. I wish I didn't have to watch him eat anymore. But the fried stuff doesn't look too bad, and it kind of smells okay.

"I think you do. You've noticed I'm a little bit strange. You moved here what, seventeen days ago?"

I nod numbly. It was seventeen days ago exactly that we pulled into Thunder Bay.

"I thought so. For the past seventeen days, I've had the worst psychic headache of my life. The kind that actually throbs and makes a home behind my left eye. Makes everything smell like salt. It's only now that we're talking that it's going away." He wipes his mouth, gets serious all of a sudden. "It's hard to believe, but you've got to. I only get these headaches when something bad is going to happen. And it's never been this bad before."

I lean back and sigh. "Just what do you think you're going to help me with? Who do you think I am?" Sure, I think I know the answers to these questions already, but it doesn't hurt to double-check. And besides, I feel at a complete disadvantage, totally off my game. I'd feel better if I could stop this infernal interior monologue. Maybe I should just vocalize everything. Or constantly think in images: kitten playing with ball of yarn, hot-dog vendor on street corner, hot-dog vendor holding kitten.

Thomas wipes the corner of his mouth with his napkin. "That's a nifty piece of hardware you've got in your bag there," he says. "Old Mrs. Dead-Eyes seemed pretty impressed by it." He snaps his chopsticks together and picks up a piece of the deep-fried stuff, then shoves it into his mouth. As he chews, he talks, and I wish he wouldn't. "So I'd say you're some kind of ghost-slayer. And I know you're here for Anna."

I should probably ask what he knows. But I don't. I don't want to talk to him anymore. He already knows too much about me.

Fucking Daisy Bristol. I'm going to tear him a new one, sending me here where there's a telepathic tagalong lying in wait, and he didn't even warn me.

Looking at Thomas Sabin now, there's a cocky little smirk on his pale face. He pushes his glasses up on his nose in a gesture so quick and easy I can tell he does it often. There's so much confidence in those shifty blue eyes; he could never be convinced that his psychic intuition was wrong. And who knows how much he's been able to read out of my mind.

Impulsively, I pluck a deep-fried circle of fish off of the platter and pop it into my mouth. There's some kind of sweet and savory sauce on it. It's surprisingly good, heavy and chewy. But I'm still not touching the fish eggs. I've had enough of this. If I can't make him believe I'm not who he says I am, I at least have to throw him off his cocky horse and send him packing.

I knit my brows in an expression of puzzlement.

"Anna who?" I say.

He blinks, and when he starts to sputter I lean forward on my elbows. "I want you to listen to me very carefully, Thomas," I say. "I appreciate the tip. But there is no cavalry, and I am not recruiting. Do you understand?" And then, before he can protest, I think *hard*, I think of every grisly thing I've ever done, the myriad of ways I've seen things bleed and burn and twist apart. I send him Peter Carver's eyes exploding in their sockets. I send him the County 12 Hiker, bleeding black ooze, the skin pulling dry and tight to his bones.

It's like I've hit him in the face. His head actually rocks back and sweat immediately begins to bead on his forehead and upper lip. He swallows, the lump of his Adam's apple bouncing up and down. I think the poor kid might actually lose his sushi.

He doesn't protest when I call for the bill.

CHAPTER SIX

I let Thomas drive me home. After I was less defensive, he didn't get on my nerves as much. On my way up the porch steps I hear him roll down his window and ask awkwardly if I'm going to be at the Edge of the World party. I don't say anything. Seeing those deaths shook him up pretty good. More and more he seems to me just a lonely kid, and I don't want to tell him again to stay away from me. Besides, if he's so psychic then he shouldn't have to ask.

When I get inside I set my bag down on the kitchen table. My mom is there, chopping herbs for what might be dinner or might be one of her wide variety of magic spells. I see strawberry leaves and cinnamon. That's either a love spell or the beginnings of a tart. My stomach rolls over and taps my shoulder, so I head to the refrigerator to make a sandwich.

"Hey. Dinner's going to be ready in an hour."

"I know, but I'm hungry now. Growing boy." I put out mayonnaise, Colby jack, and deli bologna. As my hands move for the bread I'm thinking of everything I need to do for tonight. The athame is clean, but that doesn't really matter. I don't anticipate seeing anything dead, no matter what the school rumors say. I've never heard of any ghost attacking a group of more than ten. That stuff only happens in slasher movies.

Tonight is about breaking in. I want to hear Anna's story. I want to know the people who can lead me to her. For all that Daisy could tell me—her last name, her age—he couldn't tell me where she haunted. All he knew was that it was her family home. I could, of course, go to the local library and trace the Korlovs' residence. Something like Anna's murder had to make the papers. But what fun would that be? This is my favorite part of the hunt. Getting to know them. Hearing their legends. I want them to be as large in my mind as they can possibly be, and when I see them I don't want to be disappointed.

"How was your day, Mom?"

"Fine," she says, bent over her chopping block. "I've got to call an exterminator. I was storing a box of Tupperware in the attic and saw a rat tail disappear behind one of the wall boards." She shudders and makes yuck noises with her tongue.

"Why don't you just let Tybalt up there? That's what cats are for, you know. Catching mice and rats."

Her face becomes a horrified squint. "Yish. I don't want him to get worms chewing on some nasty rat. I'll just call an exterminator. Or you can go up and set some traps."

"Sure thing," I say. "But not tonight. Tonight I've got a date."

"A date? With who?"

"Carmel Jones." I smile and shake my head. "It's for the job. There's a party at some kind of waterfall park tonight and I should be able to get some decent information."

My mom sighs and goes back to chopping. "Is she a nice girl?"

As usual, she's fixating on the wrong part of the news.

"I don't like the idea of you using these girls all the time."

I laugh and jump up on the countertop to sit beside her. I steal a strawberry. "You make it sound so dirty."

"Using for a noble purpose is still using."

"I've never broken any hearts, Mom."

She clucks her tongue. "You've never been in love, either, Cas."

A conversation about love with my mother is worse than the talk that involves birds and bees, so I mumble something around my sandwich and duck out of the kitchen. I don't appreciate the implication that I'm going to hurt someone. Doesn't she think I'm careful? Doesn't she know the trouble I go to in order to keep people at arm's length?

I chew harder and try not to get myself worked up. She's just being a mom, after all. Still, all these years of me not bringing friends home should give her a clue.

But now's not the time to be thinking of this. These are complications I don't need. It'll happen, sometime, I'm sure. Or maybe not. Because no one should get caught up in this, and I can't imagine ever being finished. There will always be more dead, and the dead will always kill.

Carmel picks me up a little after nine. She looks great, in some kind of strappy pink top and a short khaki skirt. Her blond hair hangs loose between her shoulders. I should smile. I should say something nice, but I find myself holding back. My mother's words are interfering with my job.

Carmel drives a silver Audi that's a couple of years old, and it hugs the curves as we flash past strange street signs that look like Charlie Brown's t-shirt, and others proclaiming that apparently a moose is going to attack the car. It's getting close to dusk and the light is turning orange; the humidity in the air is breaking and the wind is strong as a hand against my face. I want to hang my entire head out of the window like a dog. As we leave the city behind my ears prick backward, listening for her—for Anna—wondering if she can feel me moving away.

I can feel her there, mingled into the mud of a hundred other ghosts, some shuffling and harmless, others full of rage. I can't imagine what it is to be dead; it's a strange idea to me, having known so many ghosts. It's still a mystery. I don't quite understand why some people stay and others don't. I wonder where those who leave have gone. I wonder if the ones that I kill go to the same place.

Carmel's asking me about my classes and about my old school. I flop out some vague answers. The scenery has become instantly rural, and we pass through a town where half of the buildings are molded out and falling down. There are vehicles parked in yards, caked with years of rust. It reminds me of places that I've been before and it occurs to me that I've been through too many places; that there might be nothing new anymore.

"You drink, right?" Carmel asks me.

"Yeah, sure." I don't, not really. I've never had the opportunity to get into the habit.

"Cool. There's always bottles, but somebody usually manages to get a keg set up in the back of their truck." She hits her turn signal and pulls off the road into a park. I can hear the ominous rush of the falls from somewhere behind the trees. The drive went fast; I didn't pay attention to much of it. I was too busy thinking about the dead, and about one dead girl in particular, wearing a beautiful dress, stained red with her own blood.

The party goes as parties go. I'm introduced to a multitude of faces that I'll try to connect to names later and fail. The girls are all giggly and eager to impress the others in attendance. The guys have grouped together and left the majority of their cerebrums in their cars. I've made it through two beers; this third one I've been holding for the better part of an hour. It's pretty boring.

The Edge of the World doesn't feel like the edge of anything, unless you take it literally. We're all gathered along the sides of the falls, strings of people standing witness to the passing of brown water over black rocks. There isn't really that much water to speak of. I heard someone say that it was a dry summer. Still, the gorge that the water has cut over time is awesome, a sheer drop on both sides, and in the center of the falls there is a towering rock formation that I would like to climb, if only I had better shoes.

I want to get Carmel alone, but since we got here, Mike Andover has been interrupting her at every opportunity and trying to stare me down so forcefully that it's like being hypnotized. And every time we get him to go away, Carmel's friends Natalie and Katie appear, looking at me expectantly. I'm not even sure which is which—they're both brunettes and they have extremely similar features, right down to matching hair clip things. I feel myself smiling a lot, and I have this odd urge to be witty and clever. The pressure is pulsing at my temples. Every time I say something they giggle, look at each other for permission to laugh, and look back at me again, waiting for my next zinger. God, living people are irritating.

Finally, some girl named Wendy starts throwing up over the side of the railing, and the distraction is enough for me to take Carmel by the arm and walk with her alone along the wooden walkway. I wanted to make it all the way to the other side, but when we get to the center, staring down over the drop of the falls, she stops.

"Are you having fun?" she asks, and I nod. "Everybody likes you."

I can't imagine why. I haven't said a single interesting thing. I don't think that there's anything interesting about me, except for the thing that I don't tell anyone about.

"Maybe everybody likes me because everybody likes *you*," I say pointedly, and I expect her to scoff, or to make some remark about flattery, but she doesn't. Instead she just nods quietly like I'm probably right. She's smart, and aware of herself. I wonder what she was doing dating someone like Mike. Someone from the Trojan Army.

Thinking of the Army makes me think of Thomas Sabin. I thought he'd be here, skulking around in the trees, dogging my every move like a lovesick . . . well, like a lovesick schoolboy, but I haven't seen him. After some of the hollow conversations I've had tonight, I kind of regret that.

"You were going to tell me about ghosts," I say. Carmel blinks at me and then starts to smile.

"I was." She clears her throat and does her best to start, laying out the technical specs of last year's party: who was there; what they were doing; why they came with this or that person. I guess she wants me to have a full and realistic picture. Some people need that, I suppose. Personally, I'm the type who likes to fill in the blanks and make it my own. It's probably better that way than it really was.

She finally gets to the dark, a dark filled with intoxicated and unreliable kids, and I hear a thirdhand recounting of ghost stories that were told that night. About swimmers and hikers who died at Trowbridge Falls, where the party was that year. About how they liked to try to make you have the same accident that they did, and more than one person had been victim to an invisible push at the cliff edge, or an invisible hand dragging them down into the river current. That part makes me prick up my ears. From what I know of ghosts, it sounds probable. In general, they like to pass around the badness that happened to them. Take the hitchhiker for example.

"Then Tony Gibney and Susanna Norman come screaming down off of one of the trails, shouting about how they
were assaulted by something while they were making out."
Carmel shakes her head. "It was getting pretty late, and a
lot of us really were kind of freaked, so we got into our
cars and took off. I was riding with Mike and Chase, Will
was driving, and as we left the park, something jumped
down in front of us. I still don't know where it came from,
if it was running down the hill, or if it had been perched in
a tree. It looked like a big, shaggy cougar or something.
Well, Will hit the brakes and the thing just stood there for
a second. I thought it was going to jump on the hood and
I swear, I would have screamed. But instead, it bared its
teeth and hissed, and then—"

"And then?" I prod, because I know that I'm supposed to.

"And then it moved out of our headlights, stood up on
two legs, and walked away into the woods."

I start laughing and she hits me on the arm. "I'm not
good at telling this," she says, but she's trying not to laugh
too. "Mike does it better."

"Yeah, he probably uses more swear words and crazy
hand gestures."

"Carmel."

I turn around and there's Mike again, with Chase and
Will on either hip, spitting Carmel's name out of his mouth
like a shot of sticky web. It's strange how just the sound of
someone's name can be made to act like a branding.

"What's so funny?" Chase asks. He puts his cigarette
out on the railing and places the old butt back into his

pack. I'm sort of grossed out, but impressed with his eco-consciousness.

"Nothing," I reply. "Carmel just spent the last twenty minutes telling me how you guys all met Sasquatch last year."

Mike smiles. There's something different. Something's off, and I don't think it's just the fact that they've all been drinking. "That story is true as shit," he says, and I realize that what's different is he's being friendly to me. He's looking at me instead of at Carmel. Not for one second do I take this to be genuine. He's just trying something new. He wants something, or worse, he's going to try to get one over on me.

I listen as Mike tells me the same story that Carmel just finished, only with lots more swear words and hand gestures. The versions are surprisingly similar, but I don't know if that means they're probably accurate, or just that they've both told the story a lot. When he's done, he sort of wavers where he's standing, looking lost.

"So you're into ghost stories?" Will Rosenberg asks, filling the space.

"Love them," I say, standing up a little straighter. There's a damp breeze coming off the water in all directions and my black t-shirt is starting to cling to me, giving me a chill. "At least when they don't end with a cat-type Yeti crossing the road but not bothering to attack anybody."

Will laughs. "I know. That's the kind of story that should end with the punch line, 'a little pussy never hurt anybody.' I tell them to add it, but nobody listens."

(64)

I laugh too, even though I hear Carmel mutter toward my shoulder about how disgusting that is. Oh well. I like Will Rosenberg. He's actually got a brain. Of course, that makes him the most dangerous of the three. From the way that Mike is standing, I know he's waiting for Will to set something up, to get something going. Out of sheer curiosity I decide to make it easy for him.

"Know any better ones?" I ask.

"I know a few," he says.

"I heard from Natalie that your mom's some kind of a witch," Chase interrupts. "No shit?"

"No shit." I shrug my shoulders. "She tells fortunes," I say to Carmel. "She sells candles and stuff online. You wouldn't believe how much money there is in it."

"Cool," Carmel says, and smiles. "Maybe she can read mine sometime."

"Jesus," Mike says. "Just what this town needs: another goddamn weirdo. If your mom's a witch, what does that make you? Harry Potter?"

"Mike," Carmel says. "Don't be a jerk."

"I think that's a lot to ask," I say softly, but Mike ignores me and asks Carmel why she's bothering to hang around such a freak. It's very flattering. Carmel's starting to look nervous, like she thinks that Mike might lose it and try to punch me over the wooden rail and down into the shallow water. I glance over the edge. In the dark I can't really make out how deep it might be, but I don't think it would be deep enough to cushion a fall, and I'd probably break my neck on a rock or something. I'm trying to stay cool and collected, keeping my hands in my pockets. Just the same, I hope my look of indifference is driving him nuts, because the comments he made about my mom, and about me being some kind of wimpy boy wizard, pissed me off. If he took me over the edge of the falls right now, I'd probably wind up stalking the wet rocks, dead and looking for him, unable to rest until I'd eaten his heart.

"Mike, chill," Will says. "If he wants a ghost story, let's give him the good one. Let's give him the one that keeps the junior high kids up at night."

"What's that?" I ask. The hair is prickling up on the back of my neck.

"Anna Korlov. Anna Dressed in Blood."

Her name moves through the dark like a dancer. Hearing it in someone else's voice, outside of my own head, makes me shiver.

"Anna dressed in blood? Like Cinderella dressed in yellow?" I make light, because it will frustrate them. They'll try harder to make her horrible, to make her terrifying, which is exactly what I want. But Will looks at me funny, like he's wondering why I know that nursery rhyme.

"Anna Korlov died when she was sixteen," he says after a moment. "Her throat was cut from ear to ear. She was on her way to a school dance when it happened. They found her body the next day, already covered with flies, and her white dress stained with blood."

"They said it was her boyfriend, didn't they?" Chase supplies like the perfect audience plant.

"They thought maybe." Will shrugs. "Because he left

town a few months after it happened. But everyone saw him at the dance that night. Asking about Anna, and figuring that she'd just stood him up.

"But it doesn't matter how she died. Or who killed her. What matters is that she didn't stay dead. About a year after they found her, she showed up back in her old house. See, they sold it after Anna's mom kicked off from a heart attack six months earlier. This fisherman and his family bought it and moved in. Anna killed everyone. Tore them limb from limb. She left their heads and arms in piles at the foot of the stairs and hung their bodies in the basement."

I look around at the pale faces of the small crowd that has gathered. Some of them look uncomfortable, including Carmel. Most of them just look curious, waiting for my reaction.

I'm breathing faster, but I make sure to sound skeptical when I ask, "How do you know it wasn't just some drifter? Some psychopath who happened to break into the house while the fisherman was out?"

"Because of how the cops covered it up. They never made any arrests. They barely even investigated. They just sealed off the house and pretended nothing had happened. It was easier than they thought. People are actually pretty willing to forget a thing like that."

I nod. That's true.

"That and there were words, written in blood all over the walls. *Annan talo*. Anna's house."

Mike grins. "Plus, there's no way somebody could have

torn a body up like that. The fisherman was a two-hundred-fifty-pound dude. She tore his arms and head off. You'd have to be built like The Rock, be high on meth, and take a shot of adrenaline to the heart to be able to twist a two-hundred-fifty-pound dude's head clean off."

I snort through my nose, and the Trojan Army laughs.

"He doesn't believe us," Chase moans.

"He's just scared," Mike says.

"Shut up," Carmel snaps, and takes me by the arm. "Don't pay any attention to them. They've wanted to mess with you from the minute they saw we might be friends. It's ridiculous. This is grade-school bullshit, like saying 'Bloody Mary' in front of a mirror at slumber parties."

I'd like to tell her that this is nothing at all like that, but I don't. Instead I squeeze her hand reassuringly and turn back to them.

"So where's the house?"

And of course, they glance at each other like that was exactly what they wanted to hear.

CHAPTER SEVEN

We leave the falls and drive back toward Thunder Bay, coasting beneath amber streetlights and going too fast through blurred traffic signals. Chase and Mike are laughing with their windows rolled down, talking of Anna, making her legend grow larger. The blood in my ears sings so strongly that I'm forgetting to look for street signs, forgetting to map my way.

It took a bit of finesse for them to leave the party behind, to convince the others to keep on drinking and enjoying the edge of the world. Carmel actually had to pull a move that was essentially "Hey, what's that over there?" on Natalie and Katie before diving into Will's SUV. But now we're just streaking through the summer air.

"Long drive," Will says to me, and I remember that he was the designated driver last year at the Trowbridge Falls party too. He makes me curious; his DD status makes it seem like he's hanging out with these knobs just to fit in, but he's too smart, and something in his demeanor makes him seem like he's the one moving the pieces without the others knowing. "She's out a ways. To the north."

"What're we going to do when we get there?" I ask, and everyone laughs.

Will shrugs. "Drink some beers, throw some bottles at the house. I don't know. Does it matter?"

It doesn't. I won't kill Anna tonight, not in front of all these people. I just want to be there. I want to feel her behind a window, watching, staring out at me, or maybe retreating deeper inside. If I'm honest with myself, I know that Anna Korlov has gotten into my mind like few ghosts have before her. I don't know why. There is only one ghost aside from her that has occupied my thoughts like this, that has brought up such a stirring of feeling, and that is the ghost who killed my father.

We're driving close to the lake now, and I can hear Superior whisper to me in waves about all of the dead things she hides beneath her surface, staring through the depths with murky eyes and fish-bitten cheeks. They can wait.

Will takes a right onto a dirt road and the tires of the SUV grumble and lurch us back and forth. As I look up, I can see the house, abandoned for years and beginning to tilt, just a crouching black shape in the dark. He stops at what used to be the end of the driveway and I get out. The headlights flash on the base of the house, illuminating peeling gray paint and flat, rotten boards, a porch overtaken by grasses and weeds. The old driveway was long; I'm at least a hundred feet from the front door.

"You sure this is it?" I hear Chase whisper, but I know

that it is. I can tell by the way the breeze moves my hair and clothes but doesn't disturb anything else. The house is tensely controlled, watching us. I take a step forward. After a few seconds, their hesitant footsteps crunch behind me.

On the drive up they told me that Anna kills anyone who enters her home. They told me about drifters who stumbled in looking for a place to sleep, only to be eviscerated when they lay down. They couldn't have possibly known this, of course, though it's probably true.

There's a sharp sound behind me followed by fast footfalls.

"This is stupid," Carmel snaps. The night has gotten colder and she's put on a gray cardigan over her tank top. Her hands are stuffed into the pockets of her khaki skirt and she has her shoulders hunched. "We should have just stayed at the party."

Nobody listens. They're all just taking swills of beer and talking too loud to cover their nervousness. I creep toward the house with careful steps, my eyes moving from window to window, anxious for movement that shouldn't be there. I duck as a beer can goes winging past my head to land in the driveway and bounce up toward the porch.

"Anna! Hey, Anna! Come out and play, you dead bitch!"

Mike is laughing, and Chase tosses him another beer. Even in the growing dark I can see that his cheeks are flushed with booze. He's starting to waver on his feet.

I glance between them and the house. As much as I'd like to investigate further, I'm going to stop. This isn't right. Now that they're here and afraid, they're laughing at her, trying to turn her into a joke. Crushing their full beer cans against their heads feels like a great idea, and yes, I feel the hypocrisy in my wanting to defend something that I'm trying to kill.

I look past them at Carmel fidgeting from foot to foot, hugging herself against the chill lake breeze. Her blond hair is wispy in the silver light, strands of spider web around her face.

"Come on guys, let's get out of here. Carmel's getting nervous, and there's nothing in there anyway besides spiders and mice." I push my way past, but Mike and Chase grab me by each arm. I notice that Will has gone back to stand with Carmel and is talking to her quietly, leaning down and gesturing toward the waiting car. She shakes her head and takes a step toward us, but he holds her back.

"No way we're leaving without looking inside," Mike says. He and Chase turn me around and walk me up the driveway like prison guards escorting an inmate, one at each shoulder.

"Fine." I don't argue as much as I maybe should. Because I *would* like to get a closer view. I'd just rather they not be here when I did it. I wave to Carmel to tell her everything's fine and shrug the guys off.

When my foot hits the first moldy board of the porch steps I can almost feel the house constrict, like it's breathing in, awakening after being so long untouched. I walk up the last two stairs and stand, alone, before the dark gray of the door. I wish I had a flashlight or a candle. I can't tell what color the house used to be. From a distance it seemed like it was once gray, that the paint peelings were slivers of gray falling to the ground, but now that I'm closer they seem rotted and black. Which is impossible. Nobody paints a house black.

The tall windows on either side of the door are caked over with dirt and dust. I walk to the left and rub my palm across the glass in a quick circle. Inside, the house is mostly empty, except for a few pieces of furniture scattered about. There is a sofa in the center of what must've been a living room, covered in a white sheet. The remains of a chandelier hang from the ceiling.

Despite the dark, I can see the interior easily. It's lit with grays and blues that seem to come from nowhere. There is something strange about the light that I can't process initially, until I realize that nothing is casting a shadow.

A whisper makes me remember that Mike and Chase are here. I start to turn to tell them it's nothing I haven't seen before, and could we please get back to the party, but in the reflection in the window I see that Mike is holding a piece of broken board, aiming at my skull with his arms raised above his head . . . and I get the feeling that I'm not going to be saying anything for quite some time.

I wake up to the smell of dust and the sensation that most of my head is lying in shards somewhere behind me. Then I blink. Each breath I take sends up a small puff of gray across aging and uneven floorboards. Rolling onto my back, I realize that my head is still intact, but my brain hurts so badly that I have to close my eyes again. I don't know where I am. I don't remember what I was doing before I got here. All I can think of is the fact that my brain feels like it's sloshing around in there unattached. An image pops into my head: some Neanderthal oaf swinging a board. The pieces of the puzzle start falling into place. I blink again in the strange gray light.

The strange gray light. My eyes flash wide. I'm inside the house.

My brain shakes itself off like a dog ditching water and a million questions fly from its fur. How long have I been unconscious? What room am I in? How do I get out? And of course, the all important: Did those assholes leave me here?

My last question is answered quickly by Mike's voice.

"See, I told you I didn't kill him." He taps his finger against the glass and I twist toward the window to stare up at his grinning idiot face. He says something stupid about how I'm a dead man and that this is what happens to guys who mess with his property. That's when I hear Carmel shouting that she's going to call the cops, asking in a panicked voice if I've at least woken up yet.

"Carmel!" I shout, struggling up onto my knee. "I'm okay."

"Cas," she shouts back. "These jerks— I didn't know, I swear."

I believe her. I rub the back of my head. My fingers come away with a little bit of blood. Actually, it's a lot of blood, but I'm not worried, because head wounds leak like water from a faucet even when the injury is barely more than a paper cut. I put my hand back on the floor to push myself up and the blood mixes the dust into a gritty red-dish paste.

It's too soon to get up. My head is swimmy. I need to lie back down. The room is starting to move on its own.

"Jesus, look at him. He's down again. We should prob-ably get him out of there, man. He could have a concus-sion or something."

"I hit him with a board; of course he's got a concussion. Don't be an idiot."

Look who's talking, I would like to say. All of this feels very surreal, very disconnected. It's almost like a dream.

"Let's just leave him. He'll find his own way back."

"Dude, we can't. Look at his head; it's bleeding all over the place."

As Mike and Chase argue back and forth over whether to babysit me or let me die, I feel myself slipping back down into darkness. I think this might actually be it. I've actually been murdered by the living—pretty unthinkable.

But then I hear Chase's voice go up about five or so oc-taves. "Jesus! Jesus!"

"What?" Mike shouts, his voice irritated and panicky at the same time.

"The stairs! Look at the fucking stairs!"

I force my eyes open and will my head to lift up an inch or two. At first I don't see anything extraordinary about the stairs. They're a bit narrow, and the banister has been bro-ken in no less than three places. But then I look up farther.

It's her. She's flickering in and out like an image on a

computer screen, some dark specter trying to fight her way out of the video and into reality. When her hand grips the rail she becomes corporeal, and it whines and creaks beneath the pressure.

I shake my head softly, still disoriented. I know who she is, I know her name, but I can't think of why I'm here. It occurs to me suddenly that I'm trapped. I don't know what to do. I can hear the repeated panicked prayers of Chase and Mike as they argue about whether or not to run or try to get me out of the house somehow.

Anna is descending upon me, coming down the stairs without taking any strides. Her feet drag horribly along like she can't use them at all. Dark, purplish veins cut through her pale white skin. Her hair is shadow-less black, and it moves through the air as though suspended in water, snaking out behind and drifting like reeds. It's the only thing about her that looks alive.

She doesn't wear her death wounds like other ghosts do. They say her throat was cut, and this girl's throat is long and white. But there is the dress. It's wet, and red, and constantly moving. It drips onto the ground.

I don't realize that I've scooted back against the wall until I feel the cold pressure against my back and shoulder. I can't take my eyes off her eyes. They're like oil drops. It's impossible to tell where she's looking, but I'm not foolish enough to hope that she can't or hasn't seen me. She is terrible. Not grotesque, but otherworldly.

My heart is pounding in my chest, and the ache in my head is unbearable. It tells me to lie down. It tells me that

I can't get out. I don't have the strength to fight. Anna is going to kill me, and I'm surprised to find that I would rather it be one like her, in her dress made of blood. I would rather succumb to whatever hell she has in mind for me than give up quietly in a hospital somewhere because someone hit me in the head with a piece of plank board.

She's coming closer. My eyes are drifting shut, but I can hear her movements whisper through the air. I can hear each fat drop of blood strike the floor.

I open my eyes. She's standing above me, the goddess of death, black lips and cold hands.

"Anna." My mouth curls into a weak smile.

She looks down at me, a pathetic thing shoved up against her wall. Her brow creases as she floats. And then she jerks her gaze away toward the window above my head. Before I can move, her arms shoot forward and break through the glass. I hear Mike or Chase or both of them screaming almost in my ear. Farther away, I hear Carmel.

Anna has pulled Mike through the window and into the house. He's screaming and bawling like a caught animal, twisting in her grip and trying to keep from looking at her face. His struggles don't seem to bother her. Her arms are as immobile as marble.

"Let me go," he stammers. "Let me go, man, it was just a joke! It was just a joke!"

She sets him on his feet. He's bleeding from cuts on his face and hands. He takes one step backward. Anna bares her teeth. I hear my voice coming from somewhere else, telling her to stop or just screaming, and Mike doesn't have any time to scream before she thrusts her hands into his chest, tearing through skin and muscle. She pushes her arms out to the sides, like she's forcing her way through a closing door, and Mike Andover is torn in half. Both halves fall to their knees, jerking and skittering like insect parts.

Chase's screams are coming from farther away. A car starts up. I'm scrambling away from the mess that used to be Mike, trying not to look at the half of his body that is still connected to his head. I don't want to know if he's still alive. I don't want to know that he's watching the other half of him twitch.

Anna is looking down at the corpse calmly. She looks at me for a long moment before turning her attention back to Mike. When the door bursts open she doesn't seem to notice, and then I'm being dragged by my shoulders from behind, pulled out of the house and away from the blood, my legs thumping down the front porch steps. When whoever it is lets go of me, they drop me too suddenly on my head, and I don't see anything anymore.

CHAPTER EIGHT

Hey. Hey, man, are you waking up?"
I know that voice. I don't like that voice. I crack
my eyes open, and there's his face, hovering over me.

"You had us worried there for a while. We probably
shouldn't have let you sleep so long. We probably should
have taken you to a hospital, but we couldn't really think
of anything to say."

"I'm fine, Thomas." I reach up and rub my eyes, then
gather my will and sit up, knowing that my world is about
to swim and slosh hard enough that I might throw up.
Somehow, I manage to swing my legs down to rest on the
floor. "What happened?"

"You tell me." He lights a cigarette. I wish he'd put it
out. Beneath his scraggly hair and glasses he looks like a
twelve-year-old who swiped a pack from his mother's purse.
"What were you doing in the Korlov house?"

"What were you doing following me?" I return, accepting the glass of water he holds out.

"What I said I was going to do," he replies. "Only I

never figured you'd need so much help. Nobody fucking goes into her house." His blue eyes peer at me like I'm some kind of novelty idiot.

"Well, I didn't just walk in and fall down."

"I didn't think so. But I can't believe they did that, dumped you in the house and tried to kill you."

I look around. I have no idea what time it is, but the sun is out and I'm in some kind of antique store. It's cluttered, but full of nice things, not piles of old junk that you sometimes see in the seedier places. Still, it smells like old people.

I'm sitting on a dusty old couch near the back, with a pillow that is mostly saturated with my dried blood. At least I hope it's my dried blood. I hope I wasn't sleeping on some hepatitis-riddled rag.

I look at Thomas. He seems mad. He hates the Trojan Army; no doubt they've been picking on him since kindergarten. A skinny awkward kid like him, someone who claims to be psychic and hangs out in dusty curio shops, was probably their favorite target for swirlies and atomic wedgies. But they're harmless pranksters. I don't think they were really trying to kill me. They just didn't take her seriously. They didn't believe the stories. And now one of them is dead.

"Shit," I say out loud. There's no telling what's going to happen to Anna now. Mike Andover wasn't one of her usual transients or runaways. He was one of the school jocks, one of the party boys, and Chase saw everything. I can only hope that he was too scared to go to the cops.

Not that cops can stop Anna anyway. If they went into that house, there would only be more dead. Maybe she wouldn't show herself to them at all. And besides, Anna is mine. The image of her conjures itself in my mind for a second, looming and pale and dripping red. But my injured brain can't hold her.

I look over at Thomas, still nervously smoking.

"Thanks for pulling me out," I say, and he nods.

"I didn't want to," he says. "I mean, I did want to, but seeing Mike laying in a sloppy pile didn't exactly make me excited about it." He sucks on his cigarette. "Jesus. I can't believe he's dead. I can't believe she killed him."

"Why not? You believed in her."

"I know, but I'd never actually seen her. Nobody sees Anna. Because if you see Anna—"

"You don't live to tell anyone about it," I finish dismally.

I look up at the sound of footsteps on the brittle floorboards. Some old guy has come in, the kind of old guy with a twisting gray beard that ends in a braid. He's wearing a very well-worn Grateful Dead t-shirt and a leather vest. There are strange tattoos up and down his forearms— nothing that I recognize.

"You're a damn lucky kid. I have to say that I expected more from a professional ghost killer."

I catch the bag of ice he tosses to me for my head. He's smiling through a face like leather and peering through wire specs.

"You're the one who tipped off Daisy." I know it instantly. "I thought it was little old Thomas, here."

A smile is my only reply. But it's enough.

Thomas clears his throat. "This is my grandfather, Morfran Starling Sabin."

I have to laugh. "Why do you goth types always give yourselves weird names?"

"Strong words coming from somebody walking around calling himself Theseus Cassio."

He's a salty old dude, and immediately likable, with a voice that belongs in a black-and-white spaghetti western. I'm not put off by the fact that he knows who I am. In fact, I'm almost relieved by it. I'm happy to come across another member of this peculiar underground, where people know my job, know my reputation, know my father's reputation. I don't live my life like a superhero. I need people to point me in the right direction. I need people who know who I really am. Just not too many. I don't know why Thomas didn't say as much when he found me by the cemetery. He had to be so damned cryptic.

"How's your head?" Thomas asks.

"Can't you tell, psychic boy?"

He shrugs. "I told you; I'm not that psychic. My grandpa told me you were coming and that I should look out for you. I can read minds sometimes. Not yours today. Maybe it's the concussion. Maybe I just don't need to anymore. It comes and goes."

"Good. That mind-reader shit gives me the willies." I look over at Morfran. "So, why did you send for me? And why didn't you have Daisy set up a meeting for when I got here, rather than sending Mentok the Mind Taker?" I jerk my head toward Thomas and immediately curse myself for trying to be a smartass. My head is not healthy enough for smartassery.

"I wanted you here quickly," he explains with a shrug. "I knew Daisy, and Daisy knew you, personal. He said you didn't like to be bothered. But I still wanted to keep tabs. Ghost killer or not, you're just a kid."

"Okay," I say. "But what's the rush? Hasn't Anna been here for decades?"

Morfran leans against the glass counter and shakes his head. "Something's changing with Anna. She's angrier these days. I'm linked to the dead—more so than you are in many ways. I see them, and I feel them, thinking, thinking about what they want. It's been that way since—"

He shrugs. There's a story there. But it's probably his best story, and he doesn't want to give it away so early on.

He rubs his temples. "I can feel it when she kills. Every time some unfortunate stumbles into her house. It used to be nothing more than an itch between my shoulder blades. These days it's a full-on twist of my insides. Way things used to be, she wouldn't have even come out for you. She's long dead and no fool, knows the difference between easy prey and trust fund babies. But she's getting sloppy. She's going to get herself on the front-page news. And you and I both know that some things are better kept a secret."

He sits down in a wingback chair and claps his hand against his knee. I hear the clicking of dog toenails on the floor and pretty soon a fat black Lab with a graying nose waddles in to put its head on his lap.

I think back to the events of the night before. She was nothing like I expected, though now that I've seen her I have a hard time remembering what I did expect. Maybe I thought she'd be a sad, frightened girl who killed out of fear and misery. I thought she'd trundle down the stairs in a white dress with a dark stain at the collar. I thought she would have two smiles, one on her face and one on her neck, wet and red. I thought she would ask me why I was in her house, and then come at me with razored little teeth.

Instead I find a ghost with the strength of a storm, black eyes, and pale hands, not a dead person at all but a dead goddess. Persephone back from Hades, or Hecate half-decayed.

The thought makes me shiver a little, but I choose to blame the blood loss.

"What are you going to do now?" Morfran asks.

I look down at the melting bag of ice, tinged pink with my rehydrated blood. Item number one is to go home and shower, and try to keep my mom from freaking out and slathering me with more rosemary oil.

Then it's back to school, to do some damage control with Carmel and the Trojan Army. They probably didn't see Thomas pull me out; they probably think I'm dead and are having a very dramatic cliff-side meeting to decide what to do about Mike and me, how to explain it. No doubt Will has some great suggestions.

And after that, it's back to the house. Because I have seen Anna kill. And I have to stop her.

I luck out with my mom. She isn't home when I get there, and there's a note on the kitchen counter telling me that my lunch is in a bag in the refrigerator. She doesn't sign it with a heart or anything, so I know she's annoyed that I stayed out all night and didn't call. Later I'll think of something to tell her that doesn't involve me being bloody and unconscious.

I don't luck out with Thomas, who drove me home and then followed me up the porch steps. When I come downstairs from my shower, my head still throbbing like my heart has taken up a new residence behind my eyeballs, he's sitting at my kitchen table, having a stare-down with Tybalt.

"This is no ordinary cat," Thomas says through his teeth. He is staring unblinking into Tybalt's green eyes—green eyes that flicker to me and seem to say, *This kid is a knob.* His tail twitches at the tip like a fishing lure.

"Of course he isn't." I rifle through the cabinet to chew some aspirin, a habit I picked up after reading Stephen King's *The Shining*. "He's a witch's cat."

Thomas breaks eye contact and glares at me. He knows when he's being made fun of. I smile at him and toss him a can of soda. He cracks it very close to Tybalt and the cat hisses and jumps off of the table, growling irritably as he passes me. I reach down to scratch his back and he whacks me with his tail to tell me he wants this scruffy character out of his house.

"What're you going to do about Mike?" Thomas's eyes are wide and round over the rim of his Coke can.

"Damage control," I say, because there's nothing else I

can do. I'd have more options if I hadn't been unconscious all last night, but that's spilled milk. I need to find Carmel. I need to talk to Will. I need to shut them both up. "So you should probably take us to school now."

He raises his eyebrows like he's surprised that I've ceased attempting to ditch him.

"What did you expect?" I ask. "You're in it. You wanted in on whatever this is, well, congratulations. No time for second thoughts."

Thomas swallows. To his credit, he doesn't say anything.

When we walk into school, the hallways are empty. For a second I think that we're busted, screwed, that there is some kind of candlelight vigil for Mike going on inside every closed door.

Then I realize that I'm an idiot. The halls are empty because we're in the middle of third period.

We make stops off at our respective lockers and evade the questions of roaming faculty. I'm not going to class. We're just going to wait around until lunch, hovering near Carmel's locker in the hopes that she's here and not pale and sick and lying in bed at home. But even if she is, Thomas says he knows where she lives. We can make a stop there later. If I have any luck left, she won't have talked to her parents yet.

When the bell rings it just about jolts me out of my skin. It does nothing for my headache. But I blink hard and peer through the crowd, an endless flow of similarly dressed bodies striding into the hallways. I sigh with relief when I see Carmel. She looks a little pale, like she might have been crying or throwing up, but she's still dressed well and carrying books. Not terribly worse for wear.

One of the brunettes from last night—I don't know which one, but I'll call her Natalie—bounces up to her elbow and starts prattling away about something. Carmel's reaction is Oscar-worthy: the cock of her head and attentive gaze, the roll of her eyes and laughter, all so easy and genuine. Then she says something, some diverting something, and Natalie turns and bounces away. Carmel's mask slides off again.

She's less than ten feet from her locker when she finally raises her eyes high enough to notice I'm standing in front of it. Her eyes go wide. She says my name loudly before glancing around and walking closer, like she doesn't want to be heard.

"You're . . . alive." The way she chokes on the phrase speaks of how strange she feels to be saying it. Her eyes move up and down my body, like she expects me to be oozing blood or have a bone exposed. "How?"

I nod to Thomas, who is skulking to my right. "Thomas pulled me out."

Carmel spares him a glance and a smile. She doesn't say anything else. She doesn't hug me, like I sort of thought she might. The fact that she doesn't makes me like her more for some reason.

"Where's Will? And Chase?" I ask. I don't ask whether anyone else knows. It's obvious by the demeanor of the halls, the way that everyone is walking around chattering like normal, that nobody else does. But we still need to settle things. Get our stories straight.

"I don't know. I don't see them until lunch. I'm not sure how many classes they'll be going to anyway." She looks down. She's getting the urge to talk about Mike. To say something that she feels like she should say, like she's sorry, or how he wasn't really all that bad and didn't deserve what happened to him. She's biting her lip.

"We need to talk to them. All together. Find them at lunch and tell them I'm alive. Where can we meet?"

She doesn't answer right away, fidgeting around. Come on, Carmel, don't disappoint me.

"I'll bring them to the football field. Nobody will be using it."

I nod quickly and she walks off, glancing back once like she's making sure that I'm still there, that I'm real and she hasn't gone crazy. I notice that Thomas is staring after her like a very sad, loyal hound dog.

"Dude," I say, and head off toward the gym, to go through it out to the football field. "Now's not the time." Behind me I hear him mutter that it's always the time. I let myself smirk for a minute before wondering what I'm going to do to keep Will and Chase on a leash.

CHAPTER NINE

When Will and Chase get to the football field, they find Thomas and me sacked out on the bleachers, staring at the sky. The day is sunny, mellow, and warm. Mother Nature does not mourn for Mike Andover. The light feels fantastic on my throbbing head.

"Jesus," one of them says, and then there are a whole lot of expletives that don't bear repeating. The tirade finally ends with, "He really is alive."

"No thanks to you dicks." I sit up. Thomas sits up too, but stays slightly hunched. These jerks have kicked him around one too many times.

"Hey," Will snaps. "We didn't do anything to you, understand?"

"Keep your fucking mouth shut," Chase adds, pointing a finger at me. For a minute I don't know what to say. I hadn't thought that they would be coming to try to keep *me* quiet.

I brush off the knee of my jeans. There's a bit of dust on them from where I leaned against the underside of the bleacher. "You guys didn't try to do anything to me," I say honestly. "You brought me to a house because you wanted to freak me out. You didn't know that your friend would wind up getting torn in half and disemboweled." That was cruel. I admit it. Chase goes immediately pale. Mike's last moments are playing behind his eyes. For a second, I soften, but then my throbbing head reminds me that they tried to kill me.

Standing beside them but down a bleacher, Carmel hugs herself and looks away. Maybe I shouldn't be so angry. But what, is she kidding me? Of course I should be. I'm not happy about what happened to Mike. I never would have let it happen if they hadn't rendered me useless with a board to the head.

"What should we tell people about Mike?" Carmel asks. "There are going to be questions. Everyone saw him leave the party with us."

"We can't tell them the truth," Will says ruefully.

"What is the truth?" Carmel asks. "What happened in that house? Am I really supposed to believe that Mike was murdered by a ghost? Cas—"

I meet her eyes levelly. "I saw it."

"I saw it too," Chase adds, looking like he might throw up.

Carmel shakes her head. "It's not real. Cas is alive. Mike is too. This is all just some messed-up prank that you all cooked up to get back at me for breaking up with him."

"Don't be so self-obsessed," Will says. "I saw her arms reach through the window. I saw her pull him in. I heard someone scream. And then I saw Mike's silhouette split in two." He looks at me. "So what was it? What was living in that house?"

"It was a vampire, man," Chase stutters.

Idiot. I ignore him completely. "Nothing was living in that house. Mike was killed by Anna Korlov."

"No way, man, no way," Chase says with increasing panic, but I don't have time for his waves of denial. Luckily, neither does Will, who tells him to shut up.

"We tell the cops that we drove around for a while. Then Mike got mad about Carmel and Cas and got out of the truck. None of us could stop him. He said he was going to walk home, and since it wasn't that far away, we didn't think anything of it. When he didn't show at school today, we figured that he was hungover." Will's jaw is set. He can think on his feet, even when he doesn't want to. "We'll have to put up with a few days or weeks of search parties. They'll question us some. And then they'll give up."

Will's looking at me. No matter how big a dick Mike was, he was Will's friend, and now Will Rosenberg is trying to wish me out of existence. If there wasn't anyone else watching, he might even try it—tap his heels together three times or something.

And maybe he's right. Maybe it is my fault. I could have found another way to Anna. But to hell with that. Mike Andover hit me across the back of the head with a plank and threw me in an abandoned house, all because I talked to his ex-girlfriend. He didn't deserve to be split down the middle, but he had a kick in the nuts coming to him at the very least.

Chase is holding his head in his hands, talking to himself about how messed up this is, what a nightmare it's going to be to lie to the cops. It's easier for him to focus on the non-supernatural aspect of the problem. It's easier for most people. That's what allows things like Anna to stay secret for so long.

Will pushes him in the shoulder. "What do we do about her?" Will asks. For a second I think he's talking about Carmel.

"You *can't* do anything about her," Thomas says, speaking for the first time in what feels like decades, catching on before I do. "She's out of your league."

"She killed my best friend," Will spits. "What am I supposed to do? Nothing?"

"Yeah," Thomas says, and he's got a shrug and a lopsided smirk to go with it that's going to get him punched in the face.

"Well, we have to do *something*."

I look at Carmel. Her eyes are wide and sad, her blond hair hanging across them in streaks. This is as emo as she has probably ever looked.

"If she's real," she continues, "then we probably should. We can't just let her keep on killing people."

"We won't," Thomas says to her comfortingly. I'd like to toss him down the bleachers. Didn't he hear my "now's not the time" speech?

"Look," I say. "We're not all going to jump in a green van and go take her out with the help of the Harlem Globetrotters. Anyone who goes back into that house is dead.

And unless you want to end up torn down the middle and staring at a pile of your own guts on the floor, you'll stay away." I don't want to be so harsh with them, but this is a disaster. Someone I've involved is dead, and now all these other newbs want to join him. I don't know how I've managed to get myself in such a clusterfuck. I've messed things up so quickly.

"I'm going back," Will says. "I've got to do something."

"I'm going with you," Carmel adds, and glares at me like she's daring me to try to stop her. She's obviously forgetting that I was staring into a dead face crisscrossed with dark veins less than twenty-four hours ago. I'm not impressed by her tough-cookie routine.

"Neither one of you is going anywhere," I say, but then I surprise myself. "Not without being prepared." I glance at Thomas, whose mouth is hanging slightly ajar. "Thomas has a grandfather. Some old spiritual guy. Morfran Starling. He knows about Anna. We need to talk to him first, if we're going to do anything." I cuff Thomas in the shoulder and he tries to piece a normal expression back on his face.

"How do you kill something like that anyway?" Chase asks. "Stake her through the heart?"

I'd like to mention again that Anna isn't a vampire, but I'll wait until he suggests silver bullets to shove him off the bleachers.

"Don't be dumb," Thomas scoffs. "She's already dead. You can't kill her. You've got to banish her or something. My grandfather's done it once or twice. There's this big spell, and candles and herbs and stuff." Thomas and I share a look. The kid really does come in handy now and again. "I can take you to him. Tonight, if you want."

Will is looking at Thomas, and then at me, and then at Thomas again. Chase looks like he wishes he didn't have to pretend to be such a big strong meathead all the time, but whatever, that's the bed he's made for himself. Carmel is just staring at me.

"Okay," Will says finally. "Meet us after school."

"I can't," I say quickly. "Mom stuff. But I can be at the shop later."

They all make their way down the bleachers clumsily— which is the only way to go down bleachers. Thomas smiles as they go.

"Pretty good, huh?" He grins. "Who says I'm not psychic?"

"Probably just women's intuition," I reply. "Just be sure that you and old Morfran give them a convincing enough wild-goose chase."

"Where are you going to be?" he asks, but I don't answer. He knows where I'm going. I'm going to be with Anna.

CHAPTER TEN

I'm staring up at Anna's house again. The logical part of my brain tells me that it's just a house. That it's what's inside that makes it horrifying, that makes it dangerous, that it can't possibly be tilting toward me like it's hunting me through the overgrowth of weeds. It can't possibly be trying to jerk free of its foundation and swallow me whole. But that's what it looks like it's doing.

Behind me, there is a small hiss. I turn around. Tybalt is standing with his forepaws on the driver's side door of my mom's car, looking out through the window.

"That's no lie, cat," I say. I don't know why my mom had me bring him along. He's not going to be able to help. When it comes to usefulness he's more like a smoke detector than a hunting dog. But when I got home after school, I told my mom where I was going and what had happened—leaving out the part where I almost got killed and one of my classmates was split in two—and she must have guessed there was more to the story, because I'm wearing a fresh coating of rosemary oil in a triangle on my forehead, and she made me take the cat. Sometimes I don't think she has any idea of what it is that I do out here.

She didn't say much. It's always there, on the tip of her tongue, to tell me to stop. To tell me it's dangerous, and that people get killed. But more would be killed if I didn't do my job. It's the job that my father started. It's what I was born for, my legacy from him, and that's the real reason she keeps quiet. She believed in him. She knew the score, right up until the day he was murdered—murdered by what he thought was just another in a long line of ghosts.

I pull my knife out of my backpack and slide it free. My father left our house one afternoon carrying this knife, just like he had since before I was born. And he never came back. Something got the best of him. The police came a day later, after my mother reported him missing. They said that my father was dead. I skulked in the shadows while they questioned my mother and eventually the detective whispered his secrets: that my father's body had been covered in bites; that chunks of him had been missing.

For months my father's gruesome death plagued my thoughts. I imagined it in every possible way. I dreamed of it. I drew it on paper with black pen and red crayon, stick skeleton figures and waxy blood. My mother tried to heal me; singing constantly and leaving the lights on, trying to keep me out of the dark. But the visions and nightmares didn't stop until the day I picked up the knife.

They never caught my father's killer, of course. Because my father's killer was already dead. So I know what it is that I'm meant to do. Looking up at Anna's house now,

I'm not afraid, because Anna Korlov is not my end. Some-day, I'm going back to the place where my father died, and I'm going to drag his knife across the mouth of the thing that ate him.

I take two deep breaths. My knife stays out; there's no need for pretense. I know that she's in there, and she knows that I'm coming. I can feel her watching. The cat looks at me with reflector-eyes from inside the car, and I can feel those eyes on me too as I move up the weeded driveway toward the front door.

I don't think there's ever been a quieter night. No wind, no bugs, no nothing. The sound of the gravel under my shoes is painfully loud. It's pointless to try to be stealthy. It's like being the first one awake in the morning, when every move you make is as loud as a foghorn, no matter how quiet you try to be. I want to stomp up these front porch steps. I want to break one off, pull it up and use it to batter down the door. But that would be rude, and be-sides, I don't need to. The door is already open.

Eerie gray light is leaking out without casting a beam. It just sort of melts with the dark air, like an illuminating fog. My ears strain to hear anything; in the distance I think I hear the low rumble of a train, and there's a leath-ery squeak as I tighten my grip on my athame. I walk through the door and close it behind. I don't want to give any ghost the opportunity for a cheap B-movie scare by slamming it shut.

The foyer is empty, the staircase bare. The skeleton of the ruined chandelier hangs on the ceiling without twinkling, and there's a table covered in a dusty sheet that I could swear wasn't here last night. There is something off about this house. Something besides the presence that obviously haunts it.

"Anna," I say, and my voice rolls into the air. The house eats it up without an echo.

I look to my left. The place where Mike Andover died is empty save for a dark, oily stain. I have no idea what Anna has done with the body, and honestly, I'd rather not think about it.

Nothing moves, and I'm in no mood to wait. Just the same, I don't want to face her on the stairs. She has too much of an advantage, being as strong as a Viking goddess and undead and everything. I walk farther into the house, winding my way carefully through the scattered and dust-sheeted furniture. The thought crosses my mind that she may be lying in wait, that the lumpy sofa isn't a lumpy sofa at all, but a dead girl covered in veins. I'm just about to stab my athame through it for good measure when I hear something shuffle behind me. I turn.

"Jesus."

"Has it been three days already?" the ghost of Mike Andover asks me. He's standing near the window he was pulled through. He's in one piece. I crack a tentative smile. Death, it seems, has made him wittier. But part of me suspects that what I'm looking at isn't really Mike Andover at all. It's just the stain on the ground, raised by Anna, made to walk and talk. But just in case it isn't . . .

"I'm sorry. For what happened to you. It wasn't supposed to."

Mike cocks his head. "It's never supposed to. Or it's always supposed to. Whatever." He smiles. I don't know if it's meant to be friendly, or ironic, but it's definitely creepy. Especially when he abruptly stops. "This house is wrong. Once we're here we never leave. You shouldn't have come back."

"I've got business here," I say. I try to ignore the idea that he can never leave. It's too terrible and too unfair.

"The same business that I had here?" he asks in a low growl. Before I can reply, he's ripped in two by invisible hands, an exact replay of his death. I stumble back and my knees run into a table or something, I don't know what and don't really care. The shock of seeing him collapsed into two grisly wet puddles again makes me disregard the furniture. I tell myself it was a cheap trick, and that I've seen worse. I try to get my breathing to slow down. Then, from the floor, I hear Mike's voice again.

"Hey, Cas."

My eyes travel over the mess to find his face, which is twisted around, still attached to the right side of his body. That's the side that kept the spine. I swallow hard and keep from looking at the exposed vertebrae. Mike's eye rolls up at me.

"It only hurts for a minute," he says, and then he sinks into the floor, slowly, like oil into a towel. His eye doesn't close when it disappears. It keeps on staring. I really could have lived without that little exchange. As I continue to watch the dark spot on the floor, I realize that I'm holding my breath. I wonder how many people Anna has actually killed in this house. I wonder if they are all still here, shells of them, and if she could raise them up like marionettes, shuffling toward me in various states of decay.

Get it under control. Now's not the time to panic. Now's the time to squeeze my knife and realize too late that something is coming up behind me.

There's a flicker of black hair around my shoulder, two or three inky tendrils reaching out to beckon me closer. I spin and slice through the air, half expecting her to not be there, to have disappeared in that one instant. But she didn't. She hovers before me, half a foot off the ground.

We hesitate a second and regard each other, my brown eyes peering directly into her oily ones. She'd be about five foot seven if she was on the floor, but since she's floating six inches off of it I almost have to look up. My breathing seems loud inside my head. The sound of her dress dripping is soft as it bleeds onto the floor. What has she become since she died? What power did she find, what anger, that allowed her to be more than just a specter, to become a demon of vengeance?

The path of my blade sheared the ends off her hair. The pieces float down and she watches them sink into the floorboards, like Mike did moments ago. Something passes across her brow, a tightening, a sadness, and then she looks at me and bares her teeth.

"Why have you come back?" she asks. I swallow. I don't

know what to say. I can feel myself backing up even though I tell myself not to.

"I gave you your life, packaged as a gift." The voice coming out of her cavernous mouth is deep and awful. It is the sound of a voice without breath. She still carries the faintest Finnish accent. "Did you think it was easy? Do you want to be dead?"

There's something hopeful in the way she asks that last part, something that makes her eyes keener. She glances down at my knife with an unnatural twitch of her head. A grimace takes hold of her face; expressions pass crazily, like ripples on a lake.

Then the air around her wavers and the goddess before me is gone. In her place is a pale girl with long, dark hair. Her feet are firmly planted on the ground. I look down at her.

"What is your name?" she asks, and when I don't answer, "You know mine. I saved your life. Isn't it only fair?"

"My name is Theseus Cassio," I hear myself say, even though I'm thinking what a cheap trick this is, and a stupid one. If she thinks I won't kill this form then she's dead wrong, no pun intended. But it's a good disguise, I'll give her that. The mask that she's wearing has a thoughtful face and soft, violet eyes. She's wearing an old-fashioned white dress.

"Theseus Cassio," she repeats.

"Theseus Cassio Lowood," I say, though I don't know why I'm telling her. "Everyone calls me Cas."

"You've come here to kill me." She walks around me in

a wide circle. I let her get just past my shoulders before I turn too. There's no way I'm letting her behind my back. She might be all sweet and innocent now, but I know the creature that would come bursting out if given the chance.

"Someone's already done that," I say. I won't tell her pretty stories about how I'm here to set her free. It would be cheating, putting her at ease, trying to get her to walk into it. And besides, it's a lie. I have no idea where I'm sending her, and I don't care. I just know that it's away from here, where she can kill people and sink them into this godforsaken house.

"Someone did, yes," she says, and then her head twists around and snaps back and forth. For a second her hair starts to writhe again, like snakes. "But you can't."

She knows that she's dead. That's interesting. Most of them don't. Most are just angry and scared, more an imprint of an emotion—of a horrible moment—than an actual being. You can talk to some of them, but they usually think you're someone else, someone from their past. Her awareness throws me off a beat; I use my tongue to buy some time.

"Sweetheart, my father and I have put more ghosts in the ground than you can count."

"Never one like me."

There is a tone in her voice when she says this that isn't quite pride, but something like it. Pride tinged with bitterness. I stay quiet, because I'd rather she not know that she's right. Anna is like nothing I've ever seen before. Her strength seems limitless, along with her bag of tricks. She's not some shuffling phantom, pissed off about being shot to death. She's death itself, gruesome and senseless, and even when she's dressed in blood and veins I can't help but stare.

But I'm not afraid. Strong or not, all I need is one good strike. She's not beyond the reach of my athame, and if I can get to her, she'll bleed out into the ether just like all the rest.

"Perhaps you should fetch your father to help you," she says. I squeeze my blade.

"My father's dead."

Something passes across her eyes. I can't believe it's regret, or embarrassment, but that's what it looks like.

"My father died too, when I was a girl," she says softly. "A storm on the lake."

I can't let her keep on like this. I can feel something in my chest softening, ceasing to growl, completely despite myself. Her strength makes her vulnerability more touching. I should be beyond this.

"Anna," I say, and her eyes snap to mine. I raise the blade and the flash of it reflects in her eyes.

"Go," she orders, queen of her dead castle. "I don't want to kill you. And it seems that I don't have to, for some reason. So go."

Questions pop into my mind at this, but I stubbornly plant my feet. "I'm not leaving until you're out of this house and back in the ground."

"I was never in the ground," she hisses through her teeth. Her pupils are growing darker, the blackness swirling outward until all the white is gone. Veins creep across her cheeks to find homes at her temples and throat. Blood bubbles up from her skin and spills down the length of her, a sweeping skirt dripping to the floor.

I thrust with my knife and feel something heavy connect with my arm before I'm tossed into the wall. Fuck. I didn't even see her move. She's still hovering in the middle of the room where I used to be. My shoulder hurts a lot where I connected with the wall. My arm hurts a lot where it connected with Anna. But I'm fairly hardheaded, so I scramble up and go for her again, going in low this time, not even trying for the kill but just for a slice of something. At this point, I'd settle for hair.

The next thing I know, I'm across the room again. I've skidded across it on my back. I think there are splinters in my pants. Anna continues to hover, regarding me with ever increasing resentment. The sound of her dress dripping onto the floorboards reminds me of a teacher I used to have who would slowly tap his temple when he was really annoyed with my lack of studying.

I get back on my feet, this time more slowly. I hope it looks more like I'm carefully planning my next move and less like I'm in large amounts of pain, which is the real reason. She's not trying to kill me and it's starting to piss me off. I'm being batted around like a cat toy. Tybalt would find this hilarious. I wonder if he can see from the car.

"Stop this," she says in her cavernous voice.

I run at her, and she grabs me by the wrists. I struggle, but it's like trying to wrestle concrete.

"Just let me kill you," I mutter in frustration. Rage lights up her eyes. For a second I think what a mistake I've made, that I forgot what she really was, and I'm going to wind up just like Mike Andover. My body actually scrunches up, trying to keep from being torn in two.

"I'll never let you kill me," she spits, and shoves me back toward the door.

"Why? Don't you think it would be peaceful?" I ask. I wonder for the millionth time why I can never seem to stop running my mouth.

She squints at me like I'm an idiot. "Peaceful? After what I've done? Peace, in a house of torn-apart boys and disemboweled strangers?" She pulls my face very close to hers. Her black eyes are wide. "I can't let you kill me," she says, and then she shouts, shouts loud enough to make my eardrums throb as she's throwing me out through the front door, clear past the broken stairs and onto the overgrown gravel of the driveway.

"I never wanted to be dead!"

I hit the ground rolling and look up just in time to see the door slam. The house looks still and vacant, like nothing has happened there in a million years. I gingerly test my limbs and find that they're all in working order. Then I push myself up to my knees.

None of them ever wanted to be dead. Not really. Not even the suicides; they changed their minds at the last minute. I wish I could tell her so, and tell her cleverly, so she wouldn't feel so alone. Plus it'd make me feel like less of a moron after being tossed around like an anonymous henchman in a James Bond movie. Some professional ghost killer I am.

As I walk to my mom's car, I try to get it back under control. Because I am going to get Anna, no matter what she thinks. Both because I've never failed before, and also because in the moment she told me she couldn't let me kill her, she sounded like she sort of wished that she could. Her awareness makes her special in more ways than one. Unlike the others, Anna regrets. I rub the ache along my left arm and know I'll be covered with bruises. Force isn't going to work. I need a plan B.

CHAPTER ELEVEN

My mom lets me sleep through most of the day, and when she finally wakes me up it's to tell me she's brewed a bath of tea leaves, lavender, and belladonna. The belladonna is in there to temper my rash behavior, but I don't refuse. I hurt all over. That's what getting thrown around a house all night by the goddess of death will do to you.

As I sink into the tub, very slowly, with a grimace on my face, I start to think of my next move. The fact of the matter is, I'm outmatched. It hasn't happened very often, and never to this degree. But occasionally, I need to ask for help. I reach for my cell phone on the bathroom counter and dial an old friend. A friend for generations, actually. He knew my dad.

"Theseus Cassio," he says when he picks up. I smirk. He'll never call me Cas. He finds my full name just too amusing.

"Gideon Palmer," I say back, and picture him on the other end of the line, on the other side of the world, sitting in a proper English house that overlooks Hampstead Heath in northern London.

"It's been too long," he says, and I can see him crossing or uncrossing his legs. I can almost hear the mutter of the tweed through the phone. Gideon is a classic English gent, sixty-five if he's a day, with white hair and glasses. He's the kind of man with a pocket watch and long shelves of meticulously dusted books that reach from floor to ceiling. He used to push me on the rolling ladders when I was a kid and he wanted me to fetch some weird volume on poltergeists, or binding spells, or whatever. My family and I spent a summer with him while my dad was hunting a ghost that was stalking Whitechapel, some kind of Jack the Ripper wannabe.

"Tell me, Theseus," he says. "When do you anticipate returning to London? Plenty of things that go bump in the night to keep you busy. Several excellent universities, all haunted to the gills."

"Have you been talking to my mother?"

He laughs, but of course he has. They've stayed close since my dad died. He was my dad's . . . I guess mentor is the best word. But more than that. When Dad was killed, he flew over the same day. Held me and my mother together. Now he starts going off on this spiel about how applications are going to have to go out next year, and how I'm really quite lucky that my father provided for my education and I won't have to mess around with student loans and that business. It really is lucky because a scholarship for this rolling stone is just not in the cards, but I cut him off. I have more important and pressing issues.

"I need help. I've run into a completely sticky mess."

"What sort of sticky mess?"

"The dead sort."

"Of course."

He listens while I tell him about Anna. Then I hear the familiar sound of the ladder rolling and his soft huffs as he climbs it to reach for a book.

"She's no ordinary ghost, that seems certain," he says.

"I know. Something's made her stronger."

"The way she died?" he asks.

"I'm not sure. From what I've heard, she was just murdered like so many others. Throat slit. But now she's haunting her old house, killing whoever steps inside, like some goddamn spider."

"Language," he chides.

"Sorry."

"She's certainly not just some shifting wraith," he mutters, mostly to himself. "And her behavior is far too controlled and deliberate for a poltergeist—" He pauses, and I can hear pages being flipped. "You're in Ontario, you say? The house isn't sitting on some native burial ground?"

"I don't think so."

"Hmm."

There are a couple more *hmm*s before I suggest that I just burn the house down and see what happens.

"I wouldn't recommend that," he says sternly. "The house could be the only thing binding her."

"Or it could be the source of her strength."

"Indeed it could be. But this warrants investigation."

"What kind of investigation?" I know what he's going to say. He's going to tell me not to be a layabout and to get out there and do the legwork. He's going to tell me that my father never shied away from cracking a book. Then he's going to grumble about the youth of today. If he only knew.

"You're going to need to find an occult supplier."

"Huh?"

"This girl must be made to give up her secrets. Something has—happened to her, something has affected her and before you can exorcise her spirit from that house, you must find out what it is."

That's not what I expected. He wants me to do a spell. I don't do spells. I'm not a witch.

"So what do I need an occult supplier for? Mom's an occult supplier." I look down at my arms under the water. My skin is starting to tingle, but my muscles feel fresh and I can see even through the darkened water that my bruises are fading. My mom is a great herbal witch.

Gideon chuckles. "Bless your dear mother, but she's no occult supplier. She's a gifted white witch, but she has no interest in what needs to be done here. You don't need a circle of posies and chrysanthemum oil. You need chicken feet, a banishing pentagram, some kind of water or mirror divination, and a circle of consecrated stones."

"I also need a witch."

"After all these years, I trust you have the resources to find at least that."

I grimace, but two people have come to mind. Thomas, and Morfran Starling.

"Let me finish researching this, Theseus, and I'll e-mail you in a day or two with the complete ritual."

"All right, Gideon. Thanks."

"Of course. And Theseus?"

"Yes?"

"In the meantime, get out to the library and try to find out what you can about the way this girl died. Knowledge is power, you know."

I smile. "Legwork. Right." I hang up the phone. He thinks I'm a blunt instrument, nothing but hands and blade and agility, but the truth is I've been doing legwork, doing research, since before I even started using the athame.

After Dad was murdered, I had questions. Trouble was, nobody seemed to have any answers. Or, as I suspected, nobody wanted to give me any answers. So I went looking on my own. Gideon and my mom packed us up and moved us out of the Baton Rouge house we were staying in pretty quickly, but not before I managed to make a trip back to the dilapidated plantation where my father met his end.

It was an ugly fucking house. Even angry as I was, I didn't want to go in. If it is possible for an inanimate object to glare, to growl, then that's exactly what this house did. In my seven-year-old mind I saw it pull aside the vines. I saw it wipe away the moss and bare its teeth. Imagination is a wonderful thing, right?

My mom and Gideon had cleared the place days before, throwing runes and lighting candles, making sure my dad was at rest, making sure the ghosts were gone. Still, when I walked up that porch I started crying. My heart told me that my dad *was* there, that he hid from them to wait for me, and that any minute he would open the door, smiling this great, dead smile. His eyes would be gone, and there would be huge, crescent-shaped wounds on his sides and arms. This sounds stupid, but I think I started crying harder when I opened the door myself and he *wasn't* there.

I breathe deep and smell tea and lavender. It brings me back into my body. Remembering that day, exploring that house, my heart is pounding in my ears. On the other side of the front door I found signs of a struggle and turned my face away. I wanted answers but I didn't want to imagine my dad beat to hell and back. I didn't want to think of him being scared. I walked past the cracked banister and headed instinctively for the fireplace. The rooms smelled like old wood, like rot. There was also the fresher scent of blood. I don't know how I knew what the smell of blood was, any more than I knew why I walked straight to the fireplace.

There was nothing in the fireplace but decades-old charcoal and ash. And then I saw it. Just a corner of it, black like the charcoal but somehow different. Smoother. It was conspicuous and ominous. I reached out and pulled it from the ash: a thin black cross, about four inches in height. There was a black snake curled around it, carefully woven from what I knew instantly was human hair.

The certainty that I felt when I grasped that cross was the same certainty that coursed through me when I picked up my father's knife seven years later. That was the moment that I knew for sure. That's when I knew that whatever coursed through my father's blood—whatever magical thing that allowed him to slice through dead flesh and send it out of our world—it flowed in my veins too.

When I showed the cross to Gideon and my mother, and told them what I'd done, they were frantic. I expected them to soothe me, to rock me like a baby and ask me if I was all right. Instead, Gideon grasped my shoulders.

"Don't you ever, ever go back there!" he shouted, and shook me so hard my teeth clacked together. He took the black cross from me and I never saw it again. My mother just stood far away and cried. I'd been scared; Gideon had never done anything like that to me before. He'd always been grandfatherly, sneaking me candy and winking, that sort of thing. Still, Dad had just been murdered, and I was angry. I asked Gideon what the cross was.

He stared down at me coldly, and then drew his hand back and cracked me across the face so hard that I hit the floor. I heard my mom sort of whimper, but she didn't intervene. Then they both walked out of the room and left me there. When they called me in for dinner, they were smiling and casual, like nothing had even happened.

It was enough to scare me into silence. I never brought it up again. But that doesn't mean I forgot, and for the last ten years I've been reading, and learning, wherever I could. The black cross was a voodoo talisman. I haven't figured out the significance of it, or why it was adorned with a snake made of human hair. According to lore, the sacred snake feeds on its victims by eating them whole. My father was taken in chunks.

The problem with this research is I can't ask the most reliable sources I have. I'm forced to sneak around and talk in code, to keep Mom and Gideon in the dark. Also making things difficult is that voodoo is some disorganized shit. Everyone seems to practice it differently and analysis is damned near impossible.

I wonder about asking Gideon again, after this business with Anna is over. I'm older now, and proven. It wouldn't be the same this time. And even as I think that, I sink farther into my tea bath. Because I still remember the feel of his hand across my cheek, and the blank fury in his eyes, and it still makes me feel like I'm seven.

After I get dressed, I call Thomas and ask him to pick me up and take me to the shop. He's curious, but I manage to hold him at bay. These are things that I need to say to Morfran too, and I don't want to have to say them twice.

I'm bracing myself for a lecture from my mother about missing school and some grilling about why I needed to call Gideon, which she no doubt overheard, but as I walk down the stairs I can hear voices. Two female voices. One is my mother's. The other is Carmel's. I tramp down the staircase and they come into view, thick as thieves. They're sitting in the living room in adjacent chairs, leaning toward each other and chatting away with a tray of cookies between them. Once both my feet are on the ground level, they stop talking and smile at me.

"Hey, Cas," Carmel says.

"Hey, Carmel. What are you doing here?"

She reaches around and pulls something out of her schoolbag. "I brought your assignment from bio. It's a partner's assignment. I thought we could do it together."

"That was nice of her, wasn't it, Cas?" my mother says. "You don't want to fall behind on your third day."

"We could get started on it now," Carmel suggests, holding out the paper.

I walk up and take it from her, glance over it. I don't know why it's a partner's assignment. It's nothing more than finding a bunch of answers from the textbook. But she's right. I shouldn't fall behind. No matter what other important, lifesaving stuff I've got going on.

"This was really cool of you," I say, and I mean it, even though there is some other motive at work here. Carmel doesn't give a crap about biology. I'd be surprised if she went to class herself. Carmel got the assignment because she wanted an excuse to talk to me. She wants answers.

I glance at my mom, and she's giving me this creepy once-over. She's trying to see how the bruises are healing. She'll be relieved that I called Gideon. When I came home last night I looked beaten half to death. For a second I thought she was going to lock me in my room and dunk me in rosemary oil. But my mom trusts me. She understands what I need to do. And I'm grateful to her for both of those things.

I roll up the bio assignment and tap it in my hand.

"Maybe we can work at the library," I say to Carmel, and she shoulders her bag and smiles.

"Take one more cookie for the road, dear," Mom says. We both take one, Carmel a bit hesitantly, and head for the door.

"You don't have to eat it," I say to Carmel once we're on the porch. "Mom's anise cookies are definitely an acquired taste."

Carmel laughs. "I had one in there and almost couldn't do it. They're like dusty black jellybeans."

I smile. "Don't tell my mom that. She invented the recipe herself. She's totally proud of them. They're supposed to bring you luck or something."

"Maybe I should eat it then." She looks down at it for a long minute, then lifts her eyes and stares intently at my cheek. I know there's a long streak of black bruise across the bone. "You went back to that house without us."

"Carmel."

"Are you crazy? You could have been killed!"

"And if we had all gone, we would all have been killed. Listen, just stick with Thomas and his grandfather. They'll figure something out. Keep your cool."

There's a definite chill on the wind, an early taste of fall, twisting through my hair with ice-water fingers. As I stare up the street, I see Thomas's Tempo puttering toward us, complete with replacement door and a Willy Wonka bumper sticker. The kid rides in style, and it makes me grin.

"Can I meet you at the library in an hour or so?" I ask Carmel.

She follows my gaze and sees Thomas coming closer.

"Absolutely not. I want to know what's going on. If you think for a minute that I believed any of that nonsense Morfran and Thomas were trying to tell us last night . . . I'm not stupid, Cas. I know a diversion when I see one."

"I know you're not stupid, Carmel. And if you're as smart as I think you are, you'll stay out of this and meet me at the library in an hour." I go down the porch steps and walk down my driveway, making a little rolling gesture with my fingers so Thomas won't pull in. He gets it and slows down just enough for me to open the door and vault inside. Then we drive away, leaving Carmel staring after us.

"What was Carmel doing at your place?" he asks. There's more than just a little jealousy there.

"I wanted a backrub and then we made out for about an hour," I say, and then cuff him in the shoulder. "Thomas. Come on. She was dropping off my bio assignment. We'll meet her at the library after we talk to your granddad. Now tell me what happened with the boys last night."

"She really likes you, you know."

"Yeah, well, you like her better," I say. "So what happened?" He's trying to believe me, that I'm not interested in Carmel and that I'm enough of a friend to him to respect his feelings for her. Oddly enough, both of these things are true.

Finally, he sighs. "We led them on a royal goose chase, just like you said. It was a blast. We actually had them convinced that if they hung sacks of sulfur above their beds, she wouldn't be able to attack them in their sleep."

"Jesus. Don't make it too unrealistic. We need to keep them busy."

"Don't worry. Morfran puts on a good show. He conjured blue flame and did a fake trance and everything. Told them he would work on a banishing spell, but it would take the light of the next full moon to finish it. Think that'll be enough time?"

Normally I'd say yes. After all, it's not a matter of locating Anna. I know just where she is.

"I'm not sure," I reply. "I went back last night and she kicked my ass all around the room."

"So what're you going to do?"

"I spoke to a friend of my dad's. He said we need to figure out what's giving her all this extra strength. Know any witches?"

He squints at me. "Isn't your mom one?"

"Know any *black* witches?"

He squirms around a bit and then shrugs. "Well, me, I guess. I'm not really that good, but I can cast barriers and make the elements work for me and stuff. Morfran is, but he doesn't practice much anymore." He makes a left turn and pulls up outside of the antique shop. Through the window I can see the grizzled black dog, its nose up against the glass and its tail thumping against the ground.

We go inside and find Morfran standing behind the counter pricing a new ring, something handsome and vintage with a large black stone.

"Know anything about spell-craft and exorcism?" I ask.

"Sure," he says without looking up from his work. His black dog has finished welcoming Thomas and moves to rest heavily against his thigh. "This place was haunted as shit when I bought it. Sometimes still is. Things come in with their owners still attached, if you know what I mean."

I look around the shop. Of course. Antique stores must almost always have a wraith or two swirling around. My eyes fall on a long oval mirror set onto the back of an oak dresser. How many faces have stared into it? How many dead reflections wait there and whisper to each other in the dark?

"Can you get me some supplies?" I ask.

"What sort?"

"I need chicken feet, a circle of consecrated stones, a banishing pentagram, and some kind of divination thingy."

He gives me the stink eye. "Divination thingy? Sounds pretty technical."

"I don't have the details yet, okay? Can you get them or not?"

Morfran shrugs. "I can send Thomas down to Superior with a bag. Pull thirteen stones from the lake. They don't come more consecrated than that. The chicken feet I'll have to order in, and the divination thingy, well, I'm betting that you want a mirror of some kind, or possibly a scrying bowl."

"A scrying bowl sees the future," Thomas says. "What would he want with that?"

"A scrying bowl sees whatever you want it to see," Morfran corrects him. "As for the banishing pentagram, I think it might be overkill. Burn some protective incense, or some herbs. That should be plenty."

"You do know what we're dealing with here, don't you?" I ask. "She's not just a ghost. She's a hurricane. Overkill is fine by me."

"Listen, kid. What you're talking about is nothing more than a trumped-up séance. Summon the ghost and bind it in the circle of stones. Use the scrying bowl to get your answers. Am I right?"

I nod. He makes it sound so easy. But for someone who doesn't do spells and spent the last night being tossed like a rubber ball, it's going to be damn near impossible.

"I've got a friend in London doing the specifics. I'll have the spell in a few days. I might need a few more supplies, depending."

Morfran shrugs. "Best time to do a binding spell is during the waning moon anyway," he says. "That gives you a week and a half. Plenty of time." He squints at me and looks a whole lot like his grandson. "She's getting the better of you, isn't she?"

"Not for long."

The public library isn't all that impressive to look at, though I suppose I've been spoiled growing up with my dad and his friends' collections of dusty tomes. It does, however, have a pretty decent local history collection, which is what's really important. Since I've got to find Carmel and settle this whole bio assignment business, I put Thomas on the computer, searching through the online database for any record of Anna and her murder.

I find Carmel waiting at a table back behind the stacks.

"What's Thomas doing here?" she asks as I sit down.

"Researching a paper." I shrug. "So what's the bio assignment about?"

She smirks at me. "Taxonomic classification."

"Gross. And boring."

"We have to make a chart that goes from phylum to species. We got hermit crabs and octopus." She furrows her brow. "What's the plural for octopus? Is it 'octopuses'?"

"I think it's octopi," I say, spinning the open textbook toward me. We might as well get started, even though it's the last thing I want to be doing. I want to be getting newsprint on my fingers with Thomas, searching out our murdered girl. I can see him at the computer from where I'm sitting, hunched over toward the screen, clicking away feverishly with the mouse. Then he writes something on a scrap of paper and gets up.

"Cas," I hear Carmel say, and from the tone of her voice she's been talking for a while. I put on my very best charming smile.

"Hm?"

"I said, do you want to do the octopus, or the hermit crab?"

"Octopus," I say. "They're good with a little olive oil and lemon. Lightly fried."

Carmel makes a face. "That's disgusting."

"No, it isn't. I used to eat it with my dad all the time in Greece."

"You've been to Greece?"

"Yeah," I say, talking absently while I flip through pages of invertebrates. "We lived there for a few months when I was about four. I don't remember very much."

"Does your dad travel a lot? For work or something?"

"Yeah. Or at least he did."

"He doesn't anymore?"

"My dad's dead," I say. I hate telling people this. I never know exactly how my voice is going to sound saying it, and I hate the stricken looks they get on their faces when they don't know what to say back. I don't look at Carmel. I just keep reading about different genuses. She says she's sorry, and asks how it happened. I tell her he was murdered, and she gasps.

These are the right responses. I should be touched by her attempt to be sympathetic. It isn't her fault that I'm not. It's just that I've seen these faces and heard these gasps for too long. There's nothing about my father's murder that doesn't make me angry anymore.

It strikes me suddenly that Anna is my last training job. She's incredibly strong. She's the most difficult thing I can imagine facing. If I beat her, I'll be ready. I'll be ready to avenge my father.

The idea makes me pause. The idea of going back to Baton Rouge, back to that house, has always been mostly abstract. Just an idea, a long-range plan. I suppose that for all of my voodoo research, part of me has been procrastinating. I haven't been particularly effective, after all. I still don't know who it was that killed my dad. I don't know if I would be able to raise them, and I'd be all on my own. Bringing Mom is out of the question. Not after years of hiding books and discreetly clicking out of websites when she walked into the room. She'd ground me for life if she even knew I was thinking of it.

A tap on my shoulder brings me out of my daze. Thomas sets a newspaper down in front of me—a brittle, yellowed old thing that I'm surprised they let out of the glass.

"This is what I could find," he says, and there she is, on the front page, beneath the headline that reads "Girl Found Slain."

Carmel stands up to get a better view. "Is that—?"

"It's her," Thomas blurts excitedly. "There aren't that many other articles. The police were dumbfounded. They hardly even questioned anybody." He's got a different newspaper in his hands; he's riffling through it. "The last one is just her obituary: Anna Korlov, beloved daughter of Malvina, was laid to rest Thursday in Kivikoski Cemetery."

"I thought you were researching a paper, Thomas," Carmel comments, and Thomas starts to sputter and explain. I don't care a lick about what they're saying. I'm staring at her picture, a picture of a living girl, with pale skin and long, dark hair. She's not quite daring to smile, but her eyes are bright, and curious, and excited.

"It's a shame," Carmel sighs. "She was so pretty." She reaches down to touch Anna's face, and I brush her fingers away. Something's happening to me, and I don't know what it is. This girl I'm looking at is a monster, a murderer. This girl for some reason spared my life. I carefully trace along her hair, which is held up with a ribbon. There's a warm feeling in my chest but my head is ice-cold. I think I might pass out.

"Hey, man," Thomas says, and shakes my shoulder a little. "What's wrong?"

"Uh," I sort of gurgle, not knowing what to say to him, or myself. I look away to buy time, and see something that makes my jaw clench. There are two police officers standing at the library desk.

Saying anything to Carmel and Thomas would be stupid. They'd instinctively look over their shoulders and that would be suspicious as hell. So I just wait, discreetly tearing Anna's obituary out of the brittle newspaper. I ignore Carmel's furious hiss of "You can't do that!" and put it into my pocket. Then I discreetly cover the newspaper up with books and schoolbags and point down to a picture of a cuttlefish.

"Any idea where that fits in?" I ask. They're both looking at me like I've come unglued. Which is fine because the librarian has turned and pointed at us. The cops are starting to make their way back to our table, just like I knew they would.

"What are you talking about?" Carmel asks.

"I'm talking about the cuttlefish," I say mildly. "And I'm telling you to look surprised, but not too surprised."

Before she can ask, the tramping noise of two men laden down with cuffs, flashlights, and sidearms is loud enough to warrant turning around. I can't see her face, but I hope she doesn't look as mortifyingly guilty as Thomas does. I lean into him and he swallows and pulls himself together.

"Hi, kids," the first cop says with a smile. He's a stout, friendly looking guy who's about three inches shorter than me and Carmel. He handles this by staring Thomas directly in the eyes. "Doing some studying?"

"Y-yeah," Thomas stutters. "Is there something wrong, Officer?"

The other cop is poking around our table, looking at our open textbooks. He's taller than his partner, and leaner, with a hawk's nose full of pores and a small chin. He's bug ugly, but I hope not mean.

"I'm Officer Roebuck," the friendly one says. "This is Officer Davis. Mind if we ask you kids some questions?"

A group shrug passes amongst us.

"You all know a boy by the name of Mike Andover?"

"Yes," Carmel says.

"Yes," Thomas agrees.

"A little," I say. "I just met him a few days ago." Damn this is unpleasant. Sweat is breaking out on my forehead and I can't do anything about it. I've never had to do this before. I've never gotten anyone killed.

"Did you know that he's disappeared?" Roebuck watches us each carefully. Thomas just nods; so do I.

"Have you found him yet?" Carmel asks. "Is he all right?"

"No, we haven't found him. But according to eyewitnesses, you two were among the last people seen with him. Care to tell us what happened?"

"Mike didn't want to stay at the party," Carmel says easily. "We left to go hang somewhere else, we didn't exactly know where. Will Rosenberg was driving. We were out on back roads off of Dawson. Pretty soon Will pulled over and Mike got out."

"He just got out?"

"He was upset about me hanging with Carmel," I interrupt. "Will and Chase were trying to make nice, calm him down, but he wouldn't go for it. He said he was going to walk home. That he wanted to be by himself."

"You are aware that Mike Andover lived at least ten miles from the area you're talking about," Officer Roebuck said.

"No, I didn't know," I reply.

"We tried to stop him," Carmel pipes up, "but he wouldn't listen. So we left. I thought he would just call later, and we'd go pick him up. But he never did." The ease of the lie is disturbing, but at least it explains the guilt clearly written on all of our faces. "He's really missing?" Carmel asks shrilly. "I thought—I hoped it was just a rumor."

She sells it for us all. The cops visibly soften at her worry. Roebuck tells us that Will and Chase took them out to where we dropped Mike off, and that there was a search party started. We ask if we can help but he waves us off like it's better left to professionals. In a few hours Mike's face should be plastered all over the news. The entire city should have mobilized into the woods with flashlights and raingear, combing for traces of him. But somehow I know that they won't. This is all Mike Andover is going to get. One lame search party and a few questioning cops. I don't know how I know. Something in their eyes, like they're walking half-asleep. Like they can't wait for it to be over, for hot meals in their bellies and their feet up on the couch. I wonder if they can sense that there's more going on here than they can deal with, if Mike's death is broadcasting on a low frequency of the weird and unexplainable, telling them in a soft hum to just leave it alone.

After a few more minutes officers Roebuck and Davis say their good-byes to us and we sink back into our chairs.

"That was . . ." Thomas starts, and doesn't finish.

Carmel gets a call on her cell and picks it up. When she turns away to talk I hear her whisper things like "I don't know" and "I'm sure they'll find him." After she hangs up her eyes are strained.

"Everything okay?" I ask.

She holds her phone up sort of listlessly. "Nat," she says. "She's trying to comfort me, I guess. But I'm not in the mood for a girls' movie night, you know?"

"Is there anything we can do?" Thomas asks gently, and Carmel starts riffling through papers.

"I'd just like to get this bio homework done, honestly," she says, and I nod. We should take time for some normalcy now. We should work and study and prepare to ace our quiz Friday. Because I can feel the newspaper clipping in my pocket like it weighs a thousand pounds. I can feel that photo of Anna, staring out from sixty years ago, and I can't help myself from wanting to protect her, wanting to save her from becoming what she already is.

I don't think there'll be much time for normalcy, later on.

CHAPTER TWELVE

I wake up covered in sweat. I had been dreaming, dreaming of something leaning over me. Something with crooked teeth and hooked fingers. Something with breath that smelled like it had been eating people for decades without brushing in between. My heart's pounding in my chest. I reach under my pillow for my dad's athame, and for a second I could swear my fingers close on a cross, a cross twisted round with a rough snake. Then my knife handle is there, safe and sound in its leather sheath. Fucking nightmares.

My heart starts to slow down. Glancing down at the floor, I see Tybalt, who is glaring at me with a puffed-up tail. I wonder if he had been sleeping on my chest and I catapulted him off when I woke. I don't remember, but I wish that I did, because it would've been hilarious.

I think about lying back down, but don't. There's that annoying, tense feeling in all of my muscles, and, even though I'm tired, what I really want to do is some track and field—throw a shot put and run some hurdles. Outside, the wind must be blowing, because this old house creaks and groans on its foundation, floorboards moving like dominoes so they sound like fast footsteps.

The clock by my bed reads 3:47. For a second I blank on what day it is. But it's Saturday. So at least I don't have to be up for school tomorrow. Nights are starting to bleed together. I've had maybe three good nights of sleep since we got here.

I get out of bed without thinking and pull on my jeans and a t-shirt, then stuff my athame into my back pocket and make my way down the stairs. I pause only to put on my shoes and slide my mom's car keys off the coffee table. Then I'm driving through dark streets under the light of a growing moon. I know where I'm going, even though I can't remember deciding to do it.

I park at the end of Anna's overgrown driveway and get out of the car, still feeling like I'm mostly sleepwalking. None of the nightmare tension is gone yet from my limbs. I don't even hear the sound of my own feet on the rickety porch steps, or feel my fingers close around the doorknob. Then I step in, and fall.

The foyer is gone. Instead I drop about eight feet and faceplant in dusty, cold dirt. A few deep breaths get the wind back in my lungs and on reflex I pull my legs up, not thinking anything but *what the fuck?* When my brain switches on again I wait in a half-crouch and flex my quads. I'm lucky to have both of my legs still in working order, but where the hell am I? My body feels just about ready to run out of adrenaline. Wherever this is, it's dark, and it smells. I try to keep my breathing shallow so I don't panic, and also so I don't breathe in too much. It reeks of damp and rot. Lots of things have either died down here or died elsewhere and been stuffed here.

That thought makes me reach back for my knife, my sharp, throat-cutting security blanket, as I look around. I recognize the ethereal gray light from the house; it's leaking down through what I guess are floorboards. Now that my eyes are adjusted, I see that the walls and floor are part dirt and part rough-cut stone. My mind does a quick replay of me walking up the front porch steps and coming through the door. How did I end up in the basement?

"Anna?" I call softly, and the ground lurches beneath my feet. I steady myself against a wall, but the surface under my hand isn't dirt. It's squishy. And moist. And it's breathing.

The corpse of Mike Andover is half-submerged in the wall. I was resting my hand against its stomach. Mike's eyes are closed, like he's sleeping. His skin looks darker and looser than it was before. He's rotting, and from the way he's situated in the rocks, I get the impression that the house is slowly taking him over. It's digesting him.

I move away a few steps. I'd really rather he not tell me about it.

A soft shuffling sound gets my attention and I turn to see a figure hobbling toward me, like it's drunk, wobbling and lurching. The shock of not being alone is momentarily eclipsed by the heaving of my stomach. It's a man, and he reeks of piss and used-up booze. He's dressed in dirty clothes, an old tattered trench coat and pants with holes in the knees. Before I can get out of the way, a look of fear crosses his face. His neck twists around on his shoulders like it's a bottle cap. I hear the long crunch of his spinal cord and he crumples to the ground at my feet.

I'm starting to wonder if I ever woke up at all. Then, for some reason, my father's voice bubbles up between my ears.

"Don't be afraid of the dark, Cas. But don't let them tell you that everything that's there in the dark is also there in the light. It isn't."

Thanks, Dad. Just one of the many creepy pearls of wisdom you had to impart.

But he was right. Well, right about the last part at least. My blood is pounding and I can feel the jugular vein in my neck. Then I hear Anna speak.

"Do you see what I do?" she asks, but before I can answer, she surrounds me with corpses, more than I can count, strewn across the floor like trash, and piled up to the ceiling, arms and legs arranged together in a grotesque braid. The stench is horrible. In the corner of my eye, I see one move, but when I look closer I realize that it's the movements of bugs feeding on the body, twisting beneath the skin and lifting it in impossible little flutters. Only one thing on the bodies moves of its own power: The eyes roll lazily back and forth in their heads, mucus-covered and milky, like they're trying to see what's happening to them but no longer have the energy.

"Anna," I say softly.

"These are not the worst," she hisses. She's got to be kidding. Some of these corpses have had horrible things done to them. They're missing limbs or all of their teeth. They're covered in dried blood from a hundred crusted-over cuts. And too many of them are young. Faces like mine or younger than mine, with the cheeks torn away and mold on their teeth. When I look back behind me and realize that Mike's eyes have opened, I know I have to get out of here. Ghost-hunting be damned, to hell with the family legacy, I'm not staying one minute longer in a room filling up with bodies.

I'm not claustrophobic, but right now I seem to have to tell myself so very loudly. Then I see what I didn't have time to before. There's a staircase, leading up to the main level. I don't know how she had me step directly into the basement, and I don't care. I just want back up in the foyer. And once I'm up there, I want to forget what's residing underneath my feet.

I make for the stairs, and that's when she sends the water, gushing in and rising up from everywhere—cracks in the walls, seeping up right through the floor. It's filthy, as much slime as it is liquid, and in seconds it's creeping up to my waist. I start to panic as the corpse of the bum with the broken neck floats past. I do *not* want to be swimming with them. I don't want to think about everything that's under the water, and my mind's eye makes up something really stupid, like corpses from the bottom of the stacks opening their jaws suddenly and scrambling out along the floor, hurrying to grab my legs like crocodiles. I push past the bum, bobbing like a wormy apple, and am surprised to hear a little moan escape my lips. I'm going to gag.

I make it to the stairs just as a pillar of corpses shifts and collapses with a sick splash.

"Anna, stop!" I cough, trying to keep the green water out of my mouth. I don't think I'm going to make it. My clothes are as heavy as in a nightmare and I'm crawling up the steps in slow motion. Finally I slap my hand onto dry floor and jerk myself onto the ground level.

Relief lasts about half a second. Then I shriek like a chicken and throw myself away from the basement door, expecting water and dead hands coming to drag me back down. But the basement is dry. The gray light spills down and I can see down the steps and a few feet of floor. It's all dry. There's nothing there. It looks like any cellar that you might store canned goods in. To make me feel even stupider, my clothes aren't wet either.

Damn Anna. I hate that time-space manipulation, hallucination, whatever. You never get used to it.

I stand up and brush my shirt off even though there's nothing to brush off, looking around. I'm in what used to be the kitchen. There's a dusty black stove and a table with three chairs. I'd really like to sit down on one, but the cupboards start opening and closing by themselves, drawers slamming shut and the walls starting to bleed. Slamming doors and smashing plates. Anna is acting like a common poltergeist. How embarrassing.

A sense of safety settles on my skin. Poltergeists I can take. I shrug my shoulders and walk out of the kitchen and into the sitting room, where the dust-sheeted sofa looks comfortingly familiar. I collapse down on it in what I hope looks like a pretty decent impression of bravado. Never mind that my hands are still shaky.

"Get out!" Anna shouts from directly over my shoulder. I peek over the back of the couch and there she is, my goddess of death, her hair snaking out in a great black cloud, her teeth grinding hard enough to make living gums bleed. The impulse to spring up with my athame at the ready makes my heart beat double time. But I take a deep breath. Anna didn't kill me before. And my gut has a hunch that she doesn't want to kill me now. Why else would she waste time on the corpse-filled light show downstairs? I give her my best cocky grin.

"What if I won't?" I ask.

"You came to kill me," she growls, obviously deciding to ignore my question. "But you can't."

"What part of that actually makes you angry?" Dark blood moves through her eyes and skin. She's terrible, disgusting—a killer. And I suspect that I am completely safe with her. "I will find a way, Anna," I promise. "There will be a way to kill you, to send you away."

"I don't want to be away," she says. Her whole form clenches and the darkness melts back inside, and standing before me is Anna Korlov, the girl from the newspaper photo. "But I deserve to be killed."

"You didn't once," I say, not exactly disagreeing. Because I don't think those corpses downstairs were just creations of her imagination. I think that somewhere, Mike Andover probably is getting slowly eaten by the walls of this house, even if I can't see it.

She's shaking her arm, down near the wrist where there are lingering black veins. She shakes harder and closes her eyes, and they disappear. It strikes me that I'm not just looking at a ghost. I'm looking at a ghost, and at something that was done to that ghost. They are two different things.

"You have to fight that, don't you?" I say softly.

Her eyes are surprised.

"In the beginning, I couldn't fight it at all. It wasn't me. I was insane, trapped inside, and this was just a terror, doing horrible things while I watched, curled up in a corner of our mind." She cocks her head and hair falls softly down her shoulder. I can't think of them as the same person. The goddess and this girl. I can picture her peering out of her own eyes like they're nothing but windows, quiet and afraid in her white dress.

"Now our skins have grown together," she goes on. "I am her. I am it."

"No," I say, and the minute I do, I know it's true. "You wear her like a mask. You can take it off. You did it to spare me." I stand and walk around the sofa. She looks so fragile, compared to what she was, but she doesn't back away, and she doesn't break eye contact. She's not afraid. She's sad, and curious, like the girl in the photograph. I wonder what she was when she was alive, if she laughed easily, if she was clever. It's impossible to think that much of that girl remains now, sixty years and god knows how many murders later.

Then I remember that I'm really pissed. I wave my hand back toward the kitchen and basement door. "What the hell was that about?"

"I thought you should know what you're dealing with."

"What? Some bratty girl throwing a hissy fit in the kitchen?" I narrow my eyes. "You were trying to scare me off. That sad little display was supposed to send me running for the hills."

"Sad little display?" she mocks me. "I bet you almost wet yourself."

I open my mouth and quickly shut it. She almost made me laugh, and I'd still like to be pissed. Only not literally. Oh crap. I'm laughing.

Anna blinks and smiles, fleetingly. She's trying not to laugh herself.

"I was . . ." She pauses. "I was angry with you."

"For what?" I ask.

"For trying to kill me," she says, and then we both do laugh.

"And after you tried so hard to not kill *me*." I smile. "I guess it must've seemed pretty rude." I'm laughing with her. We're having a conversation. What is this, some kind of twisted Stockholm syndrome?

"Why are you here? Did you come to try to kill me again?"

"Oddly enough, no. I—I had a bad dream. I needed to talk to someone." I ruffle my hand through my hair. It's been ages since I've felt so awkward. Maybe I've never felt this awkward. "And I guess I just figured, well, Anna must be up. So here I am."

She snorts a little. Then her brow furrows. "What could I say to you? What could we talk about? I've been out of the world for so long."

I shrug. The next words leave my mouth before I know what's happening. "Well, I was never really in the world in the first place, so." I clench my jaw and look down at the floor. I can't believe I'm being so emo. I'm complaining to a girl who was brutally murdered at sixteen. She's trapped in this house of corpses and I get to go to school and be a Trojan; I get to eat my mom's grilled peanut butter and Cheez Whiz sandwiches and—

"You walk with the dead," she says gently. Her eyes are luminous and—I can't believe it—sympathetic. "You've walked with us since . . ."

"Since my father died," I say. "And before that he walked with you and I followed. Death is my world. Everything else, school and friends, they're just things that get in the way of my next ghost." I've never said this before. I've never allowed myself to think it for more than a second. I've kept myself focused, and in doing so have managed to not think too much about life either, about *living*, no matter how hard my mom pushed me to have fun, to go out, to apply to colleges.

"Were you never sad?" she asks.

"Not a lot. I had this higher power, you know? I had this purpose." I reach into my back pocket and pull out my athame, drawing it from its leather. The blade shines in the gray light. Something in my blood, the blood of my father and his before him, makes it more than just a knife.

"I'm the only one in the world who can do this. Doesn't that mean it's what I'm supposed to do?" As the words leave my mouth I resent them. They take away all of my choices. Anna crosses her pale arms. The tilt of her head sweeps her hair over her shoulder and it's strange to see it lying there, just regular, dark strands. I'm waiting for it to twitch, to move into the air on that invisible current.

"Having no choice doesn't seem fair," she says, seeming to read my mind. "But having all of them isn't really easier. When I was alive, I could never decide what I wanted to do, what I wanted to become. I loved to take pictures; I wanted to take pictures for a newspaper. I loved to cook; I wanted to move to Vancouver and open a restaurant. I had a million different dreams but none of them was stronger than the rest. In the end they probably would have paralyzed me. I would have ended up here, running the boarding house."

"I don't believe that." She seems like such a force, this reasonable girl who kills with a turn of her fingers. She would have left all this behind, if she'd had the chance.

"I honestly don't remember," she sighs. "I don't think I was strong in life. Now it seems like I loved every moment, that every breath was charmed and crisp." She clasps her hands comically to her chest and breathes in deep through her nose, then blows it out in a huff. "I probably didn't. For all my dreams and fancies, I don't recall being . . . what would you call it? Perky."

I smile and she does too, then tucks her hair behind her ear in a gesture that is so alive and human that it makes me forget what I was going to say.

"What are we doing?" I ask. "You're trying to get me to not kill you, aren't you?"

Anna crosses her arms. "Considering that you *can't* kill me, I think that would be a wasted effort."

I laugh. "You're too confident."

"Am I? I know that what you've shown me aren't your best moves, Cas. I can feel the tension in your blade from holding back. How many times have you done this? How many times have you fought and won?"

"Twenty-two in the last three years." I say it with pride. It's more than my father ever did in the same amount of time. I'm what you might call an overachiever. I wanted to be better than he was. Faster. Sharper. Because I didn't want to end up like he ended up.

Without my knife I'm nothing special, just a regular seventeen-year-old with an average build, maybe a bit on the skinny side. But with the athame in my hand you'd think I was a triple black belt or something. My moves are sure, strong, and quick. She's right when she says she hasn't seen my best, and I don't know why that is.

"I don't want to hurt you, Anna. You know that, don't you? It's nothing personal."

"Just like I didn't want to kill all of those people rotting in my basement." She smiles ruefully.

So they were real. "What happened to you?" I ask. "What makes you do this?"

"None of your business," she replies.

"If you tell me . . ." I start but don't finish. If she tells me, I can figure her out. And once I figure her out, I can kill her.

Everything is becoming more complicated. This questioning girl and that wordless black monster are one and the same. It isn't fair. When I slide my knife through her, will I cut them apart? Will Anna go to one place and it to another? Or will Anna get sucked away to whatever void the rest go to?

I thought I'd put these thoughts out of my mind a long time ago. My father always told me that it wasn't our place to judge, that we were only the instrument. Our task was to send them away from the living. His eyes had been so certain when he'd said it. Why don't I have that kind of certainty?

I lift my hand slowly to touch that cold face, to graze my fingers along her cheek, and am surprised to find it soft, not made of marble. She stands paralyzed, then hesitantly lifts her hand to rest on mine.

The spell is so strong that when the door opens and Carmel comes through it, neither of us moves until she says my name.

"Cas? What are you doing?"

"Carmel," I blurt, and there she is, her figure framed in the open door. She's got her hand on the knob and it looks like she's shaking. She takes another tentative step into the house.

"Carmel, don't move," I say, but she's staring at Anna, who backs away from me, grimacing and grabbing hold of her head.

"Is that her? Is that what killed Mike?"

Stupid girl, she's coming farther into the house. Anna is retreating as fast as she can on unsteady feet, but I see that her eyes have gone black.

"Anna, don't, she doesn't know," I say too late. Whatever it is that allows Anna to spare me is obviously a one-time deal. She's gone in a twist of black hair and red blood, pale skin and teeth. There's a moment of silence and we listen to the drip, drip, drip of her dress.

And then she lunges, ready to thrust her hands into Carmel's guts.

I jump and tackle her, thinking the minute I collide with that granite force that I am an idiot. But I do manage to alter her course, and Carmel jumps to the side. It's the wrong way. She's farther away from the door now. It occurs to me that some people only have book smarts. Carmel is a tame house cat and Anna will make lunch of her if I don't do something. As Anna crouches on the ground, the red of her dress flowing sickly onto the floor, her hair and eyes wild, I hurtle myself toward Carmel and put myself between them.

"Cas, what were you doing?" Carmel asks, terrified.

"Shut up and get to the door," I yell. I hold my athame out in front of us even though Anna isn't afraid. When she springs, it's for me this time, and I grab on to her wrist with my free hand, using the other to try to keep her at bay with my knife.

"Anna, stop this!" I hiss, and the white comes back into

her eyes. Her teeth are grinding as she spits her words through them.

"Get her out of here!" she moans. I shove her hard to knock her back one more time. Then I grab Carmel and we dive through the door. We don't turn until we're down the porch steps and back on dirt and grass. The door has shut and I hear Anna raging inside, breaking things and tearing things up.

"My god, she's awful," Carmel whispers, burying her head in my shoulder. I squeeze her softly for a moment before pulling free and walking back up the porch steps.

"Cas! Get away from there," Carmel shouts. I know what she thinks she saw, but what I saw was Anna trying to stop. When my foot hits the porch, Anna's face appears at the window, her teeth bared and veins standing out against white skin. She slams her hand against the glass, making it rattle. There is dark water standing in her eyes.

"Anna," I whisper. I go to the window, but before I can put my hand up she floats away and turns, glides up the stairs, and disappears.

CHAPTER THIRTEEN

Carmel won't stop chattering at me as we stomp quickly down the gravel of Anna's unkempt driveway. She's asking a million questions that I'm not paying attention to. All I can think is that Anna is a murderer. Yet Anna is not evil. Anna kills, but Anna doesn't want to kill. She's not like any other ghost I've faced. Sure, I've heard of sentient ghosts, those who seem to know that they're dead. According to Gideon they're strong, but rarely hostile. I don't know what to do. Carmel grabs me by the elbow and I spin around.

"What?" I snap.

"Do you want to tell me exactly what you were doing in there?"

"Not really." I must've slept longer than I thought I did—either that or I was talking to Anna longer than I thought I was, because buttery shafts of light are breaking through the low clouds in the east. The sun is gentle but feels harsh to my eyes. Something occurs to me and I blink at Carmel, realizing for the first time that she's really here.

"You followed me," I say. "What're you doing here?"

She shifts her weight around awkwardly. "I couldn't sleep. And I wanted to see if it was true, so I went over to your house and saw you leaving."

"You wanted to see if what was true?"

She looks at me from under her lashes, like she wants me to figure it out for myself so she doesn't have to say it out loud, but I hate that game. After a few long seconds of my annoyed silence, she breaks.

"I talked to Thomas. He says you . . ." She shakes her head like she feels stupid for believing it. I'm mostly feeling stupid for trusting Thomas. "He says you kill ghosts for a living. Like you're a ghostbuster or something."

"I'm *not* a ghostbuster."

"Then what were you doing in there?"

"I was talking to Anna."

"Talking to her? She killed Mike! She could've killed you!"

"No she couldn't." I glance up at the house. I feel strange, talking about her so close to her home. It doesn't feel right.

"What were you talking to her about?" Carmel asks.

"Are you always so nosy?"

"What, like it was personal?" she snorts.

"Maybe it was," I reply. I want to get out of here. I want to drop my mom's car off and have Carmel take me to wake up Thomas. I think I'll rip the mattress right out from under him. It'll be fun to watch him bounce groggily on his box springs. "Listen, let's just get away from here, okay? Follow me back to my place and we can take your car to Thomas's. I'll explain everything, I promise," I add when she looks skeptical.

"Okay," she says.

"And Carmel."

"Yeah?"

"Don't ever call me a ghostbuster again, all right?" She smiles, and I smile back. "Just so we're clear."

She brushes past me to get into her car, but I grab her by the arm.

"You haven't mentioned Thomas's little blurt to anyone else, have you?"

She shakes her head.

"Not even Natalie or Katie?"

"I told Nat that I was meeting you so she'd cover for me if my parents called her. I told them I was staying at her place."

"What did you tell her we were meeting for?" I ask. She gives me this resentful look. I suppose that Carmel Jones only meets boys secretly at night for romantic reasons. I run my hand roughly through my hair.

"So, what, I'm supposed to make something up at school? Like we made out?" I think I'm blinking too much. And my shoulders are stooped so I feel about half a foot shorter than she is. She stares at me, bemused.

"You're not very good at this, are you?"

"Haven't had a whole lot of practice, Carmel."

She laughs. Damn, she really is pretty. No wonder Thomas spilled all my secrets. One bat of her eyelashes probably knocked him over.

"Don't worry," she says. "I'll make something up. I'll tell everybody you're a great kisser."

"Don't do me any favors. Listen, just follow me to my place, okay?"

She nods and ducks into her car. When I get into mine, I want to press my head into the steering wheel until the horn goes off. That way the horn will cover my screams. Why is this job so hard? Is it Anna? Or is it something else? Why can't I keep anyone out of my business? It's never been this difficult before. They accepted any cheesy cover story I made up, because deep down they didn't want to know the truth. Like Chase and Will. They swallowed Thomas's fairy story pretty easily.

But it's too late now. Thomas and Carmel are in on the game. And the game is a whole lot more dangerous this time around.

Does Thomas live with his parents?"

"I don't think so," Carmel says. "His parents died in a car accident. A drunk driver crossed the line. Or at least that's what people at school say." She shrugs. "I think he just lives with his grandpa. That weird old guy."

"Good." I pound on the door. I don't care if I wake up Morfran. The salty old buzzard can use the excitement. But after about thirteen very loud and rattling knocks, the door whips open and there's Thomas, standing before us in a very unattractive green bathrobe.

"Cas?" he whispers with a frog in his throat. I can't help but smile. It's hard to be annoyed with him when he looks like an oversize four-year-old, his hair stuck up on one side and his glasses only on halfway. When he realizes that Carmel's standing behind me, he quickly checks his face for drool and tries to smooth his hair down. Unsuccessfully. "Uh, what are you doing here?"

"Carmel followed me out to Anna's place," I say with a smirk. "Want to tell me why?" He's starting to blush. I don't know if it's because he feels guilty or because Carmel is seeing him in his pajamas. Either way, he steps aside to let us in and leads us through the dimly lit house to the kitchen.

The whole place smells like Morfran's herbal pipe. Then I see him, a hulking, stooped-over figure pouring coffee. He hands me a mug before I can even ask. Grumbling at us, he leaves the kitchen.

Thomas, meanwhile, has stopped shuffling around and is staring at Carmel.

"She tried to kill you," he blurts, wide-eyed. "You can't stop thinking about the way her fingers were hooked at your stomach."

Carmel blinks. "How did you know that?"

"You shouldn't do that," I warn Thomas. "It makes people uncomfortable. Invasion of privacy, you know."

"I know," he says. "I can't do it very often," he adds to Carmel. "Usually only when people are having strong or violent thoughts, or keep thinking of the same thing over and over." He smiles. "In your case, all three."

"You can read minds?" she asks incredulously.

"Sit down, Carmel," I say.

"I don't feel like it," she says. "I'm learning so many interesting things about Thunder Bay these days." Her arms cross over her chest. "You can read minds, there's something up there in that house killing my ex-boyfriends, and you—"

"Kill ghosts," I finish for her. "With this." I pull out my athame and set it on the table. "What else did Thomas tell you?"

"Just that your father did it too," she said. "I guessed that it killed him."

I give Thomas the eye.

"I'm sorry," he says helplessly.

"It's okay. You've got it bad. I know." I smirk and he looks at me desperately. As if Carmel doesn't know already. She'd have to be blind.

I sigh. "So now what? Can I possibly tell you to go home and forget about this? Is there any way that I can avoid us forming some peppy group of—" Before my mouth can finish, I lean forward and groan into my hands. Carmel gets it first, and laughs.

"A peppy group of ghostbusters?" she asks.

"I get to be Peter Venkman," says Thomas.

"Nobody gets to be anybody," I snap. "We are not ghostbusters. I've got the knife, and I kill the ghosts, and I can't be tripping over you the whole time. Besides, it's obvious that I would be Peter Venkman." I look sharply at Thomas. "You would be Egon."

"Wait a minute," says Carmel. "You don't get to call the shots. Mike was my friend, sort of."

"That doesn't mean you get to help. This isn't about re-venge."

"Then what is it about?"

"It's about . . . stopping her."

"Well, you haven't exactly done a great job of that. And from what I saw, it didn't even look like you were trying." Carmel has her eyebrow raised at me. The look is giving me some kind of hot feeling in my cheeks. Holy shit, I'm blushing.

"This is stupid," I blurt. "She's tough, okay? But I have a plan."

"Yeah," Thomas says, rising to my defense. "Cas has it all worked out. I've already got the rocks from the lake. They're charging under the moon until it wanes. The chicken feet are on backorder."

Talking about the spell makes me uneasy for some reason, like there's something that I'm not putting together. Something that I've overlooked.

Someone comes through the door without knocking. I barely notice, because that makes me feel like I've over-looked something too. After a few seconds of prodding my brain, I glance up and see Will Rosenberg.

He looks like he hasn't slept in days. His breathing is heavy and his chin is lolling toward his chest. I wonder if he's been drinking. There are dirt and oil stains on his jeans. The poor kid's taking it hard. He's staring at my knife on the table, so I reach up and take it, then slide it into my back pocket.

"I knew there was something weird about you," he says. The scent of his breath is sixty percent beer. "This is all because of you, somehow, isn't it? Ever since you came here, something's been wrong. Mike knew it. That's why he didn't want you hanging around Carmel."

"Mike didn't know anything," I say calmly. "What happened to him was an accident."

"Murder is no accident," Will mutters. "Stop lying to me. Whatever you're doing, I want in."

I groan. Nothing is going right. Morfran comes back into the kitchen and ignores all of us, instead staring into his coffee like it's super interesting.

"Circle's getting bigger," is all he says, and the problem that I couldn't think of snaps into place.

"Shit," I say. My head falls back so I'm looking at the ceiling.

"What?" Thomas asks. "What's wrong?"

"The spell," I reply. "The circle. We've got to be in the house to cast it."

"Yeah, so?" Thomas says. Carmel gets it right away; her face is downcast.

"So Carmel went into the house this morning and Anna almost ate her. The only person who can be in the house safely is me, and I'm not witchy enough to cast the circle."

"Couldn't you hold her off long enough for us to cast it? Once it was up, we'd be protected."

"No," Carmel says. "There's no way. You should have seen him this morning; she swatted him like a fly."

"Thanks," I snort.

"It's true. Thomas would never make it. And besides, doesn't he have to concentrate or something?"

Will jumps forward and grabs Carmel by the arm. "What are you talking about? You went in that house? Are you crazy? Mike would kill me if anything happened to you!"

And then he remembers that Mike's dead.

"We've got to figure out a way to cast that circle and do that spell," I think out loud. "She'll never tell me what happened on her own."

Morfran finally speaks. "Everything happens for a reason, Theseus Cassio. You've got less than a week to figure it out."

Less than a week. Less than a week. There's no way I can become a competent witch in less than a week, and I'm certainly not going to get any stronger or more able to control Anna. I need backup. I need to call Gideon.

We're all standing around in the driveway, having disbanded in the kitchen. It's a Sunday, a lazy, quiet Sunday, too early even for churchgoers. Carmel is walking with Will to their cars. She said she was going to follow him home, hang out with him awhile. She was, after all, the closest to him, and she couldn't imagine that Chase was being much comfort. I imagine she's right. Before she went, she took Thomas off to the side and whispered with him for a few moments. As we watch Carmel and Will walk away, I ask him what that was all about.

He shrugs. "She just wanted to tell me she was glad that

I told her. And she hopes that you're not mad at me for spilling, because she'll keep the secret. She just wants to help." And then he goes on and on, trying to draw attention to the way that she touched his arm. I wish that I hadn't asked, because now he won't shut up about it.

"Listen," I say. "I'm glad Carmel's noticing you. If you play your cards right, you might have a shot. Just don't invade her mind too much. She was pretty creeped out by that."

"Me and Carmel Jones," he scoffs, even as he stares hopefully after her car. "In a million years maybe. More likely she'll end up comforting Will. He's smart, and one of the crowd, like her. He's not a bad guy." Thomas straightens his glasses. Thomas isn't a bad guy either, and someday maybe he'll figure that out. For now I tell him to go put some clothes on.

As he turns and walks back up the drive, I notice something. There's a circular path near the house that connects to the end of the driveway. At the fork of it is a small white tree, a birch sapling. And hanging from the lowest branch is a slim black cross.

"Hey," I call out, and point to it. "What's that?"

It isn't him who answers. Morfran swaggers out onto the porch in his slippers and blue pajama pants, a plaid robe tied tight around his extensive belly. The getup looks ridiculous in contrast to that braided, mossy rock 'n' roll beard, but I'm not thinking about that now.

"Papa Legba's cross," he says simply.

"You practice voodoo," I say, and he hmphs in what I think is an affirmative. "So do I."

He snorts into his coffee cup. "No, you don't. And you shouldn't, neither."

So it was a bluff. I don't practice. I learn. And here is a golden opportunity. "Why shouldn't I?" I ask.

"Son, voodoo is about power. It's about the power inside you and the power you channel. The power you steal and the power you take from your goddamn chicken dinner. And you've got about ten thousand volts strapped to your side in that bit of leather there."

I instinctively touch the athame in my back pocket.

"If you were voodoo and channeling that, well, looking at you would be like watching a moth fly into a bug zapper. You would be lit up, 24/7." He squints at me. "Maybe someday I could teach you."

"I'd like that," I say as Thomas bursts back onto the porch in fresh but still mismatched clothes. He scampers down the porch steps.

"Where are we going?" he asks.

"Back to Anna's," I say. He turns sort of green. "I need to figure this ritual out or a week from now I'll be staring at your severed head and Carmel's internal organs." Thomas turns even greener, and I clap him on the back.

I glance back at Morfran. He's eyeballing us over his coffee mug. So voodooists channel power. He's an interesting guy. And he's given me way too much to think about to sleep.

On the drive over, the high from the events of last night starts to wear off. My eyes feel like sandpaper, and my head is lolling, even after downing that cup of paint thinner that Morfran called coffee. Thomas is quiet all the way to Anna's. He's probably still thinking about the feel of Carmel's hand on his arm. If life were fair, Carmel would turn around and look into his eyes, see that he's her willing slave, and be grateful. She'd lift him up and he wouldn't be a slave anymore, he'd just be Thomas, and they'd be glad to have each other. But life isn't fair. She'll probably end up with Will, or some other jock, and Thomas will suffer quietly.

"I don't want you anywhere near the house," I say to snap him out of it and make sure he doesn't miss the turn. "You can hang in the car, or follow me up the driveway. But she's probably unstable after this morning, so you should stay off the porch."

"You don't have to tell me twice," he snorts.

When we pull into the driveway, he elects to stay in the car. I make my way up alone. When I open the front door, I look down to make sure I'm stepping into the foyer and not about to fall face-first into a boatload of dead bodies.

"Anna?" I call. "Anna? Are you all right?"

"That's a silly question."

She's just come out of a room at the top of the stairs. She's leaning against the rail, not the dark goddess, but the girl.

"I'm dead. I can't be all right any more than I can be not all right."

Her eyes are downcast. She's lonely, and guilty, and trapped. She's feeling sorry for herself, and I can't say that I blame her.

"I didn't mean for anything like that to happen," I say honestly, and take a step toward the staircase. "I wouldn't have put you in that situation. She followed me."

"Is she all right?" Anna asks in a curiously high voice.

"She's fine."

"Good. I thought I might have bruised her. And she has such a pretty face."

Anna isn't looking at me. She's fiddling with the wood of the railing. She's trying to get me to say something, but I don't know what it is.

"I need you to tell me what happened to you. I need you to tell me how you died."

"Why do you want to make me remember that?" she asks softly.

"Because I need to understand you. I need to know why you're so strong." I start thinking out loud. "From what I know of it, your murder wasn't that strange or horrific. It wasn't even that brutal. So I can't figure out why you are the way you are. There has to be something . . ." When I stop, Anna is staring at me with wide, disgusted eyes. "What?"

"I'm just starting to regret that I didn't kill you," she says. It takes my sleep-deprived brain a minute to understand, but then I feel like a total ass. I've been around too much death. I've seen so much sick, twisted shit that it rolls off my tongue like nursery rhymes.

"How much do you know," she asks, "about what happened to me?"

Her voice is softer, almost subdued. Talking about murder, spitting out facts is something I grew up around. Only now I don't know how to do it. With Anna standing right in front of me, it's more than just words or pictures in a book. When I finally spit it out, I do it quickly and all at once, like pulling off a Band-Aid.

"I know that you were murdered in 1958, when you were sixteen. Someone cut your throat. You were on your way to a school dance."

A small smile plays on her lips but doesn't take hold. "I really wanted to go," she says quietly. "It was going to be my last one. My first and last." She looks down at herself and holds out the hem of her skirt. "This was my dress."

It doesn't look like much to me, just a white shift with some lace and ribbons, but what do I know? I'm not a chick, for one, and for two, I don't know much about 1958. Back then it might have been the bee's knees, as my mom would say.

"It isn't much," she says, reading my mind. "One of the boarders we had around that time was a seamstress. Maria. From Spain. I thought she was very exotic. She'd had to leave a daughter, only a little younger than me, when she came here, so she liked to talk to me. She took my measurements and helped me to sew it. I wanted something more elegant but I was never that good at sewing. Clumsy fingers," she says, and holds them up like I'll be able to see what a mess they can make.

"You look beautiful," I say, because it's the first thing that pops into my stupid, empty head. I consider using my athame to cut my tongue out. It's probably not what she wanted to hear, and it came out all wrong. My voice didn't work. I'm lucky it didn't do the Peter Brady and crack. "Why was it going to be your last dance?" I ask quickly.

"I was going to run away," she says. Defiance shines in her eyes just like it must have then, and there's a fire behind her voice that makes me sad. Then it goes out, and she seems confused. "I don't know if I would have done it. I wanted to."

"Why?"

"I wanted to start my life," she explains. "I knew I would never do anything if I stayed here. I would've had to run the boarding house. And I was tired of fighting."

"Fighting?" I take another step up closer. There's a tail of dark hair falling down her shoulders, which slump as she hugs herself. She's so pale and small, I can hardly imagine her fighting anyone. Not with her fists anyway.

"It wasn't fighting," she says. "And it was. With her. And with him. It was hiding, making them think I was something weaker, because that's what they wanted. That's what she told me my father would have wanted. A quiet, obedient girl. Not a harlot. Not a whore."

I take a deep breath. I ask who called her that, who would say that, but she's not listening anymore.

"He was a liar. A layabout. He played love to my mother but it wasn't real. He said he would marry her and then he would have all the rest."

I don't know who she's talking about, but I can guess what "all the rest" was.

"It was you," I say softly. "It was you he was really after."

"He would . . . corner me, in the kitchen, or outside by the well. It was paralyzing. I hated him."

"Why didn't you tell your mother?"

"I couldn't . . ." She stops and starts again. "But I couldn't let him. I was going to get away. I would have." Her face is blank. Not even the eyes are alive. She's just moving lips and voice. The rest of her has gone back inside.

I reach up and touch her cheek, cold as ice. "Was it him? Was he the one who killed you? Did he follow you that night and—"

Anna shakes her head very fast and pulls away. "That's enough," she says in a voice that's trying to be hard.

"Anna, I have to know."

"Why do you have to know? What business is it of yours?" She puts her hand to her forehead. "I can hardly remember myself. Everything's muddy and bleeding." She shakes her head, frustrated. "There's nothing I can tell you! I was killed and it was black and then I was here. I was this, and I killed, and *killed*, and couldn't stop." Her breath hitches. "They did something to me but I don't know what. I don't know how."

"They," I say curiously, but this isn't going any further. I can literally see her shutting down, and in another couple of minutes, I might be standing here trying to hold on to a girl with black veins and a dripping dress.

"There's a spell," I say. "A spell that can help me understand."

She calms a bit and looks at me like I'm nuts. "Magic spells?" A disbelieving smile escapes. "Will I grow fairy wings and jump through fire?"

"What are you talking about?"

"Magic isn't real. It's make-believe and superstition, old curses on the tongues of my Finnish grandmothers."

I can't believe that she's questioning the existence of magic when she's standing before me dead and talking. But I don't get the chance to convince her, because something starts to happen, something twisting in her brain, and she twitches. When she blinks, her eyes are far away.

"Anna?"

Her arm shoots out to keep me back. "It's nothing."

I peer closer. "That wasn't nothing. You remembered something, didn't you? What is it? Tell me!"

"No, I—it wasn't anything. I don't know." She touches her temple. "I don't know what that was."

This isn't going to be easy. It's going to be damned near impossible if I don't get her cooperation. A heavy, hopeless feeling is creeping into my exhausted limbs. It feels like my muscles are starting to atrophy, and I don't have that much muscle to begin with.

"Please, Anna," I say. "I need your help. I need you to let us do the spell. I need you to let other people in here with me."

"No," she says. "No spells! And no people! You know what would happen. I can't control it."

"You can control it for me. You can do it for them too."

"I don't know why I don't have to kill you. And by the

way, isn't that enough? Why are you asking for more favors?"

"Anna, please. I need at least Thomas, and probably Carmel, the girl you met this morning."

She looks down at her toes. She's sad, I know she's sad, but Morfran's stupid "less than a week" speech is ringing in my ears, and I want this over with. I can't let Anna stay for another month, possibly collecting more people for her basement. It doesn't matter that I like talking to her. It doesn't matter that I like her. It doesn't matter that what happened to her wasn't fair.

"I wish you would leave," she says softly, and when she looks up I see that she's almost crying, and she's looking over my shoulder at the door or maybe out the window.

"You know I can't," I say, mirroring her words from moments ago.

"You make me want things that I can't have."

Before I can figure out what she means, she sinks through the steps, down, deep into the basement where she knows I won't follow.

Gideon calls just after Thomas drops me off at my house.

"Good morning, Theseus. Sorry to wake you so early on a Sunday."

"I've been up for hours, Gideon. Already hard at work." Across the Atlantic, he is smirking at me. As I walk into the house, I nod good morning to my mother, who is chasing Tybalt down the stairs and hissing that rats aren't good for him.

"What a shame," Gideon chuckles. "I've been waiting around to call you for hours, trying to let you get some rest. What a pain that was. It's nearly four in the afternoon here, you know. But I think I've got the essence of that spell for you."

"I don't know if it'll matter. I was going to call you later. There's a problem."

"What sort?"

"The sort that no one can get into the house but me, and I'm no witch." I tell him a little more about what's happened, for some reason leaving out the fact that I've been having long talks with Anna at night. On the other end I hear him cluck his tongue. I'm sure he's rubbing his chin and cleaning his glasses too.

"You've been completely unable to subdue her?" he asks finally.

"Completely. She's Bruce Lee, the Hulk, and Neo from *The Matrix* all rolled into one."

"Yes. Thank you for the entirely incomprehensible pop-culture references."

I smile. He knows perfectly well who Bruce Lee is, at least.

"But the fact remains that you must do the spell. Something about the way this girl died is imbuing her with terrible power. It's just a matter of finding secrets. I remember a ghost that gave your father some trouble in 1985. For some reason it was able to kill without ever being corporeal. It was only after three séances and a trip to a Satanic church in Italy that we discovered that the only thing allowing it to remain on the earthly plane was a spell placed on a rather ordinary stone chalice. Your father broke it and just like that, no more ghost. It will be the same for you."

My father told me that story once, and I remember it being much more complicated than that. But I let it go. He's right anyway. Every ghost has its own methods, its own bag of tricks. They have different drives and different wants. And when I kill them, they each go their own way.

"What will this spell do exactly?" I ask.

"The consecrated stones form a protective circle. After it is cast, she'll have no power over those within it. The witch performing the ritual can take whatever energies possess the house and reflect them into a scrying bowl. The scrying bowl will show you whatever you seek. Of course it's not as simple as all that; there's some chicken feet and an herbal blend which your mother can help with, then some chanting. I'll get the text to you via e-mail."

He makes it sound so easy. Does he think I'm exaggerating? Doesn't he get how hard it is for me to admit that Anna can take me anytime she wants? Toss me like a rag doll, give me noogies and atomic wedgies, and then point and laugh?

"It isn't going to work. I can't cast the circle. I've never had the knack for witchcraft. Mom must've told you. I messed up her Beltane cookies every year until I was seven."

I know what he's going to tell me. He's going to sigh and advise that I get myself back to the library, start talking to people who might know what happened. Try to figure out a murder that's been cold for over fifty years. And that's what I'll have to do. Because I'm not putting Thomas or Carmel in danger.

"Hm."

"Hm, what?"

"Well, I'm just thinking over all the rituals I've done in my years of parapsychology and mysticism—"

I can actually hear his brain turning. He's got something, and I start to get hopeful. I knew he was worth more than just bangers and mash.

"You say you have some adepts at your disposal?"

"Some what?"

"Some witches."

"I've got one witch, actually. My friend Thomas."

On Gideon's end, there is an intake of breath followed by a pleased pause. I know what the old scone is thinking. He's never heard me use the phrase "my friend" before. He'd better not be getting emotional.

"He's not that advanced."

"If you trust him, that's all that matters. But you'll need more than him. Yourself and two others. Each must represent a corner of the circle. You'll cast the circle outside, you see, and move into the house ready to work." He pauses to think some more. He's very pleased with himself. "Trap your ghost in the center and you'll be completely safe. Tapping her energy will also make the spell more potent and revealing. It might just weaken her enough for you to finish the job."

I swallow hard and feel the weight of the knife in my back pocket. "Absolutely," I say. I listen for another ten minutes as he goes over the particulars, thinking the whole time about Anna and what she's going to show me. At the end of it I think I remember most of what I'm supposed to do, but still ask that he e-mail me a set of instructions.

"Now who will you get to complete the circle? Those with a connection to the ghost are best."

"I'll get this guy, Will, and my friend Carmel," I say. "And don't say anything. I know I'm having some trouble keeping people out of my business."

Gideon sighs. "Ah, Theseus. This was never meant to keep you alone. Your father had many friends, and he had your mother, and you. As time goes by, your circle will get larger. It's nothing to be ashamed of."

The circle's getting bigger. Why does everyone keep saying that? Big circles are more people to trip over. I have got to get out of Thunder Bay. Away from this mess and back to my routine of move, hunt, kill.

Move, hunt, kill. Like lather, rinse, and repeat. My life, stretched out in a simple routine. It feels empty and heavy at the same time. I think of what Anna said, about wanting what she can't have. Maybe I understand what she meant.

Gideon is still talking.

"Let me know if there's anything you need," he says. "Even though I'm just dusty books and old stories from an ocean away. The real work is for you to do."

"Yes. Me and my friends."

"Yes. Smashing. You'll be just like those four chaps in the movie. You know the one, with the oversized marsh-mallow."

You've got to be kidding me.

CHAPTER FOURTEEN

My mom and I sit in her car on the edge of the school parking lot, watching buses roll in and unload, spilling students onto the sidewalk to rush in through the doors. The whole process is like something in an industrial plant—a bottling factory in reverse.

I told her what Gideon said and asked for her help making the herbal blend, which she said she'd do. I notice that she's looking a little frayed around the edges. There are dark, pinkish-purple circles under her eyes, and her hair is dull. Usually it shines like a copper pot.

"You okay, Mom?"

She smiles and looks over at me. "Sure, kiddo. Just worried about you, like always. And Tybalt. He woke me up last night, jumping at the attic trapdoor."

"Damn it, I'm sorry," I say. "I forgot to go up and set the traps."

"It's okay. I heard something move up there last week, and it sounded a lot bigger than a rat. Can raccoons get into attics?"

"Maybe it's just a bunch of rats," I suggest, and she shudders. "You'd better get somebody out there to check it out."

She sighs and taps the steering wheel. "Maybe." She shrugs.

She seems sad, and it occurs to me that I don't know how she's getting on here. I haven't helped her with much on this move—not around the house, not with anything. I've barely even been there. Glancing into the backseat, I see a cardboard box filled with enchanted candles of various colors, ready to be sold in a local bookshop. Normally I would have loaded them for her and tied the proper labels on with lengths of colored cord.

"Gideon says you've made some friends," she says, looking into the school crowd like she might be able to pick them out. I should've known Gideon would spill. He's like a surrogate parent. Not like a stepfather, exactly—more like a godfather, or a sea horse who wants to stuff me into his pouch.

"Just Thomas and Carmel," I say. "The ones you've met before."

"Carmel's a very pretty girl," she says hopefully.

"Thomas seems to think so."

She sighs, then smiles. "Good. He could use a woman's touch."

"Mom," I groan. "Gross."

"Not that kind of touch," she laughs. "I mean he needs someone to clean him up. Make him stand up straight. That boy is all wrinkles. And he smells like an old man's pipe." She fishes around in the backseat for a second, and her hand comes back full of envelopes.

"I was wondering what happened to all my mail," I say,

flipping through them. They're open already. I don't mind. They're just ghost tips, nothing personal. In the middle of the stack is a large letter from Daisy Bristol. "Daisy wrote," I say. "Did you read it?"

"He just wanted to know how things were going for you. And to tell you everything that's happened to him in the last month. He wants you to come to New Orleans for some witch spirit skulking around the base of a tree. Supposedly she used to use the thing for sacrifices. I didn't like the way he talked about her."

I smirk. "Not every witch is good, Mom."

"I know. I'm sorry for reading your mail. You were too focused to notice it anyway; most of them just sat on the mail desk. I wanted to handle it for you. Make sure you weren't missing anything important."

"Was I?"

"A professor in Montana wants you to come and slay a Wendigo."

"Who am I? Van Helsing?"

"He says he knows Dr. Barrows, from Holyoke."

I snort. "Dr. Barrows knows that monsters aren't real."

My mother sighs. "How do we know what's real? Most of the things you've put away could be called a monster by someone."

"Yeah." I put my hand on the door. "You're sure you can get the herbs I need?"

She nods. "You're sure you can get them to help you?"

I look at the crowd. "We'll see."

The hallways today look like something out of a movie. You know, the ones where the important characters walk in slow motion and the rest of the people just whip by as different flesh- and clothes-colored blurs. I caught glimpses of Carmel and Will in the crowd, but Will was walking away from me, and I couldn't get Carmel's attention. I never saw Thomas, despite going to his locker twice. So I try to stay awake during geometry. I don't do a great job. They shouldn't be allowed to teach math so early in the morning.

Midway through a lesson on proofs, a folded rectangle of paper finds its way onto my desk. When I open it I see a note from Heidi, a pretty blond-haired girl who sits three rows back. She's asking if I need help studying. And whether I want to go see the new Clive Owen movie. I tuck the note into my math book like I'll answer it later. I won't, of course, and if she asks about it, I'll tell her I'm doing fine on my own, and maybe some other time. She might ask again, two or three more times maybe, but after that she'll get the hint. It probably seems mean, but it isn't. What's the point in seeing a movie, starting up something that I can't finish? I don't want to miss people, and I don't want them to miss me.

After class I slide out the door quick and get lost in the crowds. I think I hear Heidi's voice call my name but I don't turn around. There's work to be done.

Will's locker is the closest. He's there already with—as usual—Chase hanging on his hip. When he sees me, his eyes do this shifty thing from right to left, like he doesn't think we should be seen talking.

"What's up, Will?" I ask. I nod at Chase, who gives me this stone face like I'd better be careful or he's going to pound me at any minute. Will doesn't say anything. He just glances my way and keeps on doing what he's doing, switching out his textbooks for his next class. I realize with sort of a jolt that Will hates me. He's never liked me, out of loyalty to Mike, and now he hates me, because of what happened. I don't know why I haven't realized it before. I guess I never give too much thought to the living. In any case, it makes me glad to tell him what I have to tell him, about being part of the spell. It'll give him some closure.

"You said you wanted in. Here's your chance."

"What chance is that?" he asks. His eyes are cold and gray. Tough and smart.

"Can't you get your flying monkey out of here first?" I motion toward Chase, but neither moves. "We're doing a spell to bind the ghost. Meet me at Morfran's shop after school."

"You're such a freak, man," Chase spits at me. "Bringing this shit in here. Making us talk to the police."

I don't know what he's whining about. If the cops were as casual as they were with me and Carmel, what's the big deal? And I have to believe that they were, because I was right about them. Mike's disappearance spawned only one small search party that combed the hills for about a week.

There were a few newspaper articles that quickly fell off the front page.

Everyone is swallowing the story that he up and ran away. It's only expected. When people see something supernatural, they rationalize it down to earth. The cops in Baton Rouge did it with my dad's murder. They called it an isolated act of extreme violence, probably perpetrated by someone traveling through the state. Never mind that he'd been fucking *eaten*. Never mind that no human could have taken such big bites.

"At least the cops don't think you're involved," I hear myself say absently. Will slams his locker shut.

"That's not what matters," he says in a low voice. He looks at me hard. "This had better not be another runaround. You'd better show."

As they walk away, Carmel appears at my shoulder.

"What's with them?" she asks.

"They're still thinking about Mike," I say. "Is there something strange about that?"

She sighs. "Just that we seem to be the only ones. I thought, after it happened, that I'd be surrounded by a herd of people asking a million questions. But not even Nat and Katie ask anymore. They're more interested in how things are going with you, whether we're a hot item and when I'm going to bring you around to parties." She looks at the passing crowd. A lot of girls smile and some call out to her and wave, but none of them comes over. It's like I'm wearing people repellent.

"I think they're getting sort of pissed off," she goes on.

"Because I haven't wanted to hang out lately. It's shitty I guess. They're my friends. But . . . everything I want to talk about I can't say to them. It feels so separate, like I've touched something that's taken the color out of me. Or maybe I'm in color now and they're black and white." She turns to me. "We're in on the secret, aren't we, Cas? And it's taking us out of the world."

"That's usually the way it works," I say softly.

At the shop after school, Thomas bounces around behind the counter—not the one where Morfran rings up sales of hurricane lamps and porcelain washbasins, but the one in the back, stocked with jars of things floating in murky water, crystals covered in dust cloth, candles, and bundles of herbs. Upon closer inspection, I notice that a few of the candles are my mother's handiwork. How crafty of her. She didn't even tell me they'd met.

"Here," Thomas says, and pushes something up to my face that looks like a bundle of twigs. Then I realize they're dried chicken feet. "They just came in this afternoon." He shows them to Carmel, who tries to make an expression that is more impressed and less disgusted. Then he bounces off behind the counter again and disappears, rummaging around.

Carmel chuckles. "How long are you staying in Thunder Bay after all this is over, Cas?"

I glance at her. I hope she hasn't fallen into her own lie to Nat and Katie—that she's not caught up in some damsel fantasy where I'm the big bad ghost slayer and she'll constantly need rescuing.

But no. I'm stupid to think so. She isn't even looking at me. She's watching Thomas.

"I'm not sure. Maybe a little while."

"Good," she says, smiling. "In case you didn't notice, Thomas is going to miss you when you go."

"Maybe he'll have someone else to keep him company," I say, and we look at each other. There's a current in the air for a second, a certain understanding, and then the door jingles behind us and I know that Will's here. Hopefully without Chase.

I turn around and wishes are horses. He's alone. And three sheets of pissed off, from the looks of it. He stalks in with his hands stuffed into his pockets, glaring at the antiques.

"So what's the deal with this spell?" he asks, and I can tell he feels awkward using the word "spell." That word doesn't belong in the mouths of people like him, rooted in logic and so in tune to the waking and working world.

"We need four people to cast a binding circle," I explain. Thomas and Carmel gather around. "Originally it was just going to be Thomas casting a circle of protection in the house, but since Anna would shred him a new face, we came up with Plan B."

Will nods. "So what do we do?"

"Now we practice."

"Practice?"

"Do you want to mess up inside that house?" I ask, and Will shuts up.

Thomas stares at me blankly until I give him the nudging eyes. This is his show now. I gave him a copy of the spell to review. He knows what needs to be done.

He shakes himself awake and grabs the written copy of the spell off the counter. Then he walks around each of us, taking us by the shoulders and positioning us where we need to be.

"Cas stands in the west, where things end. Also because then he'll be the first one in the house in case this doesn't work." He places me in the west. "Carmel, you're north," he says, and gingerly takes her by the shoulders. "I'm in the east, where things begin. Will, you'll be the south." He takes his place and reads over the paper for probably the hundredth time. "We'll cast the circle in the driveway, lay a formation of thirteen stones, and take our positions. We'll have Cas's mom's herb potion in bags around our necks. It's a basic mixture of protective herbs. The candles get lit from the east, counterclockwise. And we'll chant this." He hands the paper over to Carmel, who reads it, makes a face, and passes it to Will.

"Are you fricken serious?"

I don't argue. The chant does seem stupid. I know magic works, I know it's real, but I don't know why it has to be so damn fruity sometimes.

"We chant it continuously as we go into the house. The consecrated circle should come with us, even though we leave the stones behind. I'll be carrying the scrying bowl. When we get inside, I'll fill the bowl and we'll get started."

Carmel looks down at the scrying bowl, which is a shining silver dish.

"What are you going to fill it with?" she asks. "Holy water or something?"

"Probably Dasani," Thomas replies.

"You forgot the hard part," I say, and everyone looks at me. "You know, the part where we have to get Anna inside the circle and throw chicken feet at her."

"Are you serious?" Will groans again.

"We don't *throw* the chicken feet." Thomas rolls his eyes at us. "We set them nearby. Chicken feet have a calming effect on spirits."

"Well, that won't be the hard part," Will says. "The hard part'll be getting her inside our human circle."

"Once she's inside, we'll be safe. I'll be able to reach in and use the scrying bowl without even being afraid. But we can't break the circle. Not until the spell is finished and she's weak. And even then we should probably get the heck out of there."

"Great," Will says. "We can practice everything but the thing that might get us killed."

"It's the best we can do," I say. "So let's get chanting." I try not to think about what rank amateurs we are and how silly this is.

Morfran whistles as he walks through his shop, ignoring us completely. The only thing that betrays that he knows what we're up to is the fact that he flips the sign on the door of the shop from "Open" to "Closed."

"Wait a minute," Will says. Thomas was just about to start chanting, and the interruption really takes the wind out of his sails. "Why are we going to get out of there after the spell? She'll be weak, right? Why don't we kill her then?"

"That's the plan," Carmel replies. "Isn't it, Cas?"

"Yeah," I say. "Depending on how things go. We don't know if it'll even work." I'm not being terribly convincing. I think I said most of that while staring at my shoes. As luck would have it, Will is the one who notices. He takes a step back from the circle.

"Hey! You can't do that during the spell," Thomas yelps.

"Shut up, freak," Will says dismissively, and my hackles rise. He looks at me. "Why should it be you? Why does it have to be you who does it? Mike was my best friend."

"It has to be me," I say flatly.

"Why?"

"Because I'm the one who can use the knife."

"What's so hard about it? Slash and stab, right? Any idiot could do it."

"It wouldn't work for you," I say. "For you it would be just a knife. And just a knife isn't going to kill Anna."

"I don't believe it," he says, and plants his feet.

This sucks. I need Will in on this, not only because he completes the circle, but because part of me does feel like I owe him, like he should be involved. Of the people I know, Anna has cost him the most. So what am I going to do?

"We'll take your car," I say. "Everyone. Let's go. Right now."

Will drives suspiciously with me in the passenger seat. Carmel and Thomas are in the back, and I don't have time to ponder just how sweaty Thomas's palms are getting. I need to prove to them—all of them—that I am what I say I am. That this is my calling, my mission. And maybe, after getting soundly beaten by Anna (whether I'm subconsciously allowing it or not), I need to once again prove it to myself.

"Where are we going?" Will asks.

"You tell me. I'm no Thunder Bay expert. Take me where the ghosts are."

Will digests this information. He licks at his lips tensely and glances at Carmel in the rearview mirror. Even though he seems nervous, I can tell he already has a good idea of where to go. We all grab on to something as he does an unexpected U-turn.

"The cop," he says.

"The cop?" Carmel asks. "You're not serious. That's not real."

"Until a few weeks ago, none of this was real," Will replies.

We drive across town, through the retail district and into the industrial. The scenery changes every few blocks, from trees ripe with golden and reddish foliage to streetlights and bright plastic signs, and finally to railroad tracks and stark, unlabeled cement buildings. Beside me, Will's face is grim and not at all curious. He can't wait to show me whatever it is that he's got up his sleeve. He's hoping that I'll fail the test, that I'm full of smoke and mirrors and bullshit.

Behind me, on the other hand, Thomas looks like an excited beagle who doesn't know he's being taken to the vet. I have to admit that I'm sort of excited myself. There've been few opportunities to show off my work. I don't know what I'm looking forward to more: impressing Thomas, or shoving Will's smug expression down his throat. Of course, Will has to come through first.

The car slows almost to a crawl. Will is peering out at buildings to his left. Some look like warehouses, others like low-rent apartment complexes that haven't been used for a while. All are the color of washed-out sandstone.

"There," he says, and mutters, "I think," under his breath. We park in an alley and get out together. Now that he's here, Will seems a little less eager.

I take my athame out of my bag and sling it over my shoulder, then hand the bag off to Thomas and nod to Will to lead the way. He takes us around the front of the building and down two more, until we get to one that looks like an old apartment. There are residential-style windows at the top with paned glass and an unused window box. I peer along the side and see a fire escape with the ladder hanging down. I test the front door. I don't know why it's unlocked, but it is, which is good. We'd have cut a damned conspicuous picture if we'd had to shimmy up the side.

When we walk into the building, Will motions to head up the stairs. The place has that boarded-up smell, sour and unused, like too many different people have lived here and each left behind a lingering scent that doesn't mix well with the others.

"So," I say. "Isn't anybody going to tell me what we're about to walk into?"

Will doesn't say anything. He just glances at Carmel, who dutifully speaks.

"About eight years ago, there was a hostage situation in the apartment upstairs. Some railroad worker went crazy, locked his wife and daughter in the bathroom and started waving a gun around. The cops got called in, and they sent up a hostage negotiator. It didn't exactly go well."

"What do you mean by that?"

"She means," Will cuts in, "that the hostage negotiator got himself shot in the spine, right before the perp shot himself in the head."

I try to digest this information and not make fun of Will for using the word "perp."

"The wife and daughter got out okay," Carmel says. She sounds nervous, but excited.

"So what's the ghost story?" I ask. "Are you bringing me into an apartment with some trigger-happy railroad worker?"

"It isn't the railroad worker," Carmel answers. "It's the cop. There've been reports of him in the building after he died. People have seen him through the windows and heard him talking to someone, trying to convince them not to do it. Once they say he even talked to a little boy down on the street. He hung his head out the window and yelled at him, told him to get out of there. Scared him half to death."

"Could be just another urban legend," Thomas says.

But in my experience, it usually isn't. I don't know what I'm going to find when we get up to this apartment. I don't know if we'll find anything, and if we do, I don't know if I should kill him. After all, nobody mentioned the cop actually harming anybody, and it's always been our practice to leave the safe ones alone, no matter how much they wail and rattle their chains.

Our practice. The athame is a heavy weight on my shoulder. All my life I've known this knife. I've watched the blade move through light and air, first in my father's hand and then in my own. The power in it sings to me—it courses through my arm and into my chest. For seventeen years it has kept me safe and made me strong.

The blood tie, Gideon always told me. *The blood of your ancestors forged this athame. Men of power, bled their warrior, to put the spirits down. The athame is your father's, and it is yours, and you both belong to it.*

That's what he told me. Sometimes with fun hand gestures and a little bit of miming. The knife is mine, and I love it, like you would love any faithful hound dog. Men of power, whoever they were, put my ancestor's blood—a warrior's blood—into the blade. It puts the spirits down, but I don't know where. Gideon and my father taught me never to ask.

I'm thinking so hard about this that I don't notice I'm leading them right into the apartment. The door has been left ajar and we've walked right into the empty living room. Our feet strike the bare flooring—whatever was left over after all the carpeting was pulled up. It looks like chipboard. I stop so fast that Thomas runs into my back. For a minute, I think the place is empty.

But then I see the black figure huddled in the corner, near the window. It's got its hands over its head and it's rocking back and forth, muttering to itself.

"Whoa," Will whispers. "I didn't think anyone would be here."

"No one *is* here," I say, and feel them tense as they catch my meaning. It doesn't matter if this is what they meant to bring me to. Seeing it for real is a completely different ballgame. I motion for them to stay back, and walk in a wide arc around the cop to get a better view. He's got his eyes wide open; he looks terrified. He's muttering and chittering like a chipmunk, all nonsense. It's disturbing to think how sane he must've been when he was alive. I pull my athame out, not to threaten him but just to have it out, just in case. Carmel gives a little gasp, and for some reason that gets his attention.

He fixes his shiny eye on her. "Don't do it," he hisses. She backs up a step.

"Hey," I say softly, and get no response. The cop has his eyes on Carmel. There must be something about her. Maybe she reminds him of the hostages—the wife and daughter.

Carmel doesn't know what to do. Her mouth is open, the beginning of a word caught in her throat, and she's looking quickly from the cop to me and back again.

I feel a familiar sharpening. That's what I call it: a

sharpening. It isn't that I start to breathe harder, or that my heart speeds up and pounds in my chest. It's subtler than that. I breathe deeper, and my heart beats stronger. Everything around me slows down, and all of the lines are crisp and clear. It has to do with confidence, and my natural edge. It has to do with my fingers humming as they squeeze the handle of my athame.

I never once had this feeling when I went up against Anna. It's what I've been missing, and maybe Will was a blessing in disguise. This is what I'm after: this edge, this living on the balls of my feet. I can see everything in an instant: that Thomas is genuinely thinking about how to protect Carmel, and that Will is trying to work up the nerve to try something himself, to prove that I'm not the only one who can do this. Maybe I should let him. Let the ghost of the cop give him a scare and put him back in his place.

"Please," Carmel says. "Just calm down. I didn't want to come here in the first place, and I'm not who you think I am. I don't want to hurt anybody!"

And then something interesting happens. Something I haven't seen before. The features on the cop's face change. It's almost impossible to see, like picking out the current of a river moving beneath the surface. The nose broadens. The cheekbones shift downward. The lips grow thinner and the teeth shift inside the mouth. All of this has happened in two or three blinks of an eye. I'm looking at another face.

"Interesting," I mutter, and my peripheral vision registers

Thomas giving me the is-that-all-you-can-say? face. "This ghost isn't just the cop," I explain. "It's both of them. The cop and the railroad worker, trapped together in one form." This is the railroad worker, I think, and I glance down at his hands just as he's lifting one to aim a gun at Carmel.

She shrieks, and Thomas grabs her and pulls her down. Will doesn't do much of anything. He just starts saying, "It's just a ghost, it's just a ghost" over and over very loudly, which is pretty damn stupid. I, on the other hand, don't hesitate.

The weight of my athame moves easily in my palm, flipping so the blade isn't pointed ahead but back; I'm holding it like the guy from *Psycho* did when he was hacking through that chick in the shower scene. But I'm not using it to hack. The sharp side of the blade is facing up, and as the ghost raises the gun on my friends, I jerk my arm toward the ceiling. The athame connects and slices most of the way through his wrist.

He howls and steps back; I do too. The gun drops to the ground without a noise. It's eerie, the sight of something that should make a racket and yet you don't even hear a whisper. He looks at his hand in puzzlement. It's hanging by a thread of skin, but there isn't any blood. When he plucks it off, it dissolves into smoke: oily, cancerous tendrils. I don't think I need to tell anyone not to breathe it in.

"So what, that's it?" Will asks in a panicked voice. "I thought that thing was supposed to kill it!"

"It isn't an 'it,'" I say evenly. "It's a man. Two men. And they're already dead. This sends them where they need to be."

The ghost comes at me now. I've gotten his attention, and I duck and pull back so easily, so swiftly, that none of his attempts to strike even come close. I slice off more of his arm as I duck underneath it, and the smoke dances around and disappears in the disturbance my body made.

"Every ghost goes differently," I tell them. "Some die again like they think they're still alive." I duck another one of his attacks and land an elbow to the back of his head. "Others melt into puddles of blood. Others explode." I look back at my friends, at their wide eyes paying rapt attention. "Some leave things behind—ashes, or stains. Some don't."

"Cas," Thomas says, and points behind me, but I already know that the ghost is on his way back. I sidestep and slice through his rib cage. He goes down on one knee.

"Every time is different," I say. "Except for this." I look directly at Will, ready to go to work. It's at that moment that I feel the ghost's hands grip both of my ankles and pull me off of my feet.

Did you hear that? Both hands. Yet I distinctly remember cutting one of them off. This strikes me as very interesting just before my head bonks off of the chipboard floor.

The ghost lunges for my throat and I just barely hold him off. Looking at the hands, one is different. It's slightly more tanned, and has a completely different shape: longer fingers, ragged nails. I hear Carmel yell at Thomas and Will that they should help me, and that's the last thing I want. It would take the piss out of the whole thing.

Still, as I'm rolling around with my jaw clenched, trying to angle my knife toward the guy's throat, I wish that I were built more like Will's football-playing physique. My leanness makes me agile and quick, and I'm pretty wiry, but when it comes to this up-close-and-personal stuff, it'd be nice to be able to hurl someone across the room.

"I'm fine," I say to Carmel. "I'm just figuring him out." The words come out in an unconvincing, strained groan. They're staring at me, wide-eyed, and Will takes a jerky step forward.

"Stay back!" I shout as I manage to get my foot into the guy's stomach. "It's just going to take more," I explain. "There are two guys inside here, get it?" My breathing is heavier. Some sweat trickles into my hair. "No big deal . . . it just means I have to do everything twice."

At least I hope so. It's the only thing I can think of to try, and really it boils down to a desperate slice and dice. This isn't what I had in mind when I suggested we go a-hunting. Where are the nice, easy ghosties when you need them?

I steel myself and kick out hard with my foot, heaving the cop/railroad worker back off of me. Scrambling up, I get a better grip on the athame and refocus. He's set to charge, and when he does I start slicing and cutting like a human Cuisinart. I hope it looks a lot cooler than I think it does. My hair and clothes are moving in a breeze I can't feel. Black smoke erupts from below me.

Before I'm finished—before *he's* finished— I can hear two distinct voices, layered on top of each other, like some somber harmony. In the midst of my slicing, I find myself looking into two faces occupying the same space: two sets of teeth gnashing, and one blue eye, one brown. I'm glad I was able to do this. The uneasy, ambiguous feeling I had when we came in is gone. Whether or not this ghost has ever harmed anyone, it has surely harmed itself, and wherever I'm sending them has to be better than this, trapped in the same form with the person you hate, driving each other more and more mad with every day, week, *year* that passes.

In the end, I stand alone in the center of the room, curls of smoke fading and dispersing into the ceiling. Thomas, Carmel, and Will are standing in a huddle, staring at me. The cop and the railroad worker are gone. So is the gun.

"That was—" is all Thomas can muster.

"That was what I do," I say simply, and wish I was less out of breath. "So no more arguments."

Four days later I'm sitting on the counter in the kitchen, watching my mom wash some funny-looking roots, which she then shaves and chops to be added to the herbs we'll wear around our necks tonight.

Tonight. It's finally here. It seems like it's taken forever, and I still wish I had one more day. I've found myself in Anna's driveway every night, just standing there, unable to think of anything to say. And every night she comes to the window and stares out at me. I haven't been sleeping much, though some of that is attributable to the nightmares.

The dreams have been worse since we came to Thunder Bay. The timing couldn't be worse. I'm exhausted when I shouldn't be exhausted—when I can least afford to be exhausted.

I can't remember whether my dad had the dreams or not, but even if he did he wouldn't have told me. Gideon's never mentioned anything either, and I haven't brought it up, because what if it's just me? It would mean that I'm weaker than my ancestors. That I'm not as strong as everyone expects me to be.

It's always the same dream. A figure bending over my face. I'm scared, but I also know that the figure is linked to me. I don't like it. I think it's my father.

But not really my father. My father has moved on. Mom and Gideon made sure of that; they hung around the house where he was murdered down in Baton Rouge for nights on end, casting runes and burning candles. But he was gone. I couldn't tell whether my mom was happy or disappointed.

I watch her now as she hurriedly snips and grinds different herbs, measuring them out, pouring them from the bowl of her mortar and pestle. Her hands are fast and clean. She's had to wait until the last minute because the Five Finger Grass was hard to find and she had to go through an unfamiliar supplier.

"What's this stuff for, anyway?" I ask, picking up a

piece of it. It's dehydrated and greenish brown. It looks like a piece of hay.

"It'll protect from the damage of any five fingers," she says distractedly, then looks up. "Anna does have five fingers, doesn't she?"

"On each hand," I say lightly, and set the grass back down.

"I cleaned the athame again," she says as she adds shakes of slivered colic root, which she tells me is useful to keep enemies at bay. "You'll need it. From what I read of this spell, it'll take a lot out of her. You'll be able to finish your job. Do what you came to do."

I notice she's not smiling. Even though I haven't been around much, my mom knows me. She knows when something's off, and she usually has a pretty good idea of what it is. She says it's a mom thing.

"What's wrong about this, Cassio?" she asks. "What's different?"

"Nothing. Nothing should be different. She's more dangerous than any ghost I've seen. Maybe even more than any Dad saw. She's killed more; she's stronger." I look down at the pile of Five Finger Grass. "But she's more alive, too. She's not confused. She's not some shifting, half-existent thing who kills out of fear or rage. Something did this to her, and she knows."

"How much does she know?"

"I think she knows everything, only she's scared to tell me."

My mom pushes some hair out of her eyes. "After tonight, you'll know for sure."

I shove myself off of the counter. "I think I already do," I say angrily. "I think I know who killed her." I haven't been able to stop thinking about it. I keep thinking about the man who terrorized her, this young girl, and I want to pound his face in. In a robotic voice, I tell my mother what Anna told me. When I look at her, she's wearing big soft cow's eyes.

"It's terrible," she says.

"Yeah."

"But you can't rewrite history."

I wish that I could. I wish this knife was good for something besides death, that I could cut through time and walk into that house, into that kitchen where he trapped her, and get her out of there. I would make sure she had the future she should have had.

"She doesn't want to kill people, Cas."

"I know. So how can I—"

"You can because you have to," she says simply. "You can because she needs you to."

I look at my knife, resting in its jar of salt. Something that smells like black jellybeans permeates the air. My mom is chopping another herb.

"What's that?"

"Star anise."

"What's it for?"

She smiles a little bit. "Smells pretty."

I breathe deep. In less than an hour everything will be ready, and Thomas will pick me up. I'll take the small velvet bags secured with long strings and the four white pillar candles infused with essential oil, and he'll have the scrying bowl and his bag of stones. And we'll go to try to kill Anna Korlov.

CHAPTER FIFTEEN

The house is waiting. Everyone standing around me in the driveway is scared to death of what's inside, but I'm more creeped out by the house itself. I know it's dumb, but I can't help but feel like it's watching, and maybe smiling, grinning at our childish attempts to stop it, laughing off its foundation as we shake chicken feet in its direction.

The air is cold. Carmel's breath comes in hot little puffs. She's got on a dark gray corduroy jacket and a red loose-knitted scarf; buried inside the scarf is my mother's bag of herbs. Will showed up in a letterman jacket, of course, and Thomas looks as scruffy as ever in his beat-up Army fatigue coat. He and Will are huffing in the dirt, arranging the stones from Lake Superior around our feet in a four-foot circle.

Carmel walks up to stand beside me while I stare at the house. My athame is hanging over my shoulder by its strap. I'll put it in my pocket later. Carmel sniffs at her herb bag.

"Smells like licorice," she says, and sniffs at mine to make sure they're the same.

"That's smart of your mom," Thomas says from behind us. "It wasn't in the spell, but it never hurts to add some luck."

Carmel smiles at him in the shiny dark. "Where'd you learn all this stuff?"

"My grandpa," he answers proudly, and hands her a candle. He hands another to Will, and then gives me mine. "Ready?" he asks.

I look up at the moon. It's bright, and cold, and still looks full to me. But the calendar says that it's waning, and people get paid to make calendars, so I guess that we're ready.

The circle of stones is only about twenty feet from the house. I take my place in the west and everyone else moves to take theirs. Thomas is trying to balance the scrying bowl in one hand while holding the candle with the other. I can see a bottle of Dasani water sticking out of his pocket.

"Why don't you give the chicken feet to Carmel," I suggest when he tries to hold them between his ring and pinky fingers. She holds her hand out gingerly, but not too gingerly. She's not as girly as I thought she'd be when I first met her.

"Do you feel it?" Thomas asks, his eyes bright.

"Feel what?"

"The energies are moving."

Will looks around skeptically. "All I feel is cold," he snaps.

"Light the candles, counterclockwise from the east."

Four small flames ignite and illuminate our faces and chests, revealing expressions that are part wonder, part fear, and part feeling stupid. Only Thomas is unperturbed. He's barely with us anymore. His eyes are closed, and when he speaks, his voice is about an octave lower than usual. I can tell Carmel's scared, but she doesn't say anything.

"Start chanting," Thomas commands, and we do. I can't believe it but none of us mess up. The chant is in Latin, four words repeated over and over. They sound stupid on our tongues, but the longer we do it the less stupid it *feels*. Even Will is chanting his heart out.

"Don't stop," says Thomas, opening his eyes. "Move toward the house. Don't break the circle."

When we move together I feel the power of the spell. I feel us all walking, all of our legs, all of our feet, joined together with invisible thread. The flames of the candles stand up strong without flickering, like solid fire. I can't believe that it's Thomas doing all this—short, awkward Thomas, hiding all of this power inside a fatigue jacket. We drift together up the steps, and before I can think, we're at her door.

The door opens. Anna looks out at us.

"You've come to do it," she says sadly. "And you should." She looks at the others. "You know what happens, when they come inside," she warns. "I can't control it."

I want to tell her it'll be all right. I want to ask her to try. But I can't stop chanting.

"He says it'll be all right," Thomas says from behind me,

and my voice nearly falters. "He wants you to try. We need you inside the circle. Don't worry about us. We're protected."

For once I'm glad that Thomas reached into my head. Anna looks from him to me and back again, then slips silently away from the door. I cross the threshold first.

I know when the others are inside, not only because our legs are moving as one, but because Anna starts to change. Veins snake up her arms and neck, winding through her face. Her hair becomes slick and shimmering black. Oil covers her eyes. The white dress saturates through with bright red blood, and the moonlight bounces off it, making it shine like plastic. It runs down her legs to drip onto the floor.

Behind me, the circle doesn't hesitate. I'm proud of them; maybe they are ghostbusters after all.

Anna's hands are clenched in fists so tight that black blood begins to seep through her fingers. She's doing as Thomas asked. She's trying to control it, trying to control the urge to tear the skin from their throats, to pull the arms from their shoulders. I lead the circle forward and she squeezes her eyes shut. Our legs move faster. Carmel and I pivot so we're facing each other. The circle is opening up, letting Anna pass through into the center. For a minute, Carmel is obstructed completely. All I see is Anna's bleeding body. Then she's inside, and the circle closes back up.

We're just in time. It was all she could do to hold herself in, and now her eyes and mouth open wide in a deafening scream. She slashes the air with hooked fingers and I feel

Will's foot slip back, but Carmel's thinking fast and lays the chicken feet below where Anna hovers. The ghost quiets, no longer moving, but regarding each of us with hatred as she twists around slowly.

"The circle is cast," Thomas says. "She is contained."

He kneels and we all kneel with him. It's strange, the sensation that all of our legs are one leg. He places the silver scrying bowl down on the floor and uncaps his bottle of Dasani.

"It works as well as anything else," he assures us. "It's clean and clear and conductive. Needing holy water, or water from an earthen spring . . . it's just snobbery." The water falls into the bowl with a crystalline, musical sound, and we wait until the surface is still.

"Cas," Thomas says, and I look at him. With a start I realize that he didn't say anything out loud. "The circle binds us. We're inside each other's minds. Tell me what you need to know. Tell me what you need to see."

This is all far too weird. The spell is strong—I feel grounded and high as a kite at the same time. But I feel rooted. I feel safe.

Show me what happened to Anna, I think carefully. *Show me how she was killed, what gives her this power.*

Thomas closes his eyes again, and Anna starts to shiver in midair, like she has a fever. Thomas's head falls. For a second I think he's passed out and we're in trouble, but then I realize that he's just staring into the scrying bowl.

"Oh," I hear Carmel whisper.

The air around us is changing. The *house* around us is

changing. The strange, gray light slowly warms, and the dust sheets melt off of the furniture. I blink. I'm looking at Anna's house, the way it must have been when she was alive.

There's a woven rug on the floor of the sitting room, which is lit up by hurricane lamps that make the air yellow. Behind us, we hear the door open and shut, but I'm still too busy looking at the changes, at the photos hanging on the walls and the rusty red embroidery on the sofa. If I look closer, I can see that it's not really that fine; the chandelier is tarnished and missing crystals, and there's a rip in the fabric of the rocking chair.

A figure moves through the room, a girl in a dark brown skirt and plain gray blouse. She's carrying schoolbooks. Her hair is tied up in a long, brown ponytail, secured with blue ribbon. When she turns at a sound on the staircase, I see her face. It's Anna.

Seeing her alive is indescribable. I thought once that there couldn't be much left of the living girl inside of what Anna is now, but I was wrong. As she looks up at the man on the staircase, her eyes are familiar. They're hard and knowing. They're irritated. I know without looking that this is the man she told me about—the man who was going to marry her mother.

"And what did we learn in school today, dear Anna?" His accent is so strong that I can barely make out the words. He walks down the stairs, and his steps are infuriating— lazy and confident and too full of their own power. There's a slight limp to his stride, but he's not really using the wooden cane he's carrying. When he walks around her, I'm reminded of a shark circling. Anna's jaw tightens.

His hand comes up over her shoulder and he traces a finger across the cover of her book. "More things that you don't need."

"Mama wishes for me to do well," Anna replies. It's the same voice I know, just with a stronger flavor of Finnish. She spins around. I can't see, but I know she's glaring at him.

"And so you will." He smiles. He has an angular face and good teeth. There's a five o'clock shadow on his cheeks, and he's starting to go bald. He wears what's left of his sandy blond hair slicked back. "Smart girl," he whispers, lifting a finger to her face. She jerks away and runs up the stairs, but it doesn't look like fleeing. It looks like attitude.

That's my girl, I think, and then remember I'm in the circle. I wonder how much of my thoughts and feelings are running through Thomas's mind. Inside the circle, I hear Anna's dress dripping and sense her shudder as the scene progresses.

I keep my eyes on the man: Anna's would-be stepfather. He's smirking to himself, and when her door closes on the second floor, he reaches into his shirt and pulls out a bundle of white cloth. I don't know what it is until he puts it to his nose. It's the dress she sewed for the dance. The dress she died in.

Fucking pervert, Thomas thinks inside of our heads. I clench my fists. The urge to run at the man is overwhelming, even though I know I'm watching something that happened sixty years ago. I'm watching it like it's playing on a projector. I can't change any of it.

Time shifts ahead; the light changes. The lamps seem to get brighter and figures flash by in dark blurry clumps. I can hear things, muffled conversations and arguments. My senses struggle to keep up.

There's a woman at the foot of the stairs. She's wearing a severe black dress that looks like it must be scratchy as hell, and her hair is pulled back in a tight bun. She's looking up at the second floor, so I can't see her face. But I can see that she's holding Anna's white dress in one hand and shaking it up and down. In the other, she's clutching a string of rosary beads.

I feel more than hear Thomas sniff. His cheeks twitch—he's caught wind of something.

Power, he thinks. *Power from the black.*

I don't know what he means. I don't have time to wonder.

"Anna!" the woman shouts, and Anna appears, coming out from the hall at the top of the stairs.

"Yes, Mama?"

Her mother holds up the dress in her fist. "What is this?"

Anna seems stricken. Her hand flies to the rail. "Where did you get that? How did you find that?"

"It was in her room." It's him again, walking out of the kitchen. "I heard her say she was working on it. I found it for her own good."

"Is it true?" her mother demands. "What is the meaning of it?"

"It's for a dance, Mama," Anna says angrily. "A dance at school."

"This?" Her mother holds the dress up and spreads it out with both hands. "This is for dancing?" She shakes it in the air. "Whore! You will not go dancing! Spoiled girl. You will not leave this house!"

At the top of the stairs, I hear a softer, sweeter voice. An olive-skinned woman with long black hair in a braid takes Anna by the shoulders. This must be Maria, the seamstress who was Anna's friend, who left her own daughter behind in Spain.

"Do not be angry, Mrs. Korlov," Maria says quickly. "I help her. It was my idea. Something pretty."

"You," Mrs. Korlov spits. "You've made it worse. Whispering your Spanish filth into my daughter's ears. She has become willful since you came. Proud. I won't have you whispering to her anymore. I want you out of this house!"

"No!" Anna shouts.

The man takes a step closer to his fiancée. "Malvina," he says. "We do not need to lose boarders."

"Hush, Elias," Malvina snaps. I'm beginning to understand why Anna couldn't just tell her mother what Elias was after.

The scene speeds up. I can feel more than see what's happening. Malvina throws the dress at Anna and orders her to burn it. She slaps her across the face when she tries to convince her to let Maria stay. Anna is crying, but only the Anna in the memory. The real Anna is hissing as she watches, black blood boiling. I feel like doing a mixture of the two.

Time moves ahead, and my eyes and ears strain to follow Maria as she goes, leaving with only one suitcase. I hear Anna ask what she's going to do, begging her to stay close by. And then all but one of the lamps goes out, and the windows outside are dark.

Malvina and Elias are in the sitting room. Malvina is knitting something out of dark blue yarn and Elias is reading the newspaper, smoking a pipe. They look miserable, even in their evening routines of pleasure. Their faces are slack and bored, mouths drawn in thin, grim lines. I have no idea how this courtship went, but it had to be about as interesting as watching bowling on TV. My mind moves to Anna—*all* of our minds move to Anna—and as if we summoned her, she comes down the stairs.

I have the strange sensation of wanting to squeeze my eyes shut while not being able to take them off something. She's wearing the white dress. It's the dress that she'll die in, but it doesn't look the same on her now as it did then.

This girl, standing at the foot of the staircase, holding a cloth bag and watching the surprised and increasingly furious expressions of Malvina and Elias, is incredibly alive. Her shoulders are square and strong, and her dark hair hangs in still waves down her back. She lifts her chin. I wish I could see her eyes, because I know that they're sad and triumphant.

"What do you think you are doing?" Malvina demands. She's looking at her daughter in horror, like she doesn't know who she is. The air around her seems to ripple, and I get a whiff of the power Thomas was talking about.

"I'm going to the dance," Anna replies calmly. "And I am not coming home."

"You will go to no dance," Malvina says acidly, rising up from her chair like she's stalking prey. "You will go nowhere in that disgusting dress." She advances on her daughter, squinting and swallowing hard, like she might be sick. "You wear white like a bride, but what man will take you after you let schoolboys lift your skirts!" She rears her head back like a viper and spits in Anna's face. "Your father would be ashamed."

Anna doesn't move. The only thing that betrays any emotion is the rapid rising and falling of her ribs.

"Papa loved me," she says softly. "I do not know why you don't."

"Bad girls are as useless as they are stupid," Malvina says with a wave of her hand. I don't know what she means. I think her English is faltering. Or maybe she's just dumb. I think that might be it.

There's bile in my throat as I watch and listen. I've never heard anyone speak to their kid this way. I want to reach out and shake her until she gets some sense. Or at least until I hear something crack.

"Go upstairs and take it off," Malvina orders. "And bring it down to burn."

I see Anna's hand tighten on her bag. Everything she owns is held in a small brown cloth and tied together with string. "No," she replies calmly. "I'm leaving here."

Malvina laughs. It's a brittle, rattling sound. A dark light comes into her eyes.

"Elias," she says. "Take my daughter up to her room. Get her out of this dress."

My God, Thomas thinks. In the corner of my eye, I see Carmel put her hand to her mouth. I don't want to see this. I don't want to know this. If that man touches her, I'll break the circle. I don't care if it's just a memory. I don't care if I need to know. I'll break his neck.

"No, Mama," Anna says fearfully, but when Elias moves toward her, she widens her stance. "I will not let him near me."

"I will be your father soon, Anna," Elias says. The words make me sick to my stomach. "You must obey me." His tongue flickers across his lips eagerly. Behind me I hear my Anna, Anna Dressed in Blood, begin to growl.

As Elias advances, Anna turns and runs for the door, but he catches her by the arm and twists her around, so close that her hair flies against his face, so close that she must be able to feel the thick heat of his breath. His hands are already searching, clawing at her dress, and I look at Malvina only to see a terrible expression of pleased hatred. Anna is thrashing and screaming through her teeth; she swings her head back and connects with Elias's nose, not hard enough to make it bleed but hard enough to sting like a mother. She manages to pull herself free and scrambles toward the kitchen and the back door.

"You will not leave this house!" Malvina shrieks and follows, reaching out for a handful of Anna's hair and yanking her back. "You will never, *never* leave this house!"

"I will!" Anna shouts, pushing her mother away. Malvina

falls against a large wooden dresser and stumbles. Anna circles around her, but she doesn't see Elias, recovering near the foot of the stairs. I want to yell to her to turn around. I want to tell her to run. But it doesn't matter what I want. All of this already happened.

"Bitch," he says loudly. Anna jumps. He's holding his nose and checking for blood, glaring at her. "We feed you. We clothe you. And this is your gratitude!" He holds his palm out even though there's nothing on it. Then he slaps her hard across the face and grabs her shoulders, shaking and shaking and screaming at her in Finnish that I don't understand. Her hair is flying and she's started to cry. All of this seems exciting to Malvina, whose eyes gleam as she watches.

Anna hasn't given up. She fights back and charges forward, slamming Elias into the wall against the staircase. There's a ceramic pitcher on the dresser beside them. She smashes it against the side of his head, making him roar and let go. Malvina shouts as she runs for the door, and by now there's so much screaming that I can hardly make out any of it. Elias has tackled Anna and has her by the backs of the legs. She's fallen onto the floor of the foyer.

I know that this is it even before Malvina comes out of the kitchen holding the knife. We all know it. I can feel them, Thomas, Carmel, and Will, unable to breathe, wanting more than anything to close their eyes, or to shout and actually be heard. They've never seen anything like this. They've probably never really even thought about it.

I look at Anna, facedown on the floor, terrified but not

nearly scared enough. I watch this girl, struggling to escape, not just from Elias's grip, but from everything, from this stifling house, from this life like a weight around her shoulders, dragging her down and planting her in dirt. I watch this girl as her mother bends over her with a kitchen knife and nothing but anger in her eyes. Stupid anger, baseless anger, and then the blade is at her throat, dragging across skin and opening a deep red line. *Too deep*, I think, *too deep*. I listen to Anna scream until she can't anymore.

CHAPTER SIXTEEN

Behind me I hear a thud, and I turn away from the scene, grateful for the distraction. Inside the circle, Anna is no longer hovering. She's collapsed onto the floor on her hands and knees. The black tendrils of her hair twitch. Her mouth is open like she might moan, or cry, but there is no sound. Streaky gray tears roll like charcoal-tinted water down pale cheeks. She watched her own throat get cut. She's watching herself bleed to death, redness soaking down into the house and saturating her white dancing dress. All of these things that she couldn't remember were just slapped into her face. She's growing weak.

I look back at Anna's death even though I don't want to. Malvina is stripping the body and barking orders at Elias, who flees into the kitchen and comes back with what looks like a rough blanket. She tells him to cover the body, and he does. I can tell that he can't believe what's happened. Then she tells him to go upstairs and find Anna another dress.

"Another dress? What for?" he asks, but she snaps, "Just go!" and he scampers up the steps so fast that he stumbles.

Malvina spreads Anna's dress out on the floor, so covered in red now that it's difficult to remember that it used to be white. Then she goes to the closet on the opposite side of the room and comes back holding black candles and a small black bag.

She's a witch, Thomas mentally hisses at me. *The curse. It makes perfect sense. We should have known that the killer was some kind of a witch. But we might never have guessed it was her own mother.*

Keep your eyes sharp, I shoot back at Thomas. *I might need your help figuring out what's going on here.*

I doubt it, he says, and I guess I doubt it too, watching Malvina light the candles and kneel over the dress, her body swaying as she chants in whispers, soft Finnish words. Her voice is tender, like it never was for Anna in life. The candles glow brighter. She lifts first the one on the left, and then the one on the right. Black wax spills across the stained fabric. Then she spits on it, three times. Her chanting is louder, but I don't understand any of it. I start trying to pick out words to look up later, and that's when I hear him. Thomas. He's speaking softly out loud. For a second I don't know what he's saying. I actually open my mouth to tell him to shut up, that I'm trying to listen, before I realize he's repeating her chants in English.

"Father Hiisi, hear me, I come before you low and humble. Take this blood, take this power. Keep my daughter in this house. Feed her on suffering, blood, and death. Hiisi, Father, demon-god, hear my prayer. Take this blood, take this power."

Malvina closes her eyes, holds up the kitchen knife, and passes it through the candle flames. Impossibly, it ignites, and then, in one fierce motion, she stabs the knife through the dress and into the floorboards.

Elias has come to the top of the stairs, holding a swath of clean, white fabric—Anna's replacement dress. He watches Malvina in awe and horror. It's clear that he never knew this about her, and now that he does, he'll never speak a word against her, out of sheer terror.

Firelight is shining up from the hole in the floorboards, and Malvina slowly moves the knife, stuffing the bloodied dress down into the house as she chants. When the last of the fabric disappears, she pushes the rest of the knife in to follow it and the light flashes. The floorboard is closed. Malvina swallows, and gently blows the candles out, from left to right.

"Now you'll never leave my house," she whispers.

Our spell is ending. Malvina's face is fading like a nightmare memory, turning as gray and withered as the wood she murdered Anna on. The air around us loses color and I feel our limbs beginning to unravel. We're separating, breaking the circle. I hear Thomas, breathing hard. I hear Anna too. I can't believe what I've just seen. It feels unreal. I don't understand how Malvina could murder Anna.

"How could she?" Carmel asks softly, and we all look at each other. "It was terrible. I never want to see anything like that ever again." She shakes her head. "How could she? She was her daughter."

I look at Anna, still clothed in blood and veins. Her dark-tinged tears have dried on her face; she's too exhausted to cry anymore.

"Did she know what would happen?" I ask Thomas. "Did she know what she was turning her into?"

"I don't think so. Or at least, not exactly. When you invoke a demon, you don't get to decide the specifics. You just make the request, and it does the rest."

"I don't care if she knew *exactly*," Carmel growls. "It was disgusting. It was horrible."

There are beads of sweat on all of our foreheads. Will hasn't said a thing. We all look like we've gone twelve rounds with a heavyweight.

"What are we going to do?" Thomas asks, and it doesn't look like he's able to do much of anything at the moment. I think he'll sleep for a week.

I turn away and stand up. I need to clear my head.

"Cas! Watch out!"

Carmel shouts at me but she isn't fast enough. I'm shoved from behind and as I am, I feel a very familiar weight being pulled out of my back pocket. When I turn around, I see Will standing over Anna. He's holding my athame.

"Will," Thomas starts, but Will unsheathes my knife and swings it in a wide arc, making Thomas scuttle back on his haunches to get out of the way.

"This is how you do it, isn't it?" Will asks in a wild

voice. He looks at the blade and blinks rapidly. "She's weak; we can do it now," he says, almost to himself.

"Will, don't," Carmel says.

"Why not? This is what we came here to do!"

Carmel glances at me helplessly. It *is* what we came here to do. But after what we all saw, and seeing her lying there, I know that I can't.

"Give me my knife," I say calmly.

"She killed Mike," Will says. "She killed Mike."

I look down at Anna. Her black eyes are wide and staring downward, though I don't know whether or not they're seeing anything. She's sunk onto her hip, too weak to hold herself up. Her arms, which I know from personal experience could crush cinderblocks, are shaking just trying to keep her torso off the floorboards. We've managed to reduce this monster to a quivering husk, and if ever there was a safe time to kill her, it's now.

And Will's right. She did kill Mike. She's killed dozens. And she'll do it again.

"You killed Mike," Will hisses and starts to cry. "You killed my best friend." And then he moves, stabbing downward. I react without thinking.

I lurch forward and catch him under the arm, stopping the blow from going straight through her back; instead it glances off of her ribs. Anna gives a small cry and tries to crawl away. Carmel's and Thomas's voices are in my ears, yelling at both of us to stop it, but we keep on struggling. With bared teeth, Will tries to stab her again, hacking through the air. I barely get an elbow up to knock his chin back. He stumbles away a few steps and when he charges I hit him in the face, not too hard but hard enough to make him think.

He wipes at his mouth with the back of his hand. He doesn't try to come forward again. Looking from me to Anna, he knows I won't let him past.

"What's wrong with you?" he asks. "This is supposed to be your job, right? And now we've got her and you're not going to do anything?"

"I don't know what I'm going to do," I say honestly. "But I'm not going to let you hurt her. You couldn't kill her, anyway."

"Why not?"

"Because it's not just the knife. It's me. It's my blood tie."

Will scoffs. "She's bleeding well enough."

"I didn't say the knife wasn't special. But the death blow is mine. Whatever it is that lets that happen, you don't have it."

"You're lying," he says, and maybe I am. I've never seen anyone else use my knife before. No one except my dad. Maybe all that stuff about being chosen and part of a sacred line of ghost hunters was all bullshit. But Will believes it. He starts backing away, out of the house.

"Give me my knife," I say again, watching it as it's leaving me, the metal glinting in the odd light.

"I'm going to kill her," Will promises, then turns and runs, taking my athame with him. Something inside me whimpers, something childlike and basic. It's like that scene in *The Wizard of Oz,* when that old lady throws the dog in her bike basket and rides off. My feet are telling me to run after him, tackle him and beat him about the head, take my knife back and never let it out of my sight. But Carmel's talking to me.

"Are you sure he can't kill her?" she asks.

I look back. She's actually kneeling on the floor beside Anna; she's actually had the balls to touch her, to hold her by the shoulders and look at the wound Will made. It's seeping black blood to strange effect: the black liquid is mixing with the moving blood of her dress, swirling like ink dropped into red water.

"She's so weak," Carmel whispers. "I think she's really hurt."

"Shouldn't she be?" Thomas asks. "I mean, I don't want to side with Will I'm-Bucking-for-an-Emmy-Nod Rosenberg, but isn't that why we're here? Isn't she still dangerous?"

The answers are yes, yes, and yes. I know that, but I can't seem to think straight. The girl at my feet is defeated and my knife is gone and scenes from How to Murder Your Daughter are still playing in my head. This is where it happened—this is the place where her life ended, where she became a monster, where her mother dragged a knife across her throat and cursed her and her dress and—

I walk farther into the sitting room, staring at the floorboards. Then I start stomping. Slamming my foot against the boards and jumping up and down, looking for a loose spot. It's not doing any good. I'm stupid. I'm not strong enough. And I don't even know what I'm doing.

"It's not that one," Thomas says. He's staring at the floor. He points at the board to my left.

"It's that one," he says. "And you'll need something." He gets up and runs out the door. I didn't think he had any strength left at all. The kid is surprising. And damned useful, because about forty seconds later he's back, holding a crowbar and a tire iron.

Together we hack at the floor, at first not making a dent and then slowly cracking the wood. I use the crowbar to pry up the loosest end and fall to my knees. The hole we've made is dark and deep. I don't know how it's there. I should be looking at rafters and basement, but there's only blackness. Only a moment's hesitation, and my hand is searching in the hole, feeling depths of cold. I think I was wrong, that I was stupid again, and then my fingers brush against it.

The fabric feels stiff and cool to the touch. Maybe a little damp. I pull it out of the floor where it was stuffed and sealed sixty years ago.

"The dress," Carmel breathes. "What—?"

"I don't know," I say honestly. I walk toward Anna. I have no idea what effect the dress will have on her, if anything. Will it make her stronger? Will it heal her? If I burned it, would she evaporate into thin air? Thomas would probably have a better idea. Together he and Morfran could probably come up with the right answer, and if they didn't, then Gideon could. But I don't have that kind of time. I kneel and hold the stained fabric before her eyes.

For a second she doesn't do anything. Then she struggles to her feet. I move the bloody dress up with her, keeping it at eye level. The black has receded: Anna's clear, curious eyes are there inside of the monstrous face, and for some reason that's more disconcerting than anything. My hand is shaking. She's standing before me, not hovering, just looking at the dress, crumpled and red and dingy white in some places.

Still not sure what I'm doing, or what I'm trying to do, I gather it up by the hem and slide it over her dark and writhing head. Something happens immediately but I don't know what. A tension enters the air, a cold. It's hard to explain, like there's a breeze but nothing is moving. I pull the old dress down over her bleeding one and step back. Anna closes her eyes and breathes deep. Streaks of black wax still cling to the fabric where the candles dripped during the curse.

"What's happening?" Carmel whispers.

"I don't know," Thomas answers for me.

As we watch, the dresses begin to fight each other, dripping blood and black and trying to merge together. Anna's eyes are closed. Her hands are in fists. I don't know what's going to happen, but whatever it is, it's happening fast. Every time I blink I open my eyes to a new dress: now white, now red, now blackened and mixed with blood. It's oil and paint and things sinking into sand. And then Anna throws her head back, and the cursed dress crumbles off, cracking into dust to tumble to her feet.

The dark goddess stands looking at me. Lengths of black

tendrils die in the breeze. Veins recede back into her arms and neck. Her dress is white and unstained. The wound from my knife is gone.

She puts her hand to her cheek in disbelief and looks shyly from Carmel to me, and over at Thomas, who backs up a step. Then she slowly turns and walks toward her open door. Just before she walks through it, she looks over her shoulder at me and smiles.

CHAPTER SEVENTEEN

Is this what I wanted? I set her free. I've just let the ghost I was sent to kill out of prison. She's walking softly across her porch, touching her toes to the steps, staring out into the dark. She's like any wild animal let out of a cage: cautious and hopeful. Her fingertips trace the wood of the crooked railing like it's the most wonderful thing she's ever felt. And part of me is glad. Part of me knows that she never deserved anything that happened, and I want to give her more than this broken porch. I want to give her an entire life—her whole life back, starting tonight.

The other part of me knows there are bodies in her basement, souls that she stole, and none of this was their fault either. I can't give Anna her life back because her life is already gone. Maybe I've made a huge mistake.

"We should get out of here, I think," Thomas says quietly.

I look at Carmel and she nods, so I walk toward the door, trying to keep myself between them and Anna, even though without my knife I don't know how much use I'll be. When she hears us come through the door, she turns and regards me with an arched eyebrow.

"It's all right," she says. "I won't hurt them now."

"Are you sure?" I ask.

Her eyes shift to Carmel. She nods. "I'm sure." Behind me, Carmel and Thomas exhale and awkwardly move out from my shadow.

"Are you okay?" I ask.

She thinks for a moment, trying to find the right words. "I feel . . . sane. Is that possible?"

"Probably not completely," Thomas blurts, and I elbow him in the ribs. But Anna laughs.

"You saved him, the first time," she says, looking at Thomas carefully. "I remember you. You pulled him out."

"I don't think you would have killed him anyways," Thomas replies, but some color comes up to his cheeks. He likes the idea of playing the hero. He likes that the idea is being pointed out in front of Carmel.

"Why didn't you?" Carmel asks. "Why weren't you going to kill Cas? What made you choose Mike instead?"

"Mike," Anna says softly. "I don't know. Maybe it was because they were wicked. I knew they'd tricked him. I knew they were cruel. Maybe I felt . . . sorry for him."

I snort. "Sorry for me? I could've handled those guys."

"They smashed the back of your head in with a board from my house." Anna is giving me a look with her eyebrow again.

"You keep saying 'maybe,'" Thomas breaks in. "You don't know for sure?"

"I don't," Anna replies. "Not for sure. But I'm glad," she adds, and smiles. She'd like to say more, but looks away, embarrassed or confused, I can't tell which.

"We should go," I say. "That spell took a lot out of us. We could all use some sleep."

"But you'll come back?" Anna asks, like she thinks she'll never see me again.

I nod. I'll come back. To do what, I don't know. I know that I can't let Will keep my knife, and I'm not sure if she's safe as long as he still has it. But that's dumb, because who says she's safe if I have it either? I need some sleep. I need to recoup, and regroup, and rethink everything.

"If I'm not in the house," Anna says, "call for me. I won't be far."

The idea of her running around Thunder Bay doesn't thrill me. I don't know what she's capable of, and my suspicious side whispers that I have just been duped. But there's nothing I can do about it right now.

"Was this a victory?" Thomas asks as we walk down the driveway.

"I don't know," I reply, but it sure as hell doesn't feel like one. My athame is gone. Anna is free. And the only thing that seems certain in my head and heart is that this isn't over. Already there's an emptiness, not just in my back pocket or on my shoulder, but everywhere around me. I feel weaker, like I'm leaking from a thousand wounds. That a-hole took my knife.

"I didn't know you could speak Finnish, Thomas," Carmel says from beside him.

He grins lopsidedly. "I can't. That was one hell of a spell you got for us, Cas. I'd sure like to meet your supplier."

"I'll introduce you sometime," I hear myself say. But not right now. Gideon is the last person I want to talk to, when I've just lost the knife. My eardrums would burst from all the yelling. The athame. My father's legacy. I have to get it back, and soon.

The athame is gone. You lost it. *Where is it?*"

He's got me by the throat, strangling the answers, slamming me back into my pillow.

"Stupid, stupid, STUPID!"

I wake up swinging, popped upright in my bed like a rock 'em sock 'em robot. The room is empty. *Of course it is; don't be stupid.* Using the same word on myself brings me back into the dream. I'm only half-awake. The memory of his hands on my throat is lingering. I still can't speak. There's too much tightness, there and in my chest. I take a deep breath, and when I exhale it comes out ragged, close to a sob. My body feels full of empty spaces where the weight of the knife should be. My heart is pounding.

Was it my father? The idea brings me back ten years, and the guilt of a kid balloons sharply in my heart. But no. It couldn't have been. The thing in my dream had a Creole or Cajun accent, and my father grew up in accent-neutral Chicago, Illinois. It was just another dream, like the rest, and at least I know where this one came from. It doesn't take a Freudian interpreter to realize I feel bad about losing the athame.

Tybalt jumps up onto my lap. In the scant moonlight through my window I can just make out the green oval of his irises. He puts a paw up on my chest.

"Yeah," I say. The sound of my voice in the dark is sharp and too loud. But it sends the dream farther away. It was so vivid. I can still remember the acrid, bitter smell of something like smoke.

"Meow," Tybalt says.

"No more sleep for Theseus Cassio," I agree, scooping him up and heading downstairs.

When I get there, I put some coffee on and park my butt at the kitchen table. My mom has left out the jar of salt for the athame, along with clean cloths and oils to rub it and rinse it and make it new. It's out there somewhere. I can feel it. I can feel it in the hands of someone who never should have touched it. I'm starting to think murderous thoughts about Will Rosenberg.

My mom comes down about three hours later. I'm still sitting at the table and staring at the jar as the light grows stronger in the kitchen. Once or twice my head thumped down against the wood and then bounced back up again, but I'm half a pot of coffee in now, and I feel fine. Mom is wrapped in her blue bathrobe and her hair looks comfortingly fuzzy. The sight calms me immediately, even as she glances at the empty jar of salt and puts the cover back on. What is it about the sight of your mother that makes everything fireside-warm and full of dancing Muppets?

"You stole my cat," she says, pouring herself a cup of coffee. Tybalt must sense my unrest; he's been circling around my feet off and on, something he usually only does to my mom.

"Here, have him back," I say as she comes to the table. I hoist him up. He doesn't stop hissing until she brings him down to her lap.

"No luck last night?" she asks, and nods at the empty jar.

"Not exactly," I say. "There was some luck. Luck of both kinds."

She sits with me and listens while I spill my guts. I tell her everything we saw, everything we learned about Anna, how I broke the curse and freed her. I end with my worst embarrassment: that I lost Dad's athame. I can hardly look at her when I tell her that last part. She's trying to control her expression. I don't know if that means she's upset that it's gone or if it means she knows what the loss of it must've done to me.

"I don't think you made a mistake, Cas," she says gently.

"But the knife."

"We'll get the knife back. I'll call that boy's mother, if I have to."

I groan. She just crossed the mom line from cool and comforting to Queen of Lame.

"But what you did," she goes on. "With Anna. I don't think it was a mistake."

"It was my job to kill her."

"Was it? Or was it your job to stop her?" She leans back from the table, cradling her coffee mug between her hands.

"What you do—what your dad did—it was never about vengeance. Never about revenge, or tipping the scales back to even. That's not your call."

I rub my hand across my face. My eyes are too tired to see straight. My brain is too tired to think straight.

"But you did stop her, didn't you, Cas?"

"Yes," I say, but I don't know. It happened so fast. Did I really get rid of Anna's dark half, or did I just allow her to hide it? I shut my eyes. "I don't know. I think so."

My mom sighs. "Stop drinking this coffee." She pushes my cup away. "Go back to bed. And then go to Anna and find out what she's become."

I've seen a lot of seasons change. When you're not distracted by school and friends and what movie's coming out next week, you've got time to look at the trees.

Thunder Bay's autumn is prettier than most. There's lots of color. Lots of rustle. But it's also more volatile. Frigid and wet one day, with a side of gray clouds, and then days like today, where the sun looks as warm as July and the breeze is so light that the leaves just seem to glisten as they move in it.

I've got my mom's car. I drove it up to Anna's place after dropping Mom to do some shopping downtown. She said she'd get a lift home from a friend. I was glad to hear that she'd made some friends. She does it easily, being so open and easygoing. Not like me. I don't think it was quite like my dad either, but I find that I can't really remember, and that bothers me, so I don't push my brain too hard.

I'd rather believe that the memories are there, just under the surface, whether they really are or not.

As I walk up to the house, I think I see a shadow move on the west side. I blink it off as a trick of my too-tired eyes . . . until the shadow turns white and shows her pale skin.

"I haven't wandered far," Anna says as I walk up.

"You hid from me."

"I wasn't sure right away who you were. I have to be cautious. I don't want to be seen by everyone. Just because I can leave my house now doesn't mean I'm not still dead." She shrugs. She's so frank. She should be damaged by all of this, damaged beyond sanity. "I'm glad you came back."

"I need to know," I say. "If you're still dangerous."

"We should go inside," she says, and I agree. It's strange to see her outdoors, in the sunlight, looking for all the world like a girl out picking flowers on a bright afternoon. Except that anyone looking closely would realize she should be freezing out here wearing just that white dress.

She leads me into the house and closes the door behind like any good hostess. Something about the house has changed too. The gray light is gone. Plain old white sunshine streams through the windows, albeit with a hampering of dirt on the glass.

"What is it that you really want to know, Cas?" Anna asks. "Do you want to know if I'm going to kill more people? Or do you want to know if I can still do this?" She holds her hand up before her face, and dark veins snake up to the fingers. Her eyes go black and a dress of blood erupts through the white, more violently than before, splashing droplets everywhere.

I jump back. "Jesus, Anna!"

She hovers in the air, does a little twirl like something's playing her favorite tune.

"It's not pretty, is it?" She crinkles her nose. "There aren't mirrors left here, but I could see myself in the window glass when the moonlight was bright enough."

"You're still like this," I say, horrified. "Nothing's changed."

When I say that nothing's changed, her eyes narrow, but then she exhales and tries to smile at me. It doesn't quite work, what with her looking like goth-chick Pinhead.

"Cassio. Don't you see? Everything's changed!" She lets herself down to the ground, but the black eyes and writhing hair stay. "I won't kill anyone. I never wanted to. But whatever this is, it's what I am. I thought that it was the curse, and maybe it was, but—" She shakes her head. "I had to try to do this after you left. I had to know." She looks me right in the eye. The inky dark seeps away, revealing the other Anna underneath. "The fight is over. I won. You made me win. I'm not two halves anymore. I know you must think it's monstrous. But I feel—strong. I feel safe. Maybe I'm not making sense."

It's actually fairly easy to get. For someone who was murdered the way she was murdered, feeling safe is probably top priority.

"I get it," I say softly. "The strength is what you hold on to. Kind of like me. When I walk through a haunted place with my athame in my hand, I feel strong. Untouchable. It's heady.

I don't know if most people ever feel it." I shuffle my feet. "And then I met you, and all that went down the shithole."

She laughs.

"I come in all big and bad, and you use me for a game of handball." I grin. "Makes a guy feel damn manly."

She grins back. "It made me feel pretty manly." Her smile falters. "You didn't bring it with you today. Your knife. I can always feel it when it's near."

"No. Will took it. But I'll get it back. It was my father's; I'm not letting it go." But then I wonder. "How do you feel it? What do you feel about it?"

"When I first saw you, I didn't know what it was. It was something in my ears, something in my stomach, just a humming below the music. It's powerful. And even though I knew it was meant to kill me, it drew me somehow. Then when your friend cut me—"

"He's not my friend," I say through my teeth. "Not really."

"I could feel myself draining into it. Starting to go wherever it is that it sends us. But it was wrong. It has a will of its own. It wanted to be in your hand."

"So it wouldn't have killed you," I say, relieved. I don't want Will to be able to use my knife. I don't care how childish that sounds. It's *my* knife.

Anna turns away, thinking. "No, it would have killed me," she says seriously. "Because it isn't only tied to you. It's tied to something else. Something dark. When I was bleeding, I could smell something. It reminded me a little of Elias's pipe."

I don't know where the athame's power comes from, and Gideon has never told me, if he knows. But if that power comes from something dark, then so be it. I use it for something good. As for the smell of Elias's pipe . . .

"That was probably just something you were frightened of after watching yourself be murdered," I say gently. "You know, like dreaming of zombies right after you watch *Land of the Dead*."

"*Land of the Dead*? Is that what you dream about?" she asks. "Boy who kills ghosts for a living?"

"No. I dream about penguins doing bridge construction. Don't ask why."

She smiles and tucks her hair behind her ear. When she does I feel a pull somewhere deep in my chest. What am I doing? Why did I come here? I can barely remember.

Somewhere in the house, a door slams. Anna jumps. I don't think I've ever seen her jump before. Her hair lifts up and starts to writhe. She's like a cat arching its back and puffing its tail.

"What was that?" I ask.

She shakes her head. I can't tell whether she's embarrassed or frightened. It looks like both.

"Do you remember what I showed you in the basement?" she asks.

"The tower of dead bodies? No, that slipped my mind. Are you kidding me?"

She laughs nervously, a fake little twinkle.

"They're still here," she whispers.

My stomach takes this opportunity to wring itself out,

and my feet shift underneath me without permission. The image of all those corpses is fresh in my mind. I can actually smell the green water and rot. The idea that they are now roaming through the house with wills of their own—which is what she's implying—doesn't make me happy.

"I guess they're haunting me now," she says softly. "That's why I went outside. They don't frighten me," she's quick to add. "But I can't stand to see them." She pauses and crosses her arms over her stomach, sort of hugging herself. "I know what you're thinking."

Really? Because I don't.

"I should lock myself in here with them. It's my fault, after all." Her voice isn't sulky. She's not asking me to disagree. Her eyes, focused on the floorboards, are earnest. "I wish I could tell them that I'd like to take it back."

"Would it matter?" I ask quietly. "Would it matter to you if Malvina said she was sorry?"

Anna shakes her head. "Of course not. I'm being stupid." She glances to the right, just for an instant, but I know she was looking at the broken board where we took her dress out of the floor last night. She seems almost scared of it. Maybe I should get Thomas over here to seal it off or something.

My hand twitches. I gather all my guts and let my hand stray to her shoulder. "You're not being stupid. We'll figure something out, Anna. We'll exorcise them. Morfran will know how to get them to move on." Everyone deserves some comfort, don't they? She's out now; what's done is done, and she has to find some kind of peace. But even now, dark and distracting memories of what she's done are racing behind her eyes. How is she supposed to let that go?

Telling her not to torture herself would make it worse. I can't give her absolution. But I want to make her forget, even just for a while. She was innocent once, and it kills me that she can never be innocent again.

"You have to find your way back into the world now," I say gently.

Anna opens her mouth to speak, but I'll never know what she was going to say. The house literally lurches, like it's being jacked up. With a very large jack. When it settles, there's a momentary jarring, and in the vibration a figure appears in front of us. It slowly fades in from shadow until he stands there, a pale, chalky corpse in the still air.

"I only wanted to sleep," he says. It sounds like he's got a mouthful of gravel, but upon closer inspection I realize it's because all of his teeth have come loose. It makes him look older, as does the sagging skin, but he couldn't have been more than eighteen. Just another runaway who stumbled into the wrong house.

"Anna," I say, grabbing her arm, but she won't let herself be dragged back. She stands without flinching as he stretches his arms wide. The Christlike pose makes it worse when the blood starts seeping through his ragged clothes, darkening the fabric everywhere, on every limb. His head lolls and then whips back and forth wildly. Then it snaps upright and he screams.

The sound of ripping that I hear isn't only his shirt. Intestines spill out in a grotesque rope and hit the floor. He starts to fall forward, toward her, and I grab and yank hard enough to pull her to my chest. When I put myself between her and him, another body crashes through the wall, sending dust and splinters everywhere. It flies across the floor in scattered pieces, ragged arms and legs. The head stares at us as it skids, baring its teeth.

I'm in no mood to see a blackened, rotting tongue, so I wrap my arm around Anna and pull her across the floor. She moans softly but lets herself be pulled, and we rush through the door into the safety of daylight. Of course when we look back there's no one there. The house is unchanged, no blood on the floor, no cracks in the wall.

Staring back through her front door, Anna looks miserable—guilty and terrorized. I don't even think, I just pull her closer and hold her tight. My breath moves quickly in her hair. Her fists are trembling as she grips my shirt.

"You can't stay here," I say.

"There's nowhere else for me to go," she replies. "It isn't so bad. They're not that strong. A display like that, they can probably only manage once every few days. Maybe."

"You can't be serious. What if they get stronger?"

"I don't know what we could have expected," she says, and steps away, out of my reach. "That all this would come without a price."

I want to argue, only nothing sounds convincing, even in my head. But it can't be like this. It'll drive her insane. I don't care what she says.

"I'll go to Thomas and Morfran," I say. "They'll know

what to do. Look at me," I say, lifting her chin. "I won't let it stay like this. I promise."

If she cared enough to make a gesture, it would be a shrug. To her, this is fitting punishment. But it did shake her up, and that keeps her from really arguing. When I move to my car, I hesitate.

"Will you be all right?"

Anna gives me a wry smile. "I'm dead. What could happen?" Still, I get the feeling that while I'm gone, she's going to spend most of her time outside the house. I walk off down the driveway.

"Cas?"

"Yeah?"

"I'm glad you came back. I wasn't sure if you would."

I nod and put my hands in my pockets. "I'm not going anywhere."

Inside the car, I blare the radio. It's a good thing to do, when you're sick to death of creepy silence. I do it a lot. I'm just settling into my groove with some Stones when a news report cuts through the melody of "Paint It, Black."

"The body was found just inside the gates of Park View Cemetery, and may have been the victim of a satanic ritual. Police can't comment yet on the identity of the victim, however Channel 6 has learned that the crime was particularly brutal. The victim, a man in his late forties, appeared to have been dismembered."

CHAPTER EIGHTEEN

The images before me may as well be news footage played on mute. Lights on all of the squad cars ring out in red and flashing white, but there are no sirens. The police walk around in drab black jackets, their chins tucked low and somber. They're trying to seem calm, like this happens every day, but some of them look like they'd rather be off in the bushes somewhere throwing up their donuts. A few use their bodies to obscure the view of nosy camera lenses. And somewhere in the center of it all is a body, torn to pieces.

I wish I could get closer, that I kept a spare press pass in the glove compartment or had the money to keep a few cops in my pocket. As it is, I'm lingering on the edges of the press crowd, behind the yellow tape.

I don't want to believe that it was Anna. It would mean that man's death is on my hands. I don't want to believe it because it would mean that she's incurable, that there is no redemption.

As the crowd watches, the police exit the park with a

gurney. On top of it is a black bag that should normally be shaped like a body but instead looks like it's been stuffed full of hockey equipment. I suppose they put him back together as well as they could. When the gurney hits the curb, the remains shift, and through the bag we can see one of the limbs fall down, clearly unattached to the rest. The crowd makes a muffled noise of disturbed disgust. I elbow my way back through them to my car.

I pull into her driveway and park. She's surprised to see me. I've been gone less than an hour. As my feet crunch up the gravel I don't know whether the noise comes from the dirt, or from my grinding teeth. Anna's expression changes from pleased surprise to concern.

"Cas? What's the matter?"

"You tell me." I'm surprised to find how pissed I am. "Where were you last night?"

"What are you talking about?"

She needs to convince me. She needs to be very convincing.

"Just tell me where you were. What did you do?"

"Nothing," she says. "I stayed near the house. I tested my strength. I—" She pauses.

"You what, Anna?" I demand.

Her expression hardens. "I hid in my bedroom for a while. After I realized the spirits were still here." The look in her eyes is resentful. It's the *there, are you happy now?* look.

"You're sure you didn't leave? Didn't try to explore

Thunder Bay again, maybe go down to the park and, I don't know, dismember some poor jogger?"

The stricken expression on her face makes the anger leak out through my shoes. I open my mouth to pull my foot out of it, but how do I explain why I'm so angry? How do I explain that she needs to give me a better alibi?

"I can't believe you're accusing me."

"I can't believe that you can't believe it," I retort. I don't know why I can't stop being so combative. "Come on. People don't get butchered in this city every day. And the very night after I free the most powerful murderous ghost in the western hemisphere, somebody shows up missing their arms and legs? It's a hell of a coincidence, don't you think?"

"But it *is* a coincidence," she insists. Her delicate hands have formed balled-up fists.

"Don't you remember what just happened?" I gesture wildly toward the house. "Tearing off body parts is, like, your MO."

"What's an 'MO'?" she asks.

I shake my head. "Don't you get what this means? Don't you understand what I have to do if you keep on killing?"

When she doesn't reply, my crazed tongue plows ahead.

"It means I get to have a serious Old Yeller moment," I snap. The minute I say it, I know that I shouldn't have. It was stupid and it was mean, and she caught the reference. Of course she would have. *Old Yeller* was made in like 1955. She probably saw it when it came out in theaters.

The look she's giving me is shocked and hurt; I don't know if any look has made me feel worse. Still, I can't quite muster an apology. The idea that she's probably a murderer holds it in.

"I didn't do it. How can you think so? I can't stand what I've already done!"

Neither of us says anything else. We don't even move. Anna is pissed off and trying very hard not to cry. As we look at each other, something inside me is trying to click, trying to fall into place. I feel it in my mind and in my chest, like a puzzle piece you know has to go somewhere so you keep trying to push it in from all different angles. And then, just like that, it fits. So perfect and complete that you can't imagine how it was without it there, even seconds ago.

"I'm sorry," I hear myself whisper. "It's just that— I don't know what's happening."

Anna's eyes soften, and the stubborn tears begin to recede. The way she stands, the way she breathes, I know she wants to come closer. New knowledge fills up the air between us and neither of us wants to breathe it in. I can't believe this. I've never been the type.

"You saved me, you know," Anna says finally. "You set me free. But just because I'm free, doesn't mean—that I can have the things that—" She stops. She wants to say more. I know she does. But just like I know that she does, I know that she won't.

I can see her talk herself out of coming closer. Calmness settles over her like a blanket. It covers up the melancholy and silences any wishes for something different. A thousand arguments pile up in my throat, but I clench my teeth on them. We're not children, neither of us. We don't believe in fairy tales. And if we did, who would we be? Not Prince Charming and Sleeping Beauty. I slice murder victims' heads off and Anna stretches skin until it rips, she snaps bones like green branches into smaller and smaller pieces. We'd be the fricking dragon and the wicked fairy. I know that. But I still have to tell her.

"It isn't fair."

Anna's mouth twists into a smile. It should be bitter—it should be a sneer—but it isn't.

"You know what you are, don't you?" she asks. "You're my salvation. My way to atone. To pay for everything I've done."

When I realize what she wants, it feels like someone kicked me in the chest. I'm not surprised that she's reluctant to go out on dates and tiptoe through the tulips, but I never imagined, after all this, that she would want to be sent away.

"Anna," I say. "Don't ask me to do this."

She doesn't reply.

"What was all this for? Why did I fight? Why did we do the spell? If you were just going to—"

"Go get your knife back," she replies, and then she fades away into the air right in front of me, back to the other world where I can't follow.

CHAPTER NINETEEN

Since Anna has been free, I haven't been able to sleep. There are endless nightmares and shadowy figures looming over my bed. The smell of sweet, lingering smoke. The mewling of the damned cat at my bedroom door. Something has to be done. I'm not afraid of the dark; I've always slept like a rock, and I've been in more than my share of dim and dangerous places. I've seen most of what there is to be afraid of in this world, and to tell you the truth, the worst of them are the ones that make you afraid in the light. The things that your eyes see plainly and can't forget are worse than huddled black figures left to the imagination. Imagination has a poor memory; it slinks away and goes blurry. Eyes remember for much longer.

So why am I so creeped out by a dream? Because it felt real. And it's been there for too long. I open my eyes and don't see anything, but I know, *I know,* that if I reached down below my bed, some decaying arm would shoot out from underneath and drag me to hell.

I tried to blame Anna for these nightmares, and then I

tried not to think of her at all. To forget how our last conversation ended. To forget that she charged me with the task of recovering my athame and, after I do, killing her with it. Air leaves my nostrils in a quick snort even as I think the words. Because how can I?

So I won't. I won't think of it, and I'll make procrastination my new national pastime.

I'm nodding off in the midst of world history. Luckily, Mr. Banoff would never realize it in a million years, because I sit in the back and he's up on the whiteboard spouting off about the Punic Wars. I'd probably be really into it, if only I could stay conscious long enough to tune in. But all I get is *blah blah, nod-off, dead finger in my ear, snap awake.* Then repeat. When the bell rings for the end of the period, I jerk and blink my eyes one last time, then heave out of my desk and head for Thomas's locker.

I lean up against the door next to his while he stuffs his books in. He's avoiding my eyes. Something's bothering him. His clothes are also much less wrinkled than usual. And they look cleaner. And they match. He's putting on the Ritz for Carmel.

"Is that gel in your hair?" I tease.

"How can you be so chipper?" he asks. "Haven't you been watching the news?"

"What are you talking about?" I ask, deciding to feign innocence. Or ignorance. Or both.

"The news," he hisses. His voice goes lower. "The guy in the park. The dismemberment." He glances around, but no one is paying any attention to him, as usual.

"You think it was Anna," I say.

"Don't you?" asks a voice in my ear.

I spin around. Carmel is right over my shoulder. She moves to stand beside Thomas, and I can tell by the way they face me that they've already discussed this at length. I feel attacked, and a little bit hurt. They've left me out of the loop. I feel like a petulant little kid, which in turn pisses me off.

Carmel goes on. "You can't deny that it's an extreme coincidence."

"I don't deny that. But it is a coincidence. She didn't do it."

"How do you know?" they ask together, and isn't that cute.

"Hey, Carmel."

The conversation stops abruptly as Katie approaches with a gaggle of girls. Some of them I don't know, but two or three are in classes with me. One of them, a petite brunette with wavy hair and freckles, gives me a smile. They all ignore Thomas completely.

"Hey, Katie," Carmel replies coolly. "What's up?"

"Are you still going to help out with the Winter Formal? Or are Sarah, Nat, Casey, and I on our own?"

"What do you mean, 'help out'? I'm the chair of that committee." Carmel looks around at the rest of the girls, perplexed.

"Well," Katie says with a direct glance at me. "That was before you got so *busy*."

I think Thomas and I would like to get the hell out of

here. This is more uncomfortable than talking about Anna. But Carmel is a force to be reckoned with.

"Aw, Katie, are you trying to stage a coup?"

Katie blinks. "What? What are you talking about? I was just asking."

"Well relax, then. The formal's not for three months. We'll meet on Saturday." She turns slightly away in an effectively dismissive gesture.

Katie's wearing this embarrassed smile. She sputters a little bit and actually tells Carmel what a cute sweater she's wearing before toddling off.

"And be sure to have two ideas for fundraisers each!" Carmel calls out. She looks back at us and shrugs apologetically.

"Wow," Thomas breathes. "Girls are bitches."

Carmel's eyes widen; then she grins. "Of course we are. But don't let that distract you." She looks at me. "Tell us what's going on. How do you know that jogger wasn't Anna?"

I wish Katie had stuck around longer.

"I know," I reply. "I've been to see her."

Sly glances are exchanged. They think I'm being gullible. Maybe I am, because it *is* an extreme coincidence. Still, I've been dealing with ghosts for most of my life. I should get the benefit of the doubt.

"How can you be sure?" Thomas asks. "And can we even take the chance? I know that what happened to her was terrible, but she's done some terrible shit, and maybe we should just send her . . . wherever it is that you send them. Maybe it would be better for everyone."

I'm sort of impressed by Thomas speaking this way, even if I don't agree. But that kind of talk makes him uncomfortable. He starts shifting his weight from foot to foot and pushes his black-rimmed glasses higher up on his nose.

"No," I reply flatly.

"Cas," Carmel starts. "You don't know that she won't hurt anyone. She's been killing people for fifty years. It wasn't her fault. But it's probably not that easy to go cold turkey."

They make her sound like a wolf who has tasted chicken's blood.

"No," I say again.

"Cas."

"No. Give me your reasons, and your suspicions. But Anna doesn't deserve to be dead. And if I put my knife in her belly . . ." I almost gag just saying it. "I don't know where I'd be sending her."

"If we get you proof . . ."

Now I get defensive. "Stay away from her. It's my business."

"Your business?" Carmel snaps. "It wasn't your business when you needed our help. It wasn't just you who was in danger that night in that house. You don't have any right to shut us out now."

"I know," I say, and sigh. I don't know how to explain it. I wish that we were all closer, that they had been my friends longer, so they might know what I was trying to say without me having to say it. Or I wish that Thomas was a better mind reader. Maybe he is, because he puts his hand on Carmel's arm and whispers that they should give me some time. She looks at him like he's gone nuts, but backs off a step.

"Are you always this way with your ghosts?" he asks.

I stare at the locker behind him. "What are you talking about?"

Those knowing eyes of his are seeking out my secrets.

"I don't know," he says after a second. "Are you always this . . . protective?"

Finally I look him in the eye. There's a confession in my throat even in the midst of dozens of students crushing the hallways on their way to third period. I can hear bits and pieces of their conversations as they go by. They sound so normal, and it occurs to me that I've never had one of those conversations. Complaining about teachers and wondering about what to do on Friday night. Who's got the time? I'd like to be talking to Thomas and Carmel about that. I'd like to be planning a party, or deciding which DVD to rent and whose house to watch it at.

"Maybe you can tell us all this later," Thomas says, and it's there in his voice. He knows. I'm glad.

"We should just focus on getting your athame back," he suggests. I nod weakly. What is it my dad used to say? Out of the frying pan and into the fire. He used to chuckle about living a life full of booby traps.

"Has anyone seen Will?" I ask.

"I've tried to call him a few times, but he ignores it," says Carmel.

"I'm going to have to get in his face," I say regretfully. "I like Will, and I know how pissed off he must be. But he can't keep my dad's knife. There's no way."

The bell rings for the start of third period. The halls have emptied without us noticing and all of a sudden our voices are loud. We can't just stand here in a cluster; sooner or later some overzealous hall monitor will chase us down. But all Thomas and I have is study hall, and I don't feel like going.

"Wanna ditch out?" he asks, reading my mind—or maybe just being an average teenager with good ideas.

"Definitely. What about you, Carmel?"

She shrugs and tugs her cream-colored cardigan tighter around her shoulders. "I've got algebra, but who needs that anyway? Besides, I haven't missed a single class yet."

"Cool. Let's go grab something to eat."

"Sushi Bowl?" Thomas suggests.

"Pizza," Carmel and I say together, and he grins. As we walk down the hall, I feel relieved. In less than a minute, we'll be out of this school and into the chilly November air, and anyone who tries to stop us is getting flown the bird.

And then someone taps my shoulder.

"Hey."

When I turn all I see is a fist in my face—that is, until I feel the multicolored dull sting you get when someone hits you square in the nose. I double over and shut my eyes. There's warm, sticky wetness on my lips. My nose is bleeding.

"Will, what are you doing?" I hear Carmel shout, and then Thomas joins in and Chase starts grunting. There are sounds of a scuffle.

"Don't defend him," Will says. "Didn't you watch the news? He got someone killed."

I open my eyes. Will is glaring at me over Thomas's shoulder. Chase is ready to jump at me, all blond spiky hair and muscle t-shirt, just aching to give Thomas a shove as soon as his designated leader gives him the go-ahead.

"It wasn't her." I sniff blood down the back of my throat. It's salty and tastes like old pennies. Wiping at my nose with the back of my hand leaves a bright red swatch.

"It wasn't her," he scoffs. "Didn't you listen to the witnesses? They said they heard wailing, and growling, but from a human throat. They said they heard a voice speaking that didn't sound human at all. They said the body was in six pieces. Sound like anyone you know?"

"Sounds like lots of someones," I snarl. "Sounds like any dime-store psycho." Except that it doesn't. And the voice speaking without sounding human makes the hairs on the back of my neck stand up.

"You're so blind," he says. "This is your fault. Ever since you came here. Mike, and now this poor schlub in the park." He stops, reaches into his jacket, and pulls out my knife. He points it at me, an accusation. "Do your job!"

Is he an idiot? He must be unhinged, pulling it out in the middle of school. It's going to get confiscated and he's going to get signed up for weekly counselor visits or expelled, and then I'm going to have to break into god knows where to get it back.

"Give it to me," I say. I sound strange; my nose has stopped bleeding but I can feel the clot in there. If I breathe through it to talk normally, I'll swallow it down and the whole thing will start over.

"Why?" Will asks. "You don't use it. So maybe I'll use it." He holds the knife out at Thomas. "What do you think happens if I cut someone alive? Does it send them to the same place it sends the dead ones?"

"You get away from him," Carmel hisses. She slides herself between Thomas and the knife.

"Carmel!" Thomas pulls her back a step.

"Loyal to him now, huh?" Will asks, and curls his lip like he's never seen anything more disgusting. "When you were never loyal to Mike."

I don't like where this is going. The truth is, I don't know what would happen if the athame was used on a living person. To my knowledge, it never has been. I don't want to think of the wound it might cause, that it might stretch Thomas's skin up over his face and leave a black hole in its wake. I have to do something, and sometimes that means being an asshole.

"Mike was a dick," I say loudly. It shocks Will into stillness, which is what I intended. "He didn't deserve loyalty. Not Carmel's, and not yours."

All his attention is on me now. The blade shines brightly under the school's fluorescent lights. I don't want my skin to stretch up over my face either, but I'm curious. I wonder if my link to the knife, my blood right to wield it, would protect me somehow. The probabilities weigh out in my head. Should I rush him? Should I wrestle it away?

But instead of looking pissed, Will grins.

"I'm going to kill her, you know," he says. "Your sweet little Anna."

My sweet little Anna. Am I that transparent? Was it obvious, the whole time, to everyone but me?

"She's not weak anymore, you idiot," I spit. "You won't get within six feet of her, magical knife or no magical knife."

"We'll see," he replies, and my heart sinks as I watch my athame, my father's athame, disappear back inside the dark of his jacket. More than anything, I want to rush him, but I can't risk someone getting hurt. To emphasize the point, Thomas and Carmel come and stand by my shoulders, ready to hold me back.

"Not here," Thomas says. "We'll get it back, don't worry. We'll figure it out."

"We'd better do it fast," I say, because I don't know whether I was telling the truth just now. Anna's got it in her head that she's supposed to die. She might just let Will in her front door to spare me the pain of doing it myself.

We decide to scrap the pizza. In fact, we decide to scrap the rest of the school day, and head instead for my place. I've turned Thomas and Carmel into a right fine pair of delinquents. On the way over, I ride with Thomas in his Tempo while Carmel follows behind.

"So," he says, then stops and chews his lip. I wait for the rest, but he starts to fidget with the sleeves of his gray hoodie, which are a little too long and are starting to fray at the edges.

"You know about Anna," I say to make it easy on him. "You know how I feel about her."

Thomas nods.

I run my fingers through my hair but it falls right back into my eyes. "Is it because I can't stop thinking about her?" I ask. "Or can you really hear what's going on in my head?"

Thomas purses his lips. "It wasn't either of those things. I've been trying to stay out of your head since you asked me to. Because we're—" He pauses and looks sort of like a sheep, all lip-chewy and lashy-eyed.

"Because we're friends," I say, and shove him in the arm. "You can say it, man. We are friends. You're probably my best friend. You and Carmel."

"Yeah," Thomas says. We must both be wearing the same expression: a little embarrassed, but glad. He clears his throat. "So, anyway. I knew about you and Anna because of the energy. Because of the aura."

"The aura?"

"It's not just a mystic thing. Probably most people can pick up on it. But I can see it more clearly. At first I thought it was just the way you were with all of the ghosts. You'd get this excited sort of glow whenever you were talking about her, or especially when you were near the house. But now it's on you all the time."

I smile quietly. She is with me all the time. I feel stupid now, for not seeing it sooner. But hey, at least we'll have this strange story to tell, love and death and blood and daddy-issues. And holy crap, I am a psychiatrist's wet dream.

Thomas pulls his car into my driveway. Carmel, only a few seconds behind us, catches up at the front door.

"Just chuck your stuff anywhere," I say as we go in. We shed our jackets and toss our book bags on the sofa. The pitter-patter of dark little feet announces Tybalt's arrival, and he climbs up Carmel's thigh to be held and petted. Thomas gives him a glare, but Carmel scoops the four-legged little flirt right up.

I lead them into the kitchen and they sit down at our rounded oak table. I duck into the refrigerator.

"There are frozen pizzas, or there's a lot of lunch meat and cheese in here. I could make some hoagie melts in the oven."

"Hoagie melts," Thomas and Carmel agree. There's a brief moment of smiling and blushing. I mutter under my breath about auras starting to glow, and Thomas grabs the dish towel off the counter and throws it at me. About twenty minutes later we're munching on some pretty excellent hoagie melts, and the steam from mine seems to be loosening up the old blood still stuck up my nose.

"Is this leaving a bruise?" I ask.

Thomas peers at me. "Nah," he says. "Will can't hit for beans, I guess."

"Good," I reply. "My mom's getting seriously tired of

doctoring me. I think she's done more healing spells on this trip than our last twelve trips combined."

"This was different for you, wasn't it?" Carmel asks between bites of chicken and Monterey Jack. "Anna really knocked you for a loop."

I nod. "Anna, and you, and Thomas. I've never faced anything like her. And I've never had to ask civilians to come take care of a haunting with me."

"I think it's a sign," Thomas says with his mouth full. "I think it means you should stay. Give the ghosts a rest for a little bit."

I take a deep breath. This is probably the only time in my life that I could be tempted by that. I remember being younger, before my dad was killed, and thinking that it might be nice if he gave it up for a while. That it might be nice to stay in one place, and make some friends, and have him just play baseball with me on a Saturday afternoon instead of being on the phone with some occultist or burying his nose in some old moldy book. But all kids feel that way about their parents and their jobs, not just the ones whose parents are ghost hunters.

Now I'm having that feeling again. It would be nice to stay in this house. It's cozy and it has a nice kitchen. And it would be cool to be able to hang out with Carmel and Thomas, and Anna. We could graduate together, maybe go to college near each other. It'd be almost normal. Just me, my best friends, and my dead girl.

The idea is so ridiculous that I snort.

"What?" Thomas asks.

"There's nobody else to do what I do," I reply. "Even if Anna isn't killing anymore, other ghosts are. I need to get my knife back. And I'm going to have to get back to work, eventually."

Thomas looks crestfallen. Carmel clears her throat.

"So, how do we get the knife back?" she asks.

"He's obviously in no mood to just hand it over," Thomas says sulkily.

"You know, my parents are friends with his parents," Carmel suggests. "I could ask them to lean on them, you know, tell them that Will stole some big family heirloom. It wouldn't be lying."

"I don't want to answer that many questions about why my big family heirloom is a deadly looking knife," I say. "Besides, I don't think parents are enough pressure this time. We're going to have to steal it."

"Break in and steal it?" Thomas asks. "You're nuts."

"Not that nuts." Carmel shrugs. "I've got a key to his house. My parents are friends with his, remember? We've got keys to each other's houses in case somebody gets locked out, or a key gets lost, or somebody needs to check in while the other is out of town."

"How quaint," I say, and she smirks.

"My parents have keys for half the neighborhood. Everyone is just dying to exchange with us. But Will's family is the only one with a copy of ours." She shrugs again. "Sometimes it pays to have a whole city up your butt. Mostly it's just annoying."

Of course Thomas and I have no idea what she means.

We've grown up with weird witch parents. People wouldn't exchange keys with us in a million years.

"So when do we do it?" Thomas asks.

"ASAP," I say. "Sometime when no one's there. During the day. Early, right after he leaves for school."

"But he'll probably have the knife on him," Thomas says.

Carmel pulls her phone out. "I'll start a rumor that he's been carrying a knife around school and someone should report him. He'll hear about it before morning and play it safe."

"Unless he decides to just stay home," Thomas says.

I give him a look. "Have you ever heard the term 'Doubting Thomas'?"

"Doesn't apply," he replies smugly. "That refers to someone being skeptical. I'm not skeptical. I'm pessimistic."

"Thomas," Carmel croons. "I never knew you were such a brain." Her fingers work feverishly at her phone keypad. She's already sent three messages and gotten two back.

"Enough, you two," I say. "We're going in tomorrow morning. I guess we'll miss first and second period, probably."

"That's okay," Carmel says. "Those were the two periods we made it to today."

Morning finds me and Thomas huddled down in his Tempo, parked around the corner from Will's house. We've got our heads pulled low inside of our hooded sweatshirts and our eyes are shifty. We look exactly like you'd expect someone to look if they were minutes away from committing a major crime.

Will lives in one of the wealthier, more well-preserved areas of the city. Of course he does. His parents are friends with Carmel's. That's how I have a copy of his house keys jangling around in my front pocket. But unfortunately that means there might be lots of busybody wives or housekeepers peeking out of windows to see what we're up to.

"Is it time?" Thomas asks. "What time is it?"

"It isn't time," I say, trying to sound calm, like I've done this a million times. Which I haven't. "Carmel hasn't called yet."

He calms down for a second and takes a deep breath. Then he tenses and ducks behind the steering wheel.

"I think I saw a gardener!" he hisses.

I haul him back up by his hood. "Not likely. The gardens have all gone brown by now. Maybe it was someone raking leaves. Either way, we're not sitting here in ski masks and gloves. We're not doing anything wrong."

"Not yet."

"Well, don't act suspicious."

It's just the two of us. Between the time of the plan hatching and the time of the plan execution, we decided that Carmel would be our plant. She'd go to school and make sure that Will was there. According to her, his parents leave for work long before he leaves for school.

Carmel objected, saying we were being sexist, that she should be there in case something went wrong, because at least she'd have a reasonable excuse to be dropping by. Thomas wouldn't hear of it. He was trying to be protective, but watching him bite his lower lip and jump at every tiny movement, I think I might've been better off with Carmel. When my phone starts vibrating, he jerks like a startled cat.

"It's Carmel," I tell him as I pick up.

"He's not here," she says in a panicked whisper.

"What?"

"Neither of them are. Chase is gone too."

"What?" I ask again, but I heard what she said. Thomas is tugging on my sleeve like an eager elementary schooler. "They didn't go to school," I snap.

Thunder Bay must be cursed. Nothing goes right in this stupid town. And now I've got Carmel worrying in my ear and Thomas conjecturing in my other ear and there are just too many damn people in this car for me to think straight.

"What do we do now?" they ask at the same time.

Anna. What about Anna? Will has the athame, and if he got wind of Carmel's decoy texting trick, who knows what he might have decided to do. He's smart enough to pull a double cross; I know that he is. And, for the last few weeks at least, I've been dumb enough to fall for one. He could be laughing at us right now, picturing us ransacking his room while he walks up Anna's driveway with my knife and his blond lackey in tow.

"Drive," I growl, and hang up on Carmel. We've got to

get to Anna, and fast. For all I know, I might already be too late.

"Where?" Thomas asks, but he's got the car started and is pulling around the block, toward the front of Will's house.

"Anna's."

"You don't think . . ." Thomas starts. "Maybe they just stayed home. Maybe they're going to school and they're just late."

He keeps on talking but my eyes notice something else as we pass by Will's house. There's something wrong with the curtains in a room on the second floor. It isn't just that they're drawn when every other window is clear and open. It's something about the way that they're drawn. They seem . . . messy, somehow. Like they were thrown together.

"Stop," I say. "Park the car."

"What's going on?" Thomas asks, but I keep my eyes trained on the second-floor window. He's in there, I know he is, and all of a sudden I'm mad as hell. Enough of this bullshit. I'm going in there and I'm getting my knife back and Will Rosenberg had better get out of my way.

I'm out before the car even stops. Thomas scrambles behind me, fumbling with his seatbelt. It sounds like he half falls out of the driver's side door, but his familiar clumsy footfalls catch up and he starts asking a million questions.

"What are we doing? What are you going to do?"

"I'm going to get my knife back," I reply. We haul ass

up the driveway and bound up the porch steps. I shove Thomas's hand away when he goes to knock and use the key instead. I'm in a mood, and I don't want to give Will any more warning than I have to. Let him try to keep it from me. Let him just try. But Thomas grabs my hands.

"What?" I snap.

"Use these at least," he says, holding out a pair of gloves. I want to tell him that we aren't cat-burglarizing anymore, but it's easier to just put them on than to argue. He puts on a pair himself, and I twist the key in the lock and open the door.

The only thing good about going into the house is that the need for quiet is keeping Thomas from poking me with questions. My heart is hammering away inside my ribs, silent but insistent. My muscles are tense and twitchy. It isn't at all like stalking a ghost. I don't feel certain or strong. I feel like a five-year-old in a hedge maze after dark.

The interior of the place is nice. Hardwood floors and thick-carpeted rugs. The banister leading upstairs looks like it's been treated with wood polish every day since it was carved. There is original art on the walls, and not the weird modern kind either—you know, the kind where some skinny bastard in New York declares some other skinny bastard a genius because he paints "really fierce red squares." This art is classic, French-inspired shore-scapes and small, shadowed portraits of women in delicate lace dresses. My eyes would normally spend more time here. Gideon schooled me in art appreciation at the V&A in London.

Instead, I whisper to Thomas, "Let's just get my knife and get out."

I lead the way up the stairs and turn left at the top, toward the room with the drawn curtains. It occurs to me that I could be completely wrong. It might not be a bedroom at all. It might be storage, or a game room, or some other room that would conceivably have its curtains shut. But there's no time for that now. I'm in front of the closed door.

The handle turns easily when I try it and the door swings partially open. Inside is too dark to see well, but I can make out the shape of a bed and, I think, a dresser. The room is empty. Thomas and I slide in like old pros. So far, so good. I pick my way toward the center of the room. My eyes blink to activate better night vision.

"Maybe we should try to turn on a lamp or something," Thomas whispers.

"Maybe," I reply absently. I'm not really paying attention. I can see a little bit better now, and what I'm seeing, I don't like.

The drawers of the dresser are standing open. There are clothes spilling out of the tops, like they've been rifled through in a hurry. Even the placement of the bed looks strange. It's sitting at an angle toward the wall. It's been moved.

Turning in a circle, I see that the closet door is thrown open, and a poster near it is half torn down.

"Someone's been here already," Thomas says, dropping the whisper.

I realize that I'm sweating and wipe at my forehead with the back of my glove. It doesn't make sense. Who would have been here already? Maybe Will had other enemies. That's a hell of a coincidence, but then, coincidences seem to be going around.

In the dark, I sort of see something next to the poster, something on the wall. It looks like writing. I step closer to it and my foot strikes something on the floor with a familiar thump. I know what it is even before I tell Thomas to turn on the light. When the brightness floods the room, I've already started backing out, and we see what we've been standing in the middle of.

They're both dead. The thing that my foot struck was Chase's thigh—or what's left of it—and what I thought was writing on the wall is actually long, thick sprays of blood. Dark, arterial blood in looping arcs. Thomas has grabbed my shirt from behind and is making this panicky gasping sound. I pull gently free. My head feels disconnected and clinical. The instinct to investigate is stronger than the urge to run.

Will's body is behind the bed. He's lying on his back and his eyes are open. One of the eyes is red, and I think at first that all the vessels have popped, but it's only red from a blood splash. The room around them is demolished. The sheets and blankets are torn off and are lying in a heap by Will's arm. He's still wearing what I assume were his pajamas, just a pair of flannel pants and a t-shirt. Chase was dressed. I'm thinking these things like a CSI person might, ordering them and making note of them, to keep myself from thinking about what I noticed the moment the lights came on.

The wounds. There are wounds on both of them: bright, red, and still seeping. Large, ragged crescents of missing muscle and bone. I would know these wounds anywhere, even though I've only seen them in my imagination. They're bite marks.

Something ate them.

Just like it ate my father.

"Cas!" Thomas shouts, and from the tone of his voice I know he's said my name a few times already and gotten no response. "We've got to get out of here!"

My legs are rooted. I can't seem to do anything, but then he's got me around the chest, holding my arms down and dragging me out. It isn't until he flicks the light off and the scene in the room goes black that I shake him off and start to run.

CHAPTER TWENTY

"What do we do?"

That's what Thomas keeps asking. Carmel has called twice, but I keep ignoring it. What do we do? I have no idea. I'm just sitting quietly in the passenger seat while Thomas drives nowhere in particular. This must be what catatonia feels like. There are no panicked thoughts running through my head. I'm not making plans or evaluating. There is only a gentle, rhythmic repetition. *It is here. It is here.*

One of my ears picks up Thomas's voice. He's on the phone to someone, explaining what we found. It must be Carmel. She must've given up on me and tried him, knowing she'd get an answer.

"I don't know," he says. "I think he's freaking out. I think he might have lost it."

My face twitches like it wants to react and rise to the challenge, but it's sluggish, like coming off of Novocain at the dentist. Thoughts drip into my brain slowly. Will and

Chase are dead. The thing that ate my father. Thomas is driving to nowhere.

None of the thoughts run into each other. None of them make much sense. But at least I'm not scared. Then the faucet drips faster, and Thomas shouts my name and hits me in the arm, effectively turning the water back on.

"Take me to Anna's," I say. He's relieved. At least I've said something. At least I've made some kind of decision, some executive order.

"We're going to do it," I hear him say into the phone. "Yeah. We're going there now. Meet us there. Don't go in if we're not there first!"

He's misunderstood. How can I explain? He doesn't know how my father died. He doesn't know what this means—that it has finally caught up with me. It has managed to find me, now, when I'm practically defenseless. And I didn't even know it was looking. I could almost smile. Fate is playing a practical joke.

Miles go past in a blur. Thomas is chattering encouraging things. He peels into Anna's driveway and gets out. My door opens a few seconds later and he hauls me out by the arm.

"Come on, Cas," he says. I look up at him gravely. "Are you ready?" he asks. "What are you going to do?"

I don't know what to say. The state of shock is losing its charm. I want my brain back. Can't it just shake itself off like a dog already and get back to work?

Our feet crunch up the cold gravel. My breath is visible

in a bright little cloud. To my right, Thomas's little clouds are showing up much faster, in nervous huffs.

"Are you okay?" he asks. "Man, I've never seen anything like that before. I can't believe that she— That was—" He stops and bends over. He's remembering, and if he remembers too hard, or too well, he might throw up. I reach an arm out to steady him.

"Maybe we should wait for Carmel," he says. Then he pulls me back.

Anna's door has opened. She's coming out onto the porch, softly, like a doe. I look at her spring dress. She makes no move to wrap herself up, though the wind must be moving across her like sharp sheets of ice. Her bare, dead shoulders can't feel it.

"Do you have it?" she asks. "Did you find it?"

"Do you have what?" Thomas whispers. "What's she talking about?"

I shake my head as a reply to them both, and walk up the porch steps. I go right past her, into the house, and she follows.

"Cas," she says. "What's wrong?" Her fingers brush my arm.

"Back off, sister!" Thomas squeaks. He actually shoves her and gets in between us. He's doing this ridiculous little sign-of-the-cross thing with his fingers, but I don't fault him for it. He's freaked. So am I.

"Thomas," I say. "It wasn't her."

"What?"

"She didn't do it."

I look at him calmly so he can see that the grip of shock is loosening its hold; I'm coming back to myself.

"And knock that off with your fingers," I add. "She's not a vampire, and even if she was, I don't think your phalange-cross would do anything."

He drops his hands. Relief relaxes the muscles in his face.

"They're dead," I say to Anna.

"Who's dead? And why aren't you going to accuse me again?"

Thomas clears his throat.

"Well, he's not, but I am. Where were you last night and this morning?"

"I was here," she replies. "I'm always here."

Outside, I hear the grumble of tires. Carmel has arrived.

"That was all well and good while you were *contained*," Thomas counters. "But maybe now that you're loose you go all over the place. Why wouldn't you? Why stay here, where you've been trapped for fifty years?" He looks around, nervous even though the house is quiet. There's no indication of angry spirits. "I don't even want to be here *now*."

Footsteps slam up the porch and Carmel bursts in holding, of all things, a metal baseball bat.

"Get the hell away from them!" she screams at the top of her lungs. She swings the thing in a wide arc and knocks Anna across the face. The effect is something like smacking the Terminator with a lead pipe. Anna just looks sort of surprised, and then sort of insulted. I think I see Carmel gulp.

"It's all right," I say, and the bat goes down an inch. "She didn't do it."

"How do you know?" Carmel asks. Her eyes are bright and the bat shakes in her hands. She's running on adrenaline and fear.

"How does he know what?" Anna interjects. "What are you talking about? What's happened?"

"Will and Chase are dead," I say.

Anna looks down. Then she asks, "Who's Chase?"

Could everyone stop asking so many damned questions? Or can someone else answer them, at least?

"He's one of the guys who helped Mike trick me, the night of . . ." I pause. "He was the other one by the window."

"Oh."

When I make no move to go on, Thomas tells Anna everything. Carmel cringes at the gory bits. Thomas looks at her apologetically but keeps talking. Anna listens and watches me.

"Who would do it?" Carmel asks angrily. "Did you touch anything? Did anyone see you?" She's looking from Thomas to me and back again.

"No. We were wearing gloves, and I don't think we moved anything while we were there," Thomas answers. Both of their voices are even, if a little fast. They're focusing on the practical aspects, which makes it easier. But I can't let them do it. I don't understand what's going on here and we need to figure it out. They have to know everything, or as much as I can stand to tell.

"There was so much blood," Thomas says weakly. "Who would do that? Why would someone . . . ?"

"It isn't a *who* exactly. More like a *what*," I say. I'm tired suddenly. The back of the dust-sheeted sofa looks fantastic. I lean against it.

"A 'what'?" Carmel asks.

"Yeah. A thing. It's not a person. Not anymore. It's the same thing that dismembered that guy in the park." I swallow. "The bite marks were probably sequestered. Keeping evidence close to the vest. They didn't broadcast it. That's why I didn't know sooner."

"Bite marks," Thomas whispers, and his eyes widen. "Is that what those were? They couldn't be. They were too big; there were huge chunks torn off."

"I've seen it before," I say. "Wait. That's not true. I've never actually seen it. And I don't know what it's doing here now, ten years later."

Carmel is idly clanking the top of her aluminum bat against the floor; the sound rings like an ill-tuned bell through the empty house. Without saying anything, Anna walks past her and scoops the bat up, then sets it on the padding of the sofa.

"I'm sorry," Anna whispers, and shrugs at Carmel, who crosses her arms and shrugs back.

"It's okay. I didn't even realize I was doing it. And . . . sorry for, you know, whacking you earlier."

"It didn't hurt." Anna stands beside me. "Cassio. You know what this thing is."

"When I was seven, my father went after a ghost in Baton Rouge, Louisiana." I look down at the floor, down at Anna's feet. "He never came back. It got him."

Anna puts her hand on my arm. "He was a ghost hunter, like you," she says.

"Like all my ancestors," I say. "He was like me and better than me." The idea of my father's killer, here, is making my head spin. It wasn't supposed to happen this way. I was supposed to go after it. I was supposed to be ready, and have all the tools, and I was supposed to hunt it to the ground. "And it killed him anyway."

"How did it kill him?" Anna asks softly.

"I don't know," I say. My hands are shaking. "I used to think it was because he was distracted. Or he was ambushed. I even had this idea that the knife stopped working, that after a certain time it just stops working for you, when your number is up. I thought maybe it was me who had done it. That I killed him just by growing older, and being ready to replace him."

"That's not true," Carmel says. "That's ridiculous."

"Yeah, well, maybe it is and maybe it isn't. When you're a seven-year-old kid and your dad dies and his body looks like it's been taken to a buffet for goddamn Siberian tigers, you think up a lot of ridiculous shit."

"He was eaten?" Thomas asks.

"Yeah. He was eaten. I heard the cops describing it. Big chunks taken out of him, just like what was taken out of Will and Chase."

"That doesn't necessarily mean that it's the same thing,"

Carmel reasons. "It's kind of a large coincidence, isn't it? After ten years?"

I don't say anything. I can't disagree with that.

"So maybe this is something different," Thomas suggests.

"No. This is it. It's the same thing; I know it is."

"Cas," he says. "How do you know?"

I look at him from under my brow. "Hey. I might not be a witch, but this gig does come with a few perks. I just know, okay? And in my experience, there aren't exactly a boatload of ghosts who eat flesh."

"Anna," Thomas says gently. "You've never eaten anything?"

She shakes her head. "Nothing."

"Besides," I add, "I was going to go back for it. I always intended to. But this time I was going back for real." I glance at Anna. "I mean, I thought I might. As soon as I was finished here. Maybe it knew."

"It's coming after you," Anna says absently.

I rub my eyes, thinking. I'm exhausted. Seriously dragging ass. Which doesn't make any sense, because I slept like a rock last night, for probably the first time in a week.

And then it clicks.

"The nightmares," I say. "They've been worse since I got here."

"What nightmares?" Thomas asks.

"I thought they were just dreams. Somebody leaning over me. But this whole time, it must've been like a portent."

"Like a what?" Carmel asks.

"Like a psychopomp or something. Prophecy dreams. Foretelling dreams. A warning." That gravelly voice, echoed out of the dirt and put through a buzz saw. That accent, almost Cajun, almost Caribbean. "There was this smell," I say, my nose crinkling. "Some kind of sweet smoke."

"Cas," Anna says. She sounds alarmed. "I smelled smoke when I was cut with your athame. You told me then it was probably just a memory of Elias's pipe tobacco. But what if it wasn't?"

"No," I say. But even as I say it, I remember one of my nightmares. *You lost the athame,* is what the thing said. *You lost it,* in that voice like rotting plants and razor blades.

Fear creeps up my back in cold fingers. My brain is trying to make a connection, poking carefully, dendrite seeking out dendrite. The thing that killed my father was voodoo. That much I've always known. And what is voodoo, in essence?

There's something there, some knowledge just out of the reach of light. It has to do with something Morfran said.

Carmel raises her hand like she's in class.

"Voice of reason," she says. "Whatever the thing is, and whatever the link may or may not be to the knife, or to Cas, or to Cas's father, it's killed at least two people, and eaten most of them. So what are we going to do?"

The room falls silent. I'm no use without my knife. For all I know, the thing might have taken the knife from Will, and now I've gotten Thomas and Carmel into a ginormous mess.

"I don't have my knife," I mumble.

"Don't start that," Anna says. She walks away from me sharply. "Arthur without Excalibur was still Arthur."

"Yeah," Carmel intones. "We might not have that athame, but if I'm not mistaken, we've got *her*"—she nods toward Anna—"and that's something. Will and Chase are dead. We know what did it. We might be next. So let's freaking circle the wagons and do something!"

Fifteen minutes later, we're all inside the Tempo. All four of us—Thomas and me up front, Carmel and Anna in the back. Why we didn't take Carmel's much roomier, more reliable, and less conspicuous Audi is beyond me, but that's what happens when you hatch a plan in fifteen minutes. Except that there isn't that much of a plan, because we don't really know what's happened. I mean, we've got hunches—I've got more than a hunch—but how could we make a plan when we don't know what the thing is, or what it wants?

So instead of worrying about what we don't know, we're going after what we do. We're going to find my athame. We're going to track it magically, which Thomas assures me can be done, with Morfran's help.

Anna insisted that she come along, because for all her talk of me being King Arthur, I think she knows I'm pretty much defenseless. And I don't know how well she knows her legends, but Arthur was killed by a ghost from his past that he didn't see coming. Not exactly the best comparison. Before we left the house, there was a brief discussion about trying to fudge ourselves some alibis for when the police discover Will and Chase. But that was quickly abandoned. Because really, when you may or may not be eaten in the next few days, who the hell cares about alibis?

I've got this weird, springy feeling in my muscles. Despite everything that's happened—Mike's death, seeing Anna's murder, Will and Chase's murder, and the knowledge that whatever killed my father is now here, possibly trying to kill me—I feel, okay. It doesn't make sense, I know. Everything is messed up. And I still feel okay. I feel almost safe, with Thomas and Carmel and Anna.

When we get to the shop, it occurs to me that I should tell my mother. If it really is the thing that killed my dad, she should know.

"Wait," I say after we all get out. "I should call my mom."

"Why don't you just go get her," Thomas says, handing me the keys. "She might be able to help. We can get started without you."

"Thanks," I say, and get into the driver's seat. "I'll be back as soon as I can." Anna snakes her pale leg over the front seat and drops herself down shotgun.

"I'm going with you."

I'm not going to argue. I could use the company. I start the car back up and drive. Anna does nothing but watch the trees and buildings go by. I suppose the change of scenery must be interesting to her, but I wish she would say something.

"Did Carmel hurt you, back there?" I ask just for noise.

She smiles. "Don't be silly."

"Have you been okay, at the house?"

There's a stillness on her face that has to be deliberate. She's always so still, but I get the feeling that her mind is sort of like a shark, twisting and swimming, and all I've ever seen is a glimpse of dorsal fin.

"They keep on showing me," she says carefully. "But they're still weak. Other than that, I've just been waiting."

"Waiting for what?" I ask. Don't judge me. Sometimes playing dumb is the only move you've got. Unfortunately, Anna doesn't chase the ball. So we sit, and I drive, and on the tip of my tongue are the words to tell her that I don't have to do it. I have a very strange life and she'd fit into it. Instead I say, "You didn't have a choice."

"It doesn't matter."

"How can it not?"

"I don't know, but it doesn't," she replies. I catch her smile in the corner of my eye. "I wish it didn't have to hurt you," she says.

"Do you?"

"Of course. Believe me, Cassio. I never wanted to be this tragic."

My house is cresting over the hill. To my relief, my mom's car is parked out front. I could continue this conversation. I could get in a jab, and we could argue. But I don't want to. I want to put this down and focus on the problem at hand. Maybe I'll never have to deal with this. Maybe something will change.

I pull into my driveway and we get out, but as we walk

up the porch steps, Anna starts to sniff. She's squinting like her head hurts.

"Oh," I say. "Right. I'm sorry. I forgot about the spell." I shrug weakly. "You know, a few herbs and chants and then nothing dead comes through the door. It's safer."

Anna crosses her arms and leans against the railing. "I understand," she says. "Go and get your mother."

Inside, I hear my mom humming some little tune I don't know, probably something she made up. I see her pass by the archway in the kitchen, her socks sliding across the hardwood and the tie from her sweater dragging behind on the ground. I walk up and grab it.

"Hey!" she says with an irritated look. "Shouldn't you be in school?"

"You're lucky it was me and not Tybalt," I say. "Or this sweater thing would be in shreds."

She sort of huffs at me and ties it around her waist where it belongs. The kitchen smells like flowers and persimmon. It's a warm, wintry smell. She's making a new batch of her Blessed Be Potpourri, just like she does every year. It's a big seller on the website. But I'm procrastinating.

"So?" she asks. "Aren't you going to tell me why you're not in school?"

I take a deep breath. "Something's happened."

"What?" Her tone is almost tired, like she half-expects just this sort of bad news. She's probably always expecting bad news of one kind or another, knowing what I do. "Well?"

I don't know how to tell her this. She might overreact.

But is there such a thing in this situation? Now I'm staring into a very worried and agitated mom-face.

"Theseus Cassio Lowood, you'd better spit it out."

"Mom," I say. "Just don't freak out."

"Don't freak out?" Her hands are on her hips now. "What's going on? I'm getting a very strange vibe here." Keeping her eyes on me, she stalks into the kitchen and turns on the TV.

"Mom," I groan, but it's too late. When I get to the TV to stand beside her, I see flashing police lights, and in the corner, Will and Chase's class photos. So the story broke. Cops and reporters are flooding across the lawn like ants to a sandwich crust, ready to break it down and carry it away for consumption.

"What is this?" She puts her hand to her mouth. "Oh, Cas, did you know those boys? Oh, how awful. Is that why you're out of school? Did they shut it down for the day?"

She is trying very hard not to look me in the face. She spit out those civilian questions, but she knows the real score. And she can't even con herself. After a few more seconds, she shuts the TV back off and nods her head slowly, trying to process.

"Tell me what's happened."

"I don't know quite how."

"Try."

So I do. I leave out as many details as I can. Except for the bite wounds. When I tell her about those, she holds her breath.

"You think it was the same?" she asks. "The one that—"

"I know it was. I can feel it."

"But you don't know."

"Mom. I know." I'm trying to say this stuff gently. Her lips are pressed together so tightly that they're not even lips anymore. I think she might cry or something.

"You were in that house? Where's the athame?"

"I don't know. Just, stay calm. We're going to need your help."

She doesn't say anything. She's got one hand on her forehead and the other on her hip. She's looking off into nothing. That deep little wrinkle of distress has appeared on her forehead.

"Help," she says softly, and then one more time, only harder. "Help."

I might have put her into some kind of overload coma.

"Okay," I say gently. "Just stay here. I'll get this handled, Mom. I promise."

Anna's waiting outside, and who knows what's happening back at the shop. It seems like I've taken hours on this errand, but I can't have been gone more than twenty minutes.

"Pack your things."

"What?"

"You heard me. Pack your things. This instant. We're leaving." She pushes past me and flies up the stairs, presumably to get started. I follow with a groan. There's no time for this. She's going to have to calm down and stay put. She can pack me up and toss my stuff into boxes. She can load it into a U-Haul. But my body is not leaving until this ghost is gone.

"Mom," I say, going after the last of her trailing sweater into my bedroom. "Will you stop flipping out? I'm not leaving." I pause. Her efficiency is unmatched. All of my socks are already out of my drawer and set in an ordered stack on my dresser. Even the striped ones are to one side of the plain.

"We are leaving," she says without missing a beat in her ransacking of my room. "If I have to knock you unconscious and drag you from this house, we are leaving."

"Mom, settle down."

"Do not tell me to settle down." The words are delivered in a controlled yell, a yell straight from the pit of her tensed stomach. She stops and stands still with her hands in my half-emptied drawers. "That thing killed my husband."

"Mom."

"It's not going to get you, too." Hands and socks and boxer shorts start flying again. I wish she hadn't started with my underwear drawer.

"I have to stop it."

"Let someone else do it," she snaps. "I should have told you this before; I should have told you that this wasn't your *duty* or your birthright or anything like that after your father died. Other people can do this."

"Not that many other people," I say. This is making me mad. I know she isn't trying to, but I feel like she's dishonoring my dad. "And not this time."

"You don't have to."

"I choose to," I say. I've lost the battle to keep my voice down. "If we go, it follows. And if I don't kill it, it eats people. Don't you get it?" Finally, I tell her what I've always kept secret. "This is what I've waited for. What I've trained for. I've been researching this ghost since I found the voodoo cross in Baton Rouge."

My mom slams my drawers shut. Her cheeks are red and she's got wet, shiny eyes. She looks about ready to throttle me.

"That thing killed him," she says. "It can kill you too."

"Thanks." I throw up my hands. "Thanks for your vote of confidence."

"Cas—"

"Wait. Shut up." I don't often tell my mother to shut up. In fact, I don't know if I ever have. But she needs to. Because something in my room doesn't make sense. There's something here that shouldn't be here. She follows my gaze and I want to see her react, because I don't want to be the only one seeing this.

My bed is just how I left it. The blankets are rumpled and half pulled down. The pillow has an imprint from my head.

And poking out from underneath is the carved handle of my father's athame.

It shouldn't be. It can't be. That thing is supposed to be miles away, hidden in Will Rosenberg's closet or in the hands of the ghost that murdered him. But I walk over to the bed and reach down, and the familiar wood is smooth against my palm. Connect the dots.

"Mom," I whisper, staring down at the knife. "We have to get out of here."

She just blinks at me, standing stock still, and in the quiet of the house there is an uneven creaking I don't recognize.

"Cas," my mom breathes. "The attic door."

The attic door. The sound and the phrase make something in the back of my head start to itch. It's something my mother said about raccoons, something about the way Tybalt climbed on me the day we moved in.

The quiet is sick: it magnifies every noise, so when I hear a distinct scraping, I know that what I'm hearing is the pull-down ladder being slid toward the floor in the hallway.

CHAPTER TWENTY-ONE

I'd like to leave now. I'd very much like to leave now. The hairs are up on the back of my neck and my teeth would chatter if I wasn't clenching so hard. Given the choice between fight or flight, I would choose to dive out the window, knife in my hand or not. Instead I turn and pivot closer to my mom, putting me in between her and the open door.

Footfalls hit the ladder, and my heart has never pounded so hard. My nostrils catch the scent of sweet smoke. *Stand my ground,* is what I think. After this is over, I might puke. Assuming, of course, that I'm still living.

The rhythm of the footsteps, the sound of whatever is coming down the ladder is driving both me and my mom steadily toward peeing our pants. We can't be caught in this bedroom. How I wish that weren't true, but it is. I have to make it out into the hallway and try to get us to the stairs before whatever it is blocks our escape. I grab her hand. She shakes her head violently, but I pull her along, inching toward the door, the athame held out in front of us like a torch.

Anna. Anna, come charging in, Anna, come save the day . . . but that's stupid. Anna is marooned on the damn front porch, and how would that be, if I died in here, ripped to bits and chewed on like a rubber pork chop, with her standing powerless outside.

Okay. Two more deep breaths and we go into the hall. Maybe three.

When I move I've got a clear view of the attic ladder, and also of the thing descending it. I don't want to be seeing this. All that training and all those ghosts; all that gut instinct and ability goes right out the window. I'm looking at my father's killer. I should be enraged. I should be stalking him. Instead I'm terrified.

His back is to me, and the ladder is far enough east of the stairs that we should be able to get there before he does, as long as we keep moving. And as long as he doesn't turn around and charge. Why do I think these thoughts? Besides, he doesn't seem inclined to. As we slide silently toward the staircase, he has reached the floor, and he actually pauses to put the ladder back up with a rickety shove.

At the top of the stairs, I stop, angling my mom to go down first. The figure in the hallway doesn't seem to have noticed us. He just keeps swaying back and forth with his back to me, like he's listening to some dead music.

He's wearing a dark, fitted jacket, sort of like a long suit jacket. It could be dusty black or even dark green, I can't tell. On the top of his head is a nest of dreadlocks, twisted and matted, some half-rotted and falling off. I can't see his face, but the skin of his hands is gray and cracked. Between his fingers he's twisting what looks like a long black snake.

I give my mom a gentle push to get her farther down the stairs. If she can get outside to Anna, she'll be safe. I'm getting a little tinge of bravery, just a wafting of the old Cas coming back.

Then I realize I'm full of shit when he turns and looks right at me.

I should rephrase that. I can't honestly say that he's looking right at me. Because one can never be sure that something is looking right at them if that something's eyes have been sewn shut.

And they are sewn shut. No mistaking. There are big, crisscrossed stitches of black string over his eyelids. Just the same, there is also no mistaking that he can see me. My mom speaks for both of us when she lets out a yelpy little "Oh."

"You're welcome," he says in that voice of his, the voice of my nightmares, like chewing on rusted nails.

"I have nothing to thank you for," I spit, and he cocks his head. Don't ask me how I know, but I know he's staring at my knife. He walks toward us, unafraid.

"Perhaps I should thank you, then," he says, and the accent shows. The "thank" is "tank." The "then" is "den."

"What are you doing here?" I ask. "How did you get here? How did you get past the door?"

"I've been here the whole time," he says. He's got bright

white teeth. His mouth is no bigger than any man's. How does he leave such gigantic marks?

He's smiling now, his chin tilted upward. He's got an ungainly way of moving, like lots of ghosts do. Like their limbs are stiffening, or like their ligaments are rotting away. It isn't until they move to strike that you see them for real. I won't be fooled.

"That's impossible," I say. "The spell would've kept you out." And there's no way that I've been sleeping in the same house with my father's killer this whole time. That he's been one floor above me, watching and listening.

"Spells to keep the dead out are worthless if the dead are already in," he says. "I come and go as I please. I fetch things back that foolish boys lose. And since then I've been in the attic, eating cats."

I've been in the attic, eating cats. I look closer at the black snake he's been weaving through his fingers. It's Tybalt's tail.

"You fuck—you ate my cat!" I yell, and thank you, Tybalt, for one last favor, this pissed-off rush of adrenaline. The quiet is suddenly filled with the sound of knocking. Anna heard me yell and is banging on the door, asking if I'm all right. The ghost's head snaps around like a snake, an unnatural, disturbing movement.

My mom doesn't know what's going on. She didn't know Anna was outside, so she starts clinging to me, unsure of what to be more afraid of.

"Cas, what is that?" she asks. "How are we going to get out?"

"Don't worry, Mom," I say. "Don't be scared."

"The girl we wait for is right outside," he says, and shuffles forward. My mom and I drop down a step.

I put my hand out across the railing. The athame flashes and I bring it back to eye level. "You stay away from her."

"She's what we came for." He makes a soft, hollow rustling when he moves, like his body is an illusion and he's nothing more than empty clothes.

"*We* didn't come for anything," I spit. "*I* came to kill a ghost. And I'm going to get my chance." I lunge forward, feeling my blade part the air, the silver tip just grazing his front buttons.

"Cas, don't!" my mom shouts, trying to drag me back by one arm. She needs to knock it off. What does she think I've been doing all this time? Setting elaborate traps using springs, plywood, and a mouse on a wheel? This is hand-to-hand. This is what I know.

Meanwhile, Anna is pounding harder on the door. It must be giving her a migraine to be so close.

"It's what you're here for, boy," he hisses, and takes a swing at me. It seems halfhearted; it misses by a mile. I don't think he missed because of the whole stitched-over-eye thing. He's just playing with me. Another clue is the fact that he's laughing.

"I wonder how you'll go," I say. "I wonder if you'll shrivel up, or if you'll melt."

"I won't do either of those things," he says, still smiling.

"And what if I cut off your arm?" I ask as I leap up the stairs, my knife retracted and then slicing out in a sharp arc.

"It will kill you on its own!"

He strikes me in the chest, and my mom and I fall head over ass down the steps. It hurts. A lot. But at least he's not laughing anymore. Actually, I think I finally succeeded in pissing him off. I gather my mom up.

"Are you okay? Is anything broken?" I ask. She shakes her head. "Get to the door." As she scrambles away, I stand up. He's walking down the steps without any sign of that old ghostly stiffness. He's as limber as any living, young man.

"You might just vaporize, you know," I say, because I've never been able to keep my damned mouth shut. "But personally, I hope you explode."

He takes a deep breath. And then another. And then another, and he's not letting them back out. His chest is filling up like a balloon, stretching his ribcage. I can hear the sinews in there, ready to snap. Then, before I know what's happening, his arms are thrust out toward me and he's right in my face. It happened so fast I could barely see it. My knife hand is pinned against the wall and he's got me by the collar. I'm hitting him in the neck and shoulder with my other hand, but it's like a kitten swatting yarn.

He lets go of that breath, rolling out through his lips in thick, sweet smoke, passing over my eyes and into my nostrils, so strong and cloying that my knees buckle.

From somewhere behind me, I feel my mom's hands. She's screeching my name and pulling me away.

"You'll give her to me, my son, or you'll die." And he lets me drop, back into my mother's arms. "Your body's filth will rot you. Your mind will drain out your ears."

I can't move. I can't talk. I can breathe, but not much else, and I feel far away. Numb. Sort of confused. I can feel my mom yelp and lean over me as Anna finally blows the door off its hinges.

"Why don't you take me yourself?" I hear her ask. Anna, my strong, terrifying Anna. I want to tell her to watch out, that this thing has tricks up its rotting sleeves. But I can't. So my mother and I huddle in between this hissing match of the strongest spirits we've ever seen.

"Cross the threshold, beauty girl," he says.

"You cross mine," she says back. She's straining against the barrier spell; her head must feel almost as tight as mine. A thin rivulet of black blood dribbles from her nose and over her lips. "Take the knife and come, coward," Anna shouts. "Come out and let me off this leash!"

He's seething. His eyes are on her and his teeth grind. "Your blood on my blade, or the boy will join us by morning."

I try to tighten my grip on the knife. Only I can't feel my hand. Anna is shouting something else, but I don't know what it is. My ears feel stuffed with cotton. I can't hear anymore.

CHAPTER TWENTY-TWO

The sensation is something like staying underwater for too long. I've foolishly used up all my oxygen, and even though I know the surface is just a few kicks away, I can barely get there through the suffocating panic. But my eyes open on a blurry world, and I take that first breath. I don't know if I'm gasping. It feels like I am.

The face I see upon waking is Morfran's, and it's far too close. I instinctively try to sink farther into whatever it is that I'm lying on in order to keep that mossy beard at a safer distance. His mouth is moving but no sound is coming out. It's completely silent, not even a buzz or a ringing. My ears haven't come back online yet.

Morfran has stepped back, thank god, and is talking to my mom. Then suddenly there's Anna, floating into view, settling down beside me on the floor. I try to turn my head to follow. She sweeps her fingers along my forehead but doesn't say anything. There's relief tugging at the edges of her lips.

My hearing comes back strangely. At first I can hear

muffled noises, and then when they finally become clear, they don't make sense. I think my brain figured it had been torn apart, and now it's putting out its feelers slowly, grasping at nerve endings and shouting across synapse gaps, glad to find everything still there.

"What's going on?" I ask, my brain-tentacle having finally located my tongue.

"Jesus, man, I thought you were toast," Thomas exclaims, appearing at the side of what I can see now is the same antique sofa that they put me on when I got knocked out that first night at Anna's. I'm in Morfran's shop.

"When they brought you in . . ." Thomas says. He doesn't finish, but I know what he means. I put my hand on his shoulder and give it a shake.

"I'm fine," I say, and sit up a little with only a minimal struggle. "I've been in worse scrapes."

Standing on the other side of his room with his back to all of us, acting like he's got a lot more interesting things to be doing, Morfran gives a snort.

"Not likely." He turns around. His wire specs have slid most of the way down his nose. "And you're not out of this 'scrape' yet. You been Obeahed."

Thomas, Carmel, and I all do that thing you do when someone is speaking another language: we look around at each other and then say, "Huh?"

"Obeahed, boy," Morfran snaps. "West Indian voodoo magic. You're just lucky that I spent six years on Anguilla, with Julian Baptiste. Now that was a real Obeahman."

I stretch my limbs and sit up straighter. Except for a

little tenderness in my back and side, plus the swimmy head stuff, I feel fine.

"I've been Obeahed by an Obeahman? Is this like how the Smurfs say they smurfing smurfed all the time?"

"Don't joke, Cassio."

It's my mother. She looks awful. She's been crying. I hate that.

"I still don't know how he got into the house," she says. "We were always so careful. And the barrier spell was working. It worked on Anna."

"It was a great spell, Mrs. Lowood," Anna responds gently. "I could never have crossed that threshold. No matter how much I would have liked to." When she says this last part, her irises get three shades darker.

"What happened? What happened after I blacked out, or whatever?" I'm interested now. The relief of not being dead has worn off.

"I told him to come out and face me. He didn't accept. He just smiled this terrible smile. Then he was gone. There was nothing but smoke." Anna turns to Morfran. "What is he?"

"He *was* an Obeahman. What he is now, I don't know. Any limitations he had left with his body. Now he's only force."

"What exactly is Obeah?" Carmel asks. "Am I the only one who doesn't know?"

"It's just another word for voodoo," I say, and Morfran slams his fist into the wood corner of the counter.

"If you think that then you're as good as dead."

"What are you talking about?" I ask. I haul myself to my feet, unsteadily, and Anna takes my hand. This isn't a conversation to have lying down.

"Obeah is voodoo," he explains. "But voodoo is not Obeah. Voodoo is nothing more than Afro-Caribbean witchcraft. It follows the same rules as the magic we all practice. Obeah has no rules. Voodoo channels power. Obeah *is* power. An Obeahman doesn't channel *shit*, he takes it into himself. He *becomes* the power source."

"But the cross—I found a black cross, like yours for Papa Legba."

Morfran waves his hand. "He probably started out as voodoo. He's something much, much more now. You've gotten us into a world of shit."

"What do you mean I've gotten us?" I ask. "It's not like I called him. 'Hey, guy who killed my dad, come terrorize me and my friends!'"

"You brought him here," Morfran growls. "He's been with you the whole time." He glares at the athame in my hand. "Hitching a ride on that damn knife."

No. *No.* That can't be what's happened. I know what he's saying now, and it can't be true. The athame feels heavy—heavier than before. The glint of its blade in the corner of my eye looks secretive and traitorous. He's saying that this Obeahman and my athame are linked.

My brain fights it even though I know he's right. Why else would he bring the knife back to me? Why else would Anna smell smoke when it cut her? It was tied to something else, she said. Something dark. I'd thought it was just the knife's inherent power.

"He killed my father," I hear myself say.

"Of course he did," Morfran spits. "How do you think he became connected to the knife in the first place?"

I don't say anything. Morfran is giving me the *piece it together, genius* look. We've all gotten it at one time or another. But I just got un-mojo-ed five minutes ago, so cut me some slack.

"It's because of your father," my mom whispers. And then, more to the point, "Because he ate your father."

"The flesh," Thomas says, and his eyes light up. He looks to Morfran for approval, and continues. "He's an eater of flesh. Flesh is power. Essence. When he ate your father, he took your dad's power into himself." He looks down at my athame like he's never seen it before. "The thing you called your blood tie, Cas. Now he has a link to it. It's been feeding him."

"No," I say weakly. Thomas gives me this helpless apologetic expression, trying to tell me that I wasn't doing it on purpose.

"Wait," Carmel interrupts. "You're telling me that this thing has pieces of Will and Chase? Like it carries around part of them?" She looks horrified.

I look down at the athame. I've used it to send away dozens of ghosts. I know that Morfran and Thomas are right. So just where the hell have I been sending them to? I don't want to think of this. The faces of the ghosts I've killed flash behind my closed lids. I see their expressions, confused and angry, filled with pain. I see the frightened eyes of the hitchhiker, trying to make it home to his girl. I can't say that I thought I was putting them to rest. I hoped so, but I didn't know. But I sure as hell didn't want to be doing this.

"It's impossible," I say finally. "The knife can't be tied to the dead. It's supposed to kill them, not feed them."

"That's not the Holy Grail in your hand, kid," says Morfran. "That knife was forged long ago with powers best long forgotten. Just because you use it for good now doesn't mean that's what it was made for. It doesn't mean that's all that it's capable of. Whatever it was when your dad wielded it, it isn't now. Every ghost you've slain has made this ghost stronger. He's a flesh-eater. An Obeah-man. He's a collector of power."

The accusations make me want to be a kid again. Why isn't my mommy calling them big fat liars? The seriously, completely wrong pants-on-fire kind? But my mother is standing silent, listening to all of this, and not disagreeing.

"You're saying he's been with me the whole time." I feel sick.

"I'm saying that the athame is just like the stuff we take into this shop. He's been with *it*." Morfran looks somberly at Anna. "And now he wants her."

"Why doesn't he do it himself?" I ask wearily. "He's an eater of flesh, right? Why does he need my help?"

"Because I'm not flesh," Anna says. "If I were I'd be rotten."

"Bluntly put," Carmel observes. "But she's right. If ghosts were actually flesh they'd be more like zombies, wouldn't they?"

I start to waver by Anna's side. The room is spinning slightly, and I feel her arm come around my waist.

"What does any of this matter, right now?" Anna asks. "There's something to be done. Can't this discussion wait?"

She says that for my benefit. There's an edge of protection in her voice. I look at her gratefully, standing by my side in her hopeful white dress. She's pale and slender, but no one could mistake her for weak. To this Obeahman, she must look like the feast of the century. He wants her to be his big retirement score.

"I'm going to kill him," I say.

"You're going to have to," Morfran says. "If you want to stay alive yourself."

That doesn't sound good. "What are you talking about?"

"Obeah is not my specialty. It'd take more than six years to do that, Julian Baptiste or no. But even if I was, I can't take that hex off of you. I can only counter it, and buy you time. But not much. You'll be dead by dawn, unless you do what he wants. Or unless you kill him."

Beside me, Anna tenses, and my mom puts her hand to her mouth and starts to cry.

Dead by dawn. Okay, then. I don't feel anything, not yet, except for a low, weary hum all through my body.

"What's going to happen to me, exactly?" I ask.

"I don't know," Morfran replies. "It could look like natural, human death, or it could take the form of poisoning. Either way I think you can expect some of your organs to start shutting down in the next few hours. Unless we kill him, or you kill her." He nods at Anna and she squeezes my hand.

"Don't even think about it," I say to her. "I'm not going to do what he wants. And this suicidal ghost schtick is wearing a little thin."

She lifts her chin. "I wasn't going to suggest that," she says. "If you killed me, it would only make him stronger, and then he would come back and kill you anyway."

"So what do we do?" Thomas asks.

I don't particularly like being a leader. I don't have much practice at it, and I'm much more comfortable risking just my own skin. But this is it. There's no time for excuses or second-guessing. In the thousand ways I pictured this going down, I could never have imagined it like this. Still, it's nice that I'm not fighting alone.

I look at Anna.

"We fight on our own turf," I say. "And we pull a rope-a-dope."

CHAPTER TWENTY-THREE

A more ramshackle operation I've never seen. We're driving in a nervous little caravan, stuffed into beat-up cars that leave dark exhaust trails, wondering if we're ready to do whatever it is that we're going to do. I haven't explained the rope-a-dope yet. But I think that Morfran and Thomas at least suspect what it is.

The light is starting to get golden, coming at us sideways and getting ready to turn sunset colored. Getting everything into the cars took forever—we have half of the occult merchandise from the shop packed into Thomas's Tempo and Morfran's Chevy pickup. I keep thinking of nomadic native tribes, and how they could pack up an entire civilization in an hour to follow some buffalo. When did human beings start acquiring so much crap?

When we get to Anna's house, we start to unload, lugging as much as we can. This is where I meant when I said "our own turf." My own house feels tainted, and the shop is too close to the rest of the populace. I mentioned the restless spirits to Morfran, but he seems to think they'll scuttle off into a dark corner at the presence of so many witches. I'll take his word for it.

Carmel gets into her Audi, which has been sitting here the whole time, and dumps out her schoolbag, emptying it so she can fit bunches of herbs and bottles of oil inside. I feel okay, so far. I still remember what Morfran said, about the Obeah getting worse. There's an ache forming in my head, right between my eyes, but that might be from impacting against the wall. If we're lucky, we're accelerating the timeline enough so the battle will be over before his curse even becomes a factor. I don't know how much use I'll be, if I'm writhing around in agony.

I'm trying to stay positive, which is strange, as I tend to brood. It must be this whole leader of the pack thing I'm trying on. I have to look well. I have to appear confident. Because my mother is worried to the point of prematurely graying, and Carmel and Thomas look way too pale, even for Canadian kids.

"Do you think he'll find us here?" Thomas asks as we pull a sack of candles out of his Tempo.

"I think he's always known exactly where I am," I say. "Or, at least he always knows where the knife is."

He looks back over his shoulder at Carmel, still gently packing bottles of oil and things floating in jars.

"Maybe we shouldn't have brought them," he says. "Carmel and your mom, I mean. Maybe we should send them somewhere safe."

"I don't think there is such a place," I say. "But you could take them, Thomas. You and Morfran could take them and hole up somewhere. Between the two of you, you could put up some kind of fight."

"What about you? What about Anna?"

"Well, we seem to be the ones he wants." I shrug.

Thomas scrunches his nose up in order to push his glasses higher on his face. He shakes his head.

"I'm not going anywhere. Besides, they're probably as safe here as anyplace else. They might get some crossfire but at least they're not alone, sitting ducks."

I look at him fondly. The expression he wears is sheer determination. Thomas is absolutely not naturally brave. Which makes his bravery all the more impressive.

"You're a good friend, Thomas."

He chuckles. "Yeah, thanks. Now do you want to let me in on this plan that's supposed to keep us from getting eaten?"

I grin and look back at the cars, where Anna is helping my mother with one arm and carrying a six-pack of Dasani water in the other.

"All I need from you and Morfran is a binding when he gets here," I say while I continue to watch. "And if there's anything you can do to bait the trap, that would help too."

"Should be easy enough," he replies. "There are tons of summoning spells used to call energies, or to call a lover. Your mom must know dozens. We'll just alter them. And we can charge some cord for binding. We could modify your mom's barrier oil too." He's got his brows knit as he rambles off requirements and methods.

"Should work," I say, though for the most part I have not a clue what he's going on about.

"Yeah," he says skeptically. "Now if you can just get me one point twenty-one gigawatts and a flux capacitor, we'll be in business."

I laugh. "Doubting Thomas. Don't be so negative. This is going to work."

"How do you know?" he asks.

"Because it has to." I try to keep my eyes wide open as my head really starts to pound.

Two fronts are set up in the house, which hasn't seen this much movement since . . . possibly ever. On the upper level, Thomas and Morfran are shaking a line of powdered incense along the top of the stairs. Morfran's got his own athame out, cutting the sign of the pentagram in the air. It's nowhere near as cool as mine, which I've got in its strung leather sheath, slung over my shoulder and across my chest. I've been trying not to think too much about what Morfran and Thomas said about it. It's just a thing; it's not some inherently good or inherently evil artifact. It has no will of its own. I haven't been hopping around and calling it my Precious all these years. And as for the link between it and the Obeahman, it'll sure as hell get severed tonight.

Upstairs, Morfran is whispering and turning slowly in a counterclockwise circle. Thomas takes up something that looks like a wooden hand with stretched-out fingers, and sweeps along the top of the steps with it, then lays it down. Morfran has finished his chant; he nods to Thomas, who lights a match and drops it. A line of blue flame surges up along the top floor and then smokes out.

"Smells like a Bob Marley concert in here," I say as Thomas comes downstairs.

"That's the patchouli," he replies.

"What about the wooden finger broom?"

"Comfrey root. For a safe house." He looks around. I can see the mental checklist running behind his stare.

"What were you guys doing up there, anyway?"

"That's where we'll do the binding from," he says, nodding toward the second level. "And it's our line of defense. We're going to seal the entire upper floor. Worse comes to worst, we regroup there. He won't be able to get near us." He sighs. "So I suppose I'd better go start pentagram-ing windows."

The second front is making a clatter in the kitchen. That would be my mom, Carmel, and Anna. Anna's helping Mom find her way around a wood stove as she tries to brew protection potions. I also catch a whiff of rosemary and lavender healing waters. My mother is a "prepare for the worst, hope for the best" type person. It's up to her to cast something to lure him here—aside from my rope-a-dope, that is.

I don't know why I'm thinking in code. All of this "rope-a-dope" business. Even I'm starting to wonder what I'm referring to. A rope-a-dope is a fake-out. It's a boxing strategy made famous by Ali. Make them think you're losing. Get them where you want them. And take them out.

So what's my rope-a-dope? Killing Anna.

I suppose I should go tell her.

In the kitchen, my mother is chopping some kind of leafy herb. There's an open jar of green liquid on the counter that smells like a mixture of pickles and tree bark. Anna is stirring a pot on the stove. Carmel is poking around near the basement door.

"What's down here?" she asks, and opens it up.

Anna tenses and looks at me. What would Carmel find down there, if she went? Confused, shuffling corpses?

Probably not. The haunting seems to be a manifestation of Anna's own guilt. If Carmel encountered anything, it would probably be some weak cold spots and the occasional mysterious door shutting.

"Nothing we need to worry about," I say, walking over to close it. "Things are going pretty well upstairs. How are they in here?"

Carmel shrugs. "I'm not much use. It's sort of like cooking, and I can't cook. But they seem to be doing okay." She crinkles her nose. "It's kinda slow."

"Never rush a good potion." My mother smiles. "It'll go all wonky on you. And you've been a big help, Carmel. She cleaned the crystals."

Carmel smiles at her, but gives me the eye. "I think I'll go help Thomas and Morfran."

After she goes, I wish she hadn't left. With just me, Anna, and my mom in here, the room feels strangely stuffed. There are things that need to be said, but not in front of my mother.

Anna clears her throat. "I think this is coming together, Mrs. Lowood," she says. "Do you need me to do anything else?"

My mom glances at me. "Not just now, dear. Thank you."

As we walk through the living room toward the foyer, Anna tilts her head upward to catch a glimpse of the happenings upstairs.

"You have no idea how strange it is," she says. "Having people in my house, and not wanting to break them into tiny little pieces."

"But that's an improvement, right?"

She crinkles her nose. "You're . . . what was it Carmel said earlier?" She looks down, then back at me. "An ass."

I laugh. "You're catching on."

We walk out onto the porch. I pull my jacket closed. I never took it off; the house hasn't seen heat in half a century.

"I like Carmel," says Anna. "I didn't at first."

"Why not?"

She shrugs. "I thought she was your girlfriend." She smiles. "But that's a silly reason to dislike someone."

"Yeah, well. I think Carmel and Thomas are on a collision course." We lean against the house, and I feel the rot in the boards behind me. They don't feel secure; the minute I lean back it's like I'm the one holding them up instead of the other way around.

The pain in my head is more insistent. I'm getting what feels like the start of a runner's side ache. I should see if anybody has any Advil. But that's dumb. If this is mystical, what the heck is Advil going to do about it?

"It's starting to hurt, isn't it?"

She's looking at me with concern. I guess I didn't realize I was rubbing my eyes.

"I'm okay."

"We have to get him here, and soon." She paces to the railing and comes back. "How are you going to get him here? Tell me."

"I'm going to do what you've always wanted," I say.

It takes her a moment. If it's possible for a person to look hurt and grateful at once, that's the face she makes.

"Don't get so excited. I'm only going to kill you a little bit. It'll be more like a ritual bloodletting."

She frowns. "Will that work?"

"With all of the extra summoning spells going on in that kitchen, I think so. He should be like a cartoon dog floating after the scent of a hot-dog truck."

"It will weaken me."

"How much?"

"I don't know."

Dammit. The truth is, I don't know either. I don't want to hurt her. But the blood is the key. The flow of energy moving through my blade to where-the-heck-ever should draw him like an alpha wolf's howl. I close my eyes. A million things could go wrong, but it's too late to think of anything else.

The pain between my eyes is making me blink a lot. It's

sapping my focus. I don't even know if I'll be well enough to make the cuts if the preparation takes much longer.

"Cassio. I'm afraid for you."

I chuckle. "That's probably wise." I squeeze my eyes shut. It isn't even a stabbing pain. That would be better, something with ebbs and flows so I could recover in between. This is constant and maddening. There's no relief.

Something cool touches my cheek. Soft fingers slide into the hair at my temples, pushing it back. Then I feel her brush against my mouth, so carefully, and when I open my eyes I'm staring into her eyes. I close them again and kiss her.

When it's over—and it isn't over for a while—we rest against the house with our foreheads together. My hands are on the small of her back. She's still stroking my temples.

"I never thought I'd get to do that," she whispers.

"Me neither. I thought I was going to kill you."

Anna smirks. She thinks that nothing's changed. She's wrong. Everything's changed. Everything, since I came to this town. And I know now that I was supposed to come here. That the moment I heard her story—that connection I felt, that interest—it had a purpose.

I'm not afraid. Despite the searing between my eyes and the knowledge that something is coming for me, something that could easily rip out my spleen and pop it like a water balloon, I am not afraid. She's with me. She's my purpose and we're going to save each other. We're going to save everyone. And then I'm going to convince her that she's supposed to stay here. With me.

Inside, there's a small clatter. I think my mom must've dropped something in the kitchen. No big deal, but it makes Anna jump and pull back. I flex my side and wince. I think the Obeahman might have started work tenderizing that spleen early. Just where is your spleen, anyway?

"Cas," Anna exclaims. She comes back to let me lean on her.

"Don't go," I say.

"I'm not going anywhere."

"Don't go, ever," I tease, and she makes a face like she thinks I need a throttling. She kisses me again, and I don't let go of her mouth; I make her squirm and start to laugh and try to stay serious.

"Let's just focus on tonight," she says.

Focus on tonight. But the fact that she kissed me again speaks much more loudly.

Preparations have been made. I'm lying on my back on the dust-sheeted sofa, pressing a lukewarm bottle of Dasani against my forehead. My eyes are shut. The world feels a whole lot nicer in the dark.

Morfran tried to do another clearing or counteracting or whatever, but it didn't work nearly as well as the first. He muttered chants and struck flint, sending up nice little pyrotechnics, then smudged my face and chest with something black and ashy that smelled like sulfur. The pain in my side lessened and stopped trying to reach up into my ribcage. The pain in my head was reduced to a moderate throb, but it still sucks. Morfran seemed worried, and disappointed with the results. He said it would've worked better if he'd had fresh chicken's blood. Even though I hurt, I'm still glad he didn't have access to a live chicken. What a spectacle that would have been.

I'm remembering the words of the Obeahman: that my mind would bleed out my ears or something. I hope that wasn't literal.

My mom sits on the couch near my feet. Her hand is on my shin and she's rubbing it absently. She still wants to run. Every one of her mom-instincts says to swaddle me up and take off. But she's not just any mom. She's my mom. So she sits, and gets ready to fight alongside.

"I'm sorry about your cat," I say.

"He was our cat," she replies. "I'm sorry too."

"He tried to warn us," I say. "I should have listened to the little hairball." I put down the water bottle. "I really am sorry, Mom. I'm going to miss him."

She nods.

"I want you to go upstairs before anything starts," I say. She nods again. She knows I can't focus if I'm worried about her.

"Why didn't you tell me?" she asks. "That you were searching him out all these years? That you were planning to go after him?"

"I didn't want you to worry," I say. I feel sort of stupid. "See how well it all turned out?"

She brushes my hair out of my eyes. She hates it that I let it hang in my face all the time. A concerned tension comes into her face and she looks at me closer.

"What?" I ask.

"Your eyes are yellow." I think she's going to cry again. From another room, I hear Morfran swear. "It's your liver," my mom says softly. "And maybe your kidneys. They're failing."

Well, that explains the liquefying feeling in my side.

We're alone in the living room. Everyone else has sort of scattered off to their respective corners. I suppose everyone's doing some thinking, maybe saying some prayers. Hopefully Thomas and Carmel are making out in a closet. Outside, a flash of electricity catches my eye.

"Isn't it a little late in the season for lightning?" I ask.

Morfran answers from where he's hovering in the door of the kitchen. "It isn't just lightning. I think our boy is working up some energy."

"We should do the summoning spell," my mom says.

"I'll go find Thomas." I heave myself off the sofa and make my way upstairs quietly. At the top, Carmel's voice is coming from inside one of the old guest rooms.

"I don't know what I'm doing here," she says, and her voice is scared, but also kind of snarky.

"What do you mean?" Thomas answers.

"Come on. I'm the freaking Prom Queen. Cas is like Buffy the Vampire Slayer, you, your grandpa, and his mom are all witches or wizards or whatever, and Anna is . . . Anna. What am I doing here? What use am I?"

"Don't you remember?" Thomas asks. "You're the voice of reason. You think of the things we forget about."

"Yeah. And I think I'm going to get myself killed. Just me and my aluminum bat."

"You're not. You won't. Nothing's going to happen to you, Carmel."

Their voices drop lower. I feel like some pervert eavesdropper. I'm not going to interrupt them. Mom and Morfran can do the spells on their own. Let Thomas have this moment. So I back softly down the stairs and head outside.

I wonder what things will be like after this is over. Assuming we all make it through, what's going to happen? Will everything go back to the way it was? Will Carmel eventually forget about this adventurous time with us? Will she shun Thomas and go back to being the center of SWC? She wouldn't do that, would she? I mean, she did just compare me to Buffy the Vampire Slayer. My opinion of her isn't the highest right now.

When I step out onto the porch, tugging my jacket tighter, I see Anna sitting on the railing with one leg up. She's watching the sky, and her face lit by the lightning is equal parts awe and worry.

"Strange weather," she says.

"Morfran says it's not just weather," I reply, and she makes an *I thought as much* expression.

"You look a little better."

"Thanks." I don't know why, but I feel shy. Now's not really the time for it. I walk over to her and put my arms around her waist.

There's no warmth to her body. When I put my nose

into her dark hair, there's no scent. But I can touch her, and I've come to know her. And, for whatever reason, she can say the same things about me.

I catch a whiff of something spicy. We look up. Coming from one of the upstairs bedrooms are thin tendrils of scented smoke, smoke that doesn't break up with the wind, but instead stretches out in ethereal fingers to call something forward. The summoning spells have started.

"Are you ready?" I ask.

"Always and never," she says softly. "Isn't that what they say?"

"Yes," I reply into her neck. "That's what they say."

Where should I do it?"

"Somewhere that's at least going to look like a mortal wound."

"Why not the inside of the wrist? It's a classic for a reason."

Anna sits in the middle of the floor. The underside of her pale arm swims before my compromised vision. We're both nervous, and the suggestions issuing from the upper level aren't helping.

"I don't want to hurt you," I whisper.

"You won't. Not really."

It's full-on dark, and the dry electrical storm is moving ever closer to our house on the hill. My blade, normally so sure and steady, quivers and tremors as I draw it across Anna's arm. Her black blood runs out in a thick line, staining her skin and dripping onto the dusty floorboards in heavy spatters.

My head is killing me. I need to stay clear. As we both watch the blood pool, we can feel it, a sort of quickening in the air, some intangible force that makes the hair on our arms and necks tighten and stand up.

"He's coming," I say, loudly enough that they'll be able to hear me where they all stand on the second level, watching over the railing. "Mom, get into one of the back rooms. Your work is done." She doesn't want to go, but she goes, and without a word, even though she's got a novel's worth of worries and encouragement sitting on her tongue.

"I feel sick," Anna whispers. "And it's pulling me, like before. Did you cut too deep?"

I reach for her arm. "I don't think so. I don't know." The blood is leaking, which is what we intended, but there's so much of it. How much blood does a dead girl have?

"Cas," Carmel says. There's alarm in her voice. I don't look at her. I look at the door.

Mist is coming in off of the porch, seeping in through the cracks, moving like a seeking snake across the floor. I don't know what I expected, but it wasn't this. I think I expected him to blow the door off its hinges and stand silhouetted against the moonlight, some badass eyeless specter.

The mist circles around us. In all our rope-a-dope glory, we kneel, exhausted, looking defeated. Except that Anna really does look more dead than usual. This plan could backfire.

And then the mist comes together and I'm once again staring at the Obeahman, who stares back with his stitched-over eyes.

I hate it when they don't have eyes. Empty sockets or cloudy eyeballs or eyes that just aren't where they should be—I hate all of it. It freaks me out, and that pisses me off.

Overhead, I hear chants starting, and the Obeahman laughs.

"Bind me all you want," he says. "I get what I came for."

"Seal the house," I call to them upstairs. I heave myself to my feet. "I hope you came for my knife in your gut."

"You are becoming inconvenient," he says, but I'm not thinking. I'm fighting, lunging, and trying to keep my balance through the throbbing in my head. I'm slashing and spinning against the stiffness in my side and chest.

He's quick, and ridiculously agile for something with no eyes, but I finally get through. My whole body tenses like a bow when I feel the edge of my knife slide into his side.

He feints back and puts a dead hand to the wound. My triumph is short lived. Before I know what's happened, he's come forward and smacked me into a wall. I don't realize I've hit it until I'm sliding down.

"Bind him! Weaken him!" I shout, but as I do, he skitters forward like some god-awful spider and lifts the sofa like it's inflatable, then hurls it into my team of magic-casters on the second level. They cry out at the impact, but there isn't any time to wonder if they're all right. He grabs me by the shoulder and lifts me up, then punches me into the wall. When I hear what sounds like twigs snapping, I know that it's actually a whole bunch of my ribs. Maybe the whole effing cage.

"This athame is ours," he says into my face, sweet smoke

issuing from between rancid gums. "It's like Obeah—it is *intent,* both yours and mine now, and whose do you think is stronger?"

Intent. Over his shoulder I see Anna, her eyes gone black and her body twisted, covered in the dress of blood. The wound on her arm has grown, and she lies in an oily puddle two feet across. She's staring at the floor with a blank expression. Upstairs I see the tossed sofa and a pair of legs caught underneath. I taste my own blood in my mouth. It's hard to breathe.

And then an Amazon comes out of nowhere. Carmel has jumped down the stairs, halfway down the wall. She's screaming. The Obeahman turns just in time to catch an aluminum bat in the face, and it does more than it did to Anna, maybe because Carmel is way more pissed. It knocks him down onto his knees, and she strikes again and again. And she's the prom queen who thought she wouldn't do anything.

I don't miss my chance. I stab my athame into his leg and he howls, but he manages to snake his arm out and get hold of Carmel's leg. There's a wet popping sound, and I finally see how he's able to take such large bites of people: he's got most of his jaw unhinged. He sinks his teeth into Carmel's thigh.

"Carmel!" It's Thomas, yelling as he limps his way down the stairs. He won't get to her in time—not soon enough to keep her leg in one piece—so I throw myself at the Obeahman, and my knife goes into his cheek. I'll saw his entire jaw off, I swear it.

Carmel is screeching and clinging to Thomas, who is trying to pull her from the crocodile. I twist my knife in his mouth, hoping to god that I'm not cutting her in the process, and he releases his bite with a wet smack. The entire house shakes with his fury.

Only it's not *his* fury. This isn't his house. And he's weakening. I've sliced him open enough now that we're wrestling in a sloppy mess. He's managed to pin me down as Thomas drags Carmel out of the way, so he doesn't see what I see, which is a hovering, dripping dress of blood.

I wish he did have eyes, so I could see the surprise in them when she grabs him from behind and tosses him with a crash into the banister. My Anna has lifted herself from her puddle, dressed for a fight, with writhing hair and black veins. The wound on her forearm is still bleeding. She's not quite right.

On the staircase, the Obeahman comes slowly to his feet. He dusts himself off and bares his teeth. I don't understand. The cuts in his side and his face, the wound in his leg, they aren't bleeding anymore.

"You think you can kill me with my own knife?" he asks.

I look at Thomas, who has taken off his jacket to tie around Carmel's leg. If I can't kill him with the athame, I don't know what to do. There are other ways to take down a ghost, but nobody here knows them. I can barely move. My chest feels like a bundle of loose twigs.

"It's not your knife," Anna replies. "Not after tonight."

She looks at me over her shoulder and smiles, just a little. "I'm going to give it back to him."

"Anna," I start, but I don't know what else to say. As I watch, as we all watch, she lifts her fist and strikes down into the floorboards, sending splinters and pieces of cracked wood halfway to the ceiling. I don't know what she's doing.

And then I notice the soft, red glow, like embers.

There's surprise on Anna's face that changes to happy relief. The idea was a gamble. She didn't know if anything would happen when she opened that hole in the floor. But now that it has, she bares her teeth and hooks her fingers.

The Obeahman hisses as she moves forward. Even when she's weak, she's got no equal. They trade blows. She twists his head around only to have him snap it right back again.

I have to help her. Never mind the clawing of my own bones inside my lungs. I haul myself over onto my stomach. Using my knife like a mountain climber's pick, I heave and scrape across the floor.

As the house shifts, a thousand boards and rusted nails groan out of tune. And then there are the sounds that *they* make, crashing together, the noise dense enough to make me wince. I'm amazed that they don't both shatter into bleeding pieces.

"Anna!" My voice is urgent but weak. I'm not taking in much air. They're grappling with each other, grimaces of strain on their faces. She wrenches him to the right and left; he snarls and jerks his head forward. She reels backward and sees me, coming closer.

"Cas!" she shouts through gritted teeth. "You have to get out of here! You have to get everyone out!"

"I'm not leaving you," I shout back. Or at least I think I do. My adrenaline is running low. I feel like the lights are blinking on and off. But I'm not leaving her. "Anna!"

She screams. While her attention was on me, the bastard unhinged his jaw, and now he's attached himself to her arm, dug in like a snake. The sight of her blood on his lips makes me yell. I pull my legs up under myself and vault.

I grab him by the hair and try to push him away from her. The slice I made in his face flaps grotesquely with each movement. I cut him again and use the knife to pry his teeth up, and together we use everything we have to throw him. He hits the broken staircase and falls down, sprawled and stunned.

"Cassio, you have to go *now*," she says to me. "Please."

Dust is falling around us. She's done something to the house, opened up that burning hole in the floor. I know it, and I know she can't take it back.

"You're coming with me." I take her arm, but pulling her is like trying to pull a Greek column. Thomas and Carmel are calling to me near the door, but it seems like a thousand miles away. They'll make it out. Their footsteps hammer down the front steps.

In the midst of it all, Anna is calm. She puts her hand against my face. "I don't regret this," she whispers. The look in her eyes is tender.

Then it hardens. She shoves me away, tosses me back across the room, the way I came. I roll, and feel the sick crumple of my ribs. When my head lifts, Anna is advancing on the Obeahman, still lying prone where we threw him at the foot of the stairs. She grabs him by one arm and one leg. He begins to stir as she drags him toward the hole in the floor.

When he looks with his stitched-over eyes and sees, he's afraid. He rains down blows on Anna's face and shoulders, but his punches don't look angry anymore. They look defensive. Going backward, her foot finds the hole and sinks in, the firelight glow illuminating her calf.

"Anna!" I scream as the house really starts to shake. But I can't get up. I can't do anything but watch her sink lower, watch her drag him down while he screeches and claws and tries to get free.

I throw myself over and start to crawl again. I taste like blood and panic. Thomas's hands are on me. He's trying to pull me out, just like he did weeks ago, the first time I was in this house. But that feels like years ago now, and this time I fight him off. He gives up on me and runs for the stairs, where my mom is yelling for help as the house rattles. The dust is making it harder to see, harder to breathe.

Anna, please look at me again. But she is barely visible anymore. She has sunken so deep that only a few tendrils of hair still writhe above the floor. Thomas is back, yanking and dragging me out of the house. I take a slice at him with my knife, but I don't mean it, even in my fear. When he pulls me over the front porch steps, my ribs scream as they bounce, and I'd like to stab him for real. But he's done it. He's managed to drag me to our defeated little pack at the edge of the yard. My mom is holding up Morfran, and Carmel's hobbling on one leg.

"Let go of me," I growl, or at least I think I growl. I can't tell. I can't talk well.

"Oh," somebody says.

I push myself up to look at the house. It's filled with red light. The whole thing throbs like a heart, casting a glow into the night sky. Then it implodes with a sick crash, the walls sucking in on themselves and collapsing, sending up mushrooms of dust and flying splinters and nails.

Someone covers me, protecting me from the blast. But I wanted to see it. I wanted to see her, one last time.

EPILOGUE

You wouldn't think that people would believe that we all got so incredibly beat up—in so many interesting ways—from a bear attack. Especially not when Carmel is sporting a bite mark that is a spot-on match for wounds found at one of the most horrifying crime scenes in recent history. But I never fail to be surprised by what people will believe.

A bear. Right. A bear bit Carmel in the leg and I was thrown into a tree after heroically trying to get it off her. So was Morfran. So was Thomas. Nobody except Carmel got bit, or got clawed, and my mom was completely unharmed, but hey, things like that happen.

Carmel and I are still in the hospital. She needed stitches and she's having to undergo rabies vaccinations, which sucks, but that's the price of our alibi. Morfran and Thomas weren't even admitted. I'm lying in a bed with my chest wrapped up, trying to breathe properly so I don't get pneumonia. They ran blood work on my liver enzymes, because when I came in I was still a shade of banana, but there was no damage. Everything was functioning normally.

Mom and Thomas come to visit in a steady rotation, and they wheel Carmel in once a day so we can watch *Jeopardy!* Nobody wants to say that they're relieved it wasn't worse, or that we all came out lucky, but I know that's what they're thinking. They think that it could have been a lot worse. Maybe so, but I don't want to hear it. And if it's true, then they have only one person to thank for it.

Anna kept us alive. She dragged herself and the Obeahman into God only knows where. I keep thinking of things I could have done differently. I try to remember if there was another way it could have gone. But I don't try too hard, because she sacrificed herself, my beautiful, stupid girl, and I don't want that to have been for nothing.

There's a knock at my door. I look over and see Thomas standing in the doorway. I press the button on my Posturepedic to sit up and greet him.

"Hey," he says, pulling up a chair. "Aren't you going to eat your Jell-O?"

"I effing hate green Jell-O," I reply, and push it his way.

"I hate it too. I was just asking."

I laugh. "Don't make me hurt my ribs, you dick." He smiles. I really am glad that he's all right. Then he clears his throat.

"We're sorry about her, you know," he says. "Carmel and I. We kind of liked her, even if she was creepy, and we know that you—" He breaks off and clears his throat again.

I loved her. That's what he was going to say. That's what everyone else knew before I did.

"The house was, like, insane," he says. "Like something out of *Poltergeist*. Not the first one. The one with the scary old guy." He keeps on clearing his throat. "Morfran and I went back, after, to see if anything was still there. But there was nothing. Not even her leftover spirits."

I swallow. I should be glad that they're free. But that means she's really gone. The unfairness of it almost chokes me for a second. I finally find a girl I could really be with, maybe the only girl in the world, and I had what? Two months with her? It's not enough. After everything she went through—everything I went through—we deserve more than that.

Or maybe we don't. Anyway, life doesn't work like that. It doesn't care about fair or unfair. Still, sitting in this hospital bed has given me plenty of time to think. Lately I've been thinking about a lot of things. Mostly about doors. Because that's essentially what Anna did. She opened a door, from here to someplace else. And doors can be made to swing both ways, in my experience.

"What's so funny?"

I look at Thomas, startled. I realize I've started to grin. "Just life," I say with a shrug. "And death."

Thomas sighs and tries to smile. "So, I guess you'll be transferring out soon. Off to do what it is you do. Your mom said something about a Wendigo."

I chuckle, then wince. Thomas joins in halfheartedly. He's doing his best not to make me feel guilty for leaving, to make it seem like he doesn't care one way or the other if I go.

"Where—" he starts, and looks at me carefully, trying to be delicate. "Where do you think she went?"

I look at my friend Thomas, at his sincere, earnest face. "I don't know," I say softly. There must be a devilish glint in my eye. "Maybe you and Carmel can help me figure it out."

ACKNOWLEDGMENTS

It takes a lot to get a story into the world. To thank everyone involved could fill another book. So I'll limit myself. Much of the credit goes to my agent, Adriann Ranta, and to my editor, Melissa Frain. You have both made *Anna Dressed in Blood* stronger. No book could ask for better champions. Thanks are also due to Bill and Mary Jarrett, the proprietors of the Country Cozy Bed and Breakfast in Thunder Bay, Ontario, for their hospitality and local knowledge. As usual, thanks to the street team, Susan Murray, Missy Goldsmith, and my brother, Ryan Vander Venter. Thanks to Tybalt, for being a good sport, and to Dylan, for luck.

And of course, thank you to the readers, of all types, everywhere. We need more of you.

Turn the page for an exclusive new novella
by Kendare Blake

DEAR ANNA

A Cas Lowood Novella

CHAPTER ONE

Dear Anna,

It's been ten years since you've been gone.

Well. Actually, you've been gone a lot longer than that. You were gone even when I met you. But it's been ten years since you've been gone for me. From my life. Though if you asked Thomas and Carmel, they would say you never left, that I never really let you go—even though I distinctly remember letting you go; I was the one who was on the other side, physically releasing my hand so you might be able to find some rest, but what do I know? I'm just a ghost hunter with a lifetime of knowledge.

Remember when Thomas was just a nerdy little witch who couldn't control his mind reading? Wasn't that nice?

I should start over.

Thomas and Carmel are great, they're still my friends after all these years, and they're still somehow, against all odds, together. And that's not the least bit sickly sweet and disgusting, except that it is, obviously.

They miss you, too. They are not—they insist—glad that you're gone. They just want me to miss you less. Which I don't get. It's not like I'm walking around wearing a t-shirt with your face on it. But ten years is a milestone. A decade, gone. And it's been making me think of you again, more than is usual. So Thomas, in his new age, self-aware, therapist-guru pose, suggested I write you this letter. I said, "Where am I supposed to mail it to, do you have a door to the other side hidden up your butt?" and he said, "Not yet, but I bet I could make one," because he's a new age, self-aware smart-ass.

But I'm doing it. Because ten years with Thomas has taught me that he's usually right. He was the one who came up with the idea for Low Frequencies, *the podcast we all do together as a way to monetize the ghost killing, the podcast that's kept us together through different colleges and new jobs.* Low Frequencies: A Podcast of the Dead, with Cas Lowood. *With words mostly written by Carmel, and produced by Thomas. We have some sponsors—not a lot, but enough that I can work gig jobs instead of trying to hold down an actual career. Killing the murderous dead is my career. I'm sure you knew that already. I'm sure you know that, wherever you are.*

Anyway, we have sponsors, and some Patreon support- ers, and you don't know what any of that is, or probably even what a podcast is, and I'm never going to be able to mail this letter through Thomas's butt so why am I bothering to tell you, but basically it's a recording of stories about my ghost kills. Or not the kills exactly, because no one can know about that, but about the hunts. The dead. We tell their stories. Solve their mysteries. Sometimes even officially—I've led investigators to bodies and evidence. It occasionally makes me a person of interest, but hello, ali- bis, plus lots of the murders happened before I was alive. Usually Thomas just does his "I'm a psychic, woo" routine and that's enough to satisfy them. You know people. They want to believe the easiest thing, even if it's not much of an explanation.

My mom's good, she's remarried. His name's Brad, and he works in life insurance. I don't call him Dad and he doesn't know that what I do is real, but he likes my mom's witchiness and he loves her like crazy, which is all she's ever deserved. So I like Brad. I also like that he's the one who has to live with her mean cats now.

Gideon is good, he's old, he was old when you were around, and I don't know what I'm supposed to say in this stupid letter that's going to make me suddenly stop thinking about what happened ten years ago, like I'll turn this page and close it like a book and

I stop. My hand must hover over that last "and" for five minutes, just hanging there and waiting to find the next word before I give up and almost crumple the whole letter into a ball. But I don't. I fucking handwrote it and I don't want to do it over.

I squeeze my temples between my finger and thumb, which signals the bartender that I need another scotch. I say thanks when he drops it off and he gives me a wink. He's younger than me by a few years and he's gotten to know us in the six months he's worked here. His name's Peter and he's dating a guy named Paul. The old guys at the end of the bar ask them where Mary is all the time and I think that's a joke my mom would get. Or maybe only Gideon. I asked Peter once why he works in this basement dive of dark green paint and yellowed lamplight, where the average drinking age is forty and things peak around six p.m. before the clientele trundles off to have dinner with their families, and he said that other bars were too loud, and he likes the smell. Plus, the owner doesn't mind if Paul comes in and messes around on the piano.

It smells like cheap cologne and the stale ghosts of a thousand cigars. Sometimes, it smells like a bathroom. But it's true about the piano.

The bar is called the Commodore, and Thomas and Carmel and I are regulars. It is quiet, and people mostly keep to their own drinks. Carmel can walk to the jukebox without getting overly ogled. And it's at the midpoint of six blocks from our apartments.

The bar's front door opens. I don't need to turn to see that it's Thomas because he gives me this little psychic nudge whenever he approaches—it feels like the way a deep-toned bell sounds, if that sound wasn't a sound but a feeling. It's hard to explain. I used to hate it, but now it's a comfort.

"Beer me, Pete," he says as he takes the stool on my right. Which is a joke. Thomas doesn't drink, a fact that Carmel and I have taken full advantage of over the years when we need a DD. Peter sets a glass mug on the bar and there's a small hiss as he uncaps a cold bottle of root beer. They make small talk that wraps up with Thomas taking a swig and doing his terrible "Ah, that brewski really hits the spot" bit before Peter gives him a courtesy laugh and another wink and heads down the bar to make Carmel's martini. She's never far behind.

"How was work?" I ask, and his shoulders slump with exhaustion, exaggerated but also real. Thomas is a teacher. Seventh grade. And he's a dorky one, though quite popular. Runs an IT club, and some youth robotics thing, both brave choices considering that his witchiness has a way of messing with electronics and making machinery go boom. But that's Thomas. Thomas takes the hard road. He takes his glasses off and wipes the lenses on the end of his necktie; it's raining out and they got spotty.

"I finally got Cheeto Fingers to fill out that application to coding camp."

Cheeto Fingers is one of Thomas's brightest students. She got the nickname after she was absently snacking while tinkering and gummed up one of the bots with gooey cheese dust.

"But I don't know if her parents will have the money for it."

"Well," I say, "we have the money for it. Or is that too weird?"

"It shouldn't be weird. But it might be." He rubs his temples the same way I do. "There might be some funds from the school . . . I'll have to talk to Pamela. She could maybe—" Thomas stops talking and looks up, sensing Carmel as she walks up the sidewalk before she opens the door. Watching the heads of the regulars all around the Commodore turn as she walks in is like watching a pack of dogs sight a squirrel.

"Hey, babe," she says to Thomas as she comes over and kisses him. "Hey, Cas."

"Hey, Carmel." I press my lips together as she shakes her umbrella out, flinging drops of water all over the lower legs of my pants.

"Are we just hanging at the bar or is there work?" Podcast work, she means. Which will require notepads and elbow room. A table. A little more privacy so we don't terrorize Peter with all of our murder tales.

"I don't know," says Thomas with a sly look at me. "Depends on what the next case is, and if we have a lot of research to go through or if we already know it."

If we already know it. That's another thing they want me to do, in addition to writing the stupid letter. They want me to tell Anna's story on the podcast. The story of her life as a teenager in Thunder Bay, Ontario. The story of her abuse, and her death at the hands of her mother and her son-of-a-bitch stepfather. We'll do it in a way that honors her, they say, that makes her more than just the spook of local legend. Anna, after all, is still relatively famous. And we should do it, because we loved her and we were her friends.

And because we're not the only podcast on the ghost and death circuit. There was already an episode on her from the hacks at *Uneasy Bones* last year, and when I heard it I almost lost my shit. They called her "Bloody Anna" and claimed she was a jilted teen bride, said that if you stood on the grounds where her old Victorian house used to be you could still hear her shriek like a banshee, and if you didn't wear an engagement or a wedding ring you could be snared by her curse. Which, according to them, would make sure you either never get married, or doom whoever you got engaged to to die— they couldn't even make up their minds about their own made-up crap. The murders of Mike Andover and Chase Putnam were barely covered as an afterthought. *Uneasy Bones* is *terrible*.

But as much as it pissed me off, I know that Anna wasn't out there listening to their shoddily researched and poorly produced podcast. I know that what the living still say about her doesn't matter. Carmel and Thomas want to tell her story because they think it a fitting tribute—that she deserves the same closure that we've given to other ghosts. But I can't make myself do it. Hers is the biggest story of our lives. It's the story that brought us all together and demolished an entire house. It led to us almost dying lots of times and many, many blood transfusions.

We never talk about Anna to anyone but each other. The truth of Anna is ours, and I can't help but feel that if we put it on the air it's just another means of exorcism. That we would lose that little piece of her that was ours to keep.

And just to reiterate: Fuck *Uneasy Bones* and fuck their awful, hideous voices.

They had the nerve to go to my old town, making up stories about my old girlfriend; they're lucky I didn't show up to guest host. They're lucky that Thomas didn't hex them (it's against his "witch code") and Carmel didn't punch them in the face (that's assault . . . and she doesn't do that anymore).

"I thought we'd do the County 12 Hiker," I say. "He was the last ghost before I came up to Thunder Bay. It could be kind of nice, you know? The ghost before the move that brought the *Low Frequencies* team together."

They look at each other. That couple-y look, where it seems like they're having a whole judgmental conversation in one long glance, and since Thomas is a bit of a mind reader for all I know they actually are. But I don't need his abilities to decode this one. *The ghost before the team came together. So why not the ghost that brought the team together?*

"Well," Carmel says, and then trades winks with Peter as she takes her martini off the bar—that guy's eyelids must get tired—before leading us through the Commodore to a quiet table near the back. "At least the County 12 Hiker was a guy, right? I'm tired of all these girls. Dead girls, dead girls, dead girls."

She slides into the booth and takes off the cream jacket of her matching suit set, and around the bar I hear the disappointed sighs of other patrons when she drops out of view.

"There have been a lot of dead girls in a row." Thomas is next; he takes her jacket and hangs it on the hook outside of the booth, then slips out of his own (shabbier and brown), and hangs it up, too. "But it's just that there are so many more of them."

He slides in next to Carmel and she runs fast fingers through the sides of his hair, unmessing the perpetual messiness. To unmess her own all Carmel has to do is give her head a toss: perfect, blond, umbrella-protected locks drift to her elbows.

"And doesn't that piss you off?" she asks, and bites one of the martini olives off her toothpick.

"Of course it does." Thomas looks at me, and obviously I agree.

Sometimes seeing all those dead girls' faces I feel completely useless, like I'm the cleanup crew, pushing a broom instead of wielding a knife. Being the one who has to put those girls to rest, to kill them again after someone else already killed them once, I feel worse than useless. I feel like a villain.

I said as much to my mom a few years ago. We were in Thunder Bay and I was moping, helping her make a batch of Saskatoon jam for me to smuggle back below the border. I kept dipping a sad butter knife into the last, half-empty jar of the previous batch and making that clinking-glass sound until she snatched it out of my hands. Then she asked me if I thought any of those girls would want to be what their killers had turned them into. If they would want to exist forever as the murderous dead, caught in a loop of rage, killing others like they were killed. Then she made me leave the kitchen and stop eating her jam.

"So." Thomas pulls a yellow legal pad out of his canvas backpack and jots "County 12 Hiker" across the top of the page. "What kind of background are we going to need? Do you have any notes from that summer?"

"I don't take notes." I toss a pretzel into my mouth. "Or at least I didn't back then."

"So Thomas will do background," he says, referring to himself in the third person as he writes.

"What episode goes live for next month?" asks Carmel.

"Eleanor Bixby," says Thomas. "The girl who was bricked up in the wall in Des Moines. We hunted her in June and then couldn't get around to recording until . . . September."

Eleanor Bixby. She was a challenge. She'd worked from behind the plaster, whispering to residents of the apartment building she haunted until she drove them to madness or murder, and when I got there with the athame she refused to come out. Thomas and Carmel had to put on hardhats and earplugs, and swing sledgehammers so I'd have a way in. Then

I had to go inside the walls and chase her. An extremely slow and dusty chase with a metric ton of mice for company.

"For the County 12 Hiker," Thomas goes on, keeping us on task, "by the way, what was his real name?"

I reach back through the years and try to think of that case, but most of what I remember is that sweet-ass car I used to lure out his ghost, and cozying up to our old neighbor guy all summer so he'd let me borrow it. And of course I remember the twenty minutes the hiker and I were in the car together. Twenty high-speed, burning-tires, black-blood, dead-face minutes.

"Robby something," I said. "No. I don't know. I can get you the stretch of road, and the year."

"That's not much."

"Sorry."

He makes a face—what I like to call the Thomas-as-Kermit-the-Frog face—but then Carmel runs a soothing finger along his Kermit-frowny cheek.

"Are we going to try and make this a special 'team-building' episode?" Carmel asks around the mouthful of her last olive. "Should we go down there? Record it interview-style?" The podcast narration is mostly me, but listeners like it when Thomas and Carmel talk. They say Thomas has a nice voice, and think it's funny when Carmel gives me shit.

"Might not be a bad idea, if Cas is this short on details," says Thomas. "Where would we be road-tripping to?"

"We'd be flying, sweetheart; I don't have time to road-trip." Carmel looks at me. "Unless it's in the Tri-State area."

"North Carolina."

"Get out your calendars, boys, and I'll book the flights." She takes out her phone. She'll book and she'll pay for them. Carmel's a project manager. We don't know exactly what that means. Well, I don't, anyway. She's worked at a few different companies, but the one she's at now is the most boring: software, or something. She spares us all but the most important details and any hot office gossip. I think she's bored by her job, too. But it pays well. Even if her family wasn't already rich, Carmel would be doing just fine. "How about next Friday? There's a flight out at four thirty. That's Thomas's early release day and I could leave work at two. We could rent a car, and fly back on Sunday at . . . noon."

"I'm reupholstering a living room set," I say as I start searching Airbnbs, "but I should be finished by then." These days I take a lot of gigs where I work with my hands. I've built baby cribs, rocking chairs, refinished old cabinets. Once I helped a guy build an entire tiny house. "Holy shit." I stop scrolling over a rental listing, and Thomas and Carmel lean in. "Wanna stay at our old house? It's an Airbnb now." I turn my phone to show them, a little Cape Cod house with a brick facade and a white-railed front porch where my mom liked to sit and have her coffee. Carmel takes my phone and looks through the pictures.

"It's nice. Was it this nice when you lived in it?"

"Not quite. When we were there it had wall-to-wall carpet that smelled like old cats." It drove Tybalt crazy. He'd stalk from corner to corner sniffing and snapping his long black tail back and forth, enraged we'd move him into a place that was so . . . soiled. But it was better for him than the next place, since the next place was Thunder Bay, and had the attic where he died. And just like I do whenever I remember Tybalt, I think: *Sorry I didn't listen to you better, little guy. You mean, bitey little fella.*

"That settles it, then," Carmel says and gives my phone back. "I'll get the tickets."

"It's like we're supposed to do it," says Thomas, in that witchy tone that makes the hair stand up on the backs of our necks. He does it on purpose, and Carmel gives him a whack.

"Don't weird me out, babe."

"What?" He rubs his arm. "There's not even anything there. Cas killed the County 12 Hiker years ago. This is just going to be, like, a vacation."

"A vacation in a boring town in North Carolina," I say, and sip my scotch. I wonder if Mr. Dean is still alive. I wonder if he still has that car.

"Cas Lowood."

The woman who says my name doesn't say it like a question. Like she's some curious podcast fan who thinks she recognizes my voice—which yes, has happened. We look up and recognize her immediately: long dark hair hanging over a long black jacket, light tan skin and big brown eyes that seem like they already know everything and wonder why you don't too. She's Olivia Ortecho, the host of a much more well-known podcast. *Blood Evidence.* It started as true crime and leaned into ghosts after an encounter with one in Boston, which, to be fair, was real. I know because I went out there and killed it after the episode aired. Other podcasts might suck, like *Uneasy Bones*—again, fuck you, *Uneasy Bones*—but sometimes they're a convenient source of ghost tips.

"Olivia," I say. "Hi."

She smiles, passing one smile around to all of us, and Thomas raises a hand and squeaks out a hello. Carmel leans forward on her elbows and says, "Olivia, hi. It's so lovely to see you." She smiles a smile of her own, one that I remember from high school. Olivia is pretty enough to make even Carmel's claws flick briefly out, before she remembers that she likes other women and the feeling of competition was instilled in her by the patriarchy. Thomas and I have learned much about the patriarchy, with Carmel as our teacher. Not that she has to be our teacher. See? We're good students.

"Would you like to sit down?" Carmel glances at me, a real "scoot over, you rude-o" look.

I move farther into the booth and say, "Yeah, Olivia, please sit. Have a drink with us."

She raises her arm to Peter, who is already watching with a bartender's attentive stance. "Can I get a Guinness draft, please? And I'll buy another round of whatever they're drinking." I hear his answering "You got it" as she takes off her jacket and hangs it on the booth before sliding in beside me. She shakes her hair back and shivers. "That rain is cold." Then she smiles at Thomas, still blushing into his root beer. "Carmel Jones, when are you going to take this handsome man's last name?" Carmel chuckles; she knows it's a tease, and rhetorical.

"Actually," says Thomas, "I'm pretty sure it'll be me becoming 'Mr. Jones.'"

"I still advocate for hyphenation," I say as Peter brings the drinks and sets them on the table. "Carmel Jones-Sabin, Thomas Sabin-Jones. I don't at all think it makes you sound like weird stepsiblings." Carmel throws a pretzel at me. I catch it. Eat it.

"Olivia," Carmel says, and raises her glass so we all do a quick clink-and-cheers, "what brings you to the Twin Cities?" Olivia is Northeast-based. Providence, Rhode Island.

"And directly to our regular bar," I add. Carmel gives me another look.

Olivia nods. "Never let it be said that my production assistants don't do their research." *Blood Evidence* is bigger than our podcast by ten times. Heck, maybe by twenty. She's got real sponsorship. She has offices. "Obviously there's no reason for me to come here"—she looks around at the dark green paint and dusty yellow light fixtures—"except to find you. And there's no reason to find you, unless I'm here on a murder and want to collaborate, which I don't, or to ask your permission, which I don't need, or—"

"Professional camaraderie?" Thomas suggests.

"In a manner of speaking."

"Are you recording this?" Carmel asks with another easy smile. "Or do you always draw out the suspense?"

Olivia looks at me. *They don't know why I'm here,* those eyes say. *How interesting.*

"Cas?" Carmel glances from Olivia to me. "Something you want to tell us?"

I lean back and fiddle with my drink, clinking the glass against the wood table. I should have told them, I guess, but there didn't seem to be much of a point. When I got Olivia's invitation a few weeks ago I didn't even respond. I ignored the email, figured she'd find someone else—there's no shortage of ghostly podcasts, no shortage of murder hounds. I figured I'd never hear another thing about it until the episode aired, and her assistants, or whatever, never even sent a follow-up. Yet here she is. In person.

"She's pulling a *Haunting of Hill House*."

Carmel and Thomas look at me. For a long time.

"Is the kid from *E.T.* going to be in it?" Thomas asks.

"Not the show," Olivia says, and grins. "Though that show was great. I'm getting a group of podcasters together to record a special episode. The recording would take place over a long weekend, and participation would guarantee a slice of *Blood Evidence* listeners. New subscribers, new sponsors. I would cover all expenses. And pay a stipend."

"What kind of stipend?" Carmel asks. She's always looking for ways to shore up *Low Frequencies,* so I could do it full-time one day, even though I have no problem building furniture or delivering DoorDash. Actually, I kind of like it. Everyone I bring food or chairs to is alive. But while Carmel is hashing out fees, Thomas is boring into my skull with his pesky psychic finger.

Yes, I think at him hard. *She put the money part up-front before she told you where we'd be going. I noticed that too.*

"Where is it?" Thomas asks, interrupting Carmel and Olivia's negotiations when he abruptly breaks off from our psychic convo.

"It's the Bowery Lord Fell," Olivia replies. She looks my way and her eyes take on a devious excitement that she pulls off so well it's almost impossible not to join in on. "It's a gorgeous haunted resort hotel in the mountains outside of Calgary. Think heated soaking pools, five-star dining, a spa—have you heard of it?"

"Everyone's heard of it," I say. But there was never any reason for me to go there. The Bowery Lord Fell boasts more than its share of ghosts: a few ghost brides, some haunted paintings, and I think some dead servants or some such that clank trays down empty hallways. Most haunted hotels claim one ghost. Maybe two. Stop being so greedy. A few guests have died there, like guests die anywhere, and some have died in falls on the property or out of windows. No lords though.

"Who else is going?" I ask.

"Well, it would be me, and my production team, and you and yours"—she cocks her head at Carmel and Thomas—"plus the *Ghostcasters*—" *The Ghostcasters.* A podcast of four that's half ghost hunting and half cosplay. For their intro they play the sirens from the Ecto-1 and say, "Get in losers, we're going casting." "—and the guys from *Uneasy Bones.*"

"No," I say. "No way."

"Those guys suck," Carmel agrees, and gives Olivia a regretful frown.

"Of course they suck, and they're hacks, but they consistently pull four thousand downloads per episode and just cracked six thousand on Patreon."

"We don't get anywhere near that," Thomas says. "So why do you want us?"

"Because you're . . . actually good." She sighs. "Listen, it'll be an easy getaway weekend. The hotel is partnering with us specially; we'll be the only guests for the whole three days, with full access to amenities and free rein to record. We'll take some audio of some ghostly stuff and tell the good ghostly stories, but also it'll be a cool chance for an episode about us. The ghost podcast community. This will barely be work, I promise. The hotel is pulling out all the stops since they want the episode to bring in visitors during the winter dead season, and I want a massage and a seaweed wrap, so please." She looks at us all. She doesn't say "please" like an ask.

I sit a minute, tapping the side of my drink.

"We'll think about it."

Sensing that's as close to a yes as she's going to get tonight, Olivia slurps down the last third of her beer and gets up to put her coat on. "I won't crowd you—just tell me by the end of the week. I'll need to have Jamie make your travel arrangements. You can all get into Canada, right?"

"We're from there," Carmel says, and she and Thomas raise their hands. They could have applied for naturalization off their employment green cards a long time ago but they drag their feet, like doing so would somehow rob them of their inherent Canadianness.

"Oh." Olivia straightens her black jacket. "Well. It was great seeing you. Carmel, Thomas." She looks at me. "Cas."

I give her a close-lipped smile and a half-hearted raise of my drink. Carmel says I'm a grump and I guess that's true. I don't like new people intruding on our space. I especially don't like them when they try to drag me off to luxurious ghost-themed resort vacation weekends—except when I put it like that I don't know *why* I don't like it.

Carmel cranes her neck, watching as Olivia leaves so she can give one final wave before slumping down around her half-empty martini. "Free five-star resort. Nice chunky stipend. And bonus listeners for *Low Frequencies*. Remind me again why we're not going?"

"It's not our scene," I say. "It's a waste of our time."

"So you don't think it's really haunted?" Thomas asks.

"No, it probably is haunted."

"So, explain this to me again," Carmel says with unamused eyes. "Why we will be flying to North Carolina and camping out on turnpikes instead of bouncing into luxury king beds while Thomas gets a seaweed wrap."

"It's hard to articulate." I shift in the booth, feeling the weight of the athame strapped to my ankle, and they both glance down. They know it's there. That I'm never without it, my father's knife, the knife of my bloodline, that allows me to kill the murderous dead.

Carmel nudges Thomas, a plea for him to help her out and get them to the resort, and he shrugs helplessly.

"So you won't be doing any actual work there," Thomas says. "But what's the harm in going?"

"I don't know. It feels exploitative. The dead there don't kill."

"Are you sure?" Thomas asks.

"Pretty sure. It's been since the nineties that anyone's even fallen out of a window."

"You sound almost sad about that. I think this job's making you strange and morbid."

"Says the witch tech teacher who dresses like John Constantine."

"It's. A look." Thomas grins and straightens his necktie, and Carmel grabs his arm to keep us on track.

"So the ghosts don't kill," Carmel says. "Don't they still

deserve to have their stories told? Who is the ghost, anyway?" she asks Thomas from the side of her mouth. "A dead bellhop? Business traveler who slipped in the tub?"

They try to convince me a little while longer, and it's fun watching them team up, waxing poetic about Thomas's spa treatments and Carmel's bubble baths and room-service wine, and what the hell, they do deserve it. Sure, it's a ghost-hunter puff piece and it's kind of a sellout, but after ten years of getting chased by the dead wielding axes, or jumping out of walls, or exploding into exorcist green goo that rained down upon us and required many bathings, why not go somewhere we can kick back?

"Okay, okay," I say before they can start another round of pleading and lamentation. "Fuck it. Let's go back to Canada."

Carmel, Thomas, and I stay at the Commodore for another few hours for some celebratory drinks. I don't know what we were celebrating exactly; I think they were toasting the end of my curmudgeonliness, and I didn't have the heart to tell them that it's only on pause. When we leave, we tip Peter extra to make up for our rather loud shenanigans and, like the good man he is, he makes sure we're okay to walk home, that he doesn't need to help us get Ubers or Lyfts.

I'm glad we're going. Maybe I'm even looking forward to it. What I'm not looking forward to is telling Olivia we're in. I feel like she'll gloat with those all-knowing eyes. I'll just email her. Maybe I'll just email her assistant.

As I'm wandering down the dark block toward my apartment, I spot someone waiting at the crosswalk. It isn't so late yet that it would be weird—except that they look like Olivia. Same black jacket and slim brown pants, and when she turns slightly I'm certain. But what's she doing there? She left the bar hours ago.

Oh well, my slightly intoxicated brain thinks. It's a stroke of luck. I can just tell her right now that I changed my mind. But before I can raise my hand and call out, her head twists toward me. I can't see her face in the shadows beneath the streetlights, but what I do see is that her hair begins to float.

Float—and drift like weeds in the water.

Like Anna's used to.

My legs move forward on autopilot as I try not to blink, and in the corner of my eye I register headlights, just as the girl in front of me steps backward off the sidewalk. I shout something, a name—Olivia, or maybe Anna—and dive forward. I manage to catch her and drag her back as the delivery truck splashes through the intersection, the bulk of it less than a foot away from smearing her all over the street. Olivia stumbles into me and turns around to scream at the truck in Spanish. Mostly curse words I think. I catch a few. Then she looks back at me and blinks.

"Cas?" She gives me a light shove and I move off a few steps. "What are you doing here?"

"I was leaving the Commodore. I didn't think you saw the truck."

"I didn't." She seems confused. But at least her hair is behaving like hair again. "I must've gotten turned around on the way back to my hotel." She makes a face, laughs a little. Shrugging off any weirdness, like I've seen too many people do. "I'll just get a rideshare this time."

"Where's your hotel?" I ask.

"It's the Max," she says and looks at her phone for the address. But she doesn't need to. I know it, and it's right down the street. I can even see it from where we're standing: neon blue lights casting onto the rain-wet pavement beneath a black canopy and a couple of potted ferns.

"Is that it?" I point.

She blinks at it for a long time like it can't be.

"Oh my god, yes." She smacks herself lightly in the forehead. "I guess I don't need the Lyft after all. Night, Cas."

"Night, Olivia." She starts crossing the street, but stops again, looking at the door of her hotel and then back at me like she's not quite sure if she'll make it. I don't blame her. How did she get lost out here for more than two hours? How did she not realize she should have been back already?

"Hey, Olivia," I say. "Since I found you, I might as well save myself the email: we changed our minds. *Low Frequencies* is in for the Bowery Lord Fell."

Her face lights up. "That's amazing. That's perfect." She nods and shimmies a little farther toward the Max, but I can see she's scared, and that she feels silly about it.

"I'll walk you the rest of the way," I say, and join her to cross the street. "I need to ask a few questions about the trip, if that's okay."

"Of course." She's relieved. The confidence comes back to her eyes. "My team and I are here to make sure it's all completely painless for you."

"Sure," I say, and remember black hair, floating in the breeze. Somehow I don't think "painless" is in the cards.

Chapter Two

The next morning I'm on the fence about whether to tell Thomas and Carmel what I saw. Or what I thought I saw. In the clear light of day, and without the help of several scotches, it seems like a trick. A trick of the light. A trick of my head. Maybe even a trick put on by Olivia for some reason, to lure me into her episode of ghost-pod community. I thought I saw . . . I don't know what I thought I saw. Anna? Anna's hair is not the only ghostly hair that floats. And even if it was Anna I thought I saw, Thomas is right. I've been thinking about her more lately. It's no surprise that my drunk, ghosted-up brain would take advantage of the shadows and the deserted street.

That's all it was. And once I decide that, it makes it perfectly fine to tell Thomas, so I text him during what should be his lunch period.

Ran into Olivia again after leaving the bar. Had to save her from getting hit by a truck

His reply is fast: What???

That's not the weird thing. She says she couldn't find her hotel for two hours, but it was the Max.

The hotel down the street? Thomas texts. He always texts with perfect punctuation. Because he's a teacher. I tell him he's a tech teacher and he should embrace the lingo.

Yeah
Thats still not the weird thing. The weird thing is before the truck
she looked like Anna for a minute

I wait. His response takes longer this time and I imagine him trying out a few different ones and deleting them before I get:

Wow, that's crazy. The power of the scotch?

I smirk and jump immediately into our familiar *Labyrinth* jokes.

What scotch

And he replies, The scotch with the power! And then, Seriously, though, that's weird. You OK?

Yeah.
My head playing tricks. Don't worry

But he will worry, and after ten minutes of silence my phone vibrates and it's a text from Carmel, because during those ten minutes he told her everything.

You ok? she asks.

I smile. They're a little mother-y sometimes, but I'd be lying if I said I didn't like it.

Yeah
I'm fine
Go do work

OK, she texts back. We can talk later

"We can talk later," I say out loud to no one but the chair
I'm reupholstering. Except we won't. This was enough. That
thing last night was nothing, though it occurs to me that I'm
shrugging it off like I always get on other people for doing.
But who cares, I can do it because I know I'm doing it.

And because I'm a professional.

I take out my athame and turn it over in the sunlight. It's
small and unassuming, the wooden handle warm and comfortable in my grip. Looking at it, no one could guess what it
does, or just how strong and sharp it is along both edges. I am
safe with it in my hand.

"And I would never use you to work on a chair," I say to it,
before returning it back to its sheath.

When we pull up to the front entrance of the Bowery Lord
Fell, Thomas leans across me like an excited kid to press his
nose against the tinted-glass SUV window. Olivia's team at
Blood Evidence flew us coach to Calgary International Airport and then sent a car, this hulking black thing with little
water bottles in the back and driven by a guy in one of those
kicky hats. Only Carmel is used to this and when the driver
opens our door I don't know what to tip him and neither does
Thomas, so he fumbles with his wallet while I go help with
the bags, in case we get the amount wrong.

"I only have American," Thomas says apologetically, but
the driver seems perfectly happy with that. He tells us to enjoy our stay and drives away, and we turn back to the hotel.

(342)

Or at least Thomas and I do. Carmel's been booking spa treatments on her phone since we left the airport.

The Bowery Lord Fell. It's enormous. We tilt our heads back as far as they go to catch a glimpse of the top. And there are wings. Huge wings. The thing could be a castle, and it's set atop a hill and surrounded by pines. They got a dusting of early snow earlier and the air smells clean.

"Why do I feel like we're walking into *The Shining*," Thomas says.

I smile.

"I wish." But really, good-looking as this place is, it has less the look of a hotel to me than it does an upscale sanitorium. So in the oeuvre of Jack Nicholson, this would be *One Flew Over the Cuckoo's Nest*.

"Come on," says Carmel, tucking her neck against the breeze. "Let's get checked in."

She leads the way through the expansive hotel atrium to the front desk, where there is no line, just a smiling young Asian man in a crisp white shirt and black suit vest. His golden name tag reads MERCUTIO and, as a person saddled with the name Theseus Cassio, I feel an immediate kinship.

"Carmel Jones, Thomas Sabin, and Cas Lowood," Carmel says as she leans against the granite.

"Of course," Mercutio replies. "The team from *Low Frequencies*. I love your podcast." Thomas psychically nudges me, and we're thinking the same thing: he listened to half an episode yesterday, like he did with all of the podcasts that would be staying. "We have you on the fourteenth floor."

The fourteenth floor. So, really, the thirteenth floor. I'm sure Olivia set that up, and my only hope is that in a place this big we won't be able to hear the assholes from *Uneasy Bones* braying through the walls. Mercutio gives us our room keys and he and Carmel talk a little about the spa. Then he points us to the east wing elevators. But not before he hands us a printed itinerary.

"Great," I say as I glance at it. "I feel like I'm at camp already."

"It's not so bad," Thomas says, studying it as we head for the elevators. "There's plenty of time padded for . . . *exploration*. We just have to be back down to the wine bar at seven for introductions and dinner."

Dinner with a bunch of ghost podcasters. It sounds like torture. But as we get off the elevator on the superstitiously misnomered fourteenth floor we still haven't glimpsed anyone else, and that at least gives me hope. It might actually be a peaceful, not-annoying weekend.

I go into my room, which is right next to Carmel and Thomas's, and immediately open my suitcase to grab the athame. I hate flying. I hate checking it. I clutch it to my chest for a few moments, and yes, I realize that my knife and I have an odd relationship. I look around; the room is nice, the bed expansive and outfitted with lots of pillows. There's a minibar I might raid for snacks later, and extra soap to steal in the bathroom. Really fancy, quality stuff. I might take more off the maid cart, if I can find it.

There's a knock, but not at the main door, and I open a door that I thought was a closet and find Thomas. Apparently our rooms adjoin. And theirs is a suite with an entirely separate sitting area.

"Adjoining rooms!" Thomas says happily.

"Yes, and one shared wall," I say, leaning in to peer at Carmel as she unpacks and hangs her clothes. "So no loud porking."

"I love it when you talk romance, Cas," she says. "You're a real poet. But don't worry; we can be quiet." She winks at Thomas.

"Ew," I say, teasing and loud, and shut the door between us. But I'm glad they're happy. I wish the hotel hadn't put us in an adjoining suite, but I'm glad they're happy.

I go back to the bed and flop down, turn the TV on just in case Carmel was serious, and the next thing I know Thomas is calling my name through the door. I open my eyes. It's almost seven. I fell asleep. The bed must really be comfortable.

"Coming," I say, and tuck the athame into the pocket of my jeans.

Together we make our way down to the first floor and navigate the sprawling spaces of the Bowery Lord Fell. The light in the place is hotel soft, yellow-tinted and low. Against the burnt orange rugs and dark wood tables it casts everything in what is supposed to be a comforting, drowsy glow but instead reminds me of a bad trip, the kind where you feel like your limbs won't move fast enough. We go through the atrium again, brighter and white, the ceiling trussed with thick wood beams. Mercutio's not behind the desk anymore, so I guess everyone's checked in. With us being the only guests for the weekend, the Bowery is sure to be staffed with a skeleton crew, and sure enough, when we get to the wine bar, tucked into a corner in the west wing, I'm unsurprised to see Mercutio instead behind the bar.

I'm about to order a scotch—I'm sure I'm going to need it—when Mercutio places three identical cocktails on the counter. They're served in short, rounded little champagne glasses and they're pitch-black. Garnished with a dark cherry and a blackberry on a stick.

"Our signature cocktail: the Bowery Bride."

"What's in it?" I take a sip. It's sweet and strong: alcohol, sugar, berries.

"Nothing too exotic. Vodka, creme de cassis, blackberry simple syrup. And a bit of activated charcoal, for color."

"Didn't one of the Bowery brides die of self-immolation?" Thomas asks as he peers into his glass. "Activated charcoal. That's kind of twisted."

Mercutio shrugs, and we take our drinks and tip him.

"A bride who burned herself to death." Carmel sighs as she stirs the black liquid. "Perfect. Another dead girl."

"But at least she wasn't killed by a man this time," I say as we survey the wine bar. "And actually, I heard that it wasn't self-immolation. Just a tragic accident with a candle and a lacy veil." From the look on Carmel's face I think she feels that might be worse, but she doesn't say more, just tosses her long blond hair back and lets herself be stared at by the rest of the room.

We're the last to arrive, and the bar is a group of familiar strangers: we've heard each other's voices, and seen video, but none of us have met in person. The jackoffs from *Uneasy Bones,* Russ, David, and Juan, are at a table in the middle: three guys slouched down in hooded sweatshirts with what look like the remains of three empty Bowery Brides. One of them gives me a polite nod. They don't seem hostile. They don't know I hate their guts. But they do ogle Carmel pretty hard and beside me I feel Thomas shrink.

"Don't read their minds," I say quietly.

He replies, "I don't think I can, there's not much there."

Carmel for her part, is used to it and so ignores them. She scans the room looking for Olivia, but while I see what must be part of her crew, she's not with them. The other occupied table in the bar is clearly the Ghostcasters: they're not in full cosplay glory but they are wearing t-shirts in the colors of their respective ghostbuster uniforms. When we look their way, they grin, and we go over to say hi.

"*Low Frequencies,*" says a cute, short Black girl as we approach. "We were hoping you could make it."

"Your podcast," says another Ghostcaster, a slim young person with a trans pride flag pin so I'll wait to see how they introduce themselves, "it has real gravitas."

"Like, *Dateline* gravitas," says a third, a heavyset boy with a charming smile. The fourth, another girl with a spattering of freckles across her cheeks and red-framed eyeglasses, says nothing. Just waves.

"Wow, *Dateline* gravitas," I say, trying to sound jokey and not like an asshole. "That's what we strive for." I call them girls and boys in my head because that's the only way I can think of them. They're all younger than we are, by four or five years at least. College kids. To them we're dinosaurs.

"I'm Alysha." The Black girl points around the table. "This is Lucy, and Gabe, and Adam. We all host, as you know, but Lucy does all the tech stuff producing. She's our resident Egon Spengler. And you're probably thinking that I'm Winston, but I'm not. Actually, I'm Ray Stanz. Believer, and serious scientist."

"I'm Peter Venkman," says Gabe, the heavyset boy with the good smile.

"We don't have a Peter Venkman," Alysha says, with a roll of her eyes. Then she glances at me and winks. "But we're always looking for one."

I like the Ghostcasters already.

"Well, this is Thomas Sabin." I gesture to him. "He's our producer and resident techie. So I guess he's our Egon." *Like I always told you,* I think at him, and he narrows his eyes. "And that makes Carmel Jones"—I look at Carmel—"our Janine."

Carmel takes this in stride and smiles, and the girl in the red eyeglasses kind of swoons.

"Oh my god, their Janine and their Egon are dating!"

When we seem confused, Alysha explains.

"Sorry. Lucy's a big Janine/Egon shipper. See, she—"

But before she can go into further detail, the lights in the wine bar flicker on and off. There are a few gasps. A few heads twisting around, before we hear Olivia laughing.

"I'm kidding!" She waves at us from the entrance, and makes her way to the tables. "Just a little bit of theatrics to get the evening started." She pauses as Mercutio arrives with another Bowery Bride on a small tray, then takes it and raises it in a toast. "Welcome to GhostPod Convention: Haunted Hotel." She wrinkles her nose as the guys from *Uneasy Bones* groan. "The title is a work in progress."

Behind her, the team from *Blood Evidence* has started setting up recording equipment, mics and laptops at the ready, murmuring to each other as they work, massive headphones over their ears or hung around their necks. The wine bar meet-and-greet is going on the record.

"I thought it would be nice if we got to know each other a little better. Have a few drinks. And each podcast could talk about their favorite case."

A murmur passes through the room, a rustling like feathers. We came here to share, to collaborate, but maybe now that we're here nobody's in the mood.

I know I'm still not. "And then what?" I ask.

Olivia shrugs. She's in a cream-white mock turtleneck and blue jeans, long dark hair up and secured in a bun. "Then we're free to explore. Tomorrow we reconvene to talk about the Bowery Lord Fell, and all the terrible things that have happened within its walls. Individual night recordings on Saturday, a wrap-up brunch on Sunday and we're out."

"I guess *Low Frequencies* didn't get the itinerary," says one of the a-holes from *Uneasy Bones*. I make a fist, and all three douchebags raise their chins at me. I notice Olivia glancing between us and there's a slight glimmer in her eyes. I wonder if she knew somehow about the animosity, and that's why she asked us in the first place. For the fireworks.

I guess I'd hate to disappoint her.

"You want us to talk about our favorite cases," I say. "We'll go first." Thomas and Carmel look at me. "Our favorite case was a string of murders in Thunder Bay, Ontario. Done by a ghost called Anna Dressed in Blood."

Uneasy Bones blink for a minute. Then they snort. One of them, I think his name is Russ, says, "You never covered Bloody Anna. We did."

"If by covered you mean fucked it up," I say.

"Cas," Carmel says quietly. Thomas though, seems right on board.

"She was never called 'Bloody Anna,' you dumbasses," he says. "She was Anna Korlov. Anna Dressed in Blood. And she was sixteen, not a jilted bride."

They start to laugh.

"She was no joke," I say. "She killed squatters and transients—"

"And supposedly two high school jocks," says Russ. "We know. We went there."

"There was no 'there' for you to go to. That house was gone already. The same house where Anna herself was murdered. By her own mother."

They're silent. They don't know how I can know that and I'm hoping they don't ask. And, I suppose, the house where they recorded was on the same land as Anna's Victorian—someone bought it and built something else. But it wasn't *the same*. And it sure as shit isn't haunted.

"So serious," says David, the most frequent narrator and the one with the high nasal voice. He nudges Russ and Juan. "This is why we have listeners and they have . . ." He looks Carmel up and down. "Funding by blondie."

"This blondie will cut you, you little punk," Carmel snaps.

Olivia steps in and says, "Okay, easy everybody."

But if Olivia is supposed to be in charge, she should have put that on the itinerary.

"Oh, come on," says Russ. "You know the real reason Lowood is here. It's not because of their shitty little podcast; it's because he's a murderer. He's a murderer, and you want it on record."

"GhostPod Convention," Juan adds, making sarcastic air quotes. "Shit. That's not the real episode and everyone knows it."

Carmel and Thomas look at me.

"How many bodies did you lead the cops to in the last five years?" Juan asks. "Six? Seven?"

"You're an ass," Thomas says, as the heads of the poor Ghostcasters whip back and forth like spectators at a tennis match.

"I may be an ass but unless he's a bloodhound that's a big damn coincidence."

Russ looks at Olivia. He takes his hood down so we can see his close-cut brown hair and the gauges in his ears. "But we're right, aren't we? You're not after the Bowery Fell. You're after Cas Lowood. *Blood Evidence* is a crime 'cast. You don't even do ghost shit."

I look at Olivia too. He looks so smug. Maybe he's right.

But Olivia only laughs. "I didn't think the paranoia would kick in until tomorrow."

"Look." Alysha leans back and looks at the other Ghostcasters. "Can't we just enjoy this plush-ass hotel, tell some ghost stories, and have fun? Drama, drama, drama is not our brand."

"Exactly," Olivia agrees, but I see her do a quick check-in with her team; she gets a thumbs-up for good audio. Drama may not be the brand, but it will be peppered into whatever comes out of this weekend. "Well." She sets her drink down and claps her hands against her jeans. "If we don't want to bond, how about we divide and conquer? This hotel has three prominent ghosts. Or," she corrects herself, "three prominent hauntings. The Brides in the Blue Thomasina Ballroom, the painting of the former owner of the Bowery on the third floor, and the servant hauntings of the kitchen and the basement corridor. I thought each podcast could explore on their own and discuss findings with *Blood Evidence* in the morning."

"Dibs on the painting," Carmel exclaims, and when I look at her, she cocks her head. "What? The spa is on the third floor and I want to take a gander." I roll my eyes fondly. If we let her, Carmel would record the entire weekend wrapped in seaweed with cucumber slices over her eyes. And if a ghost actually showed up to interfere . . . I'd pity them.

"We'll take the brides," says Russ, staring at us. "Dead brides is turning out to be our theme. And besides, we drank the most of them." He gestures to the empty glasses, the bottoms blackened by activated charcoal.

"I guess that leaves us the basement," Gabe says to the other Ghostcasters.

"Fine by me," says Alysha. "Basements are scarier anyway."

"Well, if anyone is disappointed by their selections, don't worry," says Olivia. "Over the course of the weekend, every podcast will have the chance to investigate them all."

CHAPTER THREE

The first thing that strikes me about the portrait of George Cedric Powell is that it's fricken huge. The figure, depicted in a gray pin-striped suit, is practically life-sized. It's disconcerting, and when we reach it we all take a big step back, because being that close feels rude, like we're infringing on George's personal space. Of course that makes it seem like we're giving him room to climb out of the frame and join us in the hall. But he wouldn't dare. With the athame in my pocket, I'd just pin him right back into it, like a butterfly in a case.

"Well, he looks," Thomas says, leaning in to peer at George's face, "distinguished."

"What's the story behind this?" Carmel asks. "Let me guess: children look at it and inexplicably start to cry."

I snort. But she takes out her phone and records a note: "To view the portrait of George Cedric Powell, the former owner of the Bowery Lord Fell that currently hangs in the third floor hall, is to be instantly reminded of mean grandfathers of times gone by."

Thomas, getting into the spirit, pulls her phone toward him and continues. "While anecdotal evidence of hauntings includes viewers fainting and the lingering scent of pipe smoke, here at *Low Frequencies* we postulate that the urge to get away from the portrait comes from the fact that George Cedric Powell looked like one angry old dude. Reported auditory phenomena in the hallway include the strange sounds of knocking, ghostly footsteps, and repeated orders to 'get off my lawn.'"

Carmel and I laugh and she stops recording. "So," she says. "Nothing real here?"

I step closer to the painting and put my hand out. It is, strangely, bare canvas not protected by glass. And if I look too long into George's eyes, they seem to rise to greet mine between blinks. Ghostly eye contact.

That little trick is pulled off by good lighting. The spotlights are arranged in such a way that they create a shadow across the figure's brow and cheekbones. Stare at it long enough, blink at the right time, and boom. Movement.

"If George is here," I say, referring to the hotel, "he's not here," I say, referring to the painting. "Or at least he isn't up for a chat."

"Good." Carmel snaps a few pictures of George and puts her phone away. "Then we can do some real exploring. Come on, babe." She drags Thomas away toward the entrance of the spa. He turns back and mouths, "Help," and I grin and wave, staying behind to spend more time with our mysterious subject.

"George, George, George," I whisper. "Why'd they single you out for this anyway? You seem like a perfectly nice old industrialist." I cock my head and study the painting. "Nice posture, clean fingernails. A very fancy cane in the shape of a—" I can't quite tell what the head of his gold-topped cane is supposed to be. A hawk, maybe? A wolf? His curled fingers obscure part of it.

"Well, it could be the murders," Olivia says from behind me, and I spin.

"Jesus." I didn't hear her come up. Damn these plush, padded carpets. I take my hand away from my pocket and the athame tucked inside. "Didn't anyone ever tell you not to sneak up on people in a haunted hotel?"

She laughs. "Sorry. So how are you and George doing? Getting acquainted?"

"I was about to invite him to my weekly card game, until you brought up the murders," I say.

"Yeah. It was a real shame. Old George's mistresses had a way of disappearing. Or dying. Two of them in childbirth, the virile old goat."

"That's terrible. But childbirth deaths don't point to murder."

"True. And there was the persistent rumor that it wasn't George at all, but his wife, Betsy." Olivia sighs. "But then, she doesn't have a portrait." She turns to me. "Having a good time? Where are Carmel and Thomas?"

"Checking out the spa," I say. "And I'm having a fine time, actually. Except for having to look at the dicks from *Uneasy Bones.*"

"Kudos to you for not taking the low-hanging fruit and calling them the Uneasy Boners. Though I do think that's what most people wind up calling them, eventually. Anyway, I know they're dicks, but they have listeners. *Low Frequencies* is good, and *Ghostcasters* is charm central, but I needed another podcast with clout if I wanted to make this worthwhile. I'm sorry if that sounds crass."

"Crass, practical." I weigh the words on my hands. "I get it."

Olivia turns back to the painting. "You know something else about this portrait?" she asks. "It's inaccurate. George Cedric Powell was actually Jorge Parada. He was from Chile."

I look closer. "I'd never have guessed."

"That's the way he wanted it. He instructed the artist to

paint him lighter. He wanted to be the white industrialist. For the good of his business."

"That's . . . a shame."

She shrugs and says something under her breath in Spanish. "That's the way it is. It was that for my family, too. My last name is supposed to be pronounced Orte-cho, not Orte-co. But everyone kept saying Orte-co, so my grandfather embraced it. He loved it. Said it was our 'American name.'"

"You could change it back," I suggest.

"Why? It's my name. And I don't have the energy to go around correcting people, either." She smiles at me, and touches my hand. "Hey, you sure you can put up with those guys?"

"It's only one weekend."

"Yeah, but I heard them downstairs calling you Cas No-wood, so . . . No actual fights, okay? Recordable fights, yes. Actual violence, no."

"The Uneasy Boners are safe from me." I narrow my eyes. "I promise."

"Thanks." She takes her hand away and sighs. "They weren't right, by the way. About me inviting you because of the rumors about your investigations. I know there's nothing to that, and so would they if they did any actual research. Anyway, I'm going to go find Thomas and Carmel. Make sure they're not trapped in the tanning beds."

I watch her go. I like Olivia. She seems really . . . capable. And she's not bad to look at. Is that why I thought I saw Anna on the corner? Does Olivia remind me of her somehow?

I close my eyes. I like and dislike people who remind me of Anna in equal measure. I like them because—obviously. I dislike them because there is no replacing her, and the thought that I might try makes my brain bristle up like a hedgehog.

Thomas and Carmel are right. I have got to get a grip.

I open my eyes. The athame rests comfortably in my hand, the yellow light glinting off the silver of the blade.

I don't remember taking it out. But there it is. The leather sheath has fallen completely out of my pocket onto the carpet, and when I bend down to grab it, the athame tugs. Or is tugged. My hand jerks hard toward the painting, and the canvas makes a terrible ripping sound as the knife sinks into it just beside George's pin-striped shoulder.

"Shit." There are times when that's the only word that comes to mind. "Shit, shit, shit, shit, shit," I say as I watch the knife in my hand drag around George's outline, like I'm trying to cut out a man-sized souvenir. How much is this portrait worth? Probably more than me and Thomas have put together. I grab onto my elbow, trying to take back control as the athame keeps cutting with that long, smooth sound—like a sharp pair of scissors through a sheaf of paper. It carves around his collar and arcs up around his head, and when the canvas slumps, the light changes on George's face and he looks pissed.

"Stop!" I shout as my hand is pulled harder and my fingers sink into the painting to the knuckle.

"Cas," Anna says.

At the sound of her voice I stumble back so hard that I hit the opposite wall.

My hand is mine again, and George stares out of the portrait at me, untouched and undamaged beneath his trick lighting. But that was her voice—Anna's voice, carried through a decade to land in my ear like I just heard it yesterday.

"What," I breathe. "The fuck?"

"What the fuck indeed," says Carmel, coming down the hall with Thomas and Olivia. "Are you okay?"

"And why do you have a knife?" Olivia asks. She glances at the portrait like she knew I was up to something.

"Family heirloom," I mutter. "I'm never really without it."

"Okay, that's weird," Olivia says. She doesn't know the half of it. She's about to ask more when we hear muffled, panicked shouts coming from downstairs. It sounds like the Ghostcasters.

We find them in the Blue Thomasina Ballroom, clustered in the center with the crew from *Blood Evidence*. They're still recording as Alysha, Gabe, and Adam try to calm a frightened-looking Lucy, who I keep wanting to call Janine. Uneasy Bones are there, too, standing around and craning curious necks.

"Is everyone okay?" Olivia asks, and hurries over to them.

"Yeah," says Alysha. "We just got spooked down in the basement."

"Spooked," Gabe says, and chuckles nervously. "Punning!"

They smile, and Adam rubs Lucy's back a little. She tries to smile too, but instead just bursts into tears. Poor kid.

As we walk over, Thomas adjusts his glasses and gazes around the space. It's nice, all cream and blue and gold, and the staircase the burning bride tumbled down is fantastic: broad and carpeted, with curving wood railings. It must have been quite the fall.

"This is nice," he says to Carmel. "We could get married in a place like this someday."

"In a ballroom where a bride burned to death?" she says, and shoves him.

"Ow, I said like this, not this." He rubs his arm and looks at me. "She's so violent."

"I can see how she'd be confused," I say. "This is the Blue Thomasina Ballroom. It's like it's already your ballroom." Like Carmel shoved him, Thomas shoves me. "Ow. So violent." We smile, and so does Carmel, only she also rolls her eyes. It's comforting to tease; it makes the air inside feel normal. But part of my mind is still on the third floor, with Anna's voice in my head, and the feel of the knife carving through canvas.

"What happened?" Olivia asks.

"We were in the basement recording," Alysha says. "We'd turned out the lights—"

"You know," supplies Adam, "for mood."

"Right. And I was reading the history of the servant ghosts out loud, like I always do, while Adam and Gabe were clowning around and bumping into laundry carts—"

"Like we always do," say Adam and Gabe.

"And all of a sudden Lucy starts screaming."

Olivia looks at her crew and gets another thumbs up for good audio.

"We couldn't see what it was," Alysha goes on. "But it was like she was being thrown."

"Thrown?" Olivia asks.

"Thrown. Back and forth down there. Except there wasn't anything touching her." Alysha keeps one hand wrapped around Lucy's as Lucy quietly sobs.

"I knew we should have called the basement," Russ says, and smacks David on the shoulder.

"Hey," I say. "Can you guys not be assholes for, I don't know, three to five minutes?"

Russ makes a face, and Juan gestures to Lucy and says, "Chill out; she's okay. She just got scared down there, which is kind of the point? You're okay, aren't you, girl? You're a professional." He actually sounds like he's trying to buck her up a little, and it kind of works: Lucy stops trembling and her color starts to come back.

"There," Juan says. "She probably just tripped over one of those empty carts. That's what you get when you go shutting the lights off."

"We had flashlights," Adam says. "And she didn't just trip.

I saw her hair move. It was standing up like somebody was pulling it, except there wasn't anyone there."

"BS. You just panicked."

"Then you go down there, bro," Gabe says, getting mad. "Let's see how you like getting your ass kicked in the dark."

"Or right here in the light, if you keep running your mouth," adds Alysha, and the guys from *Uneasy Bones* make a lot of *psh* sounds, but I notice that they do shut up.

"Well." Olivia puts her hands on her hips. "I'm glad everyone's okay, but this sounds like too good an opportunity to pass up. Let's get down to the basement to record. Any of you are welcome to join in; the corridor might get crowded but it'll open up in the laundry room." She nods to her team and they start to pack up to head downstairs.

"No."

Everyone stops. Lucy's voice is firm.

"No one should go down there." She crosses her arms and hugs herself, and Carmel catches a glimpse of something and steps closer. Gently, she lifts the loose fabric of Lucy's sleeve to reveal a dark bruise in the shape of a handprint.

"Jesus," Gabe says, and crosses himself. The bruise is already dark purple. It looks like it hurts.

"Get photos of that," Olivia says to her team. "Lucy, do you need medical attention?"

"Oh please, they probably did that themselves," David suggests, but no one bothers with a response. The handprint is massive. Far larger than could be made by any of the Ghostcasters, or by anyone else in the ballroom. Carmel, Thomas, and I trade a look as Carmel soothingly rubs Lucy's back. There are no dangerous ghosts in the Bowery Lord Fell. So who was down there with them in the basement?

Chapter Four

I never really explore hotels. Whenever I stay in one, I find my room, find the bar/restaurant, and find the front door. But hotels, especially old, grand ones like the Bowery, are vast places, full of spaces I'd never have use for. The spa. The soaking pool. The ballroom. Sitting rooms with cozy fireplaces. And this little cigar lounge tucked into the east wing that looks like the inside of a circus tent: all dark wood and white-and-red stripes. Thomas, Carmel, and I poke our heads in. It smells sweet, like old cherry tobacco, and the bartender inside gives us a cheerful hello as he wipes down glasses. I'm not exactly tired after my encounter with the portrait, and Carmel is clearly unsettled from seeing the bruise on Lucy's arm, so we shrug and go in for a drink.

"Tom," Thomas reads from the bartender's gold name tag as we sit down. "Nice to meet you. I'm a Thomas."

"A very good name, sir," Tom says. "Never a 'Tom' then? Or a 'Tommy'?"

"Not even when I was a kid. I've always been a Thomas."

The bartender, Tom, nods and sets down the glass he's been wiping. The cigar lounge is tiny; the three of us nearly fill up the bar, and I can't imagine how thick the air would be if any of us decided to actually smoke anything. "Well. What can I get you?"

"Scotch," I say.

"Bourbon," says Carmel.

"Can you shake me up a virgin Bloody Mary?" Thomas asks. "I need something spicy, for the nerves."

Tom says he'll see what he can do, and we turn away on our stools to get some privacy, or whatever privacy can be had in a bar the size of a bathroom.

"So what was that?" Carmel asks. "You don't think they could have imagined it? Or staged it?"

It had taken a while to get Lucy and the Ghostcasters calmed down. They were upstairs now, somewhere on the thirteenth/fourteenth floor, probably huddled together over mugs of hot cocoa. Blood Evidence and Uneasy Bones are still recording in the Blue Ballroom, having been talked out of their ambitions to go down to the basement. Or screamed out of them, more accurately, by Lucy's near-hysterical pleas.

"They don't seem like the kind of podcast to fake that," Thomas says. "And I could feel it . . . how scared she was. I could hear it, in here." He taps his temple.

"They weren't faking," I agree. "So what happened? There are no bad things here. Nothing but cold spots and wanderers in loops." I look at Thomas. "Do you . . . ?" I don't have to finish the sentence. Over the years Thomas's senses have attuned to the dead in ways that even mine can't—he's become sort of my new Tybalt, sniffing out ghosts. And sometimes if I drag a string across the floor he'll bat at it.

"Nothing," he says. "Only when I saw that bruise on Lucy . . ."

I know. There was something about that bruise.

"There's something about *her*," Thomas says, finishing our psychic sentence. "I don't know what it is."

"Here we are, folks," says Tom. He slides Carmel's bourbon onto the bar, ladies first, and then sets mine near my hand, and then Thomas's, a virgin Bloody Mary in a highball glass, complete with a stalk of celery and a toothpick of olives. When he set my glass down I move my hand and my knuckles brush his fingers. I hadn't realized until then. Thomas hadn't either, until he does the same thing: a light touch of contact as the drink is passed, and he stiffens when he knows what I know: that Tom is dead.

Don't say anything, I think, hard, and Thomas's eyes sink down to his tomato juice.

There's nothing wrong with Tom. He's harmless, humming as he goes back to wiping glasses, probably enjoying serving the first customers he's had in fifty years. Like most ghosts, like nearly every ghost except Anna, he doesn't seem to know he's dead.

And he'll go right on not knowing that, unless we point it out.

But here it is again. Another part of a growing mystery, another ghost who is far stronger than any ghost the Bowery Lord Fell has ever boasted having. One that walks, and talks, and touches—one who could leave a handprint on a small girl's arm. Something in me is beginning to suspect that Tom didn't exist before we got here, and even now, if we were to get up and walk out the door, we would turn around and find nothing behind us but the closed door of a broom closet.

"Are you guys having psychic conversations again?" Carmel asks, and takes a drink. "Because you know that's not fair. I—" She looks up and freezes. Thomas and I follow her gaze.

Tom is covered in blood. Covered in it, wet and red and sticky, from his slashed throat all the way down to the edge of his burgundy vest.

Thomas slips his fingers around Carmel's and squeezes. She turns to me with wide eyes; I shake my head.

"This bourbon is really excellent," she says to Tom, her voice smooth. "Really. It's just what I needed."

"I'm very glad, miss," he says, and it's hard to hear over the blood bubbling out of his mouth. "We don't keep many bourbons here. But then, you're not from the American South, are you?"

"No," she says, and even though she's a pro, it comes out as a croak. "I'm from Ontario."

"Is this you?" Thomas asks me quietly. "Is it the athame?"

Dammit, Thomas.

On the word *athame,* dead Tom hitches to a stop mid–glass cleaning. It would be like watching an animatronic break down were it not for the blood continuing to drip and his eyes, which flick to Thomas like he thinks he's the one who has it.

"It's getting late," I say, smooth as I can, and drain my scotch in one pull. I don't want to reach for my knife. I don't want to kill Tom. I don't want to do anything until I figure out what's going on. With a steady hand, I slide a bill onto the bar top.

"Very good sir," Tom says, recovering. "I'll wish you a good night."

"You too, Tom," I say as we get up and walk out of the cigar lounge. The moment we're back in the hallway I feel the air change.

"Don't look back," I order them, and Thomas and Carmel take each other by the hand.

Minibar, minibar, minibar," are the only words out of Carmel's mouth when we get to our adjoining rooms. Quick as a blink and in long smooth strides, she raids both mine and theirs, cleaning them out and carrying the goods to throw into a pile on the middle of my king-sized bed. She gestures at us to go for it as she twists the cap off a tiny Grey Goose and sucks it down like a baby with a bottle. I pick up an airplane-sized Dewar's and follow suit while Thomas grabs an Orangina and a bag of M&M'S.

"Dead bartender," Carmel says when she comes up for air. "That wasn't on the tour."

"Or on the itinerary," says Thomas. "What's going on?"

"I don't know. This place is haunted, but it's not our kind of haunted. It's not *dangerous*."

"Tell that to Lucy." Carmel free-throws her empty Grey Goose across the room to clang into the wastebasket and moves on to the one from my minibar.

"You okay?" I ask.

"Sure. I just feel like drinking." But it's more than that. Thomas and Carmel have been with me a long time. They've seen some weird shit. They've seen terrifying shit, far worse than this. But even non-psychic Carmel's senses are working on overdrive at the Bowery. Because there's something different going on here. And nobody likes a surprise ghost.

"Did you notice anything odd about that death display?" Carmel looks at Thomas when she asks that, not at me. "Anything familiar?"

He didn't. I can tell by the way his eyes light up now. But I had noticed right away.

Anna's death. A cut throat and blood saturating a white dress, painting it red. But not only that. There was always something strange about Anna's bloody dress: it seemed more than stained. It seemed like it was made of it. Made of blood. The blood on Tom's uniform had that same quality.

"I don't think that death was Tom's," I say. "I think it was Anna's, only I don't know how that's possible."

Thomas and Carmel are silent, and I wonder if they're having a little psychic tête-à-tête. Probably not; Carmel's made it pretty clear that her mind is off-limits. But I still know what they're both thinking.

I get up and drop my empty Dewar's into the trash can.

"I saw her again," I say. "Or, I heard her. On the third floor by the painting." I take a deep breath, knowing how this will sound. "I hallucinated that I was carving the figure out of the portrait, and then I heard Anna say my name in my ear. Like she was right there."

"That's why you had your knife out," says Thomas, munching nervously on M&M's the way an alcoholic would chew on aspirin.

"But it wasn't real," says Carmel. "The portrait wasn't damaged. And Anna couldn't be here—" She looks at Thomas. "Could she?"

"Anna is at rest," he replies. "On the other side. But there are clearly things at the Bowery that shouldn't be." He looks at me. "So I don't know."

I grab another itty-bitty bottle of something and crack it open without looking. Yuck. It's rum.

"I don't know either," I say, but I'm well aware that most of the evidence points to it being just me. I thought I saw Anna before we set one foot in the hotel, when I thought she was Olivia outside the bar.

Olivia.

The bar.

I look down at the miniature rum in my hand.

"We all drank Bowery Brides," I say. Could Olivia have put something in them? Some hallucinogenic to get things rolling? And at the Commodore—she ordered the drinks, but did she interact with mine? Did she hand it to me? I can't remember.

"You think it's Olivia," says Carmel. "That she's goosing the results of the weekend. But why? *Blood Evidence* is already twice the size of *Uneasy Bones,* four times the *Ghostcasters,* and how many times more than us isn't even worth mentioning."

"Maybe she put more into this than she let on. Maybe there's something going on with *Blood Evidence* behind the scenes."

"I don't know." Thomas makes a doubtful face. "I like Olivia. And I don't know what was in those Bowery Brides but I doubt it was strong enough to make that handprint bruise on Lucy."

"That's true." The power of suggestion is strong—a hallucinogenic administered in a tense, purportedly ghost-filled environment could do a lot, including the manifestation of physical phenomena—but that bruise. It feels like too much. I run my hand over my face. "Maybe we should just get some sleep. Figure this out in the morning."

"Sleep?" Thomas points to the clock. "It's not even nine."

The three of us turn, and kind of stare at it. How it is not even nine? It feels like half a day has passed since we met downstairs in the wine bar.

"Should we get some food?" Carmel asks. "I could order up room service and we can watch a movie." She gets up and dials room service, then hangs up and tries another extension. After a minute or so she puts the headset to her shoulder. "No answer from room service or the front desk."

So the restaurant it is.

Dinner was apparently on the itinerary, because when we get to the restaurant, everyone else is already there and seated. It's an extremely large dining room, full of empty tables draped in white cloth. All the tables but ours are unadorned, which makes the large communal table stand out awkwardly, set with candelabras and centerpieces of plump, white flowers with dark green leaves. Olivia is seated at the head and smiles at us, but the smile is uncomfortable. Maybe she didn't expect things to go off the rails on the first night. Maybe she's regretting not having us eat by ourselves.

I hold her gaze as we approach and she raises an eyebrow and gives me a "who knows but here we are" kind of expression, and I cannot imagine that she is the kind of person who would drug us. Carmel is right. She doesn't need to. And Thomas is right that hallucinations don't explain everything. Dead Tom wasn't only in my head.

"Our apologies for being late," Carmel says, sitting down as Mercutio pushes her chair in.

"You're doing the work of ten," I say as he places my napkin in my lap, and if he's annoyed we're late he doesn't show it, just smiles. He hands us menu cards and we order: I opt for steak, Thomas for duck, and Carmel the butternut squash risotto. We all order more drinks. Thomas is hitting the Orangina pretty hard tonight.

I notice that around the table, two chairs are empty. Lucy is missing, and so is David, one of the guys from *Uneasy Bones*.

"Lucy wasn't up for socializing," Adam explains when he catches me looking. "I'll just bring a plate up to her room."

"Is she okay?" Thomas asks.

"Yeah," says Alysha. "She had a soak in the tub and bundled herself up in one of those nice hotel bathrobes. She's bunking with me, and when I left she had built a small fort of stuff from the minibar and was watching *Jeopardy*." She snorts. "She'll be okay. Our Egon is small, but fierce."

"I can tell," I say.

"She was the one who brought us all together for the podcast, you know." Alysha sits up straight as Mercutio sets what he calls an *amuse-bouche* before her: a flat-bottomed white spoon bearing a small curl of raw fish on a dollop of something cream-colored, sprinkled with greenery and dotted with some kind of oil. "I don't eat raw things," she says, and passes hers off to Gabe. I only eat mine when Carmel gives me a look, but it's actually good. "Anyway, Lucy and I were roommates when we lived in the dorms, and she was a huge ghost nerd. Loved them since she was a kid. When she found out how into *Ghostbusters* I was, we really hit it off, and started the podcast. Gabe joined in from down the hall, and Adam answered our ad looking for a fourth."

"So," Thomas says to him, "that makes *you* the Winston."

"Pretty much," Adam says, and grins.

"See, I told you." Gabe prods Alysha with the tip of his fork. "I'm totally Peter Venkman."

"Only by default," she replies, and I laugh.

Across the table, Russ from *Uneasy Bones* clears his throat. "David went upstairs with a headache. Thanks for asking."

"Sorry," I say, in a tone of clearly not caring as Mercutio delivers the salad course. "Is he all right?"

"He's fine," says Juan, taking a roll and holding the basket out to Thomas, who also takes one. "It's just a hangover. He drank too much on the flight up." He makes a face, and I kind of smile. "David's a . . . nervous flier." I nod. I can relate.

I don't know what it is—our nerves, exhaustion—but for the duration of the meal egos and podcasting get set aside. Everyone just kind of talks. Laughs. Olivia and her crew aren't recording, and the stories we tell aren't about ghosts but the people we hunt them with. We linger after the last plate is cleared, and for a minute it feels like the weekend might get back on track. We pile onto the elevator with the Ghostcasters, Adam holding Lucy's dinner kept warm by a silver plate cover while Blood Evidence and Uneasy Bones pile onto the elevator beside us so Gabe and Juan can race the elevators to the thirteenth floor.

And then, feeling safe, we sleep.

CHAPTER FIVE

I dream of Anna. That's not uncommon. But it's become less common, over the years. Once, every dream of her felt like a visit. Now every dream feels like a memory. This dream feels like neither.

When I dream of Anna she is always alive. She is the girl I knew. But this time Anna comes to me dead. And not even that is right—her hair doesn't float like seaweed in the air; it hangs limp in her eyes. There is no power to her, no presence. She stands, like any other dead thing, before my closed door in the hotel.

I wake up and slide my hand beneath the other pillow for my athame just in time to hear frantic knocking. I sit up, already springy from the nightmare. How long have I been asleep? An hour? Maybe two? The clock by the bed says 12:00 but it's blinking, like it was unplugged and just woke up when I did.

I get out of bed, knife in hand but still in the sheath, and hesitate between the door that adjoins my room with Carmel and Thomas's and the door that leads into the hall. I don't know which one the knock came from. But the adjoining door opens first, and there's Thomas in plaid flannel pants and a gray t-shirt, Carmel behind him in a nightgown in the process of tying a robe on over it.

"Was that you?" Thomas asks blearily, and in answer, the

knocking starts again on the door to the hallway. It's loud, and strong, and ridiculously I imagine that it's her, the dead Anna I dreamed of.

"Cas! Are you in there?" Olivia calls. "Can you get up, we need some help!"

I open the door and she sighs in relief. She's still dressed, but she looks frazzled, her knowing eyes tired and red-rimmed.

"Good. Come this way." She leads us down the hall and past the elevators, toward an open door. There are voices coming from inside. Soothing voices that I recognize from *Uneasy Bones*. I expected worse. I expected screaming. Maybe because of how forcefully Olivia knocked on the door.

I peek inside, and Juan gives me a nod so we creep in. Quietly. At first I don't know what we're looking at. But the room has been . . . vandalized. Scrawling writing, in pen, in marker, in smears of lotion, covers the walls. It stretches grotesquely over the striped wallpaper. It overlaps on itself, making it impossible to read in some places. But what it says, over and over, in big script and small, is

We were asleep we were asleep we were aSLEEEEP—

And the person still writing it is David, working feverishly against the far wall as the writing moves onto the door of the balcony.

"What's happening?" I ask anyone. The hotel isn't going to be happy about this. Or then again, maybe they will be, maybe this was all planned and they'll leave it up for guests to take photos with. Olivia's assistant, Jamie, is doing that already, snapping away from all angles.

"He's sleepwalking," Russ explains. "Don't jar him awake; it could be dangerous."

"He does this sometimes," says Juan. "Falls asleep and

(370)

writes weird shit without knowing. Course he's never done it on the walls of a five-star hotel." He chuckles nervously.

Thomas steps up beside me, fully awake now and adjusting his glasses. "He's not sleepwalking. He's automatic writing. He's an automatic writer." Automatic writing. Psychography. Commonly used by mediums to converse with the dead.

"How long has he done this?" Carmel asks.

Juan shrugs. "Since he was a kid."

"How do you stop him?" asks Olivia.

"Well, he . . ." Juan stops, and we stare as David reaches a corner and stands there, his hands dropping to his sides. "He just kind of runs out of steam." Russ walks slowly toward him, and Juan says, "And now we just kind of very gently wake him up."

"Nobody knows this about you guys," I say, meaning David but also meaning *Uneasy Bones*. "You don't talk about this on the podcast."

"Nah. Only people from the old neighborhood know about David. But it's the reason for *Uneasy Bones*. People made fun of him when we were kids, you know? He got sent away for a while. When he came back it was better but nobody in the neighborhood forgot. So we took our boy and left. Started the podcast. Nothing serious, like, 'in your face, ghosts!' you know, that kind of thing." He breaks off to look at Olivia. "Are we going to have to pay for this?"

But Olivia doesn't respond. She doesn't seem horrified, or even annoyed. She whispers directions to Jamie about shots to take, angles to capture. Her phone's been out, too, and I'm sure it's been recording. I look at Olivia. I look at David. And I finally put it together.

Blood Evidence hasn't been the same podcast since they stumbled on the real ghost two years ago while investigating a string of murders. Ever since then there's been a desperation to their investigations, like they were trying to prove something.

Now we find that *Uneasy Bones* has been keeping a spirit writer in their back pocket.

And Lucy, from the *Ghostcasters*. She's wild about ghosts. Loved them since she was a kid. Maybe because she knew some.

I look at Carmel, and we look at Thomas, who feels it and turns around. I thought Olivia had selected *Low Frequencies* for this because we were good. Maybe, vainly, I even thought it was because she liked me. But we're only here because of Thomas. Woo-I'm-a-psychic Thomas.

I turn to the walls and the ghosts' repeated lament. *We were asleep.* Until Olivia brought three psychics in to wake them up.

Beside me, Carmel grabs Olivia by the arm. "What did you do?"

"I don't know what you're talking about," Olivia says and jerks away. She doesn't quite get loose; Carmel's got a good grip, but then Carmel lets go. With a small shove.

"You know exactly what I'm talking about. Why did you bring us here?"

"To record a podcast—"

"But why us? Why us specifically?"

Olivia opens her mouth. I don't know what she would have said, what terribly competent lie she had on reserve, but she doesn't get to use it. Because right then, a dead guy appears in the doorway.

He's big, wearing a black vest and a white shirt, and is maybe the bulkiest bellhop I've ever seen. Olivia doesn't know he's dead, and starts to make apologies and explanations for the damages to the room, and as I've thought so many times before, I don't know how she misses it. The bellhop's skin is gray as clay, and he stands like his legs and spine are the only parts that function. Then, of course, there's the smell he brings with him. Like wet, rocky basements.

"Olivia," I say as she steps toward him, but he doesn't seem to see her. Instead he charges right past, through the room, knocking her aside to barrel into David, sending them both crashing through the doors to the balcony and, as Russ and Juan shout, right over the edge to fall thirteen floors to the ground.

Russ races to the balcony and leans over, crying, "David! David!" and miraculously, I hear David respond, "Russ!" I race out to help and so does Juan, who shouts, "Jesus Christ— we'll pay for the damages!"

When I get to them, Russ has ahold of David by the wrist and elbow where he clings to the balcony ledge. His other arm dangles; I think it is dislocated. But we'll have to worry about that later—I need to use it just a little to pull him up and over. It makes him scream and I say, "Sorry, man," but he tumbles safely back onto the balcony. I look down to where the bellhop fell. He's there, sprawled on the flagstones. I watch him for another few seconds. He looks dead, but he was dead to begin with.

"Juan," I say, and he comes over. I point to the bellhop. "Watch that. And I mean don't take your eyes off of it. Got it?"

"Okay, okay." He nods, and I storm back into the hotel room. David could have been killed; he was only saved by his miraculous ability to cling to the side of a building like a bat, and Russ could have been pulled over after him if he wasn't careful. And while the guys from *Uneasy Bones* are dicks, I don't want to see them dead. Compounding my anger is the fact that the dead bellhop went for the psychic. So he could have gone for Thomas.

"Oh my god, is he dead?" Jamie shrieks. "Is he dead?"

I walk straight up to Olivia and get in her face. "Three

psychics in one hotel. Don't lie about this. What were you trying to do?"

"Nothing!" Her eyes are wild. "I—I just wanted the best chance. I had to know—if it was real. Or if I was going crazy." She shoves me away to pace and swear. "We've got to call the police. Why did a bellhop just dive over the fucking railing?" She's freaking out. She doesn't realize that may be the least of our problems.

There's movement in the hallway, and I grab for my athame but it's just the Ghostcasters in pajamas and robes.

"What's with all the noise?" Alysha asks. "We heard shouting."

"All right," Olivia says. The sight of the Ghostcasters seems to have calmed her, reminded her that she's supposed to be running this show. "Let's all get downstairs. We can call the police from the front desk."

"The police?" Lucy asks, and Carmel murmurs something soothing to her and kind of corrals them back out into the hall.

"David needs a doctor," says Russ, helping David up.

"We'll call that, too." Olivia presses her hands to her head. "An ambulance. We'll call an ambulance."

"What about this guy?" Juan says. He points behind him, down below the balcony. Then he turns back and does a double take. "Hey. He's gone. He's gone!" He looks at me with wide eyes, like I'm supposed to do something about it. *Juan, Juan, Juan,* I think irritably. *I fucking told you.*

CHAPTER SIX

Everyone stops off at their rooms to quickly throw on clothes, and then we go downstairs. The ghostcast convention has become a frightened and semi-wounded group of strangers who are trying to maintain their professionalism and cool during a disorienting situation. Olivia does it well. With something to do and goals in mind she's recovered that capability that I think of as essential to her, and helps Russ to support David as they make their way through the lobby to the front desk, fielding questions from confused Ghostcasters. Carmel and I hang back and let them do their panicking living-people thing while we form a kind of subconscious barrier around Thomas.

Olivia leans Russ and David against the desk and goes around behind it. She looks for Mercutio, but doesn't wait or try to find him before dialing. She tells the person on the line that there's been an accident at the Bowery Lord Fell. She tells them we need police and emergency medical services. She doesn't give the address because they don't need it, and says, "Uh-huh," a couple of times and hangs up.

"They're on their way. Said it could be about twenty minutes." She takes a breath. "Let's just go over there and wait." She points farther into the lobby, where plush white chairs and sofas await before a lit gas fireplace.

"Perfect," I mutter. "All we need now is some hot chocolate and marshmallows." I glance at Olivia. "And a few less duplicitous people."

She looks guilty, and Carmel says, "Cas." But I'm still pissed.

Olivia didn't know what she was doing, but her little experiment could have gotten someone killed, and now the place is going to be full of flashing lights and cops and they're going to question all of us and hassle me about my knife and I haven't had any sleep yet so don't "Cas" me, Carmel.

I steer clear of Olivia as everyone gets settled on the chairs and sofas to wait even though she keeps glancing my way like she wants to explain more, or maybe apologize. It's for the best. She'll have better luck in the morning after I've slept and doused myself in coffee.

Speaking of coffee, I peer around the lobby to see if Mercutio's left a pot out, but no dice. There's no sign of him anywhere, and I really do wonder if he's somehow the only hospitality staff working. Man, did he draw the short stick. Behind me, Juan walks to the fireplace and grabs the poker, brandishing it like a weapon.

"Hey," says Russ. "Don't have that in your hands when the cops get here, homie."

"Why do they even have a poker?" asks Alysha. "It's a gas fireplace."

"Ambiance?" Gabe suggests. "The illusion of authenticity?"

"But what are you going to do with it?" Lucy asks Juan. "We're safe here, aren't we?"

"Of course we are," Olivia says, but Juan rolls his eyes.

"If we're so safe then who moved that body?" He smacks the end of the poker into his palm. "I'm not putting this baby down until I see blue flashing lights."

"Maybe he just . . . got up," Alysha suggests.

"Girl, he fell thirteen floors. He's not just going to pop back up and grab somebody's luggage."

"Just—" Olivia interrupts. "It's not worth conjecturing about. Let's wait for the police." She turns to David, who's starting to look pale. "Do you need anything? Water? A blanket? I can go to the kitchen—"

He shakes his head.

So we wait. Checking our phones and watches as ten, fifteen, twenty minutes tick by. After thirty, Olivia growls and goes to the front desk to call again. When she comes back she says, "They had another call. They're still twenty minutes out."

"Another call?" Juan exclaims. "Do they not understand what happened? Did you not sound panicked enough?"

"I'm not panicked," Olivia replies. "Panic doesn't help. We're all okay. We're all safe here."

Man, she just keeps saying the wrong thing.

I move away from the group to peer out the front windows into the darkness, and Carmel and Thomas float over with me.

"Think the police can shuttle us over to a different hotel?" Thomas asks with mock cheer.

"Or maybe we can stay," says Carmel, with a look toward the third-floor spa. "As long as Lucy and David get trucked out of here and these dead folks fall back to sleep."

"I do not want to chance being massaged by a dead person," Thomas jokes back. "Cold hands." Carmel chuckles and leans against him as I continue to watch out the front windows, looking for headlights. But all that's out there is a whole lot of dark and nothing.

"These cops aren't coming," Juan says from the fireplace.

"What are you talking about, of course they are," says Alysha. But it's already been another thirty minutes.

"I don't want to have to call again," says Olivia. She looks at her smartwatch. "But how busy can they possibly be at three in the morning?"

"It's not three in the morning," says Adam. He checks his phone. "Did my phone not update?"

"Even if it didn't that wouldn't be right," Alysha says, looking over at it. "Mine says two ten."

Russ gets up and walks over to the front desk. "The wall clock says midnight. But it can't be only midnight."

Something strange has been going on with the time since we got here. I've felt it, speeding up and slowing down, winding back on itself. Thomas and Carmel look at me, realizing. Carmel says, "Shit."

Slightly curious, but mostly just looking to confirm my suspicions, I go to the front desk and pull the phone over. "When you called before," I say to Olivia as she and the others drift to the desk, "did you dial the police or emergency services?"

"I just dialed nine one one," she says. "I didn't know the nonemergency number."

I dial it again, and someone picks up.

"Nine one one, what's your emergency?"

"Yeah, hi, we've been calling from the Bowery Lord Fell. We had an attack and a fatal accident, and some of our party has been injured. We need the police and an ambulance."

"Yes, sir, those have been dispatched. They should be arriving shortly."

"How shortly?" I turn around and look out the windows. All I see is our own reflections in the glass. On the other end of the line, the operator doesn't respond. "Hello?"

"Hello. Yes sir, those have been dispatched."

"When should they arrive?"

"They should arrive in approximately twenty minutes."

"That's what you said an hour ago."

"I'm sorry, sir."

"What's your name?" I ask. "Can I get your name and ID number? For reference?"

"We've dispatched emergency services to the Bowery Lord Fell—"

"No, you haven't," I say.

On the other end, there's a long pause, and then the voice speaks again.

"If you and your party feel in any way unsafe," it says, "you are welcome to strike out from the hotel on foot."

"On foot," I say. The voice on the other end of the line doesn't really sound human anymore, and grimly, I am not surprised. We were never talking to the police. We were always talking to the hotel.

"Or," the voice says, "the staff of the Bowery will be happy to help you to depart."

I'm sure they would. I hang up the phone.

"What?" Olivia asks, even though her tone suggests she'd rather I didn't say. "What's going on? Why aren't they here yet?"

"That wasn't the cops," I say. I look at Thomas and Carmel. "We might have to find another way out of this hotel."

"What are you talking about?" Olivia asks as Thomas, brows raised, walks backward toward the front doors. They don't glide open at his approach. "So they're locked," Russ says. "It's . . . after midnight, or whatever. Maybe they lock."

Thomas turns around and tries to force the doors open but they won't budge. Getting scared, Gabe and Adam from Ghostcasters run toward the west wing to try their luck with the fire doors.

"These won't open either!" Gabe shouts across the atrium.

I walk over to Thomas to try and help, and Juan says, "Screw this. Back up." He raises the fireplace poker like a baseball bat. "What's the difference, right? We already trashed the room." He swings against the glass, and it doesn't even wobble. It's like he swung at the pavement. And seeing that—the impossible, nonsensical physics of that—cues panic in everyone. We bang against the doors and yank on them; we shout like anyone is out there to hear us call for help.

And the hotel replies. A terrible, high-pitched scream erupts from somewhere on the upper floors and grows louder as it falls toward us until a body strikes the pavement just in front of the main doors.

Alysha, Olivia, and even Carmel scream. Lucy starts to freak out and cry, and Alysha hugs her tight. "This isn't funny, this isn't funny," she shrieks, but it kind of is.

"That's very cute," I say loudly to the hotel. And to the others, "It's showing us the way out. No doors, but we're welcome to throw ourselves from a window."

I back up and start to pace. "The hotel won't let us leave," I say, perhaps a little manic. "It's tired of so many visitors coming to abuse its hot water supply and make off with its fancy toiletries. It's sealed the exits. It's messing with time."

"Cas," Carmel says. "What does that mean?"

"It means," I say, taking the athame out and drawing it sharply from its sheath, "that I am going to have to kill a lot of dead shit."

CHAPTER SEVEN

We start in the basement. The corridor that leads to the laundry room where Lucy was attacked.

Not everyone is with us as Carmel, Thomas, and I traverse the shadowy, fluorescent-lit corridor. My heroic declaration in the atrium was met with mostly snorts and eye rolls. Only Alysha and, surprisingly, Lucy elected to come. They walk along behind us, Alysha with her arm around Lucy, Lucy hiding in the crook of Alysha's shoulder while Alysha tries to keep a brave face on. She's tough, that girl. And a true Ray Stanz believer, like she said. She was also practical enough to grab a flashlight, the heavy-duty kind that security guards carry that can easily double as a weapon.

"Just how did the staff members die down here?" Carmel asks.

"Lots of different ways," Alysha says. "A heart attack next to the washing machines, a bellhop and a bartender who came down here with a guest and OD'd, and one of the maids died in a fall down those stairs we just walked down."

"I wish I would have known that," I say. "It's always good to know when you need to be ready for a disembodied shove."

"Well, if you had done your research," Alysha says archly.

"I didn't think I had to. There was nothing here." Nothing actively dangerous anyway, until three psychics and a knife that kills the dead dropped by for a visit. I glance back to check on Lucy. I'm glad she came. I didn't want her and David clustered together out of my sight. Hopefully with just him everybody else is safe up there. But if they're not, the hotel is quiet; we might be able to hear them screaming.

"So," Alysha says. "You're like, a real for-real ghost hunter."

"Yep."

"And you two are what? His ghost-hunting posse?" She looks at Carmel and Thomas and then eyes my athame. "And he's the only one with one of those? Doesn't seem fair to me."

"Unfortunately it's the only one of those in existence," Carmel says, and wrinkles her nose at me. "Well, one of two, I guess."

"Believe me," says Thomas. "If proton packs worked, I'd build a few." He pushes his glasses up with his index finger, and the Ghostcasters smile. "But to be fair, Carmel's a real whiz with an aluminum bat."

"A whiz," Lucy says, blushing. I can tell she sees him as Egon Spengler and has developed a kind of crush. "You really do sound like a middle school teacher."

We've reached the part of the corridor where it broadens into the laundry room. Around us, industrial washers and dryers sit idle, a few with doors slightly ajar. The space is washed with cold artificial light and the linoleum down here is pale green, like in an old hospital or, yes, like a laundry room. Overhead, the lights flicker and Lucy whimpers. I breathe and catch a hint of smoke.

"Did anybody die in a fire?" I ask.

"Yeah," Alysha says suspiciously. "Two guys from the cleaning staff got trapped down here when a dryer caught fire."

"I think that's what got me before." Lucy touches her arm. "When it grabbed me. It felt hot." Not hot enough to burn, thankfully. The bruise was just a bruise.

"Well," I say, "I definitely smell smoke."

"Me too," says Carmel, and I tighten my grip on the knife.

"No, no, that's me," says Juan, stepping out of the shadows behind us, and we all jump. "I was vaping."

"Who vapes a flavor that smells like smoke?" Alysha asks, and gives him a look.

"Someone who wants the smoking experience to be authentic," Juan replies. "I changed my mind after you left. Wanted to come down and help." He grins. "Or see if you were serious."

I lower the athame, which I'd raised, ready to stab any dead thing that came right through the eye. But it's only Juan, shrouded in vape smoke and still carrying the fireplace poker from upstairs. And behind him, I see the shapes of David and Russ, also coming to join in the fun.

"Fine," I say, "but if the Uneasy Boners are going to come along they all need to stay out of my way."

"No, it's just me. David's arm's broke, and Russ wanted to stay with David. I was the only one with a weapon." Juan raises the poker and I look behind him again, just in time to realize that the shapes aren't David and Russ, and for the scent of smoke and burning skin to hit me full in the face.

"Down!" I shout, and Juan cries, "What are you doing?" as I rush him and grab his shoulder to pull him out of the way just as one of the dead staff members emerges from the dark with cracked, charred fingers. He swings, missing Juan but hitting me, and I feel the familiar lightness of flight and then the impact of myself against the sides of the industrial dryers. I kind of thought I'd bounce right off with a semi-comical *dong*, but no luck. It hurts. I'm also very slightly on fire where the ghost touched me.

"Gotcha, gotcha, gotcha," Thomas says, kneeling as he whacks me repeatedly to put out the flames.

"What the hell, what the hell?" is all Juan seems capable of saying, as the two burnt dead men advance into the laundry room. He hasn't even managed one swing of his fireplace poker. Not that I entirely blame him. The ghosts are grisly, only partially burned, on their hands and up the shoulders. Their palms are the worst, practically melted, the flesh hanging off like they grabbed on to something far too hot trying to escape.

Lucy and Alysha are screaming their heads off until Carmel steps up and says, "May I?"

She deftly takes Alysha's flashlight and swings up hard, connecting with the first ghost's jaw hard enough to flip him over backward.

"Cas," she shouts, "you coming?"

"As soon as I'm done being on fire," I grumble as Thomas helps me up. But once I'm on my feet I feel the familiar click of the hunt, a satisfying sensation like snapping two Legos together. The knife in my hand feels like it was fused there and can never be dropped. I stab the first ghost in the stomach before he can get up after Carmel's shellacking, and he dissolves into ash. I bob and weave a little with the second as he tries to restart my fire, but eventually the tip of the athame sinks into his neck, and he's ash just like the first. Both go without much argument, and without a cry—I'm eye to eye with the second one as he disintegrates and the look that comes into his at the last seems like relief. Like he thinks he's being put back to sleep. But the athame doesn't put ghosts to sleep. It sends them on, takes them off this plane, and I just have to hope that's what he'd prefer.

I wipe the blade off on the leg of my jeans.

"What was that?" Juan asks, and Carmel and I deflate. It's been a long time since we've had to explain what I do to somebody, but somehow when he asks it feels wearying, like we do it every Tuesday.

Luckily, it's Alysha to the rescue.

"Haven't you been paying attention?" she asks, and takes back her flashlight. "He hunts ghosts. Like, for real. And banishes them with that—" She points to the athame. Then she smacks Juan on the shoulder. "Keep up."

I smile at her and Thomas chuckles. And then, up the stairs and far away, a lobby's worth of podcasters begin to scream.

We rush into the atrium still slightly singed and discover that the other podcasters have welcomed a plus-one: a dead man, bloated and purple at the edges, shuffles toward them with his hands outstretched. He's soaking wet, and a runner of black blood trails down his shoulder from the back of his cracked skull. As a bonus, he's also completely naked.

"What is that?" screeches Jamie, Olivia's production assistant.

"That's Fred Lavelle," Alysha supplies, stepping up beside me. "A guest who died in the seventies after slipping in the bathtub."

"Are all hotels such death traps?" Carmel asks. "Thomas, we're installing shower stickies as soon as we get home."

I start to move forward for what should be an easy kill— the ghost is entirely fixated on the group of people in front of him. The poor schlub keeps muttering about how cold the water is and asking if someone can warm it up. Of course, he's staring at Olivia when he says that part, so it's not all great, but I'll cut him some slack since he died fifty years ago. But before I can raise the athame, Russ says, "David, can you talk to him?"

"What do you mean, talk to him? What am I supposed to say?"

"Ask him if he wants a rubber duckie." Alysha shoves me. "Come on, Cas. He's kind of . . . making me sad."

Me too, and talking to the dead has never seemed to do much good, except for with Anna. But then again, I'm not David. David's a spirit writer; he's been communicating with the dead his whole life.

I look at him and nod.

"Okay." David swallows. He raises his unbroken arm, palm out and shaking. "Okay, man. Hey. It's okay, all right?"

"It's cold. The water."

"I know. I'm gonna see what we can do about that, okay?" He backs up a step, along with Russ, Olivia, and her crew, as the ghost keeps hitching forward. Every step of his feet against the floor kind of squelches, like his skin has gone spongy. Jamie and Olivia keep glancing at them, flinching, expecting the sides of his feet to split open. If they do, someone's going to barf. Come on, David.

"Do you know what's going on here?" David asks. "Do you know why you're not . . . sleeping?"

"I was in the bath. It was warm." He steps closer. David, curious, reaches forward, and I know he's wondering if his fingers will pass right through.

"Don't touch them," I caution. "It can go bad when you touch them." But if he hears my warning he does it anyway. Which figures. I did it too, the first time.

At the weight of David's hand on his shoulder, Fred Lavelle comes fully awake. The shambling, soggy slowness disappears, and his waterlogged fingers close around David's wrist.

"Shit!" David shouts, and I dart forward. So does Russ, grabbing the ghost's hand to pry it off. The drowned head jerks toward him, and behind me I hear Thomas quietly breathe, "No, ew," before the ghost opens his jaw and spews a torrent of water and black blood all over Russ. I slide up behind them and sink the athame deep, deep between Fred Lavelle's ribs. I wait just long enough for him to lean back and moan before

I jump back out, and he pops like a balloon, the juice of him spraying across the floor and a little on our shoes.

For a moment, David, Russ, and Olivia and her crew stand wide-eyed and frozen. Then Russ points at me, several feet away.

"You knew," he says. "You knew he was going to explode!"

"I guessed, after what he did to you." I gesture to his whole torso, dripping with black filth. "Also, I'd describe it more as a bursting. If he'd exploded he'd have gotten all of us no matter how far I jumped."

"What . . ." Jamie asks, her eyes shining, ". . . was that?"

"That was Fred Lavelle, I told you." Alysha puts her hand on her hip. "And I don't want to imply anything so I'm just going to ask—are the Ghostcasters the only ones who do any kind of research?"

"I know who Fred Lavelle was," Jamie snaps. "We ran down every death on the grounds months ago, suspicious or not. But Fred Lavelle died in 1972. So who the fuck was that?" She points at the pool of mushy goo, already drying and sticking to the floor. Olivia takes her by the shoulders.

"You know what it was," she says gently. "It's what we thought. Same as what we saw in Boston."

"This is not the same," Jamie whispers. "Not the same."

And it's not. It's worse. It's a hotel full of the dead, who've been woken up. But why did they wake up murderous? I get being cranky, but the murderous dead are usually special cases. They've usually been murdered themselves. Sure, there are exceptions, but this many?

"This doesn't make any sense," I say quietly. I look at Thomas and Carmel. "Every ghost we've seen tonight has come straight for us."

"Ghosts," Gabe says and chuckles. "I can't believe we're talking about this like they're real."

"Gabe, look at your shoes." Lucy points. "You just got slimed and you still don't get it?"

"Save the disbelief for later," says Carmel, and now everyone is listening. "Cas is right. None of these ghosts were killers. Not even the ones who were already active. And none of them were murdered, right?" She looks at Alysha, who shakes her head.

"Not that we know of."

"This is such bullshit!" Russ shouts. He turns around to rattle the doors, which are still sealed shut and unbreakable.

"So why are they so pissed?" Carmel asks. "It can't just be because we woke them up."

Across the room, David cradles his arm and crouches over the stain of Fred Lavelle.

"What if we'd just gotten him some hot water?" he asks.

"It wouldn't have mattered," I say. "He wouldn't have been able to feel it. No matter what he said, hot water wasn't what he really wanted."

"Then what did he want?" asks Olivia.

Thomas shrugs. "To not be dead."

The phone rings, shrill and sudden, and we all jump. After we're back in our skins, Olivia goes behind the desk and picks it up, placing it to her ear gingerly.

"Hello?"

She pauses. Then she holds the phone out to me. "It's the hotel."

I take it. "Are you ready to let us out yet?"

"If you want out," it rasps, "you'll have to get through every last one of us."

I sigh. I want to tell it I'm jet-lagged. That my friends were counting on a massage. I want to ask it if we can cut a deal, a BOGO maybe, that I'll kill one more, and it can have Russ. What I say instead is, "Fine by me," and hang up.

"Well?" Carmel asks.

"If we want out, we have to clear the hotel." I look around. There's a lot of swallowing and shifting feet. But Alysha slaps the head of her flashlight into the palm of her hand and nods. "Then let's get going," she says, and behind her, Gabe grabs one of the wooden chairs and dashes it against the wall, breaking it into pieces.

"Dude," says Juan. "You're a real beast."

"A beast who doesn't want to miss brunch tomorrow." Gabe picks through the broken chair and hands a sharp piece to Adam, who tests the point with his finger. Then he grabs a sturdy leg for himself.

"Wait, wait, wait." Adam pulls out his phone. "Playlist!" He touches the screen and the theme from *Ghostbusters* erupts through the atrium. The Ghostcasters laugh, and Thomas widens his eyes at me and mouths, "What the fuck?"

I shrug. Whatever makes them less afraid.

"Fuck it," says Russ. He wipes the last of the black from his neck and walks to Gabe for another chair leg. "Let's do it."

"As long as you know—" I hold up the athame, and Adam pauses the music. "This is the only thing that will put them down. No proton packs, no fire pokers. These ghosts are not screwing around. We go together, and we go careful."

"We'll set them up, you knock them down," says Juan.

I look at Thomas and Carmel. They know I don't involve civilians in our business. They know I don't like it. But what choice do we have?

Olivia goes behind the desk and rifles through it. She comes back with a letter opener and hands it to Jamie. "You ready?" Olivia asks.

"I guess so," I say.

"Then cue the music montage."

CHAPTER EIGHT

What follows is precisely what I expect: a slapdash, disorganized hunt that consists of me, Thomas, and Carmel out front with the rest of the podcasters creeping along behind us in a terrified, watchful crouch. Sometimes Alysha grips my arm without realizing it, and I think I feel Jamie's letter opener jabbing me in the back. I feel like the driver of the world's most frightened and least prepared clown car.

But they do surprise me, with both enthusiasm and ability: we hit the first ghost in the second-floor hallway and Gabe and Juan jump it without hesitation, beating it to the carpet with their chair leg and fireplace poker so all I have to do is stab it through the heart. As we exit the elevator on the third floor, even little Lucy gets into the spirit, grabbing a dead bellhop in some kind of judo hold, his throat bared for me to cut.

"That was kind of grisly," she says, rubbing her hands on her skirt. "Does doing this stuff all the time like, mess with your mental well-being?"

"Probably." I turn to the rest of the podcasters, standing before the elevator, which David holds open with his good arm. "So what's the report on the third floor?"

"No deaths in particular," says Jamie. "Just the painting."

Ah yes, the painting of George Cedric Powell, the wealthy industrialist builder of the Bowery, hanging around the corner down the hall, just short of the spa. "Thomas, Olivia, and I will do a sweep," I say. "Carmel, stay with the rest, and don't let the psychics bunch together." I twirl my finger at David and Lucy as Thomas and Olivia start down the corridor. Carmel rolls her eyes as from down the hall comes a distinct rip. A sound a recognize. I heard it before, in my hallucination in front of the painting. When Anna took my hand and guided my knife right through the canvas to cut George Cedric Powell out of the frame. "Stop," I say, but Thomas already has. Around the corner the ripping sound continues before it abruptly ends, and in the next moment something tall and slender walks into our field of vision. I blink hard as the piece of torn canvas turns.

"Get it," Alysha whispers as the cut figure watches us, slowly testing out its newly free canvas arms and legs. "Cas, go get it."

"Get what?" I say back. "That's not a ghost, that's a piece of paper."

At the end of the hall, the canvas figure shifts into what can only be described as a predatory stance. I still don't quite believe what I'm looking at.

"Get back in the elevator," I say calmly.

Thomas lifts a foot, and down the hall, the thing's head twists thinly toward him and it starts to scramble across the carpet, all papery legs and arms. It emits this awful, hungry screech as it comes, and I don't care if I don't believe it, I'm shouting, "Nope, nope, nope," and shoving everyone back through the doors as they scream.

"Close the door, close the door!" Gabe cries.

David cries back, "I'm trying!"

Watching the canvas race toward the shutting doors is like watching a very fast, angry spider, and I hold the athame in front of me as it jumps. The doors of the elevator close with only inches to spare.

(391)

On the elevator, everyone gives a collective shudder and one more cleansing scream as the floor lights go by.

"So no more third floor," I say, and there are no arguments.

We clear the rest of the hotel with increasing precision, and by the time we're down to the Bowery Brides we've achieved a kind of team cohesion: the podcasters have formed lines of ghost hunters like lines on a hockey team, and I deploy them like a coach, sending Carmel, Olivia, and Russ, then Gabe, Juan, and Thomas, subbing Adam for Alysha when she gets blood in her eye from a dead maid. We're so efficient by the time we hit the Blue Thomasina Ballroom that Jamie and the *Blood Evidence* production crew could have put down their weapons and picked up their mics.

"This should be it," Jamie says, scrolling through her research notes. "The two Bowery Brides. Miss Geraldine Fisher, who died in 1910 after she caught or set herself on fire just before her wedding ceremony, and Miss Cathy Wodehouse, who hung herself after the groom didn't show."

"But they both appear here?" I ask, peering around the ballroom. We're on the upper level, approaching the stairs that Geraldine fell down after her veil caught flame after passing too close to a candle.

"Maybe they became friends," Lucy suggests. "Because they have so much in common?"

"Don't say things like that," Alysha says, and prods her.

"Why not?"

"Because we're about to beat these ladies with flashlights and table legs. And I don't need to feel any worse about it."

"They might not even show," says Olivia. Her dark eyebrows raise with hope. She's been quiet since the attacks started, and seems guilty. "They're all that's left . . . maybe the hotel will cut its losses."

"No such luck," says Carmel. "Dammit." She nods toward

the broad, twisting staircase, where one of the brides has begun to flicker into being, the image of her coming up the stairs in fits and starts, blinking in, then disappearing. I see the moment she becomes corporeal: when she reaches the top step. Her shoes indent the carpet.

"Oh," Jamie breathes sadly. "Geraldine. The veil . . ." The veil is voluminous, one of those thick ones that looks half like a cloak. It falls over her brown hair and down her shoulders and back. There's a sudden chemical scent in the air, maybe something they treated the fabric with. It must have made the thing go up like a torch. Standing there before me, not on fire, she is beautiful, and hopeful, and happy. She looks at me like she thinks I might walk her down to the ceremony. But if we don't act soon, she'll burn. That's what she does, she burns, again and again, reliving her worst moment in a loop. With the new rage from the hotel in her veins, I have to imagine she'll want to spread the flames around.

Which is why we brought the bucket.

"Now, Carmel."

"But Cas. Her dress."

"Carmel," I say, cocking my eyebrow, and she sighs, then heaves the bucket and douses the ghost of Geraldine Fisher in water from head to toe. "I'm sorry," she says as the bride cries out. She's already starting to steam when I sink my blade into her belly.

"No more burning," I whisper, and Carmel tells her how pretty her gown is. I think that makes her happy, because she kind of smiles before she flakes away to charred bones and then to nothing.

"It really was beautiful," Carmel says. "She really was beautiful."

"Maybe you can wear a gown like hers one day," Thomas suggests. "When we get married."

"You want me to wear the gown that caught on fire and burned a bride to death? Babe." Carmel presses her lips together and puts the empty bucket over his head.

I turn and look around the ballroom. The guys from *Uneasy Bones* are clustered together, Juan and Russ on either side of David, their eyes roving, improvised weapons raised. The Ghostcasters look less frightened and more fascinated. And the crew from *Blood Evidence* has actually taken their phones out and look to be making production notes, pointing down to the main floor, whispering, taking photos. Back to business. Except for Olivia, who wanders a small distance away. We wait, and wait, and wait some more for the second bride to show.

"Might be time to try the doors," Thomas suggests, the empty bucket beneath his arm. "Maybe the Bowery gave up, and they're unlocked."

"Yeah," says Gabe. "We weren't even really sure the second bride was real."

"Accounts of her are hazy," Lucy agrees. "Sometimes she only appears in mirrors. Sometimes she's only a secondary scream after the first bride vanishes."

I nod. Good. I've never put this many ghosts to rest in one night. Not even during that mad dash through the suicide forest. When I think that, Thomas flinches, and I say, "Sorry." We don't talk about the suicide forest. We don't even think about it. We made a pact.

"I want all of you to know that I'm so sorry about this," says Olivia. She looks at David and his dislocated arm, at Lucy and her angry bruise. She looks at me. "I just . . . I wanted to know. I thought I had to, after Boston. I really didn't think anything would happen."

"You put all of us together because you really didn't think

anything would happen?" Russ makes a face and gestures to the black ghost muck that stains him from ears to chest.

"I don't think I wanted it to be true," Olivia says. "I think I set this all up because then when nothing happened I could be satisfied. Like I could know for sure. I think I was trying to disprove it, if that makes sense."

"You could have told us that," says Carmel. "Instead of using us as unwitting bait."

"I know."

"Cas almost didn't come. And then where would you be?"

"I know." Olivia looks down. Her long, dark hair has come out of its bun and hides her like a curtain, so well that I almost don't see the green-gray rope slide around her neck.

"Olivia!"

Her eyes widen as the noose of the second Bowery Bride yanks her off her feet. The ghost appears behind her and drags her back toward the railing. There is no hope or happiness in Cathy Wodehouse's eyes. Cathy Wodehouse died heartbroken, and her corporeal ghost has shunned all semblance of the blushing bride. Instead she looks the way she did when they found her, pale neck bruised and stretched, the veins in her eyes burst to red from hanging and from crying.

"Cas, get to her!"

I'm trying, but I can't. As Olivia frantically scratches at the rope, the ghost jerks her back and forth in between us. I can't use the athame without risking cutting her, and the knife must never be used on the living. Olivia reaches out to me just as the ghost pulls them both over the balcony railing. As time slows down I wonder madly if Olivia's body will hit the ballroom below or if we'll have to watch her hang, suspended midway in between. But I don't have to find out because Russ leaps and grabs her.

"Cut the rope!"

I leap too and slide the athame through it, easy as cutting a fishing line. Olivia slides to the floor, red-faced and coughing. "Are you okay?" I ask, and she nods. I look at Russ. "That's the second time you've caught someone going over a railing."

"I know, right? Hidden skills." He grins, but there's no time for quips before Lucy starts screaming. The ghost has Alysha. The rope jerks hard around her neck and lifts her, straight up into the air this time.

"I'm on it!" shouts Juan, and Gabe shouts too; they beat the ghost's legs until it drops Alysha and disappears. Only to reappear behind Carmel.

"No," Carmel declares, getting a hand up between her throat and the rope before it can tighten. She twists around and aims an elbow for Cathy Wodehouse's head, bashing her in the temple. "I don't like that she's only targeting the women," Carmel growls after the ghost disappears again. "Everyone circle up around Lucy!"

Everyone moves to do just that, but in my hand, the athame gives a little tug. Toward Adam. Ugh. Old ghosts. But the unfortunate tip makes sure that I'm right there beside him when the bride's noose starts to wind around his neck.

I step close. The athame sinks in.

"I know you died a long time ago," I mutter. "But he's a guy." I twist the knife and the last Bowery Bride fades, the shape of her stretching cruelly, jaw and neck elongating as her eyes turn white. She tears in two before she vanishes, and most of us turn our faces away.

"You okay?" I ask Adam. "That had to be jarring, on multiple levels."

"I'll process it later," he says, wiping at his neck. "Right now, let's get out of here."

None of us could agree more. We stomp down the staircase

like a herd of buffalo and jog all the way back to the atrium. Russ and Juan are the first to the doors, and my heart sinks when they don't open automatically. But maybe they really were locked. Only when they try to force their way through, the frames don't move. The glass won't break. The Bowery Lord Fell is still sealed shut.

And the phone behind the desk begins to ring.

CHAPTER NINE

Olivia answers the phone. "We killed all of them! Every one of them! So let us out!" She breathes hard into the receiver, listening. "Let us out you stupid fucking hotel! You stupid!" She brings the receiver down hard against the desk. "Fucking!" She smashes it again, this time it cracks like an egg. "Hotel!" She shoves the whole phone onto the floor. Then she kicks the desk.

"So . . . who was it?" I ask. Everyone looks at me. But Alysha laughs, so at least she thinks I'm funny.

"This is serious, Cas." Carmel puts the base of her palms to her forehead. "I do not want to be trapped in the Bowery forever. There's not enough staff. Especially since we just killed so many."

Thomas seems to agree. "So we killed all the ghosts and it didn't work. Let's think it through."

"It still doesn't make sense," Carmel mutters. "Why they woke up so angry . . ."

"We did kill them all, right?" Thomas looks at the Ghost-casters and the team from *Blood Evidence*. Jamie and Lucy check the notes on their phones. They were keeping a running floor-by-floor checklist.

"Yeah," Lucy says. "Every death, found and accounted for."

"Maybe there were some unaccounted ones?" Adam suggests. But I'm only half listening. The athame practically vibrates in my hand. I walk toward the dark glass doors as a flicker of white reflects in it. One I recognize. One I remember.

"We didn't kill them all," I say numbly.

"That's right," Carmel says after a moment. "Lucy, Jamie, what did you find about a bartender named Tom? He used to work the cigar lounge in the east wing."

"Nothing," they both reply. "We never found record of that."

And they won't. Because Tom didn't die in the hotel. I don't know if he died at all. The death he wore when he met us in the bar wasn't his.

It was hers.

Anna's. Anna, who stares back at me now, reflected in the glass.

She isn't dressed in blood anymore. Only in white. Her hair still floats, but not like it used to. It used to float as if it was suspended in water. Now it floats as if on a breeze. Is this real? Does she see me? Does she even recognize me, after all these years?

"Can anyone else see this?" I ask, and I know from their confused shuffling feet that they can't. "Can anyone see her?"

"I can see her, Cas." Thomas comes and stands beside me. "I see her."

In the reflection, Anna smiles. She looks at Thomas and smiles again. The glass goes dark.

I grip the athame tight. "Thomas, Carmel, come with me." I turn. "The rest of you stay here."

"Wait, man, where are you going?" Juan asks as we walk to the elevators.

"We're going to see Dead Tom."

Want to tell us what we're doing?" Carmel asks as we get off the elevator and head for the cigar lounge. Or at least, to the place where the cigar lounge popped itself into existence for us before. "And what it was you guys just saw in the window?"

"I told you," I say. "We're going to see Dead Tom."

"And it was Anna in the window," Thomas says quietly.

Carmel's eyes widen, her brow knits. "Was she real?" she asks after a moment. "Was she . . . okay?"

"I don't know," Thomas answers when I don't. "But I thought she looked okay. She looked good. She was smiling."

I feel their eyes but I won't meet them. They're my best friends; they know my I-don't-want-to-talk-about-it face.

"So, Dead Tom first," says Carmel, as we return to the corridor where we found the lounge.

"How is Dead Tom dead?" Thomas asks. "With no record of it?"

"I don't know if Dead Tom is dead," I say.

"He felt plenty dead to me," says Thomas.

"And he looked plenty dead to me," says Carmel.

"But it didn't look right. We all agreed. Like he'd borrowed it from someone we knew." I give them each a look. "You just thought that it was my messed-up brain that was doing it."

"But you think it was him?" asks Carmel.

"Him," I say. "It. I don't know that Tom is a ghost. I don't know if what he even *is,* is a thing that could die."

"Then I don't want to go in there," says Carmel, as the door to the cigar lounge looms open before us. "I didn't want to be trapped in the whole hotel, and I definitely don't want to be forever trapped in that bar. It's smaller than the bathroom in our apartment."

"That's because you have a plush-ass apartment, Richie Rich-pants."

We step inside. Tom is behind the bar, like I knew he would be. He greets us with a smile in his crisply ironed white shirt and crimson vest.

(400)

"There you are, sir! I have your drinks freshly prepared." He presents them, passing his hand over the glasses: a scotch, a bourbon, and Thomas's celery-stalked virgin Bloody Mary.

"What do you want?" I ask.

"Only to serve," he says in a humble, slightly stricken tone. But he doesn't look humble or stricken. Or affable, really, anymore. Despite the broad grin on his face, he's cold. Different. His eyes are darker and set deeper into his skull. His teeth are longer. I get the feeling that if we stared at him long enough he would cease to look like a person altogether.

"Serve who?"

"The dead, of course."

"We're not dead," says Carmel. She looks at Thomas. "We're not, are we?" He quickly shakes his head.

"No." Tom raises his eyebrows as he wipes the bar with a cloth. "You're not dead. Yet."

"And you think you're going to be the one to do it?" Thomas snorts. "We've faced worse than a bartender with a gold name tag."

"No," Tom says, and the room fills with a smell. The smell of water men have drowned in, of cold stone slabs that pressed the life out of bodies. The smell of ancient deaths and new, fresh ones. "You haven't." Tom looks at me. His eyes have grown hollow and his eyeballs sit lifeless in the sockets, like stones. "Killer of the dead." He breathes in, a great, sucking breath like he's pulling all the air out of the room, and when he blinks his eyes are just eyes again. "Surely you haven't spent all this time killing the dead and never thinking to come across their keeper."

"Is that what you are?" He doesn't respond. I guess that was implied. "What do you want? I mean, from me. Maybe it's this." I draw the athame from my pocket. Tom's eyes flick to it, and I don't like that. The sight of the athame usually makes ghosts back off. They sense what it is.

(401)

"Yes," he says. "I want that."

"I'm not giving you my father's knife."

"And yet you will. You may leave it on the bar. Or you may place it in my hand." He holds it out, palm up. It takes me a minute to see what's wrong with it. There are six fingers, and an extra joint each on the two in the middle.

"Were you the one who brought us here? Were you the one who woke the hotel? Was it the psychics at all?"

Tom's attention shifts to Thomas. "The presence of the odd ones made it easier."

"It's you who's making them so angry," says Carmel.

"I woke them to fight, so they fight." His eyes come back to me. "I can wake anyone to fight."

"Did you wake her?" I ask. "Is that what I've been seeing?" Tom's eyes narrow, but he doesn't reply. He doesn't seem to know who I mean. Does that mean Anna was real? I clench my teeth. I can't think about that. Not when I'm staring down an undead I-don't-know-what. "What are you?" I ask again. But Tom only repeats the order.

"You may leave it on the bar. Or you may place it in my hand."

I flip the athame in my grip. "Why don't you just take it?" I hold it out, place it right beneath his nose, and watch him sniff. Unexpected cold emanates from him and something else: a pull like from a magnet. "But you can't, can you? Because there are always rules." I take a few steps around the side of the bar. "What if I don't place it *in* your hand? What if I place it *through* your hand?" Tom's head twists to follow me. His long teeth still show but he's not smiling anymore. "What if I put it through your heart?"

I jerk forward and Tom twists to face me full on, shedding the bartender costume, skin and all. What I see underneath makes my stomach turn inside out. But I don't see it for long, because the next thing I know, I'm flying backwards and landing butt first on the carpet in the hallway. Thomas and Carmel land on either side of me, and they both grunt.

From inside the lounge, Dead Tom stares at us. At *me*. Then the door slams shut, and I know that if I were to open it again all I would find is a closet. And I know another thing. The Bowery Lord Fell is unlocked. I heard it happen in my mind—a key turned, a click.

The Bowery is just a hotel again. Maybe not even a haunted one.

"Ow," I moan, stretching my back.

"What the hell was that?" Thomas exclaims.

"Oh, you know," I say as we help each other up. "Just Dead Tom, the Dead Keeper."

"Dead Tom the Dead Keeper," says Carmel. "Can we sell that to a studio as an animated children's program?"

"It's worth a shot."

"But what exactly was he?" Thomas asks.

"I don't know." But it's a safe bet to say I'll see him again someday. The look on his face, or what passed for his face just before the door closed, was that of a wolf who'd caught a fresh scent. He's going to come for me. Eventually. "We're going into research mode—get in touch with Gideon and Morfran. But that can wait." Somewhere else in the quiet hotel, excited podcasters are screaming in the atrium as they realize that they're free to leave. "Right now, I just want to go home."

Chapter Ten

I t takes less than fifteen minutes for emergency services to reach us, once we're actually able to call them. They get David's arm in a sling and at Gabe's insistence take a look at Lucy's bruise. She wanted to hide it, because it's pretty clearly a handprint and between that, the trashed room, and the broken chair she figured we'd all get hauled in for assault and destruction of property. But she's able to convince them that David just grabbed her too hard when she tried to help him during his fall. We're also greeted by the perplexed night manager of the hotel, who had no idea we'd checked in, thanks to the hotel's time warp and to Employee of the Year Mercutio, who they have no record of as being on staff. I guess he was another of Dead Tom's tricks. Or maybe just another face for him to wear.

Olivia comes over to us, weaving through the uniforms. With order restored, she seems like herself again, though still appropriately guilty.

"So," I say. "What's the damage? How much is *Blood Evidence* on the hook for?"

"Not much, actually. They're going to waive the cleaning fees for the room David wrote all over, as long as we post pictures of it to our accounts. I think they'll also take a few themselves." She shrugs. "Maybe leave the whole thing up for people to take selfies with. As for the rest of it, the water in the ballroom carpet will dry, and the black . . . stuff . . ." She glances at it on the floor, what remains of Fred Lavelle. "That'll get mopped up. This ghost-killing thing—it's actually pretty clean."

"It's also *a secret*," says Thomas, and taps his finger to his lips.

Olivia smiles. "I guess all that's left is for someone to go up to the third floor and make sure old George got back into his portrait."

Carmel and I look at each other.

"Not it," we say.

Before we leave the Bowery for the airport, Alysha pulls me aside on the front sidewalk.

"So," she says, "Carmel told me a little about you all. What brought you all together, what makes you so damn special . . ."

"Carmel," I say, scolding. "Giving away all the intel."

"Well, if it makes you feel better she was hard to follow. Lots of mumbling about some old, dead girlfriend of yours."

I snort.

"I mean, I figured a guy like you would have a kink but that's pretty twisted."

"It's not like it sounds," I say. "All right, it was. But it wasn't that weird. You kind of had to be there."

"Well. I'd like to hear about it sometime." Alysha's bundled up against the cold, her red scarf wrapped thickly to her chin. There are Ghostbusters patches sewn onto her coat. "Carmel said you've been seeing her lately, this old girlfriend."

I look out across the pines like I might glimpse her again, a flash of white between the trees. "I don't know if that was real. I saw her the night Olivia asked us to come up here. And I saw her again, in the Bowery. I think it might have been another trick. To push me on. To get us here." A cruel thing for Dead Tom to pull out of my head. An extra bit of pain, a violation of my memories. And if it really was him, he's going to pay for it.

"Alysha," Gabe calls from beside their waiting taxi.

"Time to go." She reaches up to hug me. "You keep in touch, all right?"

"You keep that flashlight handy."

"Oh no," she says, walking away. "My ghost-beating days are *done*. I'm going to split off this podcast and pivot to knitting, or cross-stitch—or those videos where people just want you to eat food that's crunchy." She grins back at me, and we both know she's lying. The Ghostcasters have been rattled, but . . . well . . . they ain't afraid of no ghosts.

Sorry.

Back home, I reach out to Gideon and my mom, and tell them about Dead Tom, and Thomas calls his grandfather. As everyone we know cracks open old and dusty books, things go back to normal: evenings at the Commodore, weekends running DoorDash. Scouring the reliable networks for tips for the next hunt.

It's almost a month before the Ghost-con episodes on the Bowery begin to drop, first from *Blood Evidence* and then *Uneasy Bones,* and finally from *The Ghostcasters*. I don't listen to them. We don't record one of our own, despite our promise to. Olivia doesn't say a word about it, and we keep the stipend without asking. Carmel does boost the episodes on our socials though, and even though she wanted to record one of our own—for the good of *Low Frequencies,* she said—she eventually agrees that it's better this way. It even makes us seem cooler, like we were the special guests or something.

I haven't seen Anna since the night at the hotel. I haven't even dreamed of her, and the more time passes the more certain I become that she wasn't real. A fact that depresses me more than I care to admit.

I'm at my work bench sanding the edge off a freshly beveled table leg when I get a text from Thomas.

The Ghostcasters episode. You should listen to it.

Maybe later I reply, clearly meaning that I won't. And Thomas texts back.

Just the last few minutes.

He even sends a link, to really give me no choice.

I sigh, and hit play, and snort through the sirens of the Ecto-1. For the next hour I listen to Alysha, Lucy, Gabe, and Adam as they hilariously recount their time at the Bowery. Listeners will love it, even as they're comfortably sure that it's all a prank, a well-produced stunt put on by three of the best ghost podcasts in the business. They sell it well. The Bowery Lord Fell will be booked to capacity every Halloween for the next decade. I'm glad I listened, and despite the frequent mention of us I'm still caught off guard when Alysha says, "And before we end this special edition of *The Ghostcasters,* we want to give a shout-out to our new friends at *Low Frequencies.* Thomas, useful psychic, and Carmel, who swings a flashlight even better than I do. But especially to Cas. Cas Lowood, real-life action hero. Slayer of the dead. And who more than one Ghostcaster may be nursing a serious crush on."

I grin.

"But on a serious note, Cas, I know you've had some doubts about some things you've seen, about a certain ladylove who we at *The Ghostcasters* have come to think of as a guardian angel.

"I know you're not sure if that angel was real. But I think she was. I think she *did* get you there, because she knew that's where you needed to be when all that stuff went down. I think she made sure you were there to save us."

I lean back in my chair.

"And oh yeah, since we kind of forgot to say it in the midst of broken arms, choked necks, and dead bodies . . . Thanks, Cas."

The *Ghostcasters* theme music plays them out, and I turn down the volume and smile.

"Thanks, Anna."

AFTERWORD

In the fall of 2009, I met a ghost called Anna Dressed in Blood. She came to me in exactly that way, just the whisper of a name, like I was hearing the rumor of her from somewhere in the back of my brain. Over the next months, I would go on to meet young ghost hunter Cas Lowood, his mother, and their cat, Tybalt (who was actually my cat Tybalt—and yes, I got his permission for him to meet that fate), as well as Thomas and Carmel and all the rest who would come to comprise the cast of *Anna Dressed in Blood*. I still remember the moment I met the Obeahman: I was working at a horse stable in the pitch-black, predawn hours and was walking up a closed staircase toward the locked door of a hayloft. When I put my hand on the doorknob I heard him say, "I'm in the attic eating cats." And I said, "These horses can wait to eat until it's light out."

I knew when I met them that I wanted to spend as much time with them as I could. What I didn't know was that their adventure would somehow find its way to readers for more than ten years. That they would become as special to other people as they were to me. That all these years later, readers would still be asking what they're up to, and if there would ever be more to their story.

It's because of those readers (and because of the energizing passion of editor Miriam Weinberg) that I was able to reach out across the divide, to call out to Cas one more time and have him answer. It was a relief, to be honest. I'd tried reaching out lots of times and gotten nothing; I was starting to suspect the little punk was dead. Yet this time I called and there he was, Cas as ever, chattier than I was used to him being and all grown up. It was such a delight and a privilege to write him again, and I must thank the people who helped bring him and *Anna* into being in the first place: *Anna*'s original editor, Melissa Frain, and my agent, Adriann Ranta Zurhellen. These two people changed my life, and I will do anything for them besides crime. And honestly, if the crime seems justified and we can probably get away with it, I might do that, too.

I also have to thank the entire publishing team at Tor, for giving *Anna* such a great home for ten years and for relaunching her in this beautiful package. Miriam Weinberg, it has been so cool to work with you, as well as Lauren Hougen (you've copyedited me before and you're always great). Big hugs and hellos to Khadija Lokhandwala, publicity dynamo, and Kayah Hodge, marketing assistant extraordinaire.

But mostly, this is thanks to you, the readers who have kept Anna and Cas alive for so long. No small feat since one of them was already dead. At the end of this novella, Cas says, "Thanks, Anna," and I hope that in his voice you'll also hear mine.

Thanks, readers. You've made my life.

ABOUT THE AUTHOR

KENDARE BLAKE is the #1 *New York Times* bestselling author of
the Anna series, Goddess War series, Three Dark Crowns series,
and Heromaker series. Her work is sort of dark, always violent,
and features passages describing food from when she writes
while hungry. She lives and writes in Gig Harbor, Washington,
with her husband, their cat son Tyrion Cattister, red Doberman
dog son Obi-Dog Kenobi, rottie mix dog daughter Agent Scully,
and naked Sphynx cat son Armpit McGee.